Sketching Character

PAMELA LYNNE

Sketching Character

Cover art and layout by JD Smith Designs

Editing by Kristy Rawley

ISBN-13: 978-1515238607
ISBN-10: 1515238601

For Lawrence, Annabelle and Remy, who tolerated my long hours in front of the computer with more grace than their ages should allow.

Prologue

Elizabeth Bennet sat at her dressing table and examined the dark circles under her eyes as she twisted her hair into a braid. She felt like she had not slept for weeks. Her limbs were heavy and her skin ached underneath her muslin gown. Still, she prepared for her morning walk, needing the time alone in the cool autumn air to sort her thoughts before facing another day with her family.

Everyone in the house, with the possible exception of her father and middle sister Mary, were in various states of ill humor. Her mother was angry with her for refusing their cousin Mr. Collins, who, while being the stupidest man in England, would one day inherit Longbourn, her father's estate. Her eldest sister Jane was nursing heartache after being abandoned by the amiable Mr. Bingley and her youngest sister Lydia had closed herself in her room the morning after the Netherfield ball, not allowing anyone other than their maid to enter, leaving her other sister Kitty and their mother in an almost panicked state worrying for her.

Elizabeth's brow furrowed with concern for her sisters. Lydia had never been ill before, except trifling colds, and it was very unusual for her to not want to be with Kitty, cheerfully recalling events from the ball. And dear Jane, her best friend in all the world, was going about her days veiled in sadness, though one would have to be close to her to know her real feelings. She kept an air of serenity around her, a shield against their mother's negative effusions and their father's thoughtless teasing. Elizabeth could see the disappointment in her eyes, though, and her heart broke for her sister.

Elizabeth let out a long sigh as she rose and grabbed her bonnet. Before she could reach the door, she heard a soft knock, followed quickly be an equally soft, "Lizzy?"

Elizabeth smiled. "Come in, Jane."

Once inside the room, Jane immediately found herself in her sister's embrace. She stepped back and looked down into Elizabeth's eyes, which were laced with so much concern and affection. She smiled and took her hand, squeezing it gently.

"Dear Lizzy. I have come with news."

"Oh? What news do you have for me when the sun is barely up and we left each other only a few hours ago? Have the mice in the walls been whispering; do they have word on the war or possibly what the neighbors are having for breakfast?"

Jane laughed quietly, appreciating her sister's attempt to cheer her. "Silly Lizzy. No, I have come to tell you that I have had enough. I will no longer let this disappointment get the better of me. I cannot continue to mourn the loss of a man whose regard for me could not have been what we supposed, not if he could leave so easily, without even saying goodbye."

Jane knew Elizabeth had been worried about her and she hoped her new resolve to forget Mr. Bingley would have mollified her, but instead she became angry. Elizabeth knew Jane cared for Mr. Bingley and was sure the gentleman had returned those sentiments. Not for the first time in the past few days, she railed against the Netherfield party.

"Jane, I refuse to believe that. Anyone who saw the two of you together could tell he was in love with you. Even Sir William commented on it when I was dancing with Mr. Darcy. That gentleman could not have been more displeased, however. I do believe his friend and sisters must have convinced him, somehow, to stay in London. Perhaps there is a way to bring the two of you together again."

Jane patted her sister's hand and led her to sit on the bed. "Is that what you wish for me, Lizzy? Do you want to see me married to a man who is so easily swayed by his friends and family? Either he is staying in London by his own volition, which means he does not care for me, or he has succumbed to the will of his sisters and Mr. Darcy, which means his regard was too weak in the face of their objections. Either way, it would be better for us to forget about Mr. Bingley. He is obviously not a man we can rest our hopes on. I will not allow my heart to break for one who can so easily toss me aside. I will learn from this, but I will not dwell on it, and neither will you. It would not do us any good."

Elizabeth could not argue with the wisdom of Jane's words, even if she could not completely release her anger. She believed her sister had been treated badly, and she could never forgive someone for hurting the ones she loved. Very briefly, a deep voice sounded in her mind, "My temper is, perhaps, too little yielding. My good opinion, once lost, is lost forever." She closed her eyes and shook her head lightly. She would not let her thoughts drift to that dreadful man or compare herself to him in any way. Jane was right. It was best to forget about the former residents of Netherfield entirely.

"Very well, Jane. We will speak of it no more."

"Thank you, Lizzy," Jane began as she rose. "I will not keep you from your walk. I am going downstairs to ask cook to prepare a special tray for Lydia. I hope she will allow me in to see her this morning."

"The poor dear, I wish I knew what was wrong. I will try to speak to her again when I return."

The sisters parted ways in the kitchen, with Elizabeth leaving through the back door, walking determinedly toward her favorite path.

Elizabeth smiled as she made her way down the hill toward Longbourn. The exercise had done much to lift her spirits. She had rambled along at a sedate pace until she was sure she was out of sight, then broke out into a run. She *would* conquer the gloominess that had begun to settle in her heart. Each time her boot hit the ground, another negative image was expelled from her mind. Miss Bingley's catty comments scattered in the dust, Mr. Bingley's jovial face disappeared into the wind, and though it took a few more steps, Mr. Darcy's assured speech and arrogant smirk joined the others in oblivion. She ran on, pushing herself up the hill until she was breathless and her mind was blessedly clear.

Now that Jane was determined to move on from her disappointment, Elizabeth's mind settled solely on Lydia. She never thought she would miss the noise her younger sister brought to the house, but life was too quiet with her hidden away in her room. Though she was in need of correction, and her behavior often reflected poorly upon her family, Lydia was full of life, and this sudden solitude was very disturbing. Elizabeth wanted to help, but she could not know how unless Lydia spoke to her about what was wrong.

She began to contemplate what things could tempt Lydia from her room. Her first thought was to invite the officers for tea. Lydia was a fool for a man in a red coat and though Elizabeth would not generally encourage her flirting, she was desperate enough to try anything. Her thoughts naturally turned to one officer in particular. She blushed slightly remembering the attention Mr. Wickham had paid her and then became irritated thinking how he had failed to attend the Netherfield ball. He had promised to see her there and she was disappointed to hear he had business to tend to in town. She knew the real reason he did not attend. He was trying to avoid an unpleasant situation with that horrible--she stopped her thoughts before they could meander too far back into the negative. She stopped walking and breathed in deeply, closed her eyes and willed her mind back to her sister. When she opened them, a wisp of white among the greying trees caught her attention.

Elizabeth gasped when she saw Lydia in the orchard, huddled under a tree wearing only a thin shift. She ran to her and kneeled at her side.

"Lydia, you are freezing." Elizabeth took off her spencer and wrapped it around her sister. "What are you doing out here?"

Lydia's only response was a sob, so Elizabeth pulled her tight against her, rubbing her back and whispering quietly.

"Please, Lydia, tell me what troubles you."

Lydia continued weeping on Elizabeth's shoulder for several minutes and then finally looked up. Her eyes were swollen and her blond curls were matted around her face. Through ragged breaths she finally spoke.

"Oh, Lizzy. I am ruined."

Elizabeth continued to stroke her sister's hair, trying to calm her enough so she could explain. She gently pulled back and lifted Lydia's head so she could see her face.

"What do you mean, Lydia? How are you ruined?"

"He said I was ruined, that no decent man would ever want me, or any of my sisters now. I am so sorry Lizzy. I did not know what he would do."

"Liddy, I need you to calm down and tell me exactly what happened."

"After the ball, when everyone else was asleep, I left the house to meet him at the old barn. He said he would not be at the ball but still wanted to dance with me. He wanted to waltz in the moonlight with a pretty girl, he said. I thought it would be romantic and that Kitty and Maria would be so jealous. He kissed me and it felt good and I did not want him to stop. But then he started doing things that did not feel so good and I was frightened. I tried to tell him to stop, but I could not find my voice when he--hurt me. I did not know that would happen, Lizzy, I swear. I thought we would dance and maybe kiss. He had said such nice things, but when it was over, he was very cruel.

"He told me I was ruined, that I would never marry and would only be good for servicing men in the shadows. He called me a whore and said my family was ruined as well. I am so sorry, Lizzy. I am so sorry. I did not know what he was doing until it was too late to stop." Her words faded as her body once again gave way to sobs.

Elizabeth held her tight and rocked back and forth as tears streamed down her own face. She felt helpless and angry. In her heart she knew the answer to the question she was about to ask, but she had to hear Lydia say the words to know for sure.

"Liddy, who was he? Who did this to you?"

Lydia turned her head to the side and pushed the hair back from her face. In a voice so soft and broken that Elizabeth could barely hear she whispered, "It was Wickham."

Chapter 1

Elizabeth was roused from her sleep by a quick movement on the other side of the bed. Her mind was still somewhere in twilight when the sound of retching reached her ears and the smell of sickness washed over her. Coming to awareness, she quickly rolled over and sat behind her sister, rubbing circles on her back in an attempt to bring comfort.

"I am sorry, Lizzy," Lydia said after long moments hunched over the chamber pot. "I did not make it in time. It can come upon me so quick, especially at night."

Elizabeth put her arm around Lydia's shoulders and pressed tenderly. She looked down at her soiled nightgown and then at her pale face. Her sister had barely eaten in the past few weeks, and when she did it came back up with so much violence that Elizabeth wondered if it was possible to die from such an expulsion.

"Do you think you are finished?" Elizabeth's voice was soft, full of sleep and concern. At Lydia's nod, she stood and placed the pot on the bedside table. "Can you stand, dearest? We need to clean you."

Lydia stood as Elizabeth helped her out of her gown. The events of the night were now a regular occurrence and Elizabeth was prepared. She moistened a towel from a basin placed close to the fire and began to wipe away the evidence of the evening's disturbance. She drew the cloth gently over Lydia's face then cleansed the rest of her thin frame, pausing briefly over the slight protrusion just below her ribcage. They would not be able to conceal her condition much longer. The lasting evidence of Lydia's seduction was growing even as the rest of her was wasting away.

Elizabeth pulled a clean gown over her sister's head and helped her back to bed.

"How much longer will this last, Lizzy?"

Elizabeth sat next to her and stroked her face. "I know not, dearest, but from what we have been told, you should not suffer much longer." She hoped it was true. Lydia had been sick for longer than their aunt advised already.

"It is only what I deserve. I... "

"Shhh." Elizabeth leaned over and placed a soft kiss on her head. "None of that, Liddy. You must try to rest now. We begin our journey tomorrow."

She rose from the bed and donned her robe. Taking the basin from the table, she turned back to Lydia.

"I will return in a moment. Go to sleep, dearest."

Elizabeth walked Longbourn's darkened passages, reaching the servants' stairs by instinct more than by sight. She moved through the kitchen to the back door, where she slipped into boots and a cloak that waited there. She stepped through the door into the night, thankful for the cool burst of air that helped calm her own stomach. The moon was bright, lighting the way through the orchard to the brook that signaled the border of her father's property. It was the same path she had taken the day she found her sister broken and sobbing amongst the trees.

She kneeled on the bank and leaned over the water, watching the ripples move over the surface for a few moments before she emptied Lydia's refuse into the stream, disturbing the chatter of the small waves hitting the pebbles beneath. She watched the water calm once more. As Lydia's waste was carried downstream, joining the volume from each night prior, Elizabeth wondered how much of her sister was disappearing with each wave.

She sighed as she stood and arched her shoulders into a stretch. Elizabeth had not slept well for weeks. Her body was beginning to protest the lack of rest. After Lydia's confession in the orchard, Elizabeth moved her sister into her room to care for her. They shared many conversations, mostly centered on Wickham's well-executed seduction.

"He was so charming, Lizzy, always telling me how pretty I was and how much he enjoyed my company. I met him alone at times. I realize now it was wrong, but at the time it all seemed a good joke. I was sure he would propose and I would be the first to marry, and me the youngest. Oh, Lizzy, Papa was right. I am just a silly, foolish girl."

Although Lydia was frightened and ashamed, Elizabeth managed to convince her to tell their father what had happened. Elizabeth had been sure he would help and do what was necessary to ensure Wickham could never hurt anyone again. Instead, he blamed Lydia's flirtatious ways and poor judgment. He insisted no one ever know, lest they all be disgraced. His words caused an already fragile Lydia to succumb completely to her regrets, and bouts of sorrowful self-recrimination became the only utterances from her lips.

As the weeks passed, Lydia's sadness gave way to illness, causing Elizabeth's concern to grow. She had kept their secret, not even telling Jane. It was their housekeeper Hill, who had seen to the girls' care as faithfully as a mother would, who first spoke to Elizabeth about the possibilities.

"Miss Lizzy, if some man . . . hurt Miss Lydia, then her illness may be the sign of . . . the consequences."

Elizabeth dissembled a bit, but Hill insisted she would never see harm done to any of her dear girls and assured Elizabeth of her secrecy and assistance. Having an ally did little to assuage Elizabeth's panic as she wondered how she could protect her sister from scandal. She slept fitfully most nights and was awakened often when Lydia became ill.

During a fit of nerves, and before consulting her husband, Mrs. Bennet sent for the apothecary, Mr. Jones. Elizabeth refused to leave the room while he examined Lydia, and in response to the imploring look from Elizabeth, he spoke to her alone.

"It appears your sister has contracted the same condition some others have since the militia arrived. Does your father know?"

Elizabeth nodded.

"Will he do nothing?"

Elizabeth looked down and shook her head.

"I will say nothing, but it will become obvious before spring."

He informed their mother that Lydia would likely be well soon, but would perhaps benefit from the sea air if she did not improve.

Mrs. Bennet lamented her dear girl's health to anyone who would listen and soon all of Meryton knew she was unwell. Elizabeth knew she had to act soon, before suspicion arose, but had no idea where to start. The arrival of Christmas and her Aunt Gardiner provided a much needed confidant.

"Oh Lydia. Oh dear, dear girl." Mrs. Gardiner held Lydia close after they disclosed their predicament. That night, in Elizabeth's childhood room, the three women devised a plan to protect the future of the Bennets. They would tell everyone Lydia was to visit Mrs. Gardiner's relations near the sea while in truth she would stay in Lambton. They would tell no one except Mr. Gardiner and live as if everything were perfectly normal. That meant Elizabeth would go to Kent as previously planned to visit her newly married friend Charlotte instead of continuing to see to Lydia's care.

"There is only room for Lydia there, my dear, and we cannot afford to establish

a separate residence for that long. We will go to her when it is time or her laying in, but until then I am afraid she must do this on her own."

And so plans were made for Elizabeth and the Gardiners to visit the Peaks in the summer. That deception would be the final one. Lydia's child would be left in the care of Mrs. Gardiner's relations and Lydia would come home and, hopefully, heal.

The Gardiners took Jane to London with them at the turn of the New Year, leaving Elizabeth with one less person to deceive. For that she was very grateful. She had never kept anything from Jane before, and not seeing her everyday lessened the guilt, though not by much. Every time Elizabeth saw her mother's concern she felt it. Every time she saw her father's closed study door she felt it. Most of all, every time she held Lydia's hair back or embraced her while she sobbed she felt it.

How could she have been so wrong? She who prided herself on being an excellent judge of character was drawn in by charm and flattery. She was seduced as easily as Lydia, only without the ultimate consequence. Her mind repeated her conversations with Wickham over and over and in hindsight she could see how easily she had been manipulated. She hated Wickham for hurting them so horribly. She resented her father for allowing Wickham to continue in the neighborhood unpunished, and with every tear Lydia shed, her resentment grew.

The next morning they would travel to London. Under normal circumstances, it was a trip Elizabeth would have eagerly anticipated, but as it was she could only dread the journey. She and Lydia would be separated. After so many weeks seeing to her wellbeing, she would have to give her sister up to strangers and hope they would tend both her and their secret with care.

She drew one final deep breath as she reached for the door handle, preparing herself to return to her chamber, where she was sure the scent of illness lingered. She climbed the stairs and stepped quietly down the hall, entering her room to find Lydia asleep. She crawled into bed and silently prayed for strength to face the morning.

Early the next day, Elizabeth stood on the periphery of the small group gathered in front of her home, staring down at the brown patches of grass that had not yet acknowledged the passing of the season. Her foot made slow circles through the blades as she fought the tears that threatened her determination to not contribute to the emotional scene playing out before her.

"Oh, Lydia, why must you go so far away?" Mrs. Bennet broke into a sob as she held her youngest daughter close. The anguish in her mother's voice caused Elizabeth's heart to constrict as she lifted her head to look upon them. She tried to suppress the worry that always simmered beneath her skin and remain calm in the mist of her mother's pain. Elizabeth did not want Lydia to go either, but kept telling herself that if she did not, they would all be ruined.

The majority of those gathered believed Lydia was on her way to the sea side to find relief from the illness that plagued her all winter. Of the two that knew the truth, only Elizabeth was privy to the details of the plan to keep Lydia safe, and the reputation of all the Bennets intact.

"I do not understand why we cannot all go to the sea side," her mother continued. "At this time of year I am sure plenty of houses are available to lease."

"As I have said before, my dear, we cannot bear the expense of removing the entire family to the seaside."

"But she will be all alone, with no friends to comfort her." Mrs. Bennet's normally shrill voice held all the anguish of a mother worried about losing her child.

"And yet I am unmoved. You must accept whatever arrangements my brother Gardiner has made and be done with it." He spoke in the tone he always used with his wife and younger daughters: one that was a strange combination of anguish and amusement, as if he could not decide between the two and so united them into one peculiar feeling that Elizabeth once interpreted as exasperation. She now only heard weakness.

Elizabeth turned to the other holder of their secret and the tightness briefly gave way to a different turmoil. Guilt and disappointment shadowed her as she gazed at her father with a hardened expression. His words were careless and without feeing and for a moment the sounds of her mother's grief were drowned out by memories of other words that had been spoken with uncharacteristic emotion.

"*Trollop*," "*your fault*," and "*no longer my concern*," echoed in her mind as she looked at her father, her mind recalling images of Lydia's face, swollen and stained with tears, while he railed against her for "*allowing a seduction*." The fact that Lydia was still a child, *his child*, and had little idea of what was happening was of no consequence. Lydia was ruined and he would not allow her to stay at Longbourn if she was with child. She would be cut off completely, with no support or contact with anyone in the family.

Mr. Bennet must have sensed Elizabeth's stare. He turned and looked gravely upon her angry visage. He stepped toward her, placed his hands on her shoulders and looked in her eyes with what could have been fatherly concern.

"You are anxious about your trip, Lizzy? Do you fear you will regret Mr.

Collins when you see him so blissfully wed?"

It took only a moment for him to see his jest was not welcomed. Elizabeth straightened and glanced around, seeing the Lucases, who were travelling with them, were out of earshot.

"No Father. I am anxious about sending my sister to strangers when she obviously needs her family."

She looked again to Lydia who was now clinging to Kitty. They had not told their father about the pregnancy, but given his decree, he had to know the reason she was leaving. He never asked where she was to go nor offered any financial assistance. He must have assumed Mr. Gardiner was taking care of everything, if he gave it any thought at all.

"She brought this upon herself, Lizzy. Sooner or later we all must face the consequences of our actions."

Elizabeth's back stiffened further. The irony of his words was almost too much to bear. The dutiful daughter in her wanted to nod and turn away, but the protective sister could not resist a parting retort.

"Or our inaction, sir." She curtsied and walked away, leaving the man in no doubt of her lowered opinion.

Seeing the Lucases were anxious to begin the journey, Elizabeth said goodbye to her mother and sisters before placing a hand on Lydia's shoulder, silently letting her know it was time. Lydia kept her hands firmly around Kitty's as she leaned in and spoke in a soft whisper, "Keep close to Mary, Kitty, and keep to Longbourn until Jane or Lizzy return. The village holds no value equal to our sisters."

She had similar words for Mary, whose confused expression matched Kitty's. The somberness coming from her youngest sister left Mary unable to speak the usual platitudes, so she merely responded with an embrace that took Lydia by surprise, but she returned it in earnest.

Mrs. Bennet once again pulled Lydia into her arms, finally letting go when she heard her husband clear his throat.

"Be well, Lydia," he spoke hurriedly. She gave him a nod and kissed her mother's cheek.

"Goodbye, Mama," Lydia whispered through her tears and with a final look to their family, the sisters boarded the carriage, leaving those left behind to wonder if anything would ever be the same.

Fitzwilliam Darcy leaned against the doorway outside the music room of his London townhouse. His tall frame was in an unusually relaxed position as he allowed the sounds of his sister's playing to move through him. He needed to speak to her, but was reluctant to interrupt such a beautiful piece. Her fingers moved lightly over the keys, creating a soothing melody that allowed them to connect without words, only emotion. The music *was* Georgiana's emotion; she was not separate from it, but one with the chords that flowed from her instrument. He knew her moods better from what she chose to play than from the words she spoke. Her music could not dissemble, could not placate; could only tell the absolute truth. What her music told him then was that she was happy. It made what he must tell her more difficult.

He entered the room as the last notes drifted out behind him and smiled softly at the look of contentment displayed on her face. That look had disappeared just a few months prior, and seeing it now filled him with hope that she was ready to move forward.

"That was beautiful, my dear. You filled the house with warmth on this gloomy day."

Georgiana rose and smiled brightly at her brother. She walked to him and kissed his cheek, causing his smile to grow.

"I did not know I had an audience. You must alert me to your presence so that I will play a piece I know you prefer. That was just something I was toying with, it is not yet perfected."

Darcy led her to a nearby sofa and motioned for her to sit.

"It sounded perfect, quite playful and light. You have not had much time to practice as of late, which makes it more of an accomplishment." Darcy looked away, feeling a momentary twinge of guilt for her lack of practice had come by his decree.

He hardly recognized Georgiana the weeks following her rescue at Ramsgate. He considered his timely appearance as such, but to her it was interference. She was convinced Darcy had sent Wickham away, threatened him somehow into abandoning her. Her anger was unexpected and severe. Eventually she stopped speaking to him and chose instead to hide in the music room and pour her heart onto her keys.

Darcy had been torn between the role of doting brother who wanted to offer her every treat possible to tempt her out of her mood, and strict guardian who knew she must be reprimanded for her behavior. While he mostly blamed Wickham and himself for what happened, Georgiana bore some responsibility for allowing the courtship to go on in secret. So, the day before he left for Hertfordshire he laid out stringent guidelines that had to be met before she could partake in any pleasurable activity. That, unfortunately, included playing the pianoforte.

The judgment was hard to make on his part and hard to accept on hers, but the results were exactly what Darcy had hoped for. Without her favorite means of escape, she was forced to think about what she had done. Her anger turned to self-reproach, and Darcy received many letters filled with grief and apologies. His letters to her were filled with forgiveness and love, and she eventually told him everything she was feeling: shame, confusion, heartache and most of all loneliness. When he returned to London, she fell into his arms and cried like she had not since their father died. She released her emotions onto him, and they grew closer as she drew from his strength in order to heal.

"I appreciate the compliment, Brother, but I should be able to play with my eyes closed, given the amount of time I have spent in this room."

Darcy hoped the slight irritation he heard in her voice was due to her surroundings and not only her perceived imperfections.

"Do you grow tired of keeping to home, Georgie? Are you ready to venture out to shops or to visit your friends?"

Georgiana had not left the townhouse since his return to London. She seemed to always need his company, seeking reassurance that she was still loved and in fact still quite perfect in the eyes of her elder brother. He indulged her as much as he could, recognizing the insecurity behind her actions.

The look of panic that crossed her face reminded Darcy that she was still very vulnerable. Like him, she did not make friends easily, and Wickham's actions had caused her to further question her ability to judge others' intentions.

"Oh, no. Well, perhaps to the shops if you accompany me, but I would rather not see any of the girls from school just yet. I do have an idea, though." Her voice was hesitant, still displaying some of the insecurity she was bravely trying to conquer.

"Yes?"

"I would like to travel with you to Rosings this year."

Darcy was surprised. He made the trip to his aunt's estate every year and had never taken Georgiana along. He had no intention of taking her this time either, but was grieved at having to disappoint her.

"Why are you asking to come now, dear? You never have before."

Georgiana brought both hands to her lap and fidgeted as she looked down.

"I missed you when you went to Hertfordshire. I was all alone here and could do nothing but think. I do not like being inside my own head so much. What I find there is not always pleasant."

She looked at him and he could tell she was trying very hard to be convincing. It was times like this Darcy had to remind himself not to look at her as if she were still twelve and asking for an extra sweet with her tea, though she currently held the same expression.

"I will be sociable. I will speak to Anne and," she look down and frowned, "Lady Catherine. I promise not to hide in the closet like I did the last time she was here."

"No, no, I know you would not. You have grown so much since then and I have no doubt of your ability to act like a lady while in anyone's company. Besides, all the closets at Rosings are fitted with shelves, leaving an unfortunate lack of room for hiding. Richard tried just last year and ended up with a horrible cramp." They laughed together until Darcy once again took her hand in his.

"I am sorry, Georgie, but I must say no. I do not believe Rosings is a good environment for you, especially now."

"Why is that? I know Lady Catherine can be unpleasant but I believe I can manage her if you and Richard are with me."

Darcy sighed and looked at his sister closely. He never spoke to her much about their maternal relations. He strove to protect her from their manipulations and limited her time with them, just as their father had done. The difference was that their father had explained to him precisely why the Fitzwilliams were not to be trusted. Darcy had not done so with Georgiana, not wanting her innocence tainted by the knowledge that their family was filled with controlling, manipulative liars. He had done the same with Wickham, allowing her childhood memories to remain unspoiled by the truth of his character. That omission nearly cost her everything.

"Georgiana, there is more to the situation than her being unpleasant. Are you aware of the family's expectation that I marry Anne?"

She shook her head. She had very vague recollections of her cousin Anne from when the family descended upon Pemberley after their father's death. Darcy kept her in the nursery for most of their stay, but Anne would visit her occasionally.

"For years now both Lord Matlock and Lady Catherine have attempted to pressure me into marriage with Anne, to unite our two great estates they say. I have no desire to do as such, and neither does Anne, but that is of little matter. They have increased the pressure of late, and though I believe I know the true reasons behind their suit, I have said little to dissuade them. That will likely change this visit."

"If you and Anne are both against the marriage why have you said nothing? Are you afraid of what they might do?"

"I am not afraid of them. I am my own man and they have no say over my life. Anne, however, is dependent on Lady Catherine. She is not well, Georgie, and has not been for a very long time. She is weak, nothing no Fitzwilliam should ever be, and Lady Catherine has always been very dismissive of her. The one use she has of her, I believe, is to be paired with me. Once she finally sees that will not happen, I fear her dismissal of her daughter will turn into outright neglect."

"So how will this visit be different than the rest?"

"I received a letter from Anne this morning asking that I make my journey to Kent early. She believes her time is short and would like to see Fitzwilliam and me before . . . she leaves us."

Georgiana tilted her head as tears began to flow over her cheeks. Darcy handed her his handkerchief, already feeling remorse for exposing her to such sadness.

"I am a very selfish creature, wanting you to stay here with me when our cousin needs your comfort. I do not understand though, Brother. You speak of Anne with compassion and I know you love Richard, as did Father, but you say the Fitzwilliams are bad?"

Darcy nodded. It was a complicated situation, one that he only knew how to navigate because he had grown up doing so, at his parents' instruction. They gave him good principles, filled him with honor, but also caution when dealing with the world outside Pemberley.

He explained to her their parents' relationship and how their mother had always hoped for healing between the families. She encouraged the cousins to love each other and prove themselves to be worthy friends for each other. She also tried to cultivate that friendship with her own brother and sister.

"Unfortunately, Lord Matlock and Lady Catherine have proven themselves to be truly selfish creatures. I know it is hard for you to understand, but the need for power can corrupt a man's soul. They both feel that need acutely."

Georgiana became very quiet, as she contemplated all he had told her.

"I believe I can understand how that need can corrupt. Mr. Wickham felt it, did he not? The need to have some sort of power over you, over Pemberley, that he was not born to? Do our aunt and uncle attempt to manipulate you the way Wickham did me?"

Again, Darcy found himself smiling softly at his sister, wondering at her ability to comprehend the emotions at play. He quickly realized that he need not wonder since she daily sought complex streams of thought and feeling to master through music. She had the capability for profound understanding; she only needed his encouragement and honesty.

"Yes, dear, and I will not subject you to them any more than is necessary. I am sorry that I must go but I cannot deny Anne's request."

"And you will not grant mine?" Her eyes were again filled with tears. He wanted to give her what she wanted, to be her comfort until she was fully healed, but he felt protecting her was more important.

"I am sorry, Georgie. I am due at Matlock House for dinner and I must dress before Fitzwilliam arrives. Will you not retire until I return home this evening, so that we can talk more?"

"Of course, Brother." She rose and walked back to the pianoforte. She sat gracefully and placed her fingers on the keys, closed her eyes and looked down in silent communication to her partner-in-escape. Darcy walked from the room as she began to play, leaving her music to comfort her in a way he could not.

Some minutes later, Darcy leaned against the back of his dark green desk chair. He closed his eyes and drew a deep breath as he listened to the sound of his sister's playing waft in through his open study door. Her fingers landed heavily on the keys, and he could imagine the determined look on her face as she made her way through the movement. He recognized the piece as one she played whenever she sought courage.

He took a few more moments to breathe in the spirit of her song, allowing it to penetrate the barriers that kept the well-hidden stirrings of discontent at bay. The notes flowing into the room grew harsher, almost as if fighting a battle with the player, and Darcy slowly opened his eyes and glanced at his desk.

His papers were stacked neatly in the center, filled with instructions for his staff both in London and Pemberley. He lifted the ledgers that were piled over to the side and placed them in a drawer, locked it and put the key in his pocket. He fingered the stack of letters he penned earlier in the day, studying the one on top and wishing he had a few moments to spare for Bingley before his departure. Darcy was worried for his friend, who had seemed particularly careless in both his business and behavior since their return from Hertfordshire. He would take care to write to Bingley often from Kent, though he knew he would receive few letters in reply. Hopefully he would find him no worse for wear upon his return.

He reflected upon all he had accomplished in the last weeks. He had rechecked every figure from his estates, including household accounts with which he rarely bothered, trusting his housekeepers implicitly. The planting schedule for Pemberley was arranged in greater detail than previous years and the steward of his Scottish estate had seen more letters from him than they had from any prior Darcy.

Clearly, Georgiana was not the only one with a means of escape.

Chapter 2

The journey to London was tortuous. As soon as they set off, Maria proceeded to relay all of the neighborhood gossip Lydia missed during her illness. The most interesting tidbit, of course, involved Wickham.

"He is to marry Miss King, can you believe it?"

"Miss King," Elizabeth gasped. "She is very young still, and so soon after her grandfather's death."

"That is the material point is it not, Miss Eliza. She is now a rich woman, and therefore very desirable. He must strike while the iron is hot, as they say," Sir William's jovial voice resounded about them, his tone belying the seriousness of his words. Did no father take Wickham's actions seriously?

"Lizzy," Lydia leaned into her sister and Elizabeth immediately called for the carriage to stop. After Lydia expelled what little she had eaten for breakfast, Elizabeth straightened her bonnet and pelisse, and helped her back into the carriage, asking the driver to go a bit slower.

Sir William and Maria were very kind, each concerned for the girl. Elizabeth looked for suspicion in their eyes and thankfully found none. She wanted to trust Hill and Mr. Jones, but so many people knowing their secret made her nervous. Elizabeth knew the slightest hint of scandal would spread like a disease through the village and surrounding countryside. She knew without a doubt her father would say nothing and she believed the same of Hill and Mr. Jones, but she worried about her aunt's servants in London and, most of all, she did not trust Wickham. He would only implicate himself by speaking of his actions with Lydia, but was there any real danger for him if he did? Men were never ruined by their seductions. Elizabeth had nothing at her disposal to insure his silence. She could only hope.

The party arrived in London later than expected and were greeted by an enthusiastic Jane who, after warmly welcoming everyone to London, swept Lydia away to rest. The Lucases settled in to refresh themselves and Jane continued to tend Lydia, leaving Elizabeth and Mrs. Gardiner time to chat in the privacy of her aunt's chambers.

"Tell me about Longbourn, Lizzy. How is life there now?"

"Much less chaotic. With Jane gone and Lydia ill, Mama requires Kitty and Mary to be with her almost constantly. Lydia's illness has exasperated Mama's poor nerves, I am afraid. Imagine what she would be like if she knew the truth. Fortunately, there has been very little socializing. Aunt Phillips comes to visit some, but Kitty and Mary only go to church and occasionally to a shop. Thankfully Papa has taken it upon himself to accompany them, which is probably why the outings are so rare."

"You are still very angry with him?"

"How could I not be? If you had seen her, Aunt . . ." Elizabeth paused to push down a sob. "She did not want to tell him, but I was certain he would help. He is our father. Is he not supposed to protect us? He blamed her, Aunt, accused her of purposefully enticing that man. She is fifteen. She has no real education and little discipline. Every time she and Kitty spoke of the officers, every time they openly flirted, he merely rolled his eyes and called them silly. Never was there a word of caution or a reprimand. Yet, her mistakes are her own and she must bear the consequences with no help or understanding from her father. I feel as if I do not know him. Is he the same man who refused to give me to Mr. Collins? If that was based on love, why could he not share that same love with Lydia?"

"It was not love that influenced that decision, it was foolishness. Of course you could not have married Mr. Collins, but he could have encouraged a more appropriate match, perhaps with Mary or Kitty. At the very least he could have cultivated a relationship with his heir that would have resulted in feelings of sympathy or obligation toward your mother and sisters. Instead he left your futures to chance. Men like your father—*weak men*—cannot admit their mistakes. Instead they cast off blame and allow others to clean the mess they leave behind. I am sorry to speak so plainly, Lizzy. I am sure this is not helping, but I am fairly angry with him myself.

"However," her face softened as she continued, "Your father is not acting in a contrary manner to any other man of his class. No gentleman could have allowed his daughter to remain at home in that condition. In the eyes of society, Lydia is ruined, and the risk to the rest of you is too great. We should be grateful he did not force a marriage between the two."

"Yes, there is that, though I doubt he was thinking much of Lydia's future happiness. He simply could not afford to broker a marriage between his fallen daughter and her seducer. I know she could not stay home, but he did not need to be cruel. It is as if I never knew him until that day. Oh, I was never blind to his faults. I knew he was a poor husband, but because he loved me, whereas my mother did not, it did not matter. It was the same with Wickham, I now realize. He flattered me, whereas another did not, so of course every word he said was true." She drew in a shuddering breath. "Oh Aunt, not only do I hardly know myself, but I do not think I could recognize a truly good man if I were to meet one."

"Lizzy, you have not been in varied society and still have much to learn. How could you know the truth of a man's character based on mere words? A man's actions are much more telling and you knew nothing of what Wickham was about. No sheltered gentlewoman such as you could have. You must learn from this, my dear. The only good that can come from this is the ability to prevent it from happening to your family again."

She rested her head upon her aunt's shoulder for a moment before rising to look out the window.

"What else is it, Lizzy?"

"I was looking at Maria in the carriage today. She is so lively and vibrant, just as Lydia was only a few months ago. She told us Wickham is engaged to a young girl in our neighborhood, a Miss King who recently inherited ten thousand pounds. What is my silence costing her? What could it cost Maria or any other naïve girl who crosses his path? I feel so powerless. I cannot expose him without risking Lydia. I must protect her, and I will protect her, but I am endangering others by doing so. How can I live with that?"

Mrs. Gardiner stood and embraced her niece, trying to bring comfort. "Dear Lizzy. You cannot take on the problems of the world. Right now you have only the power to protect your sister. That must be your solace."

Elizabeth nodded and enjoyed a few more moments of respite in her aunt's embrace before she excused herself to rest before dinner.

Darcy stared into the flames of his study's fireplace as he swirled his brandy, bringing it to his lips but finding no comfort there. His mood had soured since the morning. The anticipation of spending the evening in his uncle's home along with having to leave his sister the next morning had him anxious.

Darcy's defensives always rose when in company with his uncle, who was far too good at reading insecurities and exploiting them to his full advantage. It annoyed him that Matlock played up their personal connection, weak as it was, to gain favor among those who so desperately wanted a piece of Darcy for themselves. Since becoming his own man, this game had been part of his life and he was tired. Darcy never truly understood why the game was played, only that he was in danger of being devoured if he ever lost.

"Father will expect you to linger a while after the other guests have gone. I believe he desires to speak about some family business."

His cousin's voice drew Darcy's attention to a dark corner of the room. Richard Fitzwilliam's tall frame draped over a chair close to the window. His brandy glass dangled from his fingers casually, as if he were not holding on to it for dear life.

"Your father will be disappointed, I am afraid. I have no intention of staying at this dinner any longer than necessary. I doubt the earl has anything to say that I would want to hear."

"Well, you will never know unless you hear him out."

Fitzwilliam was often caught between his cousin and his father. Darcy did everything he could to avoid involving him in their dealings. Truth be told, he did everything he could not to deal with Matlock at all.

"I have heard it all before, Fitzwilliam—at least a thousand times since my father died. I spend too much time at Pemberley. I should allow Georgiana to live with them at Matlock. I should not maintain a friendship with the son of a tradesman. I should be more involved in politics … as *his* supporter, of course. Most important of all I should marry Anne and claim Rosings before it is too late. Have I missed anything?"

Richard sighed. "No, Darcy, I am sure you have covered it all. What harm will it do to indulge him for a while? The Fitzwilliams are your family—your only family. Do you not owe them a bit of time to voice their concerns, not only for you but for Georgie as well?"

Darcy turned toward his cousin, amazement at his last statement clearly expressed in his features.

"Concerns? Demands, you mean. What of this renewed interest in my sister? They had ceased their efforts to get close to her until recently. You have not told them about Wickham have you?"

"Of course not, Darcy. I would never betray her like that—or you for that matter. If you will not stay after dinner, then come out with me. My brother's taming has left a hole in the London nightlife. I say we fill it. When is the last time you allowed yourself a bit of fun?"

"You and I have very different ideas of fun, Fitzwilliam. I have no interest in filling anything recently left vacant by my cousin, or anyone else for that matter. Need I remind you, again, that I will not give the most intimate parts of myself to women frequented by the dregs of society?"

"You mean the upper nobility and peers of the realm?"

"Exactly."

Fitzwilliam let out a small chuckle. "And, of course, the Darcy seed is far too superior to spread about so casually."

"Of course."

Fitzwilliam had been jesting, but Darcy was completely serious. His father had instilled in him a sense of pride and responsibility. Pemberley had grown into one of the most prosperous estates in the country, and the Darcy legacy was not only one of wealth, but of strength. No brief pleasure was worth soiling the work of generations. No Darcy had fathered a bastard nor laid with a woman outside the marriage bed, and he would not be the first.

Fitzwilliam finished his brandy then stood and shook his head. "God, Darcy, you really are an arrogant, ill-tempered ass. You have the world laid at your feet: wealth, property, position. Every woman in this town is willing to lift their skirts for you. You are the richest man in Derbyshire and could easily be the richest in Kent if you would only take it. Most men would kill for what you have and you appreciate none of it."

Darcy could not decide whether or not Fitzwilliam was teasing. His voice was hard, and there was something in his tone that almost sounded angry and resentful. He looked carefully on his cousin and spoke with calm authority, allowing only a slight edge in his voice, though he was becoming somewhat irritated with his petulance.

"I do not partake of the same pleasures as your father and that makes me unappreciative? I should squander my wealth on meaningless pursuits, lie idol while others tend my land, and use my position to make others feel inferior? I was raised to be better than that Fitzwilliam, and so were you."

Darcy hoped his words hit their intended mark, reminding his cousin that it was George Darcy, not Henry Fitzwilliam, who taught him what it meant to be a man. As a second son his presence was not necessary by his father's side, so as a child he spent much of the year at Pemberley. All of the Fitzwilliam cousins had visited there throughout their early childhood. Darcy's mother Anne had hoped that if the younger generation bonded, the rivalry that had existed between the fathers would cease. Time would tell if her efforts were fruitful.

Fitzwilliam refilled his glass. "And of course, you are above temptation. You sit in your fortress, surrounded by all the things that protect you—wealth, status and that fearsome scowl—never being touched, never allowing anyone within feet of your well-ordered existence. I wonder what will happen when something or someone is placed before you and you find them more than tolerable. What will your reaction be when there is finally a temptation you cannot conquer?" He no longer held his glass loosely, but with a grip that matched the tightness in his face.

Darcy turned back to the fire and toed at the hearth as a vision of fine eyes and a wicked, challenging smile flashed in his memory. Temptation was why he was so efficient at his desk in recent weeks, why he spent his mornings riding hard through the park, and why he had needed Georgiana's playing as much as she did. Darcy knew temptation, and he knew his reaction to said temptation was to run away like a bloody coward.

"We are all lured by something. How do we know our worth if never tested?"

Fitzwilliam gave a mirthless laugh before he downed the contents of his glass. "On the contrary, cousin, our worth is outlined by our birth. Temptations, works, actions--it all means very little in the world in which we live. Life is as random as it is harsh."

Concern overrode Darcy's irritation as he looked upon his cousin's angry, yet defeated countenance. He relaxed his stance, crossed the room and placed his hand on his shoulder.

"Have I done something to offend you, Richard? You have been unusually belligerent this evening. If it is too inconvenient for you to leave for Rosings in the morning, I understand. You can join me whenever you wish. I did not mean to be overly demanding."

Fitzwilliam's face softened in reply to Darcy's concerned expression. He returned the shoulder pat with one of his own and walked over to place his glass on the table.

"Forgive me, Darcy. You are not the only one who dreads this dinner. The air inside my parents' home has been especially thick of late."

Darcy shook his head. "There is no need to apologize. You have suffered my bad moods enough over the years. I suppose you are owed at least one of your own. Shall we get to it then?" Darcy gestured toward the door.

Fitzwilliam nodded then turned back to the bottle. "Just one more."

Chapter 3

The trip from Hertfordshire to Kent did not require a night's rest in London, but it had been planned that way to give the Bennet sisters time together as well as Sir William the opportunity to discuss business with Mr. Gardiner.

Lizzy examined her uncle, seated at the head of the table enjoying conversation with guests on either side of him. She felt great affection for the man. He was her mother's younger brother and they shared many of the same handsome features, but their similarities were only skin deep. He was charming, well read, well-spoken, and had a keen mind for business. Like her father, he did not spend much time in the bosom of his family. Unlike her father, his absence was due to his efforts to provide a better life for his wife and children. His family accepted his absence as part of life, knowing he worked hard to give them every opportunity his success could buy. He was kind, but not overly affectionate and was clearly uncomfortable when he spoke to Lydia earlier that afternoon. Elizabeth felt sympathy for him. Fifteen year old girls can be difficult for men to understand in ordinary situations, much less the one in which they found themselves. He did assure her he would see to her comfort, which gave them all a measure of peace.

Elizabeth turned her attention to the man sitting to her uncle's left. She was surprised when her aunt informed her they expected another guest for dinner. Her surprise faded when she noticed the attention that guest paid to her elder sister.

Mr. Samuel Burton was the owner of a small estate in the north who had some financial dealings with Mr. Gardiner. He stood taller than her uncle and Sir William but had not the height of some others of her acquaintance. His dark blonde hair framed his face, which was neither handsome nor unpleasant. What kept Mr. Burton from being merely average was his demeanor. An aura of confidence surrounded him, giving him an almost regal appearance. Elizabeth wondered if all gentlemen from the north held such a mien as she watched his interactions with Jane.

He had abandoned his conversation with his host and was now speaking solely to Jane, whose smile was less serene and more . . . joyful. She looked over to see the same expression lighting the gentleman's face. Elizabeth smiled. Perhaps Jane would soon have an announcement for the family. They certainly needed some good news. Reason began to rein in her hope as she remembered Mr. Bingley's happy expression when he had looked upon her sister. No, she would no longer assume affection and honorable attentions until a declaration was made. She would have to speak to Jane about protecting her heart and make sure her aunt and uncle were doing everything necessary to protect her reputation.

"Ah, my son and nephew. You have arrived at last."

Matlock stood outside the drawing room and greeted the two gentlemen. He was an imposing figure, standing nearly as tall as Darcy, armed with a smile that would appear friendly to those who did not know him well. Darcy, however, recognized it for what it was.

"I believe we are right on time, Father. Darcy would never allow us to be a moment late for any engagement." Two of the gentlemen laughed.

"No, I suppose he would not. You are, of course, on time for dinner but I had expected to see you earlier. Did my son neglect to inform you that I needed to speak to you?"

"I was informed." Darcy did not feel the need to elaborate. Matlock's irritation showed only a moment before the smile took its place.

"No matter. We can talk over brandy after dinner. We must not keep everyone waiting. We have some special guests tonight, Darcy. I think even you will approve of the company."

The earl was at his manipulative best. His smile and warm greeting foretold an evening of empty flattery and false concern over Darcy's lack of companionship. If his greeting had been more formal Darcy would have known that he would be asked to invest in some acquaintance's endeavor or align himself with a favored politician. As it was, he knew the purpose of the evening was to convince him to marry Anne.

Thus, when he entered the drawing room, Darcy became confused. Sitting among the obscenely ornate silk-covered furniture and overly perfumed greenhouse roses, were four very beautiful women. Two belonged to the house, but two were strangers. They were all finely dressed and rose gracefully when the men entered the room. Ladies Sophia and Victoria stood on the right, both standing with the confidence and poise that had been drilled into them since they were children. The jewels that hung from their necks were heirlooms, some dating back more than a century. No one could mistake them for anything but ladies, wives to peers of the realm, genuine to their surroundings of opulence.

The two that stood opposite them were dressed just as fine and their jewels shone just as brightly, though they were obviously of a newer fashion. To the casual observer, they were indeed no different than the Ladies, but Darcy's ever-present suspicion caused him to look deeper. Their demeanor was perfect for their environment, but their eyes gave away their insecurity. They knew they did not belong. He looked around the room and saw no gentlemen other than Viscount Wakely, the earl's eldest son. It seemed odd they were there without escorts. At any other party he would assume the ladies were intended for Fitzwilliam and himself, but that surely could not be the case here. If his uncle still expected him to marry Anne (and Darcy was sure he did) why was he introducing him to Miss Olivia Wallace?

"She is worse since I left Longbourn." Jane spoke softly while stroking a sleeping Lydia's hair. The evening ended early out of consideration for the travelers. Jane and Elizabeth intended to help Lydia prepare for bed, but found her already asleep when they entered Jane's room.

"She is," Elizabeth agreed. "Are you sure you want her to stay in your room? Perhaps she should be closer to our aunt or we could ask for a maid to stay with her." Elizabeth was concerned that Jane would notice the unusual rise in Lydia's stomach, especially when the rest of her was so gaunt. No, Jane was too innocent to understand the reason behind the bump, nor would she ever suspect her sisters would keep secrets.

"No, Lizzy, I want to care for her. It is only for a week and then she will be gone for many months, as will you, dear sister. I cannot help but wonder when we will all be together again."

Jane had spoken Elizabeth's greatest fear: that Lydia would not survive her illness or would be discovered and sent away for good. Not wanting Jane to see her distress, she quickly changed the subject.

"Does Mr. Burton call here often? He seemed very comfortable amongst the company."

Jane blushed slightly and Elizabeth could tell she was trying to school her features.

"He visits at least twice a week. He and our uncle have much business to discuss."

"So he only comes when Uncle is at home?" Elizabeth's eyebrow arched as Jane's blush deepened.

"Do not tease me, Lizzy."

"I am not meaning to tease, I am merely asking a question."

"I believe you asked enough questions at dinner." Jane's voice held a note of irritation that was as close to an admonishment as she could produce. Between that and the hard kick she had received under the table from her aunt, Elizabeth felt duly chastised.

"I was only trying to get to know the gentleman. You all seemed rather intimate and I felt left out." Attempting to tease her way out of trouble proved ineffectual. Jane remained firm.

"The way you asked him about his estate and his family caused me to wonder how Mama had managed to take possession of your mouth."

"Jane!" Elizabeth was shocked such a statement could come from her sweet and docile sister. It seemed as though she were protecting Mr. Burton.

"Shhh." They looked down to see that Lydia was not disturbed, then to each other. "You were nearly uncivil, Lizzy. Why?"

Elizabeth reached out and took her sister's hand. "It was fairly obvious at dinner that you like him, very much, I would wager. I do not want to see you hurt again, Janey. We barely knew Mr. Bingley, yet we were all pushing you toward him. It was very foolish to expect so much after such a short acquaintance. We did not take enough time to sketch his character and I believe our encouragement only added to your disappointment. I do not wish to make that mistake again."

"I understand your concern, Lizzy, but there is no need to worry. He is behaving as a gentleman should. He calls on me here amongst our family and has escorted me on walks, with Aunt as chaperone, of course. He talks to me. He tells me about his estate and how he wants to improve it. It is small now but he has plans to expand his fortune. His dealings with our uncle are part of those plans. He is focused and determined. His wife and children will never fear for their future."

Elizabeth took a moment to study her sister, remembering the times they had sat in a similar manner and discussed Mr. Bingley. Jane would blush and give a sweet smile while she spoke of his amiability but not much else. Not once did she have the confidence she now displayed. Elizabeth had never been more jealous of Jane—not because she was getting attention from a man, but because Elizabeth had forgotten what it was to be sure of anything.

"Well, he did say his only sister is married and does not visit often. He has that over Mr. Bingley at least."

Jane's resolve was finally broken and the two sisters giggled quietly. "You should not speak such things, Lizzy. I still believe Miss Bingley did me a great service when she warned me off her brother."

Elizabeth was pleased to see some part of Jane remained the same. She had felt friendship for Miss Bingley and, even though the acquaintance had been short, Jane would never wish to see fault in a friend.

"Very well. I will allow you to see her in such a light since it is unlikely we shall ever see any of them again. Perhaps I, too, shall look back upon the Netherfield party with fondness so you will not be alone in your delusions."

"Lizzy!" Their quiet laughter ensued for many moments until Elizabeth pulled Jane into a tight embrace.

"I have missed you so much, Janey."

This time with Jane had not only provided a short rest from the weariness that was settling in, but served to remind her of what was truly at stake. Jane was in love, or soon would be, and ruin would cost far more than society's good opinion.

Elizabeth went to bed feeling better about the separate paths each of them were taking. She still ached at the idea of leaving Lydia, but was more determined than ever to do whatever it took to protect the people she loved, no matter the cost.

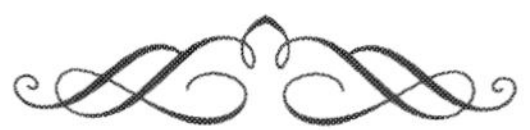

As Darcy made polite conversation, Fitzwilliam moved to the back of the room, content to observe for a while. He looked over everyone in the room, his gaze finally resting on the one he had been determined not to see. As his eyes settled on her, she laughed and the sound lifted his heart while simultaneously piercing it through. Even from the distance he could see the joy in her eyes. His attention traveled from her face down to the curve of her neck. The skin there was lily white, delicate and, he imagined, very soft. To Fitzwilliam's mind, there was no one more graceful, beautiful or seductive than the woman on his brother's arm.

"Lady Victoria is looking particularly well this evening." The sound of his father's voice caused him to start.

"All the ladies present tonight are beautiful. Are you trying to torture us lonely bachelors?"

The earl laughed. "Of course not. I am trying to end your suffering, and Darcy's."

Fitzwilliam wondered at the statement, but before he could ask, his father continued.

"I do not say it enough, I know, but I am proud of you, Richard."

"Oh?"

"Indeed. You are making your own way in the world. First sons are raised with all the privileges, never needing to worry much over the future. Frederick and Darcy could never have done the things you have. I was a second son, you know."

Fitzwilliam nodded.

"My brother Edward was as spoiled as those two, with no expectations laid upon him except to simply be first. Along with the title of Viscount, he also inherited whatever illness it is that my younger sister suffered from. It was a shame really, to lose a brother so young." Matlock did not say that he thought it was nature's way of correcting itself, filtering out the weak so the strong could prosper.

"But I did benefit from the loss. I came into everything that was to be his, including your mother. She has never forgiven me for that. Frederick it seems, has been more fortunate in his choice of wife."

"She is lovely."

"Yes. She is everything someone of her class is supposed to be. Graceful, accomplished, and she seems to be quite kind as well. She was, of course, raised to be the wife of a first son. Pity that."

The father-and-son bonding was interrupted by the call to dinner. Fitzwilliam watched Viscount Wakely escort Victoria from the room before he moved to do the same for one of his father's guests.

Once seated, Darcy surreptitiously studied the scene around him. The dining room, like the rest of the house, was a gilded spectacle. Indulgence dripped from every fixture, falling onto the inhabitants like saliva from the mouth of an overworked mare. The scent of roses followed him from the drawing room, and he would no doubt need to scrub the pungent sweetness from his skin and the end of the night.

He found the seating arrangement a bit odd as their other guest, whose name Darcy could not remember, was seated next to Matlock opposite Colonel Fitzwilliam. She was speaking of something she must have found amusing, as she was laughing quietly, but Matlock was not attending. He was occupied studying his youngest son.

Fitzwilliam was engaged in conversation with his sister-in-law, Lady Victoria. She was an attractive woman with delicate features and a cheerful disposition. Darcy had not spent much time in her company, but it was clear to him that she was intelligent and kind, though perhaps a little young to be married. She was nineteen and just the previous year had come out into society, quickly gaining the attention of Viscount Wakely, who beat out several others in the quest for her hand. While she seemed comfortable in the opulence of her surroundings, she was not one with it.

In contrast to Lady Victoria was the Countess Lady Sophia. She was a bit too comfortable in her surroundings. She was all politeness, but made little effort at conversation. She was like a bird in the clouds, seemingly weightless though firmly in her seat. She was distant—a world away from present company—and Darcy wondered just how much opium was needed to obtain such a detachment.

"If we are to be dinner companions, Mr. Darcy, we must be able to speak to one another. We cannot sit here all evening in grave silence."

Darcy turned to glance at the woman at his side. Most men would consider her beautiful. Her dark hair was swept up in tight curls with tiny pearls dotted throughout. Her ivory gown was fitted close to her body and accentuated the parts men would most like to see. Rouge enhanced her cheeks and lips, but not overly so. She was as perfect as an illustration in a book and, Darcy supposed, likely as flat.

"If you wish for conversation, Miss Wallace, I will try to oblige you. What would you like to discuss?"

"Anything will do. You are a man of the world and must know infinite topics of interest. Or, if you prefer, we may simply discuss the meal before us. The soup was served at just the right temperature, was it not, Mr. Darcy?" The playfulness of her voice caused a sudden thump in his chest. He ignored it and continued the conversation in his dullest voice.

"It was indeed, Miss Wallace."

"Oh, this will not do. We cannot speak of soup if you will only agree and be silent. There must be something I can say that will keep your interest."

"What of books, madam?"

"Books? At a dinner party hosted by a premier family of the *ton*? Surely you are teasing, for you must know that we should comment on the number of footmen present or the fineness of her ladyship's gown."

Miss Wallace's eyes lit up as her mouth curved in amusement. The thump returned and this time Darcy did not ignore it. His gaze remained fixed on the woman before him, but his mind drifted to the past, and a vision of superior beauty danced before him, tempting him to travel a different road in the morning, one that would take him north rather than to Kent.

"Mr. Darcy, you seemed so serious just now. Were you dreaming of ways to win the war, or perhaps contemplating a different haircut?"

"No indeed, madam. My mind was more agreeably engaged."

Dinner ended and the men remained in the dining room to enjoy brandy and cigars, while the ladies removed to the drawing room.

"Well, Darcy, what do you think of Miss Wallace and Miss Bradford? They are singular beauties are they not?"

"I saw nothing truly beautiful in either of them. They are no different than any of the women one would find in the drawing rooms of London on any given evening."

"Ah, that is where you are wrong, nephew. You will not often find the likes of these ladies amongst society. They are special."

Darcy's entire countenance showed his boredom with the situation. He wished the earl would just lay out his demands so he could dismiss them and go home.

"How so, my lord?"

"They are yours. Just pick one, or both if you prefer. They are already paid for, their establishments have been arranged; you just need to choose."

Darcy looked to Matlock, whose expression bore a look of triumph, then to their companions, who looked as shocked as he felt.

"I beg your pardon?"

"Come now, Darcy. I believe I finally understand why you are reluctant to marry Anne. I am embarrassed to have not thought of it before. You are a young man with desires that Anne will no doubt be unable to fulfill. I know your father raised you to have a reluctance when dealing with pleasures of the flesh and so you might find it difficult to set that aside and make arrangements for yourself, so I have done it for you. Now tell me, did you prefer the dark or the fair?"

Darcy rose from his chair and paced the length of the table and back before he finally spoke his indignity.

"Do you mean to tell me that you invited me here tonight to introduce me to potential mistresses? Have you given up the earldom to take a position as a madam? Are you arranging similar situations for all unmarried gentlemen in London, or am I the sole recipient of your generosity?"

Before Matlock could speak, Viscount Wakely joined in.

"You invited whores into your home and seated them at the same table as *my wife*?"

Darcy had maintained a distance but Wakely closed the gap between himself and his father, who stood to meet his son's anger without fear.

They stood nearly nose to nose, almost mirror images of each other. The earl's blond hair was streaked with gray and his eyes were cold, but there was no question they were father and son; the contempt they felt for each other was just as obvious.

"The way you treat your wife is of little concern to me, but mine will not be humiliated and subjected to your insanity. You must be out of your mind to act in such a manner."

The earl's only answer was to raise his eyebrows and Wakely bolted from the room.

Matlock rolled his eyes and straightened his coat. "He has become such a disappointment. If I had known that girl would have so much influence over him, I never would have allowed the marriage. She has a few Methodist tendencies, you know."

Darcy shook his head and wondered if this was part of the game or if his uncle was truly out of his wits. He turned to his cousin, who was still seated with his head resting in one hand.

"Did you know about this, Fitzwilliam?"

"No, Darcy. I knew he wanted to take you somewhere after dinner. I had no idea he would bring the entertainment to you instead."

Darcy looked at his uncle with all the contempt he had disguised the past five years. His emotions were on full display, and they spoke nothing but hatred.

"I have no interest in your women, Matlock, and I must question your judgment in allowing them in your home, with your wife and daughter no less. It is your duty to protect them, not expose them to fallen women. Have you no respect at all for them or their reputations?"

"I did this for you, Darcy. It seems you need encouragement to do your duty to your family. This has gone on long enough. You will announce your engagement to Anne during your visit to Rosings. Your honor demands it of you."

"My honor, sir, demands that I do what is best for Pemberley and Georgiana. I am resolved to act in a manner that will constitute my own happiness and that of my sister without regard to you or anyone who has their own self-interest at heart."

The earl lost his typical cool attitude and took on a heated air in response to Darcy's emphatic declaration.

"You are a Fitzwilliam. Where is your loyalty? I am your nearest relation and head of this family. I say you will marry Anne."

"I will state this one final time. You have no say as to whom I marry or how I live my life whatsoever. When I marry, whether it be to Anne or some country nobody, it will be my choice."

Without sparing another glance to either man, Darcy turned and left the room. He took no time to gather his hat or call for his carriage. He stormed into the cool air and allowed it to settle his mind and emotions as he walked the short distance to his home.

Darcy arrived to the sound of Georgiana playing softly in the music room. He wondered at the lateness of her practicing, then remembered his request that she not retire until he came home. He chose to not greet her until he was able to process everything that had just occurred. He made his way to his study where he poured a large brandy then paced the room.

Before long, his glass was empty and he had yet to make any sense of the earl's actions. His uncle was no stranger to whores, but to bring them into his home was scandalous. He poured another brandy and was about to make another circuit of the room when a knock sounded on his door.

"Enter."

His aging butler entered and offered a shallow bow. "Viscount Wakely, sir."

Darcy nodded and the butler stepped aside to allow the visitor entry before leaving and closing the door behind him.

"Can you spare one of those, cousin? You are not the only one in need of fortification."

Darcy nodded and motioned for him to help himself. "What is your father about, Wakely? What would prompt him to take such an action?"

The viscount sat heavily in a chair, bringing a leg over his knee while taking a long drink from his tumbler. "I do not know, Darcy, and frankly, I do not care. I have washed my hands of my father. I have come to warn you of the ensuing scandal."

"What do you mean?

"I am breaking from my father. I have moved Victoria to her father's house and we will stay there until I can arrange for other accommodations."

"Are you abdicating your title?"

"God no. I am simply no longer acknowledging the soulless bastard who fathered me. We will live well enough on Victoria's dowry, though we will have to leave London until the talk dies down."

"I understand your anger, but are you sure this is wise? This will affect your children someday."

"That is precisely why I am doing it, Darcy. I would rather have the respect of my wife and children than be acknowledged by the quality."

Darcy leaned against his desk and smiled. One year ago, the man before him thought only of himself and whatever easy pleasure he could find. Now he was risking his future over an insult to his wife.

"Your wife has made something of you has she not?"

"Indeed she has. All those years I spent visiting women like those my father offered you tonight, as well as the ones that came freely, I had no idea the truth of the matter. There is in fact nothing more enticing than an enthusiastic wife. Lust is a powerful thing, no doubt, but love is what will bring you to your knees."

Darcy sipped his brandy then placed it on his desk. He laced his fingers in front of him and looked down momentarily in contemplation.

"And how do you know the difference?"

Wakely's face softened as he leaned forward to rest his elbows on his knees, dangling his brandy loosely in his fingers.

"Lust is about taking. It is selfish, greedy, temporary. Love makes you want to give everything you ever had or ever will have to ensure the happiness of the one you treasure. When you love someone, you are a part of them; you claim their joys and their miseries. You defy their detractors and make a fool of yourself by trying to explain something that can only understood when it is experienced. I highly recommend it, cousin."

Wakely stood and drained his glass before returning it to the table with the decanter. He came to stand next to Darcy and placed a hand on his shoulder.

"I am truly sorry for any trouble you will have because of this, and Georgiana as well."

Darcy drew a deep breath as he contemplated the possible ramifications for his sister. Visits to the shops were out of the question now. He would not subject her to the viciousness of the *ton* while she was still so vulnerable. She would be better off at home, at Pemberley.

"I will send her to Derbyshire. She will be safe from the gossip there. It is a break in the family, rather mild by *ton* standards. You could keep this quiet, leave Matlock without any public set down."

"Yes, but his humiliation will be well worth any cuts we receive as a result. What will I lose, really? My standing with the gentlemen at the club? I prefer the company at 110 Bond Street anyway."

"Pugilism Wakely? A bit savage is it not?"

"All men have savages inside them, Darcy. It only takes the right situation to bring them out. The beast within will only be ruled by the gentleman for so long."

"And Lady Victoria does not fear your savagery?"

"She encourages it. Perhaps you will join me there when you come back from Kent, if we are still in town. I have a feeling you will need to hit something hard after your time with Lady Catherine. My brother could perhaps be of service while you are there."

"I forgot about Fitzwilliam. In my anger I left him there without much thought."

"You should not worry. I believe he is taking advantage of Father's generosity for the evening."

Darcy groaned, knowing the viscount did not refer to a meal and lodgings. They said their goodnights with promises to be in touch and wishes of safe travels. After speaking to Georgiana about her pending journey home, he retired to his chamber to contemplate his cousin's words and dream of his own enthusiastic wife.

Chapter 4

Elizabeth looked out the window at the menacing clouds that gathered in the distance ahead. The hour of their departure had promised good traveling weather, but nature had tricked them, it seemed. She heard thunder crack overhead and she jumped at the sound. She glanced at her fellow travelers to see if they noticed her reaction, but they were occupied with watching the scenery gradually fade to gray as the clouds overtook them. She found it fitting that the atmosphere outside the carriage should mirror the tumult that was raging inside her after leaving her sisters that morning. Lydia had been too tired from the short journey the previous day to farewell Elizabeth at the door, so the sisters said their goodbyes above stairs, alone. Elizabeth tried to reassure her that all would be well, but she could not tell if Lydia believed her.

"I will be with you again as soon as I can, Liddy. In the meantime, take this." Elizabeth removed the garnet cross she always wore from her neck and placed it around Lydia's.

"I cannot take this from you, Lizzy. You have no replacement for it."

"I have nothing else to give you, Lydia, and I need to know that some piece of me is there with you. Will you take it, please?"

Lydia nodded as tears streamed from her eyes. "I am frightened, Lizzy. I do not know where I am going."

"Yes you do. You are coming home. Focus on that, dear. After this is all over, you will be coming home to us." Elizabeth stroked her hair and looked in her eyes with all the confidence she could muster. "You are brave and strong and you shall conquer this."

"Are you not excited, Eliza? I have only traveled to London before and everything I am now seeing is new. Oh, I will not let this rain dampen my mood, for I am far too excited."

Elizabeth turned toward the voice and tried to keep a smile from forming as she watched Maria look warningly out the window, as if she were convincing the rain she was not impressed. Elizabeth had never thought much about Maria. She was Kitty and Lydia's friend, and she had relegated her to the "silly girl who must be tolerated" area of her mind. She was ashamed of herself for being so prejudiced and dismissive of another person. She began to search herself for other ways in which she was like her father. She, too, had some things to conquer.

The rain, falling hard upon the carriage roof, broke Elizabeth's reverie. She did not know how far they were from Bromley, but she hoped they would make it there without incident. Before the thought could completely leave her head, a sudden light filled the carriage followed by another loud crack of thunder above them, and the carriage began to speed along the road. She looked to her companions in panic, and this time they did notice.

"The lightening must have frightened the horses. Not to worry, the driver should have it under control in a moment." Sir William's words would have been reassuring if his eyes had not bulged.

Several moments passed and they were still speeding. Elizabeth's heart pounded in time to the beating of the horse's hooves as they raced in determination to flee from what frightened them. She could hear the driver shouting in an effort to control the beasts and as she reached to grasp the door handle for support, she heard a loud splitting sound. The carriage rocked and she lost her grip, landing heavily on the floor. A thought flashed in her mind of how quickly things could change: in one moment she was in a comfortable seat contemplating the past, and in the next she found herself tossed on the floor wondering about her future–as quick as a lighting strike. She felt the carriage begin to tip and she closed her eyes and braced herself for the coming impact.

"Will you please stop all that bloody racket, my head is throbbing."

"I cannot stop the bloody racket. I have not that power. It is the rain you hear."

Darcy stared at his cousin from across the carriage. Fitzwilliam had yet to open his eyes and must have sleepwalked into the conveyance that morning. He had not spoken, but groaned with each bump in the road as his head leaned against the window. The thunder must have finally roused him to consciousness.

"You must have some way to master it— you are a *Darcy* for God's sake."

"You would be surprised how little weight a great estate and proud lineage carries when trying to command the clouds. One would do much better to not find himself in a state that requires the expulsion of such noisy things as raindrops."

"The devil take you, Darcy. I swear to you one day I will see you so inebriated that you forget that proud lineage and do something human-like."

"You already have. Do you not remember my first week at Cambridge?"

"Oh yes. I had quite forgotten that." A proud smile spread across his face. Darcy thought it typical that it only took memories of his humiliation to revive his cousin.

"No doubt due to your own inebriation."

Fitzwilliam laughed outright at this, and Darcy was glad to hear it. The tension between them the previous evening was unusual. Though they often teased each other, they had not had cross words since they were children. Darcy had no true confidants, preferring to keep his own counsel on most things, but Fitzwilliam was at least able to share some of the burdens of raising Georgiana.

The colonel finally opened his eyes and leaned toward his cousin. "About last night, Darcy. I cannot comprehend at all what my father was thinking. In his twisted way, I do believe he was trying to help. He simply does not understand why you have not already married Anne."

"Fitzwilliam, you know as well as I do that Anne could never carry the burden of motherhood. Marriage would mean death for her; everyone in the family is aware except her mother and your father. Of course he does not understand why I have not married her. He cannot see anything beyond wealth and influence. He has attempted to manage my affairs for years and last night was just another example. One cannot do something so despicable and not reap the consequences, however. Your brother has already cut ties with him. He removed Lady Victoria to her father's house last night."

"What? When did this happen?"

"No doubt while you were enjoying the favors of our dinner companions."

Darcy maintained eye contact until Fitzwilliam turned to the window. He seemed to become lost for a moment until he once again looked at his cousin.

"Frederick will risk scandal because of this? He will feed Victoria to the gossips because of our father's lapse in judgment? This does not need to be made public."

Darcy nodded. "He was angry last night when he came to the townhouse. It is likely he will see things a bit differently this morning. I doubt he will publicly set down the earl, but he will no longer live in his house. He made it clear that no one is allowed to disrespect his wife in such a way.

"I have decided it would be best, should anything come of this, if Georgiana was removed from town. She is on her way to Pemberley now." He did not mention his concern lay more with the possibility that Matlock would try to see Georgiana while he was away. The man had failed to influence Darcy so he might turn his attentions to his niece instead.

"I would like to have known that. She is my ward as well, and she is dear to me, though I do wonder if she realizes that since she seems to avoid me now. I would like to have at least said goodbye."

"I did not want to leave her in town unattended. You could not say goodbye because you were indisposed."

"Yes, Darcy, let's beat that dead horse, shall we? How was she this morning?"

"Angry. She did not want to travel to Pemberley; it is too far from Kent and she is still often in need of reassurance. I promised her I would be there with her as soon as I was able. I also reminded her that we are expecting guests later in the summer, hoping to give her something to look forward to."

"What did she say to that?"

"She asked if the possibility of scandal would keep Miss Bingley away. I told her the only thing likely to do that was my marriage to someone other than Miss Bingley."

"And her response?"

"She told me to get to it."

The gentlemen laughed, causing one to wince at the sensation the brief merriment caused in his temple.

"Will you join us as well? I am sorry you have not spent much time with Georgiana these past months. She is embarrassed by her behavior in Ramsgate and still very unsure of herself. She has not wanted to be in company with anybody."

"Except you."

"I am her elder brother—it is natural that she would cling to me in times of distress."

Fitzwilliam nodded. "And how is our boy Bingley? Not yet married?"

"No he is not, though he may very well have been had I not intervened.

He came perilously close to making a most unfortunate match."

"Ah, there's the Darcy I know— full of self-righteousness and officious interference. What did you save him from—a match from his own circles rather than yours?"

"Bingley is not a social climber. This particular match would have done him no favors in society, though she is a gentlewoman. He found himself enamored with a young woman in Hertfordshire and paid her such attention that gained the notice of the locals. Especially her mother."

"And you believe her a fortune hunter?"

"Not the lady, no. I saw nothing of greed in her countenance. In fact I did not see much in her at all, certainly no affection for Bingley. That was my greatest objection, of course, but her family was also most unsuitable."

Darcy noticed Fitzwilliam's raised eyebrows and shook his head in response.

"I know what you are thinking. Who am I to judge anyone else's family? But that is my material point, Fitzwilliam. Bingley and I both know full well the challenge of having a ridiculous family. Imagine having two. I can at least walk away from mine, but Bingley cannot. He is responsible for Miss Bingley and is too soft hearted to deny the Hursts any request of his time. He would have been saddled with three very silly sisters and an ill-bred mother to go along with his own silly, ill-bred relations. It was too much to risk when the affection involved was untested."

Darcy paused for a moment and looked out the window. He could have as easily have been speaking of himself as Bingley. When he retired the previous evening he could not rest. His mind was full of his uncle and how the pending scandal, though likely to turn out to be of little importance, could affect his sister.

Sleep had little claim over him, but when it did it was filled with dreams of *her*. He was once again seated at the Matlock table with Miss Wallace at his side. Suddenly, Miss Wallace faded and Elizabeth took her place. She was luminous and he hung on her every word. She teased him, laughed at him, sent him arch looks that made his blood simmer. Words he recognized from their dance were spoken and as if by magic they were transported to the ballroom at Netherfield.

His hand held hers, and he gently traced a pattern inside her palm as he led her down the dance. Her movements were sensuous, naturally seductive, and the sway of her hips had him longing for the cradle of her thighs. When they reached the end, he turned and pulled her close. All the other faces in the ballroom disappeared as they waltzed together in the dim light. When the music ended he once again found himself at Matlock

House. Elizabeth was still with him, but instead of his aunt and uncle, he saw Mr. and Mrs. Bennet. Chatter rose around them as members of the *ton* arrived, laughing at the low bred woman who loudly proclaimed triumph. He looked to Elizabeth, whose light dimmed under the scrutiny of the bats now surrounding her. He pulled her to him, kissing her with all the passion he felt for her, but he could not drown out the noise. Eventually she faded away and he was left alone. He awoke feeling lifeless, as if his very existence had faded along with the dream.

The ache that had settled in his chest when he returned to London in November was now as familiar to him as his own face in the mirror. Elizabeth Bennet had awakened something in him, something that was natural, primal. It was lust in its basest form and he would not subject Georgiana to another outlandish family just so he could satisfy his cravings.

"You should not meddle in matters of the heart, Darcy. To be a true proficient would require you to have one yourself and I am not certain that lump of coal you have hidden in your chest qualifies." The colonel had finally opened his eyes, which were alight with amusement.

"One more remark of that nature and I shall have the driver stop and put you out on the road so you may enjoy your raindrops more intimately."

Just then the carriage slowed and Darcy looked out the window to determine the reason. He saw a carriage tipped slightly on its side, detached from its horses with one wheel split in two. Standing beside the wreckage was a woman holding some piece of clothing over her head while speaking to a man he assumed was the driver. His heart lurched, though he was at a loss as to why.

The carriage stopped and the gentlemen immediately stepped out to see if they could be of assistance. The storm they had driven through earlier had abated, and only a slight drizzle of rain fell around them. Darcy rounded the equipage then stopped dead in his tracks when the woman standing by the carriage came into full view. The driver walked back toward the equipage, where Fitzwilliam had gone, and the lady turned in his direction, giving him a clear view of her fine eyes, now full of astonishment.

"Mr. Darcy!"

"Miss Bennet!"

Elizabeth shook inside her skin as she tried to attend to the driver's words of apology while her mind raced with her emotions in a bid for control. She had never been so scared in all her life when she felt the carriage hit the ground. She could only credit a miracle for them not turning over, instead sliding into the brush along the road. She hardly finished her prayers of thanks when they stopped and she opened her eyes to see Maria clinging to her father, whose face was covered in blood.

Sir William was actually calm, taking his handkerchief to clean the blood from his face. It was a vain attempt as the blood wiped away was immediately replaced, leaving her to believe he was dying. She immediately left the carriage with the intention of going for help. The driver, who had managed to free the still frightened horses, stopped her. They were discussing what they should do when another carriage arrived.

She dismissed the driver with less civility than her normal manner, hoping to have a moment to settle her thoughts before tending her friends and whoever had stopped to, hopefully, help. She could not conceal her surprise when she turned and saw a very handsome, and familiar, face. Mr. Darcy, her nemesis from the previous autumn, was before her, staring as if she were a specter on the moors.

Darcy stood stupefied, wondering if the woman before him was real, or just another apparition his mind saw fit to conjure. It was a striking image, like so many of his dreams; Elizabeth standing in the rain, wet and distressed, waiting for him to assist, to prove himself. He needed to calm his mind and think, but it was terribly hard to do so with his heart pounding in his ears.

"What are you doing here? It is raining." God, he was an idiot.

"So it would seem, Mr. Darcy." Her sweet voice conveyed a semblance of the archness that he found so troubling, but there was something else there, too. She looked at him intently and he realized she was waiting for him to speak.

He stammered a moment and finally managed, "You are wet."

"Yes, it is an unfortunate condition one often suffers from when standing in the rain, sir." The irritation in her voice finally broke through his daze and he began to act.

"Forgive me." He took off his great coat and placed it around her shoulders. "I believe my cousin is seeing to the other passengers. Please, take shelter in my carriage while I sort out what has happened." He led her to the coach as she continued to speak.

"What happened, Mr. Darcy, is that the wheel of our carriage has broken. The horses were frightened and the driver lost control. Thankfully we did not turn over but Sir William is hurt."

"Yes, so I see. What I want to know is how that happened. The driver should have taken more care. You could have been seriously injured. Are you injured?"

He looked her over carefully from head to toe and back again. He could see no discernable injuries, just the sheer fabric of her wet dress clinging to her legs. He reached out and pulled his coat tighter around her. She was pale and shivering, but quickly stepped away from his grasp.

"No, sir, I am well, but Sir William and Maria may require your help."

Darcy looked over his shoulder to see that his cousin was tending to the Lucases, so he turned back to her.

"My cousin is with them. I shall stay with you should need assistance. Indeed, you look very ill." He helped her up the steps and was ascending himself when she stopped him.

"Sir, I assure you I am well. I only need to catch my breath without an audience. Will you oblige me?"

Her eyes were large and moist as she pleaded with him. Her voice held little of the assurance he was used to hearing from her, and he was sure she did not realize how badly she was shaking. Darcy did not wish to add to her distress by arguing. He had learned from Georgiana that sometimes it was best to walk away, if only for a short time, to allow frayed emotions to still.

"Of course, Miss Bennet, forgive me. I will go speak to the driver, but please call out if you need me."

She nodded and he left the carriage. His body fought his mind as he strode toward the driver. He felt pulled to her and wanted to care for her, hold her until the shivers stopped, and assure her she was well. He had to settle for leaving part of himself behind and hope his coat would at least provide some warmth against the chill left by the storm.

He approached the carriage and leaned over to inspect the wheel and attempted to check his emotions. The driver should have had better control over the horses. Sir William Lucas should have better trained horses and a better built carriage. Elizabeth was traveling with inferior people in an inferior rig and had been put in danger. He looked back to see that she was bent over her knees, likely trying to catch her breath, as she had said. He could not take away the fright she had suffered, but he could ensure her safe arrival to the inn at Bromley. He formed a plan to do just that as he approached the driver.

Elizabeth watched as Darcy looked at the broken wheel. When she was sure he would not return, she lowered her head to her knees and breathed deeply, determined not to dissolve into a fit of nerves like her mother. She raised her head and looked out the open door to where Mr. Darcy stood, speaking to the driver. Sir William may have been indisposed, but no one gave Mr. Darcy permission to take charge of the situation. She had managed fine without his help, and refused to acknowledge the gratitude she felt at being safe and dry.

"Officious man," she whispered as she pulled his coat tighter around her, bringing the lapel to her nose for a moment. Elizabeth could not name the sent, but recognized it from their time together at Netherfield. It permeated the fibers, and as she inhaled deeply, trying to fill herself with the warmth that was now surrounding her, her heart began to slow to normal. One more deep breath and she was calm. Her eyes remained closed as she enjoyed the scent and softness surrounding her, cocooning her from the fright she just endured. The sound of a throat clearing brought her back to her surroundings. She looked up to see Maria, as well as a strange man, looking at her.

"Oh, I am so sorry." Elizabeth moved to allow the girl entry. She looked to the gentleman, and instinctively moved closer to Maria, placing a protective arm around her.

"I am afraid we must wait for introductions, madam, for my cousin is busy trying to calm your driver. Excuse me."

She followed his movement from the carriage to stand next to Mr. Darcy who was speaking to Sir William. She watched Darcy then gesture to his men who pulled their trunks from the broken coach and brought them to his.

A few minutes later, Sir William entered the carriage, holding a handkerchief to his head. He took the seat in between the ladies and soon Mr. Darcy and the other man joined them.

"We will see you to Bromley and your driver will wait here for the men we send back for your carriage. We could see the horses just in the distance. Hopefully now that the storm as passed they will be easy to corral."

"I thank you, Mr. Darcy. Miss Eliza was determined to walk to find help, with little care for my objections. If you had not come along she would have been well on her way now."

Elizabeth's face grew warm. The concern she had felt for Sir William was quickly giving way to less charitable feelings.

"I knew you needed a doctor, sir. You are wounded. I have never before seen so much blood." Her voice was weak with the memory.

"Head wounds do tend to bleed heavily, even if not serious. I am afraid I must suggest a small breech of propriety, and ask that you allow me to exchange seats with you, madam. I believe I can be of assistance, and, perhaps Darcy can finally tell me to whom I am speaking."

Elizabeth nodded and turned to see Darcy's outstretched hand. She slipped her hand into his and he gently led her to sit at his side. He saw that she was settled before he made introductions.

"Sir William Lucas, Miss Lucas, Miss Elizabeth Bennet, may I introduce my cousin, Colonel Richard Fitzwilliam? Cousin, I had the pleasure of making their acquaintance in Hertfordshire when I was visiting Bingley."

"Darcy was just telling me of his visit. It is an amazing coincidence, is it not Darcy, that we were travelling the same road today. We were not scheduled to make our journey for a few weeks yet. Just think, Sir William, you could have a complete stranger tending your wounds now instead of a near stranger such as myself. To be in such close proximity it is only right that we should at least have an acquaintance in common."

The carriage filled with soft laughter and Elizabeth was grateful for the lightened atmosphere. She studied the colonel as he pressed the handkerchief, now spotted with blood, against Sir William. He seemed all ease and friendliness among the *near strangers* while Mr. Darcy, who had been in their company on a number of occasions, was stiff and formal, even with the intimacy of the situation.

"Miss Bennet, your gloves are soaked through. Please take mine, they did not get wet." Elizabeth turned her attention to the gentleman at her side. His countenance was indeed familiar, but his words and tone were unlike the man she had previously known. She would never have thought him so solicitous.

"That would be quite improper, Mr. Darcy."

"You are correct, Miss Bennet, but I would rather risk raised eyebrows at Bromley than your illness in Kent. You should have remained inside the carriage with Sir William and Miss Lucas."

Elizabeth became irritated by his tone and she suddenly remembered that she did not like the man who had withdrawn his care and replaced it with criticism. She did not want to feel beholden to him for anything, especially when he spoke to her so condescendingly. She was on the verge of letting him know she did not appreciate his tone when she became aware of the fact that her hands had begun to tingle with feeling when they had been numb with cold only moments earlier. She looked down to see Darcy's large but dry gloves covering her hands. He removed her wet ones and replaced them with his while they were speaking.

Gratitude finally won out over irritation. She gave him a soft smile and was inexplicably pleased to see it returned. She really must cease with thinking of the past with such bitterness that it would affect her behavior in the present. Her greatest reason to dislike the gentleman came from a truly despicable place, after all. She had been a very poor judge of character; it was one of the things she was determined to change. He was being very attentive to her needs at present, and so, at present, she thought him very kind.

"Sir William said you are on your way to visit his daughter who was recently married. Her husband is my aunt's parson, I believe." His voice was quiet, almost a whisper, yet deep, serving to veil them from the rest of the company.

"Oh, yes. I had completely forgotten that your aunt is Lady Catherine de Bourgh. Are you visiting her?"

"Yes. I travel to Rosings every Easter, but needed to make my journey a little early this year. How is your family, Miss Bennet? Are they all in good health?"

Elizabeth looked away, wishing she did not have to answer. The warmth he provided had been a much needed respite from the coldness of her continued deception. She began to wonder if saving her sister would cost her soul.

"Most of my family are well, sir. My youngest sister, Lydia, has been ill all winter. The apothecary suggested a lengthy stay at the sea side." Not exactly an untruth.

"Is she there now?" If he would stop staring, or just look away for a moment so she could be sure she gave nothing away in her expressions. But he did not. He continued to stare as if he could see straight through her.

"No sir, we have left her in London with my aunt and uncle and my sister Jane. She begins her journey next week."

"I am very sorry for her illness, Miss Bennet."

"Thank you."

He was silent for a moment and she could hear Colonel Fitzwilliam whispering to Maria to cover her father with a rug from beneath her seat. Darcy must have heard him as well, because he reached under their own and pulled out a thick covering and draped it over her. Again, she was warmed by the effort. His eyes returned to her own.

"You have been caring for Miss Lydia." He could see her fatigue. The circles under her eyes were weeks old, marring her beautiful fair skin with the signs of worry. Elizabeth gave a slight nod.

"But you have not become ill yourself?"

"No, sir, I am well."

"I am glad. I hope you will forgive me for my less than gentlemanly conduct earlier. I should have removed you from the rain instantly. I was surprised to see you. I had just been thinking about you, uh, rather, my time in Hertfordshire. It took a moment to realize it was actually you." He looked down to his hand, which was resting on the seat near her own. He could see the lines of her fingers wrapped inside his gloves, and he found comfort he did not know he needed.

"Do not trouble yourself, Mr. Darcy. I, too, was rather surprised. You have acquitted yourself admirably. I appreciate your care."

He again lifted his eyes, capturing hers in their depths.

"It is my great pleasure, Miss Bennet."

Chapter 5

Darcy's team of horses ensured their quick and safe arrival at the inn before the rain once again began to fall. Little conversation was had which, after the events of the morning, seemed to suit everyone's desires. When they stopped, Darcy turned to Elizabeth.

"There seems to be a great deal of activity today, probably due to the weather. Perhaps you would prefer to wait in the carriage while I see to our accommodations?"

"Accommodations? Are we still so far from Rosings that we need to stay at the inn?"

Darcy shook his head. "Not very far, Miss Bennet, but it would be better for Sir William to rest after losing so much blood."

Elizabeth looked at the other occupants. Maria held her father's hand as he rested his head on the back of the seat. He was pale and quiet. Colonel Fitzwilliam caught her eye and smiled. She turned back to Darcy.

"Of course, Mr. Darcy. Thank you." She smiled. "*Again.*"

Darcy nodded then looked to his cousin. "Fitzwilliam, you will stay."

Colonel Fitzwilliam responded to the demand with a tilt of the head. Darcy did not wait for anything further as he determinedly stepped from the carriage. Elizabeth noticed the interaction with amusement.

"Mr. Darcy always seems deliberate in his actions, even when the unexpected occurs. I would imagine he is quite used to giving orders."

Fitzwilliam chuckled. "He is indeed and it is many years now since I have seen him follow any. He would not have made a good soldier."

"He inherited his duties quite young, did he not, Colonel Fitzwilliam?" Sir William joined the conversation. He lifted his head but kept the cloth over his wound.

"He was two and twenty when his father died. Thankfully, my uncle was a good teacher and master. Darcy knew the estate well when he passed."

Elizabeth felt a slight pang of jealously. Her father had taught her how to laugh at people. Perhaps if she has been a boy, it would have been different. If her father had a reason to care about maintaining the estate for future generations maybe he would have been a different man. Conjectures like this were useless, of course, and she had long since given up any guilt at having not been born male. Although, she thought with some regret, Lydia could have benefited from having an elder brother.

Darcy returned to the carriage satisfied with the arrangements. "I was able to secure private rooms for each of us." He explained as he handed the women down.

Fitzwilliam laughed. "How did you manage that, cousin? They are overcrowded here, it seems. What poor souls will not have a bed tonight due to the Darcy pride?"

Elizabeth, though desperate for privacy, became alarmed at such a thought. "Mr. Darcy, it is no hardship for Maria and me to share a room. I would not want to displace anybody for the sake of my own comfort."

Darcy wanted to say that her comfort was paramount and all others could be hanged, but he chose more prudent words.

"I assure you, Miss Bennet, no one has been inconvenienced. If you are unfortunate enough to continue the acquaintance with my cousin, you will see he teases me almost as much as you do. If it sets your mind at ease, we can give up his room and relegate him to the stables."

Fitzwilliam rolled his eyes. "Yes, Darcy. Show your friends here how you treat your poor relations. Let them take back to Hertfordshire tales of your *real* character."

Elizabeth's stomach seemed to drop to her boots. It was obvious the cousins were teasing each other. She enjoyed the lightness of Darcy's voice and the glint of mischief in his eyes. He seemed almost human at that moment. But Colonel Fitzwilliam's comment reminded her that she had spread hateful gossip about Darcy throughout her neighborhood. She determined his character to be the very worst but now it was showing itself to be quite the opposite. She felt very low indeed.

"Miss Bennet?"

Elizabeth looked up to see his concern. Guilt and regret had followed her and her remorse grew as he looked upon her with such kindness.

"I am sorry, Mr. Darcy. I am very sorry . . . that we have inconvenienced you today."

"It is an honor to be of service to you, Miss Bennet. Please do not trouble yourself. I am afraid we must walk through the public rooms to get to the stairs. Shall we?"

Elizabeth nodded and they began walking. Darcy wound her hand through his arm and motioned for the others to follow. The common rooms of the inn were just that. Travelers of every class gathered in the tight spaces and, though her cursory glance told her many gentlemen were present, Darcy drew attention. It was no wonder, Elizabeth thought. The attentive, caring man she had unexpectedly spent the morning with had disappeared and was replaced with the man she knew in Hertfordshire. His tall frame was rigid and his face was fixed in an uninterested stare as if the entire place had been inspected and found lacking.

Months ago, she found this man proud and intolerable. As she walked through the room, with her dress splattered from the rain and mud and her nerves still slightly frayed, she leaned into his warmth and mirrored his expression as best she could. These strangers would not know how frightened she had been, or that she had left her ruined sister in London, or that she was wholly out of place on this man's arm. She felt him pull her closer. She did not react but allowed her gratitude to remain as hidden as every other emotion that bubbled beneath her skin. She would show him later, with a smile or a simple thank you, but now she needed to make it through the room.

Darcy's anxiety nearly matched hers, but for different reasons. He was still recovering from the shock of seeing her, but as he escorted her through the inn, his mind was set on all the eyes that were following Elizabeth. Gentlemen in name only leered at her, offering smiles that she, thankfully, seemed not to notice. When he pulled her closer, she did not react and continued to look forward, causing Darcy to believe she was just as uncomfortable as he. He thanked God he and Fitzwilliam found them on the road. If not, she would be there unprotected. A niggling feeling formed in his mind that he had traveled early to Kent for more than just Anne.

Once upstairs, they both began to breathe normally. Darcy stopped in front of a door that opened on its own. Elizabeth was surprised to see a maid waiting to attend her. She again looked at Darcy with a small smile of gratitude. She started to speak, but he stopped her with a gentle squeeze of her hand.

"Will you join us downstairs for dinner this evening? If you feel well enough, of course."

"If you wish, though I cannot promise witty conversation. My mind may be too full of other things."

"Your presence will be enough."

"Mr. Darcy, you are all politeness. Thank you." Elizabeth smiled. "*Again.*"

They shared a smile as he released her hand and stepped back. She looked down the hall to see Maria entering her room. She looked back to Darcy, who bowed slightly, then entered her chamber.

Elizabeth changed her dress and rearranged her hair with the help of the maid. She and Maria had not traveled with one and were to use the services of Charlotte's staff at Hunsford. Mr. Darcy must have noticed their lack of help and arranged for girls to attend them. She felt her cheeks flush as she remembered his kindness when he came upon them. Again she marveled at his care and determined she would not analyze the situation until she had spoken to Charlotte about it all. She could no longer rely solely on her own judgment when it came to a person's character. She had been too wrong in the past; too quick to judge. If only one good thing came from Lydia's dilemma, it would be Elizabeth's maturity and willingness to see beyond her own feelings.

As the maid pinned the last curl in place, a knock sounded on the door. The girl opened the door to let Maria through, then curtsied and left before Elizabeth could thank her.

"Oh, Mr. Darcy sent one to you, as well. Of course he did, why would he only send a maid to one of us?" Maria shook her head as she looked at the door. She clasped her hands together as she turned back to Elizabeth.

"Maria?"

"Oh, Eliza. He is just so pale. I know Colonel Fitzwilliam said the wound was not severe, but I have never even seen my father ill, let alone bleeding."

Elizabeth embraced the girl as her tears flowed. She knew too well the fright of seeing a loved one injured as well as the hurt that came with the realization that a parent is neither immortal nor infallible.

"He is well, Maria. Has a doctor come, yet?"

"Yes, he just left. I was surprised how quickly he came. He said Papa needs only rest and will be fine."

"See there? He will be himself in a day or two."

Maria continued to cry and Elizabeth could see there was no point in being rational. Sometimes a young girl just needed to feel the emotion, think the worst and then realize the world is not ending.

"Let us go downstairs. Mr. Darcy would like us to join him and his cousin for dinner. I have never eaten at an inn before but I am sure there will be ample entertainment before us. I did notice a woman wearing the ugliest hat I have ever seen when we arrived. Let us hope she has not changed it for I believe it would be excessively diverting. Shall we go pick apart all the ladies' poor choices in fashion?"

This earned a slight smile and a nod. Maria splashed water on her face and they departed for the dining room. Unfortunately, Mr. Darcy had anticipated a need for solitude rather than distraction and arranged for a meal to be served in a private room. The door remained opened while they dined. They could hear the crowd, but their company gave them no reason to laugh or poke fun as Darcy again became the somber fellow from the autumn and the Colonel spoke far too much.

"Darcy, why did you not tell me there were such beauties in Hertfordshire? You made it seem dull and tedious."

Darcy and Fitzwilliam retired not long after the rest of the party. Darcy hoped some time alone would help him put his thoughts about Elizabeth back in order. His hopes were dashed when his cousin knocked on his door.

"I must not have been speaking of the things that should catch your interest, Fitzwilliam."

"Obviously not. Miss Bennet is quite intriguing, Darcy. Do not tell me you do not agree, I saw the attention you paid her in the carriage."

"Yes, and I saw the attention you paid her at dinner. I also saw her annoyance."

Fitzwilliam laughed. "Yes, she certainly had her fill of me early on. I am sure it was merely due to fatigue."

"She *is* tired. She was affected more by the incident than she wanted us to know. She did finally admit to some soreness and a wish to rest, but that likely was a ploy to get away from you."

Fitzwilliam laughed again. "Perhaps, perhaps. She is a fiery little thing. She reminds me much of Miss Wallace."

Darcy shot his cousin a warning look.

"Come Darcy, surely you noticed the similarity. The eyes alone bore an extraordinary resemblance."

"On the contrary, there was nothing remarkable about your Miss Wallace, other than the fact she had the nerve to sit at a Lady's table. I will thank you to cease your musings. You will not compare Miss Bennet to a whore."

"You will not convince me your thoughts were purely friendly this morning, cousin. You may hide behind your propriety, but you are a man after all, and Miss Bennet is a very enticing woman."

"Fitzwilliam, I will not tell you again to cease. You are speaking of an innocent gentlewoman, not some common trollop. If you cannot be respectful then perhaps you should not speak. Must I remind you that you are supposed to be a gentleman?"

"And must I remind you, Darcy, that I am not a child? You will not speak to me as such."

"Then stay your tongue, cousin."

The tension between the men that had brewed the past few days returned as they both refused to stand down for several moments. Fitzwilliam, finally seeing the ridiculousness of the argument, stepped back.

"I will leave you now. It seems you need a nap. I will see you at breakfast."

Darcy allowed him the last word, eager to be out of his company. When he was in a better frame of mind, he would examine Fitzwilliam's odd behavior. Currently, he needed to consider his own.

He paced about the room, removing his cravat in the process. His coat and waistcoat were discarded before he sat in a chair in front of the fire. He leaned back and placed his fingers over his mouth as he contemplated the day.

His surprise at seeing Elizabeth had been great. He had not had time to accustom his mind and emotions, and like the morning she arrived at Netherfield six inches deep in mud, he was dumbstruck. He let out a long breath and settled more deeply into his seat.

"Damned bloody fool," he admonished himself.

There was no relief from his embarrassment over having been so tongue-tied in her presence. *You are wet.* Darcy rolled his eyes at his stupidity. His only comfort was that Fitzwilliam had been occupied at the time and had missed the display.

He finally allowed his mind to drift from his mortification to hers. She had not wanted his help in the beginning, he could see that upon reflection. He smiled slightly as he thought of her pride, remembering their conversation at Netherfield. Did she even realize how she clung to the very thing she accused him of having? In the end, she did seem grateful though reluctant.

A slight ache began to form in his chest. That sort of independence might be necessary among her relations, whose silly dispositions could not possibly allow for ease, but not with him. As much as he enjoyed their debates, at that moment he had no desire to be her adversary, but her comfort. The thought that she was now alone and possibly still feeling the fright from the accident or worry for her sister made him restless. He was accustomed to solving problems, but he had no claim to do so now. It was not his right to provide comfort to the woman who was now resting just a few doors down and because of that, she was suffering alone. The ache grew along with the restlessness and all he could do was pace and wait for the morning when he could, perhaps, do something for her.

Elizabeth sat on her bed, knees drawn to her chest as she contemplated the events of the day. She was tired and her body ached, but she could not quiet her mind. She could not help but wonder what force found it necessary to give her such a fright on the same day she had to leave her sisters. When she closed her eyes those brief moments before impact, all she saw were images of Lydia, sick and alone.

That Mr. Darcy should come across her in that state, wet and disconcerted, added humiliation to her fright. She must have looked truly appalling to cause his usual controlled speech to fail him. She had seen that stern disapproving glare before when she arrived at Netherfield to see Jane. Between her frightful appearance and sharp tongue, he undoubtedly had found enough fault. Perhaps *now* he would cease staring at her the way he did throughout dinner that evening.

Elizabeth placed her hands over her eyes and shook her head. After the initial shock of seeing her, he had been extremely kind and solicitous. Why must she continue to disparage him, even if just in her own mind? She had such little understanding of men. In truth, the opinions she formed of them, in general, were influenced as much by books as by actual experience. She grouped all the ones she knew into two categories: heroes and villains. And in her naiveté, she never realized the lines between the two could be fluid.

She began to shake as she stifled the sobs that finally broke through. The thin walls of the inn offered no protection, so she fell back on the bed and rolled over to hide her cries in the pillow. After several moments, she opened her eyes to see a pair of large white gloves on the table next to her. She removed them when she first entered the room to change before dinner and had forgotten to return them to Mr. Darcy. She reached out and fingered one gently, remembering the warmth they brought her in the carriage. She contemplated slipping them back on her fingers but quickly dismissed the thought as she rolled over and willed herself to sleep.

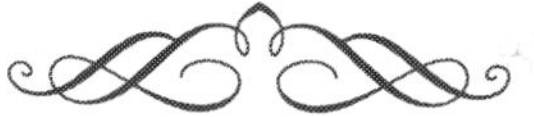

Little was said in the carriage on the road to Hunsford. Not long after they departed the inn, Sir William complained of dizziness and everyone seemed to silently agree that a noiseless ride was best. Each traveler not suffering from a spinning head was lost in their own musings. One lady was again enjoying the scenery, two gentlemen were contemplating one of the ladies, and that lady's mind was on her sister.

Elizabeth slept alone for the first time in months, but the solitude did little to help her rest. She woke in the night by instinct, but Lydia was not there to require her assistance. Sleep did not come again quickly as she wondered how Jane would cope when Lydia became ill. Her elder sister was everything good and kind and Elizabeth knew her heart would break at the sight of Lydia's discomfort. She closed her eyes and leaned her head back against the seat. She wished, again, that she had been able to stay with them. She trusted her aunt and uncle and knew their plan was best, but that logic did little to soothe her concern. It grew with every mile as she traveled further away from those who needed her most.

From his seat across from her, Darcy could see the signs of worry on Elizabeth's face. He had hoped a night's rest would soothe her anxiety from the accident, but she apparently had not slept well. He watched as she turned her head to the window, then back to rest against the seat. She was restless. He knew the feeling well and as his mind began to drift to images of them relieving their restiveness together, his cousin's cough drew his attention. Darcy looked and saw Fitzwilliam's knowing smirk.

He turned to the window and silently admonished himself to be more careful. His feelings for Elizabeth could not be shown at Rosings. Lady Catherine would devour her if she thought there was the slightest chance Elizabeth could take his attention away from Anne. He did not know what would develop between them. Now that he had seen her again, he could not deny the pull she had on him, but he could not yet be sure these emotions were lasting. Whatever might occur, he knew that while he was in her orbit, he would have to protect her from his family.

Chapter 6

Lydia pressed her forehead against her chamber window. The cold glass provided some relief to her flushed features. She had managed to not expel her breakfast, but it weighed on her stomach like an anchor. The heaviness was a constant, a solid mass in the pit of her belly that reminded her always of what she had done. Aunt Gardiner told her the sick feeling should not last much longer, but Lydia did not believe her. It would always be there, taunting her just as he had.

She opened her eyes and gazed at the street below. She had always wanted to visit London. Her dreams of town had been full of shops and parties, of making her sisters jealous that she wore the finest gowns and danced every dance. She had been so sure those things would happen, but now wondered how that could ever have come about. The Gardiners, her only acquaintances in London, never invited her to visit even though she begged on a number of occasions. Her father certainly would never bring her to town. The only way she would have managed it was through marriage.

That was no longer a possibility—Wickham was sure to tell her *that*. This would be her only trip to London and she was spending it at a window watching the people below floating up and down the street while was weighed down by the might of her sin.

"Lydia, are you well?" Jane entered the room so quietly Lydia did not hear her. She turned and gave her sister a soft smile.

"Yes, Jane. I do not think I will be ill this morning."

"Oh, that is good. Perhaps you are on your way to being well and the sea air will further your recovery. You do still look pale, though. Would you like to lie down and I can read to you?"

Lydia's smile grew. She never paid much attention to her eldest sister.

She knew Jane was beautiful because their mother always said so. Lydia never actually saw it herself until now. Jane was truly the loveliest girl she had ever known. Mr. Bingley was a fool to have left her and she was a fool to have ever thought it was Jane's fault. Her sister was an angel.

"I would like that, Jane, but please do not be angry if I fall asleep."

"Oh, you will not fall asleep. This story is too interesting." Jane spoke her usual calm way as she removed Lydia's slippers then pulled the bed-covers over her. She opened the book but before she could begin a knock was heard.

"Enter."

"Miss Jane, your aunt wanted me to tell you Mr. Burton is downstairs."

Jane blushed then looked to Lydia and back to the maid. "Please tell my aunt that I am reading to my sister this morning."

"Jane, you should go downstairs. You cannot snub a suitor just to read to me."

"I am not snubbing him. I am choosing to stay with you this morning." She looked down and smiled. "He will return." She nodded to the maid, who then departed and closed the door.

"Thank you, Jane."

"There is nowhere I would rather be, dear sister."

Darcy remembered Mrs. Collins, then Miss Lucas, to be a sensible, unaffected woman. He was surprised to see her anxiousness when he stepped out of the carriage. He was close to blaming being married to a toad for her change in demeanor when he remembered her family and dearest friend had been in an accident the day before. He gave her an understanding smile before turning to hand down Maria. Colonel Fitzwilliam did the same for Elizabeth then both gentlemen assisted Sir William.

"Oh, Maria! Eliza! I was so worried when we received Mr. Darcy's note. You must have been terrified." She embraced the ladies then moved to her father.

"Papa." She touched the bandage on his head. "Does it hurt terribly? You should have stayed at the inn longer. I would have come to you."

"Nonsense, it is just a small scrape. I became lightheaded in the carriage and the gentlemen here are being cautious. No need to worry, my dear."

Charlotte was unconvinced, but if her usually boisterous father was determined not to cause a scene, she would not either. Unfortunately the same could not be said for her husband. Shortly after introductions and greetings, he began his effusions.

"Mr. Darcy, you honor us, sir, by being of service during our time of need. Your note explaining the incident was as eloquent as it was informative. You do your aunt, Lady Catherine de Bourgh, great credit, indeed, for I know she has had influence over you since your infancy. She told me so herself."

Darcy looked at the clergyman with the same disinterest he showed him the night of the Netherfield ball. Collins stood before him, slightly hunched, with his hands clasped at his chest. Darcy half expected to see his tongue project from his mouth in search of flies. Collins tilted his head in anticipation of some sort of answer.

"Thank you," Darcy managed very dryly.

Seeing no further reply was forthcoming, Collins continued to praise Darcy, Lady Catherine, the chimney at Rosings, the fish in the ponds, the birds in the sky and the game in the woods, for surely they all bowed to the great lady's influence as well.

Taking advantage of his lesser status, and therefore anonymity in the sight of Collins, Fitzwilliam gently pulled Elizabeth aside.

"Miss Bennet, if I might have a word. I must apologize for my behavior last night. I fear I may have offended you, or at the very least annoyed you after such a trying day. My only defense can be the unexpected pleasure of encountering a lovely woman on the road to Rosings."

He expected to see a blush cover her features, but her only response was a raised eyebrow. Fitzwilliam could not tell if she was further annoyed, contemplating his sincerity, or merely waiting for him to dig himself deeper into a hole. Finally, her shoulders relaxed.

"I, too, must apologize, Colonel. I was in quite an ill humor and did little to disguise it. The mere fact that I was sitting there and you were breathing was enough to draw my ire. I should not have come down for dinner, but Maria was so distraught over her father's injury she could not sit still. I thought bringing her down to watch the crowd might distract her."

"Then Darcy arranged for a private dining room."

"He did what he thought would please us best."

"Without asking what would best please you. Yes, that is Darcy. He will ever be his own man, quite content to tend his own superior thoughts rather than observe others." He smiled.

Elizabeth shook her head. "No, Colonel, you will not get me to laugh at the man whose carriage has just brought me here."

"Very well, I will give you a few days to forget his kindness then I will regale you with stories of how many times he fell off his pony when he was first learning to ride or about the time the pigs got into the garden and Darcy squealed as if he were one of them."

That last image got the best of her and she laughed, drawing the attention of those gathered. Elizabeth composed herself quickly but not before the Colonel finally saw a blush.

"Fitzwilliam, I think it is time we left Mrs. Collins to enjoy her guests." Darcy walked to them and as he reached Elizabeth's side, Fitzwilliam stepped away to speak to Collins.

"I hope you will enjoy your stay here, Miss Bennet."

"I am sure I will. Charlotte always provides excellent company and we have much to catch up on. Please allow me to thank you again for your assistance yesterday and this morning. You did much for us that went far beyond mere courtesy."

"Think no more of it, Miss Bennet. It was no more than any friend would do."

Elizabeth's smile brightened her entire countenance and Darcy's heart raced at the sight. He must remember the whole exchange exactly as it occurred in hopes of making her smile like that again.

"I find I like the idea of being your friend very much, Mr. Darcy. You have proven yourself quite useful in dire circumstances. I look forward to seeing how gallantly you handle the familiar and mundane."

Darcy's smile tugged at something inside Elizabeth. It was not an overwhelming feeling. Rather, it was proportional to the small lifting of the corners of his mouth. It was slight, but it was there and it held great promise.

Darcy reached for her hand and bowed over it gracefully. "I am sure we will see each other again soon, madam."

"I look forward to our next meeting, sir."

Darcy nodded, then moved to say farewell to the rest of the party. After the carriage drove off and Sir William was helped into the house, followed by an effusive Collins and curious Maria, Charlotte wove her arm through Elizabeth's.

"Well, Eliza, it appears Mr. Darcy has risen in your esteem."

Elizabeth looked straight ahead as they walked through the door, her chin slightly lifted. "He is tolerable, I suppose."

The friends laughed as they entered the parlor. They settled down for quiet conversation, but each was eager for the talk that would come after the rest of the house was asleep.

"Nephew! You have finally arrived." Lady Catherine de Bourgh sat on what could only be described as a throne. The large chair was intricately carved and stood in front of an expansive tapestry. The furniture surrounding her was small in comparison, giving her the illusion of importance.

Fitzwilliam stared at the scene behind his aunt. It depicted what he assumed was heaven since tiny cherubs flew about the clouds. Two of the plump deities floated in the center, right above Lady Catherine's head and when his eyes traveled down to her, he noticed the feathers in her headpiece were arranged in such as way one could easily mistake her for an angel of an entirely different variety.

"You have redecorated, Aunt. It is . . . quite fitting for your . . . tastes."

"You will not distract me, Fitzwilliam. I am quite vexed at your tardiness. Be seated." She gestured for them to sit on either side of her. The gentlemen did as bid, sinking down on the very uncomfortable sofas.

"It can hardly be said we are late, Lady Catherine, when we have come several weeks before we were scheduled." He may have been seated below her, but his voice was commanding.

"I expected you yesterday."

"We were delayed, as you know."

"Yes, I read your note. There was no need for you to stay in Bromley yesterday. You should have deposited those travelers at the inn and come here."

"Now, Aunt, as your representatives, we could not leave an injured man and two young ladies unattended, especially as they are guests of your parson. People expect more from the nephews of someone so illustrious."

Darcy was awed by his cousin's simpering and wondered if he would attempt to catch flies. Lady Catherine also studied him for a long moment before pointing her nose upward.

"This is true. Still, I was very put out. Anne was excessively disappointed."

"Where is Anne?"

"She is resting, Darcy. You will see her tonight at dinner."

Darcy rose and Fitzwilliam followed. "Please excuse me, Lady Catherine.

I would like to change before dinner. I will see you then."

"Yes, so will I, Aunt." They both bowed and left the room. In the hall, Fitzwilliam put his hand on Darcy's shoulder.

"Lord, the old lady is in a mood."

"When have you known her not to be?"

"I remember seeing her smile once, but she was beating a servant at the time."

The jest earned a small chuckle from Darcy. The cousins parted ways, each making plans to pass the time that did not involve their aunt's company.

"Oh, Eliza, it must have been awful." Charlotte sat on Elizabeth's bed as her friend detailed the events of the day. She had shown extra care to her guests that evening, letting them know how happy she was that they were in her home and safe. Now that she was alone with Elizabeth, she could allow some of the emotions she felt to come forth. She reached for Elizabeth's hands. "Were you very frightened?"

"I was, but I did not feel it entirely until afterward. I could barely breathe when Mr. Darcy took me to his carriage."

"It must have been a shock to see him there. Given your history with the gentleman, I can imagine you were less than gracious?" Charlotte smiled.

Elizabeth laughed. "I was unpardonably rude. He should have left me in the rain, but he was very gentlemanly. What do you make of it, Charlotte? He was so arrogant and rude in Hertfordshire. Does it take a carriage accident or some sort of distress to bring out his kindness?"

"Perhaps it was seeing you in distress that brought about his change in behavior? I never believed he looked at you to find fault."

"Do not start that again or I will pinch you."

Charlotte held her hands tighter. "Then I will hold on to you while I say that Colonel Fitzwilliam seemed to pay you a great deal of attention as well."

Elizabeth pulled away and swatted her friend playfully. "Charlotte Collins, you have only been married a few months and you are already an old biddy with nothing better to do than marry off the neighborhood. I am sorry to disappoint you, but I was quite rude to the Colonel as well."

"Did your mother teach you nothing? Two eligible gentlemen were at your disposal and instead of playing the damsel, you chose to act like a shrew."

"I know, I know." Elizabeth shook her head. "It did not seem to matter, however. You can imagine how guilty I feel now. I said horrible things about Mr. Darcy in the autumn. He will never be received warmly in Meryton."

"Now, Eliza, his behavior did him no favors. He certainly was not kind and solicitous then, though he was not as bad as you were determined to believe."

Elizabeth pursed her lips in a straight line. "I *was* determined. There was no hope for him after that rude comment at the assembly. He was a guilty man based on a few words. Oh, vanity. You would think I would have none after a lifetime in Jane's shadow. I have much to learn."

"Well, Eliza, if it is humility you seek, you have come to the right place. There is no vanity that can surpass the great lady at Rosings. If we are fortunate enough to receive an invitation while you are here, you will experience such displays of wisdom and understanding that you will never feel the need to rely on your own judgment."

Elizabeth raised an eyebrow at Charlotte's biting sarcasm. She was usually more circumspect.

"Forgive me, I now sound like a bitter old woman. She has her hands in nearly every aspect of life in the parsonage and the village. I welcome the disruption in our normal routine. With her nephews visiting, she will surely have less time to summon us to tea or write notes suggesting how to better tie my boots or something else just as silly."

"She is that bad?"

"Yes. I am happy to have you to speak to about it. My husband believes every word she says and I have not met anybody with whom I feel comfortable talking on a personal level. That is certainly a disadvantage of marriage, not having a sister or friend with you."

"Well, Maria and I are here now and will be for many weeks. So, let us hope that invitation comes so that we may all commiserate on the follies of Lady Catherine de Bourgh. For now, tell me, how do you like being married?"

Charlotte tilted her head in contemplation. "I find I like it very well. Having my own home to manage is certainly preferable to following Mama's orders."

"Do you miss Meryton?"

"Not as much as I thought I would. I do miss you and Jane, but I have a purpose here. With each year that passed and I was not married the fear would be greater that I would never be more than a daughter or sister. I am still dependent, but at least now I am valuable."

"It sounds as though you are quite content. I am glad. I admit that I worried for you."

"I know. I worry for you as well, and your sisters and Maria. Meryton offers so few opportunities for gentlewomen. However, Rosings may be over flowing with possibilities."

This time Elizabeth did pinch her then shooed her out of the room. As she readied for bed she replayed Charlotte's words. She was convinced she would find Charlotte unhappy with her situation. How could she be content with such a man? But she was. Or rather, she was content with what Mr. Collins had to offer. There was great value in the ability to manage at least some part of one's own life.

Elizabeth smiled as her head rested on her pillow. What else would this visit bring? She was in a carriage accident and now she was jealous of Charlotte. The only thing that would shock her more would be a marriage proposal. Charlotte's words came back to her and she quickly rolled over and pulled the bedcoverings over her head, as if to protect herself from the vision of the possibilities at Rosings.

Chapter 7

"Cousin Elizabeth, I feel I should speak to you about what to expect when visiting Rosings." The Hunsford party was walking to the manor house when Mr. Collins fell behind his wife to speak to Elizabeth. "Her ladyship has bestowed upon you a great honor by inviting you to dine in her home amongst her eminent relations. I would hope that you respect her position and remember yours. Your usual *liveliness*, though charming, would not be appropriate in such a place as Rosings." He lifted his hand and gestured to the building that had just come into view.

"Thank you for the advice, Mr. Collins. I would not wish to offend someone of such stature. Do you have any suggestion as to how I should behave, sir?" Elizabeth's voice was light and full of amusement. She had looked forward to the evening since Colonel Fitzwilliam arrived earlier in the day with the invitation. Though she was determined to be less like her father in some ways, she still delighted in the ridiculous, which was why she could tolerate the current conversation. From what Charlotte told her, she would find much to delight in at dinner.

"I am glad you asked, cousin, for I knew not how to speak to you on the subject. Lady Catherine and her daughter expect, nay *deserve*, to receive the greater part of attention from their guests. I have observed your propensity to attract male attention and must warn you not to put yourself on display tonight. Colonel Fitzwilliam and Mr. Darcy, especially, are meant for superior companions. It would do no good to entice when no respectable offer could be made."

Before she could reply he hastened to join his wife. Elizabeth's humor in the situation turned to mortification. She knew she should not dwell on the musings of such a man, but she could not hold back the anger that grew in her chest. She took comfort in the knowledge that she was not always wrong in her judgment. Mr. Collins was exactly the small man she believed him to be in the autumn.

They soon arrived and were shown to the same room where Lady Catherine received her nephews days before. Elizabeth's breath caught for a moment as she took in her surroundings. Delightful indeed. The place dripped extravagance. She wondered which came first: the name of the estate or the gilded roses that made up the predominate theme of the room? The cherubs in the tapestry were even holding some stems.

Her attention moved to the individuals in front of her. She forced herself to look first to the center of the group, knowing Lady Catherine would be positioned there. It was not an easy task. Though she was draped in beautiful fabrics with a headpiece that would usually brook no competition, Lady Catherine was out shown by the tall figure to her left.

Mr. Darcy presented the same stern mien he had in every other drawing room she had seen him in, but he seemed far more handsome tonight than on those occasions. Now that she allowed herself to look at him without prejudice, she could see that he was indeed the best looking man she had ever met.

After introductions had been made, they were all instructed to come closer and be seated. Elizabeth sat in between Charlotte and Sir William on the sofa across from Darcy and Miss de Bourgh. Maria chose a chair close to the Colonel and Mr. Collins slipped into a low seat next to his patroness. They all waited anxiously for Lady Catherine to speak, but she seemed content to study the newcomers. Her eyes roamed over them carefully, dismissively, and after long moments focused on Elizabeth, she finally spoke.

"Your friend seems like a pretty sort of girl, Mrs. Collins. Tell me, Miss Bennet, do you play?"

"Yes, ma'am, but very ill."

"I will be the judge of that, Miss Bennet. You will play for us after dinner and I will judge your performance. You will never find a keener ear for music and, if I had ever learned, I would have been a true proficient."

Mr. Collins, who had so far no share in the conversation, took the opportunity to heap praise on her ladyship. "There can be no doubt, given your elevated tastes and superior knowledge that," his effusions were stayed with a raise of her hand.

"Tell me about your education, Miss Bennet. What school did you attend?"

"I did not attend school, ma'am. I learned at home."

"And has your governess left you?"

"We have no governess, ma'am."

"No governess? Mrs. Collins informed me you have younger sisters. Your mother must be a slave to your education."

"In some areas she has been, but we mostly were given leave to educate ourselves."

Lady Catherine took another long look at Elizabeth. "How old are you, Miss Bennet."

"I am not one and twenty."

"How old is your youngest sister? Mr. Collins informed me of her illness." She spoke as if it were her right to know everything of the Bennets.

"Fifteen."

"She is not out, then."

"All my sisters are out."

"All out at once, before the older ones are married?"

Elizabeth was entertained for the first part of the conversation, but as Lady Catherine continued to pry, she found it hard to control her impertinence.

"Yes, ma'am. My younger sisters enjoy a party as much as anyone. Why should they be forced to sit at home because I have failed to secure a suitable husband?"

Lady Catherine contemplated her words for a moment then nodded. "This is true. Your failure should not affect you sisters. While you are here, we will see what we can do to rectify the situation. You really should be married by now."

Elizabeth felt the flush on her cheeks and she looked across to Darcy to see his reaction to his aunt's rudeness. He showed no signs of embarrassment, other than a slight coloring of his cheeks. Elizabeth found herself disappointed to not have been defended. She soon admonished herself for being silly. She was, after all, nothing to the man. He had not called at the parsonage since they arrived like she had expected him to. Perhaps she had been right and he only displayed that softened version of himself when he had to play the hero. More likely he just did not think of her when she was not in front of him.

Lady Catherine's attention had finally been drawn elsewhere and as she instructed Charlotte on the proper way to polish silver; Elizabeth returned to her observations. Colonel Fitzwilliam sat next to Maria, trying to engage her in conversation. The girl was terrified in the middle of such opulence and scrutiny. Elizabeth was grateful to the Colonel for distracting her.

He was dressed in his red coat for the evening and Elizabeth thought he would be considered handsome in any other company. His blonde hair and blue eyes were very similar to his aunt's and they shared the same angular jaw line. She could easily see a resemblance between the Lady and her elder nephew but not with the younger nor her daughter. This led Elizabeth to believe both Darcy and Miss de Bourgh must favor their fathers more than their Fitzwilliam relations.

Elizabeth felt eyes on her and turned to see two sets focused in her direction. There was nothing new to be found in Darcy's stare. It was the same one that followed her in Hertfordshire in the autumn. Unlike then, she would not assume she had dirt on her face or a misaligned coiffeur. She was confused by his behavior, but rather than dwell on it, she turned her attention to Miss de Bourgh.

If Elizabeth had previously met Lady Catherine and been informed that she had a daughter, the image that would form in her mind would likely be similar to the flesh and blood woman across from her. Though she did not much resemble Lady Catherine, Anne de Bourgh had been dipped in the same extravagance as her mother. The gown she wore was not fashionable but was made of exquisite silk, probably the finest Elizabeth had ever seen. The sleeves were long and the neckline high, leaving very little of her skin uncovered. She was adorned with sapphires encased in old-fashioned settings, obviously heirlooms, and her headpiece rivaled her mother's.

Elizabeth tried to make out the color of her eyes, but the lighting was dim where they sat. She could tell, however, that Miss de Bough wore a great deal of face powder and rouge. She wondered at that since cosmetics were rarely worn that heavily, at least not in the circles to which she was accustomed. Perhaps the very rich had their own set of fashions and customs. To Elizabeth, however, it merely looked like a mask.

They were called to dinner and Collins stood and looked longingly at Lady Catherine, obviously hoping to be allowed to escort her. She dismissed him with a look and with the same motion gestured to Darcy, who then escorted both his aunt and cousin from the room. Elizabeth took Sir William's offered arm and followed.

"Darcy, Anne planned this dinner with you in mind. I believe she ordered your favorites. As you see, she sets a very elegant table."

Elizabeth looked over the table setting and the truly delicious looking duck that sat on her plate. Unbidden, the image of her mother came to her mind. Longbourn may not have had the most delicate china like she now saw, but her mother's table setting could rival that of Rosings at any meal. She was suddenly proud of her.

"It is all quite wonderful, thank you, Anne."

Elizabeth thought she heard a touch of sarcasm in his voice. She looked up and expected to see a smirk, but instead saw a warm look pass between Darcy and his dinner partner. The disappointment she felt in the drawing room threatened to sneak its way in again, but she quickly dismissed it.

As could be expected, Lady Catherine dominated the conversation during dinner. Most of her words were meant for Darcy, but she did occasionally spare some time for the rest of the party, disbursing advice and instructions on everything from proper maintenance of carpets to the context of future sermons. It must take a great deal of time and effort to learn everything there is to know about the world in order to be able to correct everyone in the room. Elizabeth wanted to ask if she herself was a slave to education.

While Lady Catherine admonished Colonel Fitzwilliam to keep his feet dry while marching on Napoleon, Elizabeth heard Darcy's deep voice address her.

"I hope you have recovered from the carriage accident, Miss Bennet."

"I am fine now, thank you, Mr. Darcy." She smiled as she answered, earning one in return.

"I am glad to hear it. Are you enjoying your visit?"

"Yes, very much. I had missed my friend."

"She seems well settled. It must de agreeable to her to be in such an easy distance to her family."

"An easy distance? It is nearly fifty miles."

Darcy shrugged. "What is fifty miles of good road? Yes, I would say that is a very easy distance."

"Near and far are relative terms, I suppose. Sometimes the distance seems insurmountable."

She saw Darcy's formal stance relax as the kind man from the inn returned. "Forgive me, Miss Bennet. That was very insensitive of me. I remember three miles was too much when your elder sister was ill. You much feel the distance from your younger sister acutely now."

His sincerity touched her. She thanked him and they each continued to look at the other, hoping one of them would find a way to carry on the conversation. Just as it seemed Darcy would do just that, Miss de Bourgh began coughing.

"Anne, what is the matter?" Lady Catherine's harsh tone made Elizabeth cringe.

"Forgive me, Mother, but I believe I need some air. Darcy, will you please escort me to the terrace."

"Of course."

Anne turned to look at Elizabeth, took her cousin's arm and walked out of the room. Elizabeth watched them go and felt something she did not recognize rise within her. The only comparison she could make was the sadness she felt when her mother would take her best dolls for Jane to play with, leaving her with the worn playthings that needed much mending. She was brought back from her musings by Colonel Fitzwilliam asking her about the society in Hertfordshire.

"Are you well, Anne?" Darcy led his cousin through the garden, taking care to keep them in view of the windows.

"I am fine Darcy. Please let us sit. I cannot hold the weight of this hat much longer." They sat on a bench overlooking the barren rose bushes.

"Why do you allow her to dress you like that? You are not a puppet for heaven's sake."

Anne let out a mirthless laugh. "Am I not? Be at ease, cousin. This does not happen every day—only when you visit. I am so thankful you only come once a year." She smiled, but it did not put him at ease.

"You should have married me when I asked you. You would be safe at Pemberley and free of all this... plumage."

"You were fourteen and I was ten. You only asked me because you thought your father would not send you back to school if you were married."

"It might have worked." He smiled. "And you would not have to live here."

"Here is my home and I will not leave it. Besides, if we had married, you would never have met Miss Bennet."

"What?"

"Do not deny it, cousin. Anyone paying attention can see you are fascinated with her. Unfortunately, Mother had started to notice."

"That is the reason for your cough?" She nodded. "Thank you. I do find her fascinating. Did you see her with your mother? She was laughing at her. Not out loud, of course, but her eyes danced with mirth. All these years I have been subjected to the foolishness of my elder relations, with their extravagance and self-importance. I have always been angry. I never once thought to laugh at them."

"Oh, Darcy." Anne's eyes softened at the idea of her favorite cousin being in love.

"Do not, Anne. I spent some time in her company in Hertfordshire and I admit to having enjoyed it. But we have only just become reacquainted. I am still reeling from the coincidence of her being here now."

"What would your Grandmama Darcy say about this *coincidence*?"

Darcy smiled. "Mórai would say fairies or sprites or some other magical force broke that carriage wheel and put Elizabeth in my path. She would say it was fate. Then Grandfather would tell her to stop talking nonsense, that the lady in question has no fortune or connections and this attraction will not likely stand the test of time."

Anne sighed and shook her head. It was always a battle with Darcy. He never allowed anything to be easy. "Well, Darcy, while you debate both sides of your nature in regard to Miss Bennet, I will give you something else to ponder. I have wanted to speak to you all week but we are never alone. Mother will try harder than ever to connect us to each other this visit."

Darcy looked into the garden. "You turn five and twenty soon."

"Yes, and Rosings will be mine. It is her greatest nightmare to lose control over this estate. She would rather sell me to Pemberley so she could remain here always." She shook her head. "She and our uncle are truly delusional. They believe we would marry, join our estates, and let them have their way over us."

"It is not a sensible thought process, but the Fitzwilliams are not sensible people. We have resisted them for so long that if we were to give in now, they would believe us broken and susceptible to their machinations."

"They will never break you, Darcy. That is why I am leaving Rosings to you."

Darcy stared for a moment then shook his head. "No, Anne. I have enough. Leave it to Fitzwilliam so that he might resign from the army and finally be autonomous."

Anne shook her head. "Fitzwilliam will never be independent. He seeks his father's approval too much. You are your own man. Wakely is his own man. Fitzwilliam never will be. Mother would not allow any wife of his to truly be mistress and Matlock would have his hand in the operations and the coffers. I will not let my father's estate fall under the control of the Fitzwilliams. It is yours, Darcy. Now, act graciously."

He took her hand. "How can I when it comes at such a cost, just like everything else I own?"

"Darcy, there is nothing to be done. I could spend my days dwelling on what ifs. What if I were a man, what if I were healthy, what if my mother had been Anne rather than Catherine? It does no good. We must make the best of what we have been given. So much has been granted to you through death, it is true. You cannot rest your thoughts solely on that. Such powerful guilt is an insult to the ones who worked hard to provide what you have. I do not mean only the land and wealth, but strength and character and love. That is what sets you apart from every other man in our family. That is why you will have Rosings."

"How is it you are so wise, Anne?"

"I believe when you are never truly part of the world, you are given leave to observe it more closely."

Darcy nodded then brought her hand to his lips. "Thank you, Anne. It is cold and we have been gone too long. Shall we join the others?"

"Yes, but do control those moony looks; you never know who is watching."

Darcy kept himself under good regulation the rest of the evening and retired with a renewed determination to check his feelings for Elizabeth Bennet. His success was short lived, however, as he found himself on the path to Hunsford the very next morning.

Chapter 8

Elizabeth sat in a chair by the window in her bedroom and looked down at the letter in her hands. Jane wrote to inform her that their uncle and sister had begun their journey to the sea side. Lydia remained in her room during her entire stay in London and was never able to keep much food down. Jane was exceedingly worried and regretted being unable to accompany them. She closed by saying how much she missed all her dear sisters but was not anxious to return to Longbourn.

Elizabeth smiled. Jane's reluctance to leave London no doubt had something to do with Mr. Burton. She was shocked that her next thought took her to the idea of Jane needing to secure the man sooner rather than later. Elizabeth rolled her eyes. She'd had entirely too many conversations with Charlotte. Although if Jane's future could be secured, Elizabeth would feel more at ease.

She folded the letter and held it to her chest, saying a quick prayer for Lydia's safe journey, then rose to take a turn about the room. She was in an ill mood when they left Rosings the night before, bringing on a head ache that made sleep difficult. She blamed Lady Catherine and her cousin for her malady, but the image in her mind that made her head ache more was that of Mr. Darcy holding Miss de Bourgh's hand as they entered the drawing room. It could easily have been familial concern, but she could not dismiss the idea that Miss de Bourgh was the superior company Mr. Darcy was meant for. Now that they were friends, she would hope that he would marry someone with some sort of personality, but rank and wealth would always win with certain gentlemen. She would be disappointed if he was one of them.

As she walked by the window, her eye was caught by the approach of two gentlemen. There could be no doubt whom they were. Her skin flushed, as would happen to any woman looking at such a sight from the privacy of her bed chamber. They walked casually up the path. One gestured here and there, turning to take in something of interest while the other looked straight ahead as if determined not to be swayed. Their step slowed as they reached the gate. She was not the only one who had seen their approach.

Elizabeth put her fingers over her mouth as she watched Mr. Collins descend upon the gentlemen. He adopted his usual stance, shoulders hunched, head down and eyes up. She could not hear what he was saying, but he continued on for some time until Colonel Fitzwilliam gestured toward Rosings. Suddenly, Mr. Collins stood straight and walked down the path. He turned back to the gentlemen and said something before going quickly on his way. She could only be grateful at the prospect of spending the morning free of her cousin's company. She hastily checked her hair and straightened her gown before leaving to greet the guests.

Whatever good humor had abandoned Elizabeth that morning found its way to Charlotte, who greeted the men with more warmth than was typical. Elizabeth worried that living with Mr. Collins was wearing on Charlotte. Thankfully, however, she was not hunched.

"You will forgive my father's absence, I hope. He is to return to Hertfordshire and is preparing for his travels. I am sure my husband will join us soon."

"Ah, we actually have a message from Mr. Collins. He learned that my aunt could be out of sorts this morning and has gone to provide assistance."

"Could be out of sorts, Colonel Fitzwilliam?"

"Yes, Mrs. Collins, there is always that possibility." Everyone but Maria and Darcy laughed. The former would not dare laugh at Lady Catherine, even from a distance. The latter was not attending.

"Are you well, Miss Bennet?"

"I am, thank you, Mr. Darcy. I admit to not sleeping well due to a head ache, but thankfully it is gone now."

"I can well imagine your head throbbing after such an evening. The old lady put on quite a show, but you performed very well, Miss Bennet. I bow to your fortitude, madam. I have seen soldiers fall before less aggression."

"Fitzwilliam," Darcy admonished.

"We are all friends here, are we not? Must we keep the same formality here as we do at Rosings? Mrs. Collins, I ask your permission to speak openly and honestly in your parlor. When I am allowed to speak in front of my aunt, I am afraid I must leave the truth behind in my chambers."

Charlotte smiled. "I would have you be yourself, Colonel Fitzwilliam."

"See there, Darcy. Mrs. Collins appreciates the value of honesty."

"Indeed I do. If we are to be truthful, then I must tell you that when your aunt asked Eliza last night if she had a governess, she dissembled a little."

"Charlotte," Elizabeth looked at her friend menacingly from her seat beside her, but it did no good.

"She, in fact, did have one, for all of a week."

Elizabeth was tempted to put a pillow over her friend's mouth for the story about to come from it was mortifying. She shook the thought from her head. Charlotte was determined and she could only laugh.

"Oh, you truly are a strange creature by way of a friend. Here I am attempting to pass myself off with some degree of credit in a part of the world where I am not well known. You will have them all believe I am a liar." Elizabeth smiled and shook her head.

"You shall have them believing that, my friend, since you are the one lying. I am telling the truth." She turned to the gentlemen. "The Bennets employed a governess for Eliza and her elder sister Jane when they were around ten and eleven. You see, Mrs. Bennet was at her wits end with her second daughter. She was never still, all her stitches were crooked and her hair was always untidy. She feared Elizabeth would never become a lady."

Elizabeth sighed. "I am afraid it is all true. It did not help that Jane was perfect. If she had done something wrong occasionally my behavior would not have seemed so odd."

"Believe that if you will, Eliza. I will not take that comfort from you. So the governess, a Mrs. Martin, arrived to teach our little gypsy how to be a lady and, apparently, only observe Jane as she was already flawless. No one could know, of course, that Mrs. Martin was afraid of everything Eliza loved, including worms and toads. After playing in the garden one afternoon, she gifted Mrs. Martin with both those things. The poor woman's screams could be heard all the way to Lucas Lodge."

Elizabeth shook her head and turned away from Charlotte, trying to subdue her smile. "I blame your brother for that. He told me she was a witch. I thought if I gave her those creatures she could conjure a spell that would keep my stiches straight without so much effort. I cannot believe you are telling this. I have long suspected, but now I have no doubt: you, Charlotte Lucas, are the devil."

"Charlotte Collins, if you please."

"Oh yes, and how clever of you to hide in a parsonage. No one would ever suspect the vicar's wife was pure evil."

Darcy looked on in amusement as the two succumbed to laughter. Elizabeth was utterly enchanting. Her natural beauty shone through in her regard for her friend. Darcy wished to see his sister sitting in Mrs. Collins' place, brightening in the joy of a shared joke. Suddenly, Elizabeth became a bit more serious as she wiped her tears away.

"We should not be laughing so, for the outcome is no so amusing. That poor woman twisted her ankle terribly when she jumped from her seat and ran out of the room. Mama said she would not pay someone who could not work and released her.

"I felt awful. I promised Papa that if he kept her on, I would be the perfect lady and be ever so diligent in my studies. He told me Mrs. Martin would no longer be able to keep up with such a mischievous little one. I asked if he could allow her to live in one of our cottages—I knew one was vacant because we used to play there. She stayed on our estate and taught several of the tenant children for a living until she passed away just a few years ago. I would go and read to her sometimes, but I do not think she enjoyed it. She always insisted on checking my reticule before she allowed me to enter the cottage. I still feel guilty. But, I did learn to behave properly, much to my mother's relief.

"So there you have it, gentlemen. If your aunt ever questions you about my lack of education, you may tell her it was not due to a lack of effort on my parents' part, but my own."

Fitzwilliam wiped the tears from his eyes as his laughter faded. Darcy had enjoyed the story of her childhood exploits just as much, but his merriment only showed in his eyes. With the exception of Georgiana, every woman he had known displayed some sort of artifice. The women in his circle were raised to look pretty in their father's parlor or on their husband's arm. His mother remained poised at all times, even when showing affection. She had primarily been reared in the drawing rooms of London, but Elizabeth was something out of nature, wild and varying, yet beautiful. He could not tear his eyes from her.

"Darcy, what do you say to a stroll through the garden?"

"If it is agreeable to the ladies, I say yes." Darcy was grateful for Fitzwilliam's suggestion. Too many parts of him were feeling confined.

They ladies retrieved their gloves and bonnets then led the way outside to Mr. Collins' garden. Not much was in bloom, but everything was manicured to near perfection. One shrub had been left to grow and as Elizabeth walked past it she wondered if Mr. Collins had plans to turn it into an effigy of Lady Catherine.

As the party made polite conversation, Darcy withdrew and stood alone looking out toward the woods. Unbidden, the image of a girl with dark, wild hair running free among the trees came to mind. He became lost to his thoughts and the images moved from Kent to Pemberley. He heard Elizabeth's laughter behind him and he imagined they were home and it was Georgiana's laugh that mixed with hers. The familiar ache was joined by a tenderness that was as surprising as it was sweet. He let a small smile escape to acknowledge the feeling, believing no one would notice.

"What about this view is worthy of one of your rare smiles, Mr. Darcy."

He turned to see Elizabeth had joined him. She did not look at him, but stared straight ahead in the same direction he had set his eyes a moment earlier. He had not been this close to her in days and he took a moment to breathe her in before replying.

"That row of trees there in the distance reminded me of home and my sister."

She turned to him. "Trees remind you of your sister?"

"Not usually, no. I sent her home to Pemberley and wonder how she is getting on. She was not happy to be leaving London."

"She enjoys the excitement of town?"

"No, it was the shorter distance to Kent that she preferred. She does not have your confidence, Miss Bennet, and prefers to be closer to her elder brother."

Elizabeth smiled softly then turned back to the view. "My sister began her journey a few days ago. I wonder how she is getting on, too."

"Missing you, I would suspect."

Elizabeth smiled and nodded. "You were very quiet in the parlor, Mr. Darcy. Were you shocked by the story of my wild childhood? Do you despise my lack schooling as much as your aunt?"

"Quite the opposite, actually. It seems you have spent your time more wisely, Miss Bennet. You are far better read than many with formal educations and you can talk your way around the best of us. You are also kind and loyal, traits that cannot be learned in a schoolroom. No one treated to the privilege of your acquaintance could ever find you lacking. You were right not to tell the full truth to my aunt. You need not perform to strangers."

She met his eye and for a moment, as her cheeks blushed beautifully, he held her captive. Her eyes searched his greedily, as if pondering some great mystery, and he could not contain the hope that she would find what she sought. Too soon, the spell was broken and she looked away, murmuring her thanks.

As they stood there, dark clouds began to gather overhead. Darcy tried to ignore the sound of his cousin's voice, but his insistence they walk back before they were drenched eventually broke through. He did not want to leave, but could not stay. Finally, he bowed.

"Good day, Miss Bennet."

"Good day, Mr. Darcy."

Elizabeth stood in place and watched the two gentlemen walk away. Her heart beat wildly in her chest after his compliment. She may not have turned his head when they first met but it seemed she was now more than tolerable. That thought pleased her entirely too much. She smirked as she moved to follow Charlotte and Maria up the path.

No one treated to the privilege of your acquaintance could ever find you lacking.

I wager he never said that *to Anne de Bourgh.*

Lydia rested her head against the seat and chewed on the ginger root her aunt gave her for the journey. It helped while resting at the inns, but nothing soothed her stomach in the carriage. It seemed to roll in time with the wheels as they carried her north.

Her uncle sat across from her and read aloud to pass the time. The words made no sense to Lydia. They ran together like the blurred images of the world coming to life she sometimes caught in her peripheral vision. She did not turn to the window, fearing the movement would bring dizziness along with the nausea, but she could tell spring was working on the landscape.

"Uncle?" He had paused reading and she took the opportunity to ask about her accommodations. "Tell me more about who I am staying with."

Mr. Gardiner looked to the maid who accompanied them to assist Lydia. She remained asleep as she had for most of the ride.

"The Baineses are distant cousins to your aunt. They are the last of her family in the area. Mr. Baines breeds hunting hounds and they lease a small farm. I am afraid you will have to forgo some of the luxuries you used to as a gentleman's daughter. You may have to help with meals or gather eggs and such. They know of your condition and will not expect too much, I am sure."

"They will take care of . . . everything . . . afterward?"

"Yes. They recently experienced a stillbirth. It was recommended that Mrs. Baines not again become with child."

Lydia nodded and said no more. The remaining hours of the journey were slow and though she was apprehensive about the situation, she would be glad to at least be out of the carriage.

"Ah, here we are. Are you ready?"

Lydia hesitated. Inside she screamed *no*. She was not ready; she did not want to spend the next months on a farm tending chickens. She wanted Lizzy and Jane. She wanted her mother. She wanted to be free of the weight that never left her. She wanted to go home.

She briefly fingered the garnet cross around her neck. "Yes, Uncle. Let us go."

Longbourn was not large when compared to a place like Netherfield. Compared to the house she now stood in front of, it was a mansion. She looked at her uncle and he held her gaze but a moment before looking away. He started toward the door but it opened before he could knock.

"Mr. Gardiner?" Lydia had expected to see a maid but the woman before them was obviously the woman of the house. "Please, come in."

They were led inside to a very small parlor. The furnishings and carpets were worn but clean. Lydia had never been inside a tenant's house at Longbourn, but she imagined one would look similar to her new home.

"Mrs. Baines, I am delighted to meet you. My wife has told me many stories of her childhood here in Lambton. You featured prominently in most of them."

Mrs. Baines stood nearly as tall as Mr. Gardiner. Her clothes were simple but neat and her dark hair was mostly hidden beneath a lace cap. Like the room where they stood, she could not be called warm, but rather, functional.

"I am happy to hear she thinks of us with fondness and that we are able to do her this service." She looked to Lydia expectably.

"This is my niece Lydia."

Lydia curtsied and Mrs. Baines merely nodded. "I am afraid my husband will be unable to receive you today, Mr. Gardiner. He had some unexpected business to attend to. He will be back this evening if you can wait."

"Oh, I had hoped to speak with him. I am afraid my own business calls me home and I must depart soon. Would you oblige me and show me around your home, madam?"

"Of course."

She led them to the other rooms of the house, which included the kitchen and a small workroom downstairs and three bedrooms plus a maid's room upstairs.

"That bedroom belongs to my son, Adam. He is with his father today. And this will be your room, Miss Lydia."

She opened the door to another modest but well-kept room. Lydia entered and saw her trunk had already been placed inside. Her footfalls echoed in the nearly empty space that contained only a bed and small table. There was no fireplace, nor window. Suddenly fatigued, Lydia sat on the bed.

"Mrs. Baines, I will take a few minutes to help my niece settle before I depart." She nodded and left them alone.

"Lydia, I am sorry I could not find a better option for you. I did not want to leave you among strangers, and these are the only family Maddy and I have outside of Meryton and London."

"Must you leave?"

"Again, I am sorry. I have little help and cannot be away for long. I must make it back to the inn before nightfall if I am to keep my schedule. We must make the best of this, dear. Here." He pulled a small purse from his pocket. "I will send the Baineses money each month for your care, but take this as well. Use it for things like paper to write to us with or sweets when you are feeling better."

She took it and nodded her thanks.

"I will be back with your aunt and sister. That time will be here before you can even blink."

"Very well. I think I would like to sleep now. Will it be alright?"

He kissed her forehead and looked her in the eye with the intent to answer the affirmative, but the words would not form.

"Rest, Lydia. I will see you soon."

He walked from the room and closed the door, but the thin walls could not contain the sound of Lydia's sobs.

Chapter 9

"Mr. Collins, your boots!" Charlotte reprimanded her husband as he came through the door covered in mud nearly to his knees.

Mr. Collins looked down and saw the extent of his untidiness. "Forgive me, my dear. I will just go and change."

"You will go through the kitchen and not my entry hall. What would Lady Catherine say if she knew you tracked mud through the home she has worked hard to improve?"

"Oh my goodness, Charlotte! Why did you not correct me before? Her ladyship would indeed be cross if she knew. I heartily chastise myself in her stead."

"Mr. Collins."

"Right, right. I will turn around and go through the kitchen."

Charlotte rolled her eyes and entered the parlor, where Elizabeth sat smiling, having overheard the entire exchange. She sat down near the window and picked up her sewing.

"Charlotte, you are brilliant. Do you often have to evoke Lady Catherine to get your husband to cooperate?"

"Her more than Jesus at times."

"Charlotte!"

"It is true. He has put so much faith in her that I fear for his well-being should she fall from her throne and somehow injure herself irrevocably."

Elizabeth laughed. "Charlotte, I cannot believe the words that come from your mouth now. "

"I know, but, believe me, I do not say these things to my husband or anyone else. I only play harridan with you, dear Eliza."

Elizabeth tilted her head in thought. "I do not know what to say. I suppose it is flattering that you feel comfortable enough to show your real personality to me. However, that nature is almost shrewish. I am not sure it is wise to be friends with such a person."

Charlotte laughed. "You will not abandon me now, Eliza. Not when I have such plans for you."

Elizabeth raised her eyebrows and began to ask what plans, but then thought better of it. "I know you wish me to ask, but I will not. It only encourages you."

Before Charlotte could explain herself, a clean Mr. Collins entered the room. He bowed then clasped his hand together.

"Oh, my dear Charlotte and my dear Cousin Elizabeth. As a man of God, I never complain about the paths he leads me on but this morning I ardently wish they would have been less muddy."

"Will you not sit down, Mr. Collins?"

"Of course, my dear." He turned to Elizabeth. "I am happy to see you are sewing, cousin. I was worried you would show the same sort of wild nature you displayed in Hertfordshire, always going on your rambles."

Elizabeth paid closer attention to her sewing and chose not to respond. She made that choice often in the last week. Rain had fallen nearly every morning, leaving the paths too muddy to travel by foot. The sun came out earlier that day and she hoped it would dry the trails enough to tread tomorrow in spite of her cousins admonishment.

"Wild behavior will have its consequence. I have just come from ministering to a family in the village. Their young unmarried daughter has become with child." He shook his head and clicked his tongue. "They were just beginning to come up in the world. Now they face ruin all because that girl could not be tamed. I told them they must send her away if they have any hope of recovery. The sin must be cleansed from the house."

Elizabeth looked at her cousin with a stern expression. "And did you have the same admonishment for the man who put her in that position?"

Mr. Collins looked confused for a moment. He studied her face then seemed to suddenly find enlightenment. "My dear cousin, I do not expect you to understand the workings of the world. That girl should have said no."

"How do you know she did not? Did you get any of the particulars before you cast your judgment?"

"What I know is that she has brought shame on her family. It would have been far better had she died rather than dishonor them in such a way. Then they could mourn openly. Now they must live with the shame of her impurity."

Elizabeth stood and walked to the window in an attempt to hide her anger. *Better had she died.* She wanted to throw something at him, or better still, strike him with her own fists. She suddenly found it fitting that this man would inherit her father's estate. His opinions certainly fell in line with the current owner.

"Mr. Collins, I do not believe it is appropriate to speak of such things in front of an unmarried woman. Thankfully Maria is helping the cook with the pies. Let us change the subject, please."

"Of course, of course. I had the pleasure of visiting Rosings today as well. I was not allowed inside because of the mud, but her ladyship is so very kind. She had one of her footmen bring books for me to read on farming and land management. She believes it is not too early to prepare for the inevitable. One never knows when the hand of the Almighty will descend upon us, taking from one and giving to another."

Elizabeth looked at the ceiling then to the wall. She was afraid she could not disguise the sheer revulsion she felt at that moment. The contentment she felt for Charlotte's situation evaporated. She could only pity her friend for being married to such a hateful man. Although she knew he was ridiculous, Elizabeth could not help but believe those words were uttered to cause her pain.

Suddenly, Charlotte rose and dropped her sewing into her basket. "Mr. Collins, I believe I need your assistance with the household accounts."

Mr. Collins looked to his wife in confusion. "Uh, um, but you have said we need only attend the accounts on Saturdays. After sundown."

She lifted her chin and clasped her hands in front of her. "Yes, Mr. Collins, I believe we should tend them now."

He rose and swallowed heavily. "In daylight?"

"Mr. Collins."

"Yes, my dear. I will, uh, go prepare the books for inspection."

Charlotte turned to Elizabeth, who was perplexed by the entire exchange. "I am sorry for my husband's poor choice of words, Eliza. I can see you are distressed. Tending the books always leaves him fatigued and he will likely remain above stairs until tomorrow." Charlotte gathered her thoughts then pulled Elizabeth into an embrace. "Mr. Collins is right that the change in ownership is inevitable. I promise you, Eliza, that I will do everything I can to see Longbourn thrive and to raise an heir worthy of your home."

Elizabeth was overcome with both sadness that Mr. Collins would one day inherit Longbourn and gratitude that Charlotte would be there, too.

"Thank you, Charlotte," Elizabeth spoke through her tears. "Would you mind if I did not join you for dinner this evening. I believe I would like to spend time writing to my sisters."

"Of course, Eliza. You have not had much solitude this week. I will bring a tray to your room."

Elizabeth hugged her friend close one more time before she retired to her chamber. She sat at the small writing desk and penned a long letter to Lydia. She told her of Kent and Rosings and how Mr. Collins was as bizarre as ever. She filled the page with words of encouragement and love and assured her they would see each other soon. Elizabeth folded the letter and added it to one she had written to her aunt. She could not send it to Lydia directly, lest someone see the direction and question who she knew in Lambton.

As promised, Charlotte brought dinner to Elizabeth's room. They spoke quietly of inconsequential things before Charlotte excused herself to have dinner with Maria. As she supposed earlier, Mr. Collins was too tired to join them.

Elizabeth did not sleep easy. Mr. Collins' words filled her dreams as scenes of her sister played in her mind. It began at the Netherfield ball. Lydia danced every dance and the blush on her cheeks made her vibrancy all the more attractive. She laughed and through her dream, Elizabeth laughed with her. Lydia moved through the line of a reel when two arms clothed in red appeared around her waist. Elizabeth could not see the man's face, but panic replaced her laugh as she saw Lydia struggle to free herself from his grasp. He released her and she fell to the floor as the other dancers moved away. Elizabeth ran to her side and gathered her up in her arms. She looked down at Lydia's face, which had become thin and ashen. She whispered her name, but Lydia did not respond; she merely faded in her sister's arms.

Elizabeth woke with a heavy heart and a renewed worry for her family. She kept Mr. Collins' words in the front of her mind as she rushed through her morning ablutions. His words had been callous, but nonetheless correct. Society would pity the Bennets if they lost their young, lively, beautiful daughter to death. They would be prayed over and cared for, offered every possible balm to soothe the heartache of loss. But losing her to a scoundrel would make them objects of scorn. They would be avoided, gossiped about and despised. The unfairness of life struck her hard as she gathered her bonnet and gloves. She needed to run. She needed to lose these thoughts to the wind if she had any hope of facing the coming weeks with any cheerfulness.

Darcy stared out his chamber window, happy to see the sun coming up over the trees. He had spent too many gloomy days inside of Rosings. The restlessness that claimed him in London was settling in again. He needed to move. Not bothering to ring for his valet, he strode to his closet and gathered his clothing. As he dressed himself his mind wondered to his last visit with Elizabeth, which had been too many days ago.

She was vivacious and warm, full of love for those she was close to. As they looked over the landscape together, it was not hard to imagine her on his arm as they toured the grounds of Pemberley. He continued those imaginings after they parted and added to them as the week drew on. They were poor substitutes for her lovely face. He missed her. He paused his musings while that thought took root. This was different from the longing he felt through the winter. That time was full of regret. This feeling was softer, sweeter, and full of hope.

He would see her today—he was determined and he would do so without Fitzwilliam. He was still angry with his cousin for his actions the previous week. Darcy had not realized when they walked to the parsonage that his cousin was well into his cups. Fitzwilliam's casualness with the ladies caused him to suspect something was not quite right. Darcy confronted him about his behavior on the walk back to Rosings and they argued vehemently, nearly coming to blows when they reached the manor.

They had barely spoken since—though Fitzwilliam had tried to raise his ire a number of times. Darcy could not understand why he was acting this way. Visiting Rosings was never pleasurable, but they had always managed to make the best of it. The tension between the two weighed on Anne, who now would only receive them separately.

Darcy blew out a long breath and rubbed his face. He could not call at the parsonage alone. Word would surely get back to Lady Catherine and she would demand to know why he was there. Anne was right when she said that her mother was more determined than ever that they marry.

His aunt used every ploy in her power that week to convince him to fulfill his duty. When trying to induce his guilt by mentioning his mother's desire to unify the family did not work, she became irate. She demanded to know if some lesser woman had bewitched him, causing him to forget what he owed to Anne.

If she suspected his interest in Elizabeth, she would exercise her power over Mr. Collins and have him send her away, or worse. She was now desperate and he had to believe she was capable of anything. He did not want to be caught off guard.

He donned his coat and decided a hard ride would clear his mind and hopefully help him determine the best plan of action. He made his way downstairs as quietly as possible and quit the house for the stables. A short time later he was riding hard toward the woods.

Elizabeth tied the ribbons of her bonnet beneath her chin as she walked down the stairs. She stepped quietly, hoping to avoid any of the household before she could walk off the stress of the night before. After she had managed to escape the house and gardens, Elizabeth inhaled the scent of earth and woods. To her, this was the smell of freedom. She could hide among the trees or run a race with the wind and no one would be the wiser—at least not until she came back with dirty petticoats.

She reached the line of the trees and was pleased to find a path soon after she ventured inside. She walked a little ways, attempting to empty her mind when she heard a thundering sound behind her. She barely had time to move to the side when a great horse, carrying a great figure, ran past her then stopped a few feet ahead.

"Miss Bennet, good morning."

"Good morning, Mr. Darcy."

It seemed for some moments this would be the extent of their conversation, as the gentleman sat on the magnificent steed and looked at her as if he expected something more. She was about to curtsy and be on her way when he dismounted.

"Do you often roam the woods so early in the morning, Miss Bennet?"

"I do at Longbourn. Today is my first opportunity to explore here at Rosings. I find the exercise to be helpful in clearing one's mind before getting on with the arduous tasks of breakfast and embroidery."

He smirked at her impertinence, the one that always left her wondering if he was offended, amused, or something else altogether. This man's character was impossible to sketch, yet, she found his presence—and that smirk—oddly familiar, like an old friend.

He finally dismounted and walked toward her. "Did you leave the inhabitants of the parsonage in good health?"

Elizabeth's irritation at the mention of the parsonage was evident. Darcy raised his eyebrow in question.

"I did not have the pleasure of seeing anyone this morning, but last evening they were all quite themselves."

"I have the impression you do not believe that is a good thing."

"You can be sure, Mr. Darcy, that I think Charlotte to be everything that is excellent and pleasant."

She received another smirk in response to her omission. He would not let it pass.

"And Mr. Collins?"

Elizabeth sighed. If he would press the subject, then she would be honest. "I cannot comprehend, Mr. Darcy, why some people must hold themselves so high above others. It seems unfair that opportunity of education and growth, not to mention fortune of birth, can be bestowed on the ridiculous. That man will inherit all that my family has and he takes every opportunity to remind me of it. And there is, of course, the matter of my unfortunate nature that leads me to do such unseemly things as love my family or walk in these woods."

Darcy searched her face for a moment. The fatigue he noticed in the carriage the morning of the accident had returned. He wanted to carry her somewhere, hold her close to him and demand that she rest. He chose instead to speak.

"What can I do, Miss Bennet? How may I help settle your mind this morning? Will you to speak to me more of your troubles?"

She gave him a soft smile then shook her head. "I thank you, Mr. Darcy, but for once in my life I am tired of words. If I were alone. . ." she paused, knowing she was about to divulge a secret that would undoubtedly shock the staid man at her side. "If I were alone I would run so fast the thoughts that plague me this morning could not catch me."

The shocked expression she expected did not emerge. Instead, his features softened as the corners of his mouth lifted just a little.

"You would like me to leave you so that you may run through the woods by yourself." It was a statement more than a question. He looked at her for a moment before he led his horse to a nearby tree and tied its reigns to a branch. "I will not give you the isolation you seek, madam. The woods are too full of dangers, especially for one who does not know their secrets."

Elizabeth knew she should be angry at his refusal, but she was too distracted by the sight of him removing his greatcoat and hat, which he carefully placed over the horse's saddle. Her heart rate quickened and she had to remind herself that he had always acted like a perfect gentleman.

"You will not leave me?" The strength she intended to display failed to materialize as he returned to her side and without it, her voice seemed but a whisper.

"No, I will not." He tilted his head and extended his hand. "I will run with you."

Elizabeth looked at his hand and then to his face. He was in earnest. She was simultaneously relieved and ashamed. She swore to herself that she would never again question his good character. Still, she did not take his hand but delivered her best impression of his amused smirk.

"Well, then, Mr. Darcy. I suggest you try to keep up."

Then she ran. As she hoped, the thoughts vanished from her mind as she felt the cool air on her face. She could feel Darcy just behind her. She turned her head and flashed him a genuine smile as she increased her pace. She could see a fork in the path ahead and stopped, trying to decide which way to take. She felt a strong hand take hers.

"This way."

He tugged her arm and they were off again. He did not release her but led her further into the trees where the path was less worn. The sun had not dried the ground there, and mud splashed around them. There was no convention in their actions. No propriety or societal expectation followed them as they moved deeper into the trees. They had escaped.

Elizabeth felt her bonnet fall from her head, but she did not stop until they reached a small clearing. They slowed and she began to take in her surroundings. When they stopped altogether, she felt him release her hand. She watched as he turned back down the path to retrieve her bonnet, which had fallen in the grass along the muddy trail.

She stepped forward into the clearing. In the weeks she had been in Kent, the foliage had gone from gray to green and the air began to warm. She closed her eyes and drew in a deep breath as she slowly turned in the sun. Spring was indeed glorious; nature's rebirth allowing mere mortals a glance at eternity, a never-ending cycle of renewal. No matter how harsh winter had blown or displayed its temper, the warmth would come, the flowers would bloom and the word would set itself right again. Elizabeth stilled her movements and allowed herself a few moments to hope her own world would right itself: Lydia's bloom would return, and the cold that had surrounded them for so many months would be replaced by a warmth that would never fade.

She lowered her chin and opened her eyes to see Darcy at her side, looking at her with that same intense gaze that had followed her in Hertfordshire. As if the sun had suddenly come down to sear her flesh, her cheeks reddened as he spoke in a deep purposeful tone.

"The wilderness suits you, Miss Bennet. You seem far more at home here among the trees than in the structured gardens. Do you often find yourself playing the part of wood nymph?"

Darcy's cheeks fared no better than Elizabeth's. In fact, his entire body seemed on fire. When he turned back after retrieving her hat, he saw what he was sure to be the most beautiful image her would ever behold. Elizabeth's face was tipped toward the sun and the breeze toyed with the chestnut locks that had fallen from their pins. He felt the blood rush through his veins. For the first time since he was a child he felt the excitement of discovery, as if he had come across some uncharted land that had grown from the earth, meant for only him to explore.

The desire he felt for her in the autumn was but a trifle compared to the emotion that now coursed through him. He thought back to what his cousin told him about the difference between lust and love. One takes while the other gives. He no longer wanted to take her; he wanted to claim her and claim the land that surrounded them for her so that she could run free and rid herself of whatever burden she had sought respite from just moments earlier. He wanted to give her all the pleasure that could be shared between them, along with his land, his fortune, and most of all his heart if she would have it.

Elizabeth, at first, thought she might wither under the heat of his gaze. His words in the parsonage garden, along with his genuine smile, had led her to believe he never disapproved of her, but she knew that her current state was far worse than the six inches of mud that covered her the first day he saw her at Netherfield. She gathered her courage and stepped back, forcing herself from the pull of his eyes.

She summoned her greatest weapon, her only defense against the confusion she always felt when in the presence of this man. She tilted her head, raised an eyebrow, and willed her voice to stay calm.

"If you are attempting to frighten me, Mr. Darcy, by reminding me of my disheveled appearance, then I must admonish you, sir, to first repair you own. I was not the only one plodding through the woods nor am I the only one to bear the evidence of my endeavor."

Her eyes traveled down to his dirt splattered breeches, then back up to his tousled mass of curls. She reached up and pulled a small clump of mud from one such curl and presented it to him along with a satisfied smirk. He laughed as he took it from her hand. Elizabeth started, thinking she might be safer under the heated glare than in the presence of the usually well-hidden dimples.

"Then we make the perfect pair, madam. I may not appear to uncommon advantage like the last time I attempted to walk with you, but I hope you will grant me the pleasure nonetheless. Shall we?"

His acknowledgment of her insult at Netherfield surprised her, and she was relieved to see that he was more amused than affronted. They began their walk around the grove quietly and she once again attempted to fill the silence.

"You are correct, sir, that I prefer the wild to the ornamental. I find more beauty in what is natural, than what is tended to perfection."

"The rose garden is not in bloom. You may yet find beauty there."

Elizabeth shrugged her shoulders slightly. "Perhaps."

"You do not find roses beautiful?"

"I find them common. You will see roses in every garden in England. I would wager, Mr. Darcy, that after two turns within those lovely walls you would not be able to find a single thing you have not seen before. They are pretty, they are prevalent, but in them I find nothing truly beautiful. Whereas here, one could explore for days, weeks perhaps, and only see a small portion of what nature has to offer. You see Mr. Darcy, I find roses quite vulgar."

He chuckled softly then after a while added, "My aunt is very fond of roses."

Elizabeth nodded. "I noticed."

They shared a knowing smile and continued their walk mostly in silence. Their heads had been cleared by the run and now their hearts were free to reign. While one was now certain there would be no future without the other in it, another was simply grateful to finally feel at ease.

Too soon, it was time to return. He offered her his arm and he gently led her down a shorter path to Hunsford. Once there, he opened the gate for her but closed it after she walked through. She turned and looked up at him questioningly.

"As much as I would like to escort you further and call on Mrs. Collins, I believe I should not appear before her so . . ."

"Unlike yourself?" She thought she could see sadness in his eyes as he nodded.

"Do you plan to walk out again tomorrow, Miss Bennet?"

"I do, sir."

"May I join you in your search for the beautiful and rare?"

"I would like that very much, Mr. Darcy, so long as you promise to return me in better condition than you have today."

"I will try my very best Miss Bennet." He bowed and as he raised back up he once again fixed his intense gaze upon her.

She curtsied and turned down the path thinking, *Dimples. Dimples are definitely safer.*

Chapter 10

Elizabeth breathed a sigh of relief as she leaned against her chamber door. She managed to make it into the parsonage and up to her room with only a maid seeing her. She looked down to her mud splattered boots and skirts and wondered if perhaps it would be better just to throw them away rather than try to clean them. If she were home, her mother would surely be thrown into a fit of nerves over the ruined gown. As she moved to the vanity, she noticed a roll and a pot of tea on the table beside her bed. She sighed. She had missed breakfast. Mr. Collins likely filled the dining room with words of disapproval for her absence, but she could not regret it.

Her time in the woods had been a balm for her frayed emotions. She had not felt such contentment in months. Mr. Darcy joining her was a welcome surprise. *I will run with you.* She loved the freedom that running provided and it had been her means of escape since she was a child. Never had she shared that precious time with anyone, not even Jane.

She blushed as she recollected the feel of his hand over hers. Strong but gentle. Those were words that were becoming very important to her, as they described Darcy entirely. Twice in recent weeks she had felt distressed. Both times he provided understanding and comfort.

She picked up the pitcher off the vanity and was relieved to find it full of water. *Dear Charlotte.* She must have anticipated Elizabeth's need to wash away evidence of her morning walk. She poured the water into the basin and wondered again at the difference between women and men. She would have to change out of her dress entirely while Darcy would only need to retrieve his great coat to hide most of his dirtied clothing. This difference in dress was only slight when compared to the judgment of others. Mr. Collins would comment on Darcy's robustness and health if he knew of their run while thoroughly chastising her for the same.

She looked in the mirror as she washed the dirt from her face. She still bore the evidence of restless sleep, but her cheeks held color and her eyes finally showed signs of life. She felt like Elizabeth again. Not the same girl she was before Lydia's illness, to be sure, but lighter than when she first arrived in Kent. Not as afraid. Hopeful. It was a good run.

She removed her dress and boots and had just finished buttoning a clean gown when a knock came.

"Yes?"

"Excuse me, miss, but Mrs. Collins is asking for you. You have a visitor."

"Thank you, I will be right down."

Elizabeth took a last look in the mirror before quitting the room. She walked down the stairs in a much more ladylike fashion than she had earlier and found Colonel Fitzwilliam sitting with Charlotte and Mr. Collins. She smiled and looked for another visitor, but the Colonel had come alone.

"Good morning Miss Bennet," Fitzwilliam addressed her as he rose from a deep bow. "I trust you are well." He smiled affably, apparently in very good spirits.

"Good morning, Colonel. I am, thank you. Is everyone at Rosings as cheerful as you today?" She took a seat between Charlotte and Maria, avoiding the disapproving glare of her cousin.

Fitzwilliam laughed. "Cheerfulness at Rosings was banished years ago. I do not believe one is allowed to enter the parlor without a scowl or at least a right and proper grimace. Darcy manages well enough, but I find myself in need of escape."

Elizabeth smiled and looked down. Did the Colonel not know of Darcy's need to escape? Was she the only one privy to that side of him, or was his behavior that morning just his way of easing her distress? No, he had been lightened by the exercise as much as she. She could tell by his expression when she turned and smiled at him. She felt Charlotte's slipper gently tap hers, bringing her attention back to Colonel Fitzwilliam.

"And you have chosen the parsonage as your refuge, sir?"

"Of course. There is no better company in all of Kent, I am sure."

"You flatter us, sir," Mr. Collins joined the conversation. "If you find her ladyship is in need of cheering, then perhaps I should walk back with you. I do hope she is not becoming ill."

"No, Mr. Collins, I believe she is quite herself."

"Well, that is certainly good to hear. I have been unable to call because of the weather. I would be forever guilty if something were to happen to her ladyship in my absence."

No one quite knew what to say to that, so the room fell silent for a moment. It seemed Mr. Collins was ready to fill the void, but Charlotte spoke first.

"Is Mr. Darcy well this morning?"

"I suppose he is. I have not seen him yet today. He saddled his horse early this morning and did not come back for breakfast, much to my aunt's displeasure."

"Mr. Darcy missed his breakfast, you say? That is most unfortunate. I do hope he did not meet with some misfortune along the trails."

Elizabeth could feel her cousin's eyes boring into her, but she would not react.

"I am sure he is fine. I wager when I return I will find him reading to Anne."

"Of course. A gentleman like Mr. Darcy does know his duty."

"Yes," Colonel Fitzwilliam stated flatly. He turned again to Elizabeth. "Miss Bennet, you are looking quite well this morning. I see the recent weather has not dampened your spirits."

"I am not formed for ill humor, sir. Although, I will admit to slight irritation after I awoke to a third, fourth, and then fifth morning of rain. What is good for the garden is quite hazardous to my state of mind."

He laughed at her teasing expression. "Let us hope your temper is not tested much more, then. We would not want your slight irritation to turn into a full on tantrum."

Elizabeth laughed and Colonel Fitzwilliam leaned forward slightly, fully taking in the sound. He took one last long look at her happy countenance then rose.

"I should be going. Thank you for the lovely company, ladies. Mr. Collins." He bowed, met the parting farewells with a smile and left the room with a bloviating Mr. Collins traveling behind.

The ladies remained in the parlor, each tending their own basket of sewing while speaking of news they had heard from Hertfordshire. Elizabeth tried to concentrate on her needlework, but too often her gaze traveled to the window where, if she bent her head just right, she could see the trees along edge of the woods.

"Charles, have you heard from Mr. Darcy regarding dinner this week? I asked you to invite him a month ago."

Bingley looked up from his plate to see his sister Caroline glaring at him. He tilted his head and responded impassively.

"I thought I had already told you he is unable to attend." He was almost sure he had, but could not be certain. His mind had not been its sharpest since his return to town in November.

"Need I remind you, Caroline, that dinner invitations are both given and received by me? We are no longer at Netherfield where you played hostess. You are in my family's home and, while my mother is not in residence, I am mistress. Charles informed me of Mr. Darcy's regrets last week. After I asked several times." Louisa Hurst looked pointedly at her brother, who was too engrossed by his eggs to notice.

"Why is he unable to come, Charles? Is it because we are not in the fashionable part of town?"

Bingley groaned inwardly at the jab against his eldest sister. Caroline and Louisa got along so well when they had another person to pick on. When left to their own devices, they turned on each other.

"No, Caroline, it is because he is not in town at all. He has made his annual trip to Kent."

"To Kent?! But he was not supposed to leave until later this week. He was to dine here before he left so that he could see the new gown I had made just for him. It shows my figure to its best advantage."

Bingley finished his eggs and finally gave Caroline his full attention. She seemed on the verge of a proper fit. She would not like his answer. "He was called to Rosings early. He sent his regrets and hopes to dine with us upon his return."

"Called to Rosings? By *Anne de Bourgh*, I suppose."

"I imagine her *fortune* is displayed to its best advantage. Give up, Caroline."

Louisa's comment sent Caroline into a panic. She stood and wrung her napkin as she walked to her brother's chair. "Charles, you must write to him. List all my virtues and accomplishments. You must not let him make the mistake of proposing to the wrong woman. You are his closest friend. He will listen to you."

"Caroline, your virtues have been on full display for a few years. If they have not impressed him by now, they never will. I will echo Louisa: give up."

Both his sisters looked at him in disbelief. He had never encouraged Caroline's pursuit of Darcy, but this was the first time he attempted to dissuade her.

"What do you know, Charles? Has he already proposed to her?"

"If Darcy were to ever confide his plans to me regarding matrimony or any other subject, I would not be free to discuss them with you, Caroline."

His sister did not relent, nor did he expect her to. "I believe I have had my fill. I think I shall go for a walk through the park this morning."

"You will not. We have calls to make and it is not even the fashionable time to walk in the park. No one will see you."

"That is the second time you have used that word this morning, Caroline. Do you not think it time to expand your vocabulary?"

Caroline sat back down in exasperation. "You are trying to vex me, Charles. I will not let you. Go for your walk and stop bothering me. Please try to be back in time to go with us on calls. It is past time for you to display *your* virtues."

"Yes, Caroline."

The Hursts indeed were not in the most sought after part of town, but they were not far from it, so Bingley made good time to Hyde Park. He had been off kilter for months—as if he had forgotten something important. He made all his usual rounds in town and enjoyed himself well enough though not with the same enthusiasm as previous seasons. He made every effort at fun, sometimes to the point of recklessness. Truth be told, he was bored of it all. He was ready for something different, but he could not name what, exactly. He was drawn from his contemplations by the sound of a child's laugh.

He looked at the water and saw a fleet of paper boats sailing with the current, much to the delight of the little observers. Something about the scene tugged at his heart and he found himself moving toward them. As he closed in on the joyful group, the sight of a woman walking to the same destination stopped him dead in his tracks.

"Miss Bennet!"

"Mr. Bingley." Jane curtseyed.

"It is a great pleasure to see you. Are you well? I can see that you are. Does this brood of sailors belong to you?"

"Yes, they are my cousins. We usually take them to the park nearer their home, but they wanted to try their boats this morning."

"You are staying with family in town?"

Jane looked confused for a moment, then replied, "Yes, I am still with my Aunt and Uncle Gardiner. I have not left town since your sister called on us in January."

Bingley's smile disappeared. "You have been in town since January? My sister called on you?"

"Yes, after I called on her some weeks prior. Did she not tell you?"

"No, she did not. I wish I had known. I would like to have called with her. It truly is a great pleasure to see you."

Jane smiled but offered no such sentiments in reply. He noticed her reluctance and started to say something else when they were joined by another. Mr. Burton tipped his head to Bingley as he offered his arm to Jane.

"Miss Bennet?" Jane gladly accepted and made introductions.

"Mr. Bingley, this is Mr. Burton. He has escorted my cousins, aunt and me to the park today. He is staying with his sister's family nearby for the season, but his estate is in Yorkshire."

Bingley studied the scene before him. Mr. Burton had obviously taken possession and Jane did not mind. "Ah, you are a northern man like myself."

"Oh? Where is your estate, sir?"

"I do not have one. Not yet." Bingley stammered out the words. If the man was trying to intimidate him, it was indeed working.

"Mr. Bingley leased an estate near Longbourn. I am afraid the neighborhood did not impress him, though." Her voice held no regrets, merely disapprobation. Bingley's heart sank.

"I would not say that, Miss Bennet. I enjoyed my time in Hertfordshire very much. I am sorry to have left without saying goodbye, but I had every intention of returning at the time."

"Your sister's letter informing us of the departure of the entire party stated otherwise. There is no need to placate me, sir. I understand the singularity of Meryton society is not for everyone."

"Truly, Miss Bennet, I found no fault with the society in Meryton. There seems to have been a great deal of misunderstanding."

Jane smiled. "It is no matter, Mr. Bingley. But, if you do not mean to return to Netherfield, perhaps it would be better for the neighborhood if you gave it up altogether. We have such unvaried company there, and my mother has four daughters to marry off."

Bingley noticed Mr. Burton pull Jane closer as the meaning behind her words sunk in.

"Ah, I see. I will think about what you have said, Miss Bennet. I must be going. My sisters are expecting me to return soon. It was good to see you again. Please give your family my regards. Mr. Burton, a pleasure."

Bingley tipped his hat and turned away. A peculiar sort of feeling settled over him as he walked. He could assume it was regret, knowing he could have seen Miss Bennet long before today had he been informed of her being in town. Would it have made a difference, though?

He looked back and saw the couple walk toward the children. For just a moment, Jane rested her head on Mr. Burton's arm and he looked down at her and smiled. Her smile in return was radiant. He had enjoyed Jane's company immensely and thought she had enjoyed his as well. No matter her level of pleasure at his attentions, she had never given him that smile. It was that which he regretted. He was not a man who inspired devotion. Perhaps it was time to become one.

"Jane Bennet, you purposefully made that man uncomfortable. Should I be worried that you are harboring disappointed hopes for Mr. Bingley?"

She looked at him in surprise.

"I followed the conversation, my dear. You thoroughly chastised him for quitting the neighborhood."

Jane sighed. "You have no need to worry. It is true that he paid me a great deal of attention while he resided at Netherfield. But it has been many months since I felt any disappointment over his departure. However uncharitable it may be, I *did* wish to chastise him. Men do not realize the scrutiny we women are placed under, especially in small communities such as Meryton. When he left, my mother, aunt and every matron we know chastised me for having failed to secure him. I was the object of pity from the entire village. I had to come here to escape it all. Hopefully, in the future Mr. Bingley will be aware of how his attentions could affect others."

"So, you did not love him?"

"Not even a little. I might have thought I did once, but that was before I truly felt love."

He presented a smile of pure adoration. "Jane. Since you all but outright told him of our understanding, can I go to your father?"

"Not yet, please. As soon as my mother hears the news, our engagement will belong to her. I am not yet ready to share. Allow me to be selfish a little longer, at least until Lizzy returns?"

"As you wish, my dear. I will accompany you and your sister back to Hertfordshire and speak to your father then. But Jane, I do insist on a short engagement."

"My darling, you will not hear me object, but in order to get your way in this, you must convince Mama."

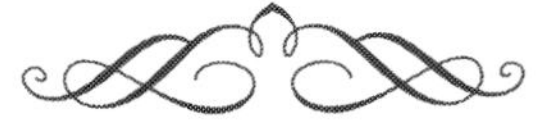

Bingley returned to the townhouse and immediately sought out his sister. He found Caroline in the drawing room, toying with her jewelry in apparent boredom.

"Caroline." His voice had taken on a determined tone, but his sister failed to notice.

"Charles, you are finally here. Are you ready to depart?"

"No, I will not be going with you today."

With this statement, Miss Bingley's attention was finally turned from her bracelets. "Charles, you must. How will you ever get married if you do not call on young ladies?"

"I would like to have called on a particular lady had I known she was in town."

"Who do you mean, Charles?" Her eyes narrowed.

"Miss Jane Bennet. You saw her in January did you not?"

Miss Bingley tilted her head and tapped her fan on her chin. "Oh, yes, I did. I had quite forgotten."

"Why did you not inform me, Caroline?"

"I thought I had. It must have slipped my mind. Why does it matter, Charles? It was months ago."

He could not be very angry with his sister, as he alone was to blame for not returning to Hertfordshire. But she had deliberately deceived him and that wounded him more than he would have thought. "I see. Well, I hope it will not happen again. Enjoy your visits today, Caroline."

He could hear her protests as he walked away, but he paid them no mind. He did not see much of either of his sisters for several days afterward until Miss Bingley entered his rooms with a bill and a questioning glare.

"Charles, there has been some mistake. My dressmaker sent this to me. Will you take care of it, please?"

"No, Caroline, I will not. You are now responsible for paying for your gowns, jewelry, and whatever else you wish to purchase. I will no longer pay your overages. If the interest from your dowry does not cover your expenditures, then you have to do without."

"Charles!" She sputtered a few words of objection that were barely heard. "When exactly did you decide this and why was I not informed?"

"Did I not tell you, Caroline? I thought I had. I suppose it must have just slipped my mind."

Chapter 11

Darcy stood at the edge of the woods waiting for Elizabeth to arrive. He rose early that morning in anticipation of seeing her. The day before had been exhilarating. Not only had he shed propriety and run through the woods with a beautiful woman, but he realized with a stark clarity that he loved her. He had struggled with the feelings for so long that finally admitting them to himself seemed monumental. He was not a patient man by nature and he fought the impulse to propose and carry her away to Pemberley as soon as possible.

Unfortunately, too many steps needed attention before that could happen. He could not propose while residing at Rosings, and he could not yet leave Anne. He felt compelled to stay at least until her birthday to help with the transition. Lady Catherine was sure to cause trouble and he feared Anne was not strong enough to handle her alone. They would likely need Fitzwilliam's military skills to remove her to the dower house, if not an entire army.

In just a moment, those thoughts no longer mattered. Elizabeth appeared on the path walking toward him. The lightness in his chest that was quickly becoming a constant swelled until it washed over him completely, brightening his entire countenance. He walked to meet her, fighting the urge to pull her into his embrace. Instead, he took her hand and brought it to his lips.

"Miss Bennet." He held her hand for a moment as he tried to form a proper sentence. All the words of admiration he wished to speak seemed inadequate, so he simply stated, "Good morning."

"Good morning, Mr. Darcy. I see you have come without your horse today. I did worry after we took this path yesterday that you had forgotten about him. Is the poor creature still tied to the tree, wondering where his master could be?"

Darcy chuckled. "Be assured, Miss Bennet, that he was retrieved and cared for. I rode him this morning and he is currently resting under that same tree. We may go in that direction and see him if you are concerned." He placed her hand on his arm and they began to walk.

"That is not necessary. I have come to realize you take prodigious good care of those around you and assume you hold your horse in the same regard as the rest of us. I should not have worried. I would prefer to walk to the grove. I have a feeling there is much to explore there."

Unconsciously, Darcy pulled her closer. He cherished her liveliness. "Indeed, Miss Bennet. I believe there are enough wonders there to satisfy even your curiosity and zeal. We may even unearth a few worms and toads."

She tipped her head up and smiled so beautifully at him that he was sure he would kiss her if she did not quickly turn away. Sadly, she did just that.

"Oh no. I have not touched a toad since that fateful day Charlotte was so kind to speak of. If you present me with one, I will be forced to act as a proper lady should and swoon from the fright of it."

"I would not dream of it, Miss Bennet. I much prefer the wood nymph I ran with yesterday to a swooning proper lady. Truly, you need only be yourself. I will keep your secrets."

Elizabeth held her breath for a moment. Darcy was teasing, of course. He did not know her secret and she would not tell him, not when it gave her such solace to be near him. She could not stand the thought of his disapprobation.

She was nervous when she woke that morning. At first she thought perhaps Darcy would regret his actions the previous day. She had always known him to be proper and correct in every manner of being. It was entirely possible he would think her a hoyden for dragging him through the woods and revert to his formal behaviors. Then she worried he would not join her at all. *That* thought was especially upsetting. But he was here, and the look on his face told her he regretted nothing and was happy to see her. No, she would not risk that by telling him her secret.

They reached the grove as the sun began to shine through the trees. Elizabeth breathed in the scent of the earth and turned to find Darcy staring at her. She wondered what went through his mind when he was so grave and silent. Whatever it was, it would not do. She would hear him speak.

"I would like to know more about you, Mr. Darcy. Will you oblige me?"

"I will say anything you wish, only you will need to ask. Though offering up pieces of myself does not come easily."

"Very well. Tell me of your sister. Is she as accomplished as Miss Bingley says?"

"No, she is far more accomplished than Miss Bingley is aware. Georgiana is very shy and does not perform for those outside the family often. Miss Bingley may have heard her play once and I am sure it was technically proficient, but nothing to what she displays to a private audience."

His features softened as he spoke and Elizabeth could tell he enjoyed talking about Miss Darcy. "You are very proud of her."

"I am. She is more than ten years my junior and looks to me as much as a father as an elder brother. She does not remember our mother and our father died when she was quite young. She was left to the care of Colonel Fitzwilliam and myself. In spite of that she has grown into a very kind and amiable girl."

"And what will you do, sir, when she marries?"

"Oh, she will not marry."

"Will she not?" He shook his head and Elizabeth laughed. "You will have her tending you in your dotage?"

"Yes." His terse answers usually annoyed her, but now she found herself charmed.

"And how will you keep her from marrying, sir? What happens when she finds some young man irresistible?"

"It is quite simple. When I notice any interest on her part, I will invite the young man to dinner. I will then loan him a book of poetry and encourage him to read to her. As we know, one good sonnet will starve away any fledgling bits of feeling."

Elizabeth looked at him in amusement. This was the second time that he had used words she had spoken at Netherfield against her. Did he forget nothing? The satisfied smile he wore was entirely too delicious.

"It seems you have it all figured out, Mr. Darcy."

The intense stare returned and Elizabeth felt her heart in her throat as it gave way to a full dimpled smile.

"Yes, Miss Bennet, I believe I have."

She tugged on his arm and moved forward a little faster. If she did not keep moving, she would surely swoon, and there was no toad close by to blame.

"What else can I ask? I heard you attended Cambridge. Did you go on a tour?"

"I did though not to the Continent. I spent many months visiting my paternal grandmother's lands of Ireland and Scotland. If not for the unrest abroad, I would have made a more traditional journey as my father did, but

I do not regret it. She was very dear to me and I am glad to have had the opportunity to learn more of her people."

"So, she is no longer with you?"

"No. Georgiana and I are all that is left on my father's side."

The sadness in his voice resonated deep within her. She wanted to embrace him but instead rested her head briefly on his arm in comfort.

"Are you close to your maternal relations, then?"

He was quiet for many moments. Elizabeth turned to him and was preparing to repeat her question when he removed her hand from his arm and walked toward a large elm. For the second time in as many days, she was treated to the sight of him removing his greatcoat. She was intoxicated by the movement and watched as he gracefully pulled the garment from his person and spread it on the ground. She never knew a man could be beautiful, but that was the only way she could describe him. He turned to her and smiled softly as he held out his hand in invitation. She floated to him and placed her hand in his. He helped her settle then sat close enough that she could feel his warmth.

"I am close to my Fitzwilliam cousins. My mother loved her nephews and niece and gathered them at Pemberley as much as possible. It was her wish that we be a part of each other's lives. Fitzwilliam was my closest friend as a child and, along with Bingley, remains so.

"We used to play in that clearing. We had grand plans to build a bridge that ran from this tree to that one across the way. We determined if we were high up our nannies would not be able to reach us and drag us to tea with Lady Catherine. It would also serve as a sort of fortress, where we could launch campaigns against our enemies."

Elizabeth smiled as she pictured the scene in her mind. "What enemies were there for two little boys to fight?"

"Fitzwilliam's elder brother, Freddy. Well, we do not call him Freddy anymore. If we did, we would need more than the acorns we used then as ammunition. He grew into his size far earlier than I and he is four years my senior. Having only sisters, you may not know this, but boys tend to play rough, even those supposedly learning to be gentlemen. Freddy often used his size to his advantage to catch me and pin me down. Richard would always defend me though he never managed to get the best of his brother, either."

Elizabeth felt there was something he was not saying. Something in his countenance, regret possibly, made her think it pained him to speak of his family. She was curious, but she would not push him.

"You have met nearly all of my family. My father has no living relations.

Well, except for Mr. Collins." It was his turn to offer comfort and he gently took her hand in his own.

"It must be heartening to have so many sisters."

"I can honestly say I have never considered that. I have neglected to tend any sort of friendship with my younger sisters. I am most sorry for that now. I can tell you that Lydia's favorite color is pink and she takes a little tea with her cream and sugar, but I was never her confidante before she became ill."

A particular type of sorrow came to Elizabeth's voice whenever she spoke of Lydia. Darcy had heard it several times and could now recognize what it contained—fear combined with guilt. He assumed the same resonated in his speech when he talked of Anne. He placed his hands on her shoulders and turned her so she could see his face.

"She will be well, Elizabeth. She is young and before this illness she was strong, was she not?" Elizabeth nodded and lowered her head. "She will be again. I can arrange for a doctor to see her if you wish."

Elizabeth was touched by his offer. Tears formed behind her closed lids in grief both for Lydia and herself. She was going to lie to him and that felt so very wrong.

"Thank you, Mr. Darcy. My uncle has arranged for her care. She is being tended most diligently, I am told." She could not look at him and she could not say more.

Darcy lightly touched her cheek, wiping away her tears with his fingertips. He traced the line of her jaw to her chin. The tenderness of his touch soothed her. She opened her eyes to find Darcy's mouth dangerously close to hers. Her eyes moved from his perfectly formed lips to his eyes. She had previously noted their brown color, but now they were dark and filled with something Elizabeth did not recognize, but instinctively wanted more of.

His other hand traveled up her arm to rest on her cheek. She leaned into him without removing her eyes from his gaze. Her heart beat wildly in her chest and she could feel her face flush as those beautiful dark orbs moved closer. Finally, she felt his lips on her cheek. They were as soft as his fingertips had been and she sighed in both relief and disappointment. She closed her eyes and allowed herself to enjoy the sensation of his nearness.

"We should go." His husky voice broke through her haze and she nodded. They rose and Darcy shook out his coat before putting it back on. He turned to Elizabeth and grasped her hands.

"You will come to me if you are ever in need of assistance, with your sister or anything else." It was not a request. He needed to know she would turn to him with her troubles. She did not respond instantly and he pulled her closer. "Elizabeth."

"Yes, Mr. Darcy. I promise to come to you if I ever need help."

He nodded and brought her hands to his lips. He walked with her to the edge of the woods and, like their last encounter, he bid her farewell before they came into view of the parsonage.

Elizabeth felt a twinge of sadness at his departure. The day before he truly had been too "unlike himself" to greet Charlotte. He was perfectly presentable now but still left her on the trail before they could be seen. She could only assume he was reluctant to be in company with her cousin. For that, she could not blame him and she resolved to think on it no more. Instead, she would contemplate the great pleasure a set of dark eyes and soft lips could bestow.

Chapter 12

The soap stung Lydia's raw hands as she plunged the gown into the basin of cold water. Her elbows and shoulders ached from the repetitive motion of scrubbing soiled garments up and down the washboard. She longed for a rest but the day was early and she had already fallen behind. Mrs. Baines would not be pleased.

Mr. Gardiner had told Lydia she would have to do small chores, but she was sure he did not mean the type of labor Mrs. Baines had demanded. Nearly as soon as he left, Lydia was told she would have to carry her own weight.

"I am sure you have a full staff of servants to tend your wants at home, Miss Lydia. But if you want to eat here, you'll have to work for it."

Lydia protested, citing her condition but her hostess would not hear it. "You should have thought about the consequences before you opened your legs for that man, now shouldn't you?"

Lydia protested no further. Guilt was a powerful motivator and Lydia worked as much as her body allowed, hoping it would allow for some sort of absolution.

She pulled the gown from the basin and twisted out the excess water. As she walked toward the rope that strung from one end of the room to the other, the heaviness in her stomach shifted and she became dizzy. She quickly found a chair and sat, placing her head in her hands to wait for the spell to pass. After several minutes she felt nearly ready to stand when she heard a loud sigh behind her. She turned to find Mrs. Baines standing on the other side of the table with her hands on her hips, showing a severe look of disapproval.

"Just what are you doing sitting, Miss Lydia? Those clothes will not wash themselves."

Lydia rose and stammered out a reply. "I felt lightheaded and needed to rest for a moment. As you can see," she gestured toward the basin. "I am almost finished."

Mrs. Baines walked to the basin, keeping her eyes on Lydia the entire time. She looked inside the tub then walked toward her.

"This has taken much too long." She shook her head and let out another long sigh. "When you are finished you will walk to the village and purchase some items for me."

Mrs. Baines remained in front of her, standing close enough that Lydia could feel her breath. The deep crevices on her face spoke of age, but given her young child and recent delivery she could not be very old. Perhaps her Aunt Gardiner's age. She had none of the serenity of her aunt, though. She seemed in a perpetual state of exasperation.

"You will take Adam with you. Do not be all day with the laundry." She turned and walked back around the table but stopped before reaching the door. "Mr. Baines will be home for dinner this evening. I would like you to eat in your room from now on when he is here." She looked at Lydia almost accusingly then turned and left.

Lydia let out a breath of relief and returned to her task, moving just a little faster than before. If Mr. Baines was to be home, she was more than happy to remain in her room. The previous times she had been in his company, he had barely spoken, but looked at her in a way that made her very uncomfortable.

When she finished she went to her room to tidy herself for her trip to the village. She was tired and did not feel up to walking that far, but would be grateful to be out of the house for a while. At least then she would not be subjected to Mrs. Baines' harsh looks and demands. She removed her apron and looked in the small hand mirror on her bedside table.

The pale skin on her face was marred with red blotches and the dark circles under her eyes made her look far older than her fifteen years. She had spent so much time wishing she was older and now fifteen felt ancient. She pulled out the drawer in the table and picked up Elizabeth's necklace and the small purse her uncle had given her. She put both in her reticule then left to find Adam and receive further instructions from Mrs. Baines.

The little boy seemed as happy as Lydia for the change of scenery, though she imagined he wandered these paths around his home often. She listened as he chatted away while the setting moved around them. Thankfully, before they reached the main road to the village, a farmer had stopped and offered them a ride in the back of his wagon. Lydia thanked God for the reprieve and begged for another on the return to the cottage. The rocking caused the weight in her stomach to twist, but she doubted she had the strength to walk without taking many rests. Failure to make it back in time for tea would only anger Mrs. Baines.

"There, Liddy, see!" Adam stood in the wagon and pointed to a tall tree standing several yards back from the road. "That's my favorite one. It has that low branch, there, you see. It makes it easier for climbing."

"Yes, Adam, I see. It is a fine tree." She grabbed him by the waist and pulled him back to sitting. "If we have time on the walk back perhaps you can show me how high you can climb."

The smile that formed on his freckled face told her he liked that idea very much. Adam was a sweet boy. He liked to talk to her and often would bring extra bread or cheese to her at night when he noticed she did not eat much at dinner. She reached down and patted his mass of red curls.

"Is there a confectioner in the village? My uncle left me a little money. Perhaps we can have a treat when we are done with the shopping. You have to promise not to tell your mother, though."

Lydia smiled as she watched him silently contemplate the reward of the treat against the risk of keeping a secret. As with most eight-year old boys, the power of the treat won out.

"I promise!"

The village of Lambton reminded Lydia very much of Meryton. So much so that she caught herself wondering if she would see any of her friends in the street. This caused the weight to sink a little and she wondered for the dozenth time if she would ever see any of them again. Elizabeth told her she would come home, but she did not believe truly her father would allow it.

Adam was delighted to see a pair of donkeys tied up beside horses outside one of the shops. While he carried on a conversation with the docile creatures, a voice to her side caught Lydia's attention.

"Mrs. Annesley, let us go in here for a moment. I would like to buy a gift for my brother."

Lydia turned to see a young gentlewoman enter the shop, followed by an older companion. Through the large picture window, she could see them browse the selection of gentlemen's hats on display. The girl looked to be her age with similar features. She was blond with a fully formed, graceful figure. She laughed at something the older woman said and Lydia's heart sank at the sound. The girl, whoever she was, was the perfect picture of innocence.

Lydia wondered about her, where she lived, who was her family. Mostly, she wondered at the seemingly randomness of life. If she were this girl instead of Lydia Bennet, would she be subjected to the ill temper of a supposed care giver? Would she have been so easily seduced? Would she feel so alone? Would a different name or place of birth even matter?

While Lydia pondered all this, the girl had moved closer to the window. She must have noticed Lydia staring at her, because she was now staring back. The two looked at each other for long moments as if trying to place where they had seen each other before. A sudden flicker appeared in the girl's eye and she tilted her head and smiled softly, as if reassuring a friend.

Lydia stepped back, feeling exposed and awkward. She wanted to hide but there was no shelter from the curious gaze of the girl in the window. She finally broke eye contact and turned away. She took Adam's hand and dragged him down the street and away from the soulful eyes of the girl she would never be.

"Fitzwilliam, may I have a word?"

"I would rather not, Darcy. I just spent the last hour in the old lady's company and I am in no mood for your admonishments at this time."

"Did I miss breakfast again?"

"You did and she is very angry. Where have you disappeared to the past two mornings?"

"I was out riding and lost track of the time." That was not entirely untrue. After leaving Elizabeth both days he required a hard ride to cool his ardor before returning to the manor.

"Well I hope you will do better tomorrow or our aunt will be breaking her fast alone. You are not the only one able to 'lose track of the time.' Perhaps I will find my own diversion or just join Anne in her chambers."

"Were you going out just now?"

"Yes."

Darcy waited for a moment but Fitzwilliam offered nothing further. He assumed his cousin was going to the parsonage and he took a moment to calm his jealousy before he spoke.

"Before you go, I would like to apologize for my behavior last week. You are correct. I am not your father and I should not admonish you as if I were."

Fitzwilliam stood silent for a few moments while contemplating the man before him. Reluctantly, it seemed, he finally spoke.

"Think on it no more, Darcy. I believe neither of us have been ourselves this visit. Rosings is not the most joyful place in England. Perhaps there is something in the air that makes us ill at ease." He continued to pull on his gloves and turned away. He suddenly stopped and looked back at his cousin. "What are your plans for the day?"

"Anne has asked me to look at some estate papers. She is preparing for next week."

Fitzwilliam looked around before he moved closer to Darcy. "She really is going to banish the old lady to the dower house?"

"That is her plan. She will need our support. You know Lady Catherine will not go willingly. In the meantime everything must look normal." He sighed. "I will miss no more meals and make every effort to tend to her babblings. It will not be easy but we must remember it is all for Anne."

"Agreed. Well, I am off."

"Fitzwilliam. Are you sure it is only the air making you ill at ease? You were very agitated in London as well."

"I am well, Darcy. If anything, perhaps I am bored. It will not last. It never does." Giving his cousin no time for further questions, he turned and walked away.

Darcy watched him go, but felt dissatisfied with the conversation. Sharing his childhood memories with Elizabeth made him feel sentimental. His mother would be disappointed in the way his friendship with Fitzwilliam had become strained. More than that, he was disappointed. He relied on the presence of few people in his life. In truth there were only a handful he truly loved or could tolerate for any length of time. Fitzwilliam was both and losing him would be a serious blow to Darcy's small circle of confidants.

Until Bingley, Wickham had been his only friend outside of the family. They played together at Pemberley as children and at one time were as close as brothers. The sting from witnessing Wickham's true character emerge remained with him and was one of the primary reasons he did not easily trust. It was also one of the reasons he became so angry with his cousin when they returned from to the parsonage the previous week. Fitzwilliam's actions and words that day reminded him very much of Wickham. He had seen Fitzwilliam misbehave before, but for another man to be anything other than proper and respectful in front of Elizabeth was forbidden.

That was why he had only kissed her cheek that morning. His lips had been so close to hers, but concern overcame desire. As much as he wanted to kiss her and take her into his arms, he would not take advantage of her worry for her sister to do so. In truth, he was only days away from being able to declare himself. He need be patient just a little while longer before he could express his feelings for her.

These morning walks, that he knew would be daily, would no doubt test his resolve. Finally admitting that he loved her did not temper the lust he had always felt for her. In fact, it seemed to fan the flames even more. He was thankful more than ever for his father's admonishments about proper behavior for a Darcy. He would enter their union with no secrets or regrets, only love and hope for the future.

Elizabeth once again sat at the window in her chamber looking down upon the guest about to enter the parsonage. For a second time, Colonel Fitzwilliam had come alone and again Elizabeth felt a subtle sting of disappointment. Coming back to the company of her cousin and his judgements made her long for more time with the man who was in every way his opposite.

She knew she should not be greedy. Darcy was a guest in his aunt's home and he must spend the majority of his time there. But, he provided such comfort that she could not help but crave more. She closed her eyes and rested her head on the window as she remembered the feel of his hand holding hers and his lips on her cheek. Strong but gentle. Her musings were interrupted by a knock on the door. With a sigh and a great deal of petulance, she rose to make her way downstairs.

Colonel Fitzwilliam greeted her with great enthusiasm. She wished she had taken a moment more to calm herself after her musings on Mr. Darcy's attentions that morning. She could still feel the flush on her cheeks. Colonel Fitzwilliam expectantly took her hand and bowed over it, causing her to blush deeper.

"Good morning, Miss Bennet."

"Good morning, Colonel."

Charlotte was the only other occupant in the parlor and as she sat, the other two did as well. They chatted amiably about nothing of importance for some time before Maria entered the room holding a letter and a satisfied smile.

"Charlotte, Eliza, you will never guess what Kitty has written." She stopped when she saw Colonel Fitzwilliam. "Oh, forgive me. I was unaware we had a guest." She gave her sister a stern glare then looked to her shoes.

Fitzwilliam laughed. "Do not mind me, Miss Lucas. I would love to hear the news from Hertfordshire. Unless, of course, it is a private matter."

"Oh, no, it is not private. I would image all of Meryton is talking about it."

Elizabeth laughed. "Then do share, Maria. Since my sister has not sent a single letter to me, you must tell all on her behalf."

Maria giggled then sat next to her sister. "You remember I told you that Mr. Wickham had been paying much attention to Mary King? Well, her uncle has taken her away and insisted on them breaking any sort of understanding between them. So you see, Mr. Wickham is safe!"

The smile disappeared from Elizabeth's face and her back stiffened. "I would sooner say Mary King is safe."

"Oh, Eliza, do not pretend to be indifferent. Mr. Wickham is a friend of yours is he not?"

"He is not, Maria. He is a man who has resided in our neighborhood for only a short time. We should not judge him to be good based merely on his own words. I beg you to be discerning when it comes to gentlemen."

"Is this George Wickham?" Colonel Fitzwilliam leaned forward in his chair and spoke to Charlotte.

"Yes, he is a member of the militia that is now quartered at Meryton. He has mentioned an acquaintance with your cousin, Mr. Darcy."

"They are acquainted, yes." He turned to Maria. "Miss Lucas, I would listen to Miss Bennet. A man is far more than his words. You must judge by his actions and if you have not known him long, you must be wary."

The ladies looked at his serious expression then to each other. Charlotte spoke for all of them.

"Thank you, Colonel Fitzwilliam. We will be sure not to put our trust in ones with whom we are not well acquainted."

"Please do. Now that I have certainly brought a dark cloud over your happy morning, I will leave you." They all rose and Fitzwilliam turned to Elizabeth and bowed. "I hope I will be welcome again tomorrow?"

Elizabeth tilted her head in confusion then turned to Charlotte, who answered his petition.

"You are always welcome, Colonel."

He bowed again then retreated from the room. As the ladies returned to their seats, Charlotte teased Elizabeth.

"You have certainly changed your opinion of Mr. Wickham. Has being in more varied company influenced you, Eliza?"

"Not at all, I assure you. Before we left Meryton my estimation of Mr. Wickham had gone through quite material a change. Perhaps, I should say that I decided to be more careful about taking the word of a man about whom we truly know nothing. There is no risk in caution."

The mention of Wickham always unsettled her and though she believed she kept her reaction well hidden, Elizabeth thought it best to change the subject. Thankfully, Maria had other gossip to share and they soon forgot about Wickham altogether.

Time passed each day in a similar fashion for the inhabitants of Hunsford and Rosings. Darcy and Elizabeth met early each morning at the edge of the woods and spent hours in discovery. They would reluctantly part for breakfast with their respective relations, each feeling strengthened by their time together.

Colonel Fitzwilliam continued to call at the parsonage and Elizabeth began to genuinely enjoy his company. Darcy told her more stories from his childhood that almost always involved his older cousins, which caused her to feel a familiarity with the colonel. She studied Fitzwilliam closely during his visits. She told herself she was looking for signs of the mischievous little boy that always protected his younger cousin. In truth, she looked for a resemblance between the two, but no matter how closely she observed, she found none.

Darcy filled his time distracting Lady Catherine from and helping Anne prepare for the coming change. It amazed him that his aunt continued in every effort to convince him to marry her daughter. Anne's weakness was obvious to everyone and Darcy wondered if Lady Catherine did not notice or did not care. While touring the land he saw that much of the estate had been neglected. Thankfully, the steward was not loyal to the current mistress. For many years he witnessed the decline of the grand estate as Lady Catherine continued to spend unwisely and pontificate from her throne. He was willing to keep their secret and help dispose the Lady to the dower house when the time came.

The two lovers each spent their nights in restless dreams. Darcy's were filled with images of his beautiful Elizabeth in their grove, in his chambers at Pemberley, at his house in London, in the wilds of Ireland. Every place he had ever been, she was there, too. The dreams began innocently enough, with her sweet voice teasing him as she danced in the sun. Inevitably, his visions would become more sensual and he would wake with an overwhelming desire to feel her skin against his. His need for her grew in time with his affection and he longed for her with his entire being.

Elizabeth's dreams were not so pleasant. Her nightmare about Lydia fading away recurred nightly but with a slight alteration. She still watched Lydia laugh happily as she danced before being taken away by the red clad arms. Now when she held Lydia she looked up to see Darcy standing over them. He was not the man from the grove, but the austere figure she met in Hertfordshire. He looked down to Lydia and back to Elizabeth. She tried to speak but no words came and eventually he turned away. When she looked back to Lydia she was gone, too, leaving Elizabeth alone and searching.

Mornings were their refuge from yearning and fear. They never spoke of their worries, but being in company together settled their rampant emotions and allowed their mutual fondness to grow into something more. Soft touches and glances were exchanged that soothed and stirred, leaving each with a sense of completeness that was felt more than recognized.

They would leave their paradise reluctantly to rejoin the world that expected their full participation in spite of their distraction. It was their attention to each other and all the feelings their closeness generated as he leaned in to kiss her cheek that caused them to miss the figure in the corner of the woods—and the shocked expression who turned away quickly in quiet fury.

Chapter 13

Elizabeth tipped her head toward the sun as a cool breeze danced across her face. Her eyes were closed and she was lost in the feeling of solidarity with the woods surrounding her. She was seated, leaning back with her arms supporting her as she enjoyed the feel of the sun's gentle morning rays warming what the wind had just left cool. She smiled brightly when a shadow suddenly interfered with her basking. She opened her eyes to see Darcy's fixed on her. The sun cast a glow around his strong frame and she wondered if Apollo himself would cut such an appealing figure if he descended to Earth. One man should not be so handsome.

"Would you be offended, Mr. Darcy, if I removed my bonnet? I would like to fully enjoy what the sky offers us this morning. That is, of course, if you would be so kind as to remove yourself from between me and my object of adulation."

Darcy chuckled and kneeled in front of her. They had met in their usual place and walked to the grove. After laying out his coat and seeing her settled in the sun, he had left her briefly and now returned with a handful of different green stems and one pink sweetbriar. She smiled, knowing that particular bloom was not easy to obtain and that he had picked it for her.

"I can hardly object to you removing your bonnet, Miss Bennet, when I have dropped my own hat there next to you." As he spoke he untied the ribbons, lifted the straw billed garment and placed it beside his own.

"It is fitting they should be placed side by side in their impropriety." Her teasing eyes softened when she saw his smile brighten his features. She loved seeing him like this, with no coat or hat and his hair tousled from the wind. He looked as natural there as she felt, so much more so than in any drawing room or assembly. She sat up and reached to smooth the wild curls but they would not be tamed.

He caught her hand and gave it a gentle kiss before releasing it and picking up the flower. He leaned forward and tucked it into one of the pins holding up her hair.

"I believe this is a much more fitting adornment for my wild rose." His voice was light and teasing and his hands were warm as they held her face. The touches they shared were much like the hats that sat beside each other on Darcy's coat: against the rules of propriety but perfectly right in their grove.

Darcy kissed her forehead then sat next to her but turned slightly away. It was not uncommon for them to enjoy a companionable silence, but after a few moments Elizabeth became restless and wanted his attention.

"What do you do there in secret, sir?"

Darcy smiled but did not look up. He kept to his task. "It is no secret." His smile grew as he saw her raised eyebrows from the corner of his eye.

"Yet you will not tell me what you are doing? Teasing man, I will think on you no longer."

Darcy laughed as she stood and walked away in a feigned huff.

"I have had the pleasure of your acquaintance long enough to know you sometimes say things you do not mean. I believe this is one of those times."

"You may believe whatever you like, Mr. Darcy, as you tend your secrets so diligently. I have no time for your musings, though you did just imply I am a liar. I am far too occupied in observing the lone bloom near the top of that tree there. It seems an odd occurrence and I should like to investigate. It may be that one of your aunt's majestic beauties is being taken over by a weed."

"Shall I retrieve it for you, my lady, so that you may determine its origins?"

Elizabeth turned to find Darcy had followed her and was now standing mere inches away.

"No, Mr. Darcy. I am not quite ready to end my speculations. The journey toward knowledge is often more enjoyable than learning the truth. Too often I am disappointed with the conclusion."

"Nothing could be disappointing here in our woods, Elizabeth. Even the weeds are made beautiful in your presence."

She never knew how to respond when he spoke such sweet words. She would like to have returned the sentiment but embarrassment swept across her in the form of a deep blush. She believed he must think her silly or unfeeling when no words came. She need not have worried. He was charmed.

He then presented her with his secret—a beautifully woven emblem made of stands of the tall grass he had picked earlier. It was fastened to several more blades tied together to form a necklace. She fingered it gently then looked at him in wonder.

"My grandmother taught me how to tie these knots when I was a child. She said keeping my hands busy would keep the devil away. Every design she showed me came with its own legend."

"It is lovely."

"Then it matches its owner perfectly."

He took it from her and slowly placed it over her head while his eyes bore into hers. He traced the blades that fell around her neck then brought his hands to cup her cheeks.

The tenderness he displayed filled Elizabeth's heart with such longing she felt she would burst. She loved him, she could not deny it, nor did she want to. The delicious pain of affection mixed with the fear that she would lose him once the truth about her sister was known.

"Will you tell me the legend of this one, Mr. Darcy?"

Darcy nodded as his thumbs caressed her cheeks. "There is so much I want to tell you, Elizabeth. I feel utterly incapable of speech when I am this close to you and you look at me with such care in your eyes."

"Then do not speak."

"Elizabeth."

There was no hesitation as they came together. His lips pressed tenderly against hers as he continued to stroke her face. After a moment he pulled back. Her eyes fluttered open and the dazed look there sent him in for more. He feathered light kisses along her cheek and up to her temple. His nose trailed down hers as his hands moved down the column of her neck. She again opened her eyes and looked into his with undisguised love and desire.

"So beautiful, Elizabeth."

Her hands had been resting on his chest but now moved to his neck and the tangle of curls that rested on his collar. Feeling completely out of control, she stepped forward and pressed her entire body against him.

"My darling Fitzwilliam." She was sure she meant to say more, but all thought left her as he bent to once again claim her mouth with his.

The force of instinct bound them together as passion took control. As their lips learned to move together, their hands explored every edge and contour they could reach. The contrast of their bodies, his hard and hers soft, added to their fervor as they anxiously explored new territory.

Underneath the burning hunger was a sweetness they both recognized. It was the ache to belong, to give over every good part of themselves to the other. It was a perfect surrender.

"Elizabeth," Darcy breathed as he pulled away. "My dearest, loveliest Elizabeth." Once again words failed him as the soft skin of her neck tempted his mouth to be of better use. As he made his way back to her lips, the words he needed to say seemed to form on their own.

"You must allow me to tell you, how ardently—"

Darcy's deep voice was suddenly interrupted by the sound of another coming through the trees. Elizabeth remained in Darcy's arms as they looked at each other in confusion. Hearing the voice again, the light of recognition dawned on Darcy's face and he released Elizabeth abruptly. He looked grimly toward the path then stooped to collect Elizabeth's bonnet. He placed it on her head then gently grabbed her shoulders and hurriedly spoke.

"Tomorrow?"

She nodded and he released her to gather his own hat and coat. By the time the intruders made themselves known, Darcy and Elizabeth were outwardly composed. Elizabeth looked to the trail to see Colonel Fitzwilliam emerge from the trees. She turned back to Darcy, whose face was set in anger. He reached for her but then stopped suddenly as his visage changed from anger to surprise. Her eyes followed his and she saw another figure had appeared.

"Anne?" The concern in Darcy's voice as he walked away tore at Elizabeth's heart. She attempted to dismiss the emotion, as it was clear Miss de Bourgh was fatigued. She should be proud that he showed such concern for his cousin, but it was hard to be rational when the man who held her close just a few moments earlier now had another woman on his arm. She was so occupied with the sight that she did not notice the colonel's approach.

"Good morning, Miss Bennet."

"Good morning, Colonel Fitzwilliam." She curtsied and tried to smile but her eyes could not leave Darcy as he spoke to Miss de Bourgh.

Colonel Fitzwilliam laughed softly. "Darcy is rather overprotective is he not? One would think Anne had never been out of doors before. He dotes too much, but he is devoted to her."

Elizabeth continued to watch the cousins exchange whispers as Colonel Fitzwilliam's words broke through any vestiges of reason that remain in her mind.

"Excuse me, Colonel Fitzwilliam, but I must get back to the parsonage. Charlotte expects me for breakfast."

"Shall I escort you, Miss Bennet?"

"No, I do not wish to disturb your morning. Good day."

"Good day, Miss Bennet."

Fitzwilliam watched her walk away with a smile then turned to make a tour of the grove before he returned to his cousins.

"Anne, what are you doing here? Did you walk from Rosings?"

"No, Darcy, not all the way. Fitzwilliam drove the phaeton to the edge of the woods. He suggested the walk and it was too tempting to resist."

"You should not have come. You tire easily."

She sighed. "I am tired. I had hoped to go further. I am indoors too much these days."

"I will retrieve my horse and take you back to the phaeton. Fitzwilliam should know better." Darcy turned to look at his cousin and saw Elizabeth had left. He could not hide his disappointment.

"Forgive me, Darcy. We interrupted something between you and Miss Bennet." She gasped as she realized what must have happened. "Darcy! Did you propose?"

He shook his head. "I had begun when I heard Fitzwilliam coming through the woods."

Anne placed her fingertips to her mouth. "Oh no! Oh, Darcy, I am so sorry. Go after her."

"No. She is likely back at the parsonage now. Mr. Collins would go straight to your mother if I called on her there."

"Has fear of my mother kept you from securing your Miss Bennet?"

"Not for myself. Lady Catherine still holds power over the parsonage and as long as Elizabeth is a guest there she is vulnerable."

Anne folded her hands in front of her and set her mouth in a thin line. "Then we shall take away her power. We are only a few days from my birthday. I believe we can contain her until then."

"What will you do, lock her in her room and post armed guards outside her door?"

"Yes. That is what we expected we would have to do on my birthday; we will just do it a little early. I will not have control legally, but I am rather sure none of the staff will mind. We can send word to Mr. Collins that she is not accepting visitors so he will not come around. Yes, we will do this today."

"Anne, you are already tired. Are you sure you have the strength to face your mother?"

"I am determined, Darcy. Your visit will end soon and I should like to get to know Miss Bennet before she returns home. My first dinner as mistress will be a celebration of your betrothal."

Anne's smile was so bright that Darcy could not help but return it. "Alright Anne, but we still have much to plan. We must find men suitable for containing your mother."

Anne laughed. "A difficult task indeed. Go fetch your horse. Here comes Fitzwilliam. He will make sure I am not carried off by any wild beast."

Darcy would like to have had words with his elder cousin about his stupidity in bringing Anne into the woods but he did not want to dampen her spirits. She had been plagued by negativity far too much so he merely nodded to Fitzwilliam as he walked past.

As he walked, Darcy replayed the events of the morning. He had not planned to ask for her hand until Lady Catherine had been dealt with, but he had been completely overcome by the sight of her basking in the sun. She was so natural and perfect in her surroundings, just like the sweetbriar he found for her.

He was glad she never shied away from his touch and allowed the chaste kisses on her hands and face. As grateful as he was, he wanted more. The sight of her leaning back, her breasts arched and lips slightly parted was nearly enough to erase every good intention from his mind. Had she not begun to tease him, then, he would have fallen to his knees, begged her to be his and taken her there under the protection of the trees.

Darcy reached his horse and mounted him, quickly prodding him into a gallop. He was anxious for the evening to come and go. He would help secure Anne's position at Rosings that night and the next day secure Elizabeth's place beside him. One more day, and his world would be right.

Elizabeth sat in the parlor with Charlotte, barely attending the conversation or the sewing in her hands. Her mind whirled in confusion while her heart rested heavily in her stomach. She had kissed Mr. Darcy. For weeks she had longed to know the sensation of being in his arms and the feeling his lips against hers. It was wonderful. It was better than anything she could have imagined.

She had given no thought to accepting his attentions. In truth, she had encouraged them. She had been selfish in her need to feel protected and willingly gave up all sense of propriety. Yet, being with him in such a way had never felt wrong. The intimacy between them was true, as if it had always been. But when they were intruded upon, it suddenly became wrong—a secret that had to be quickly hidden.

Elizabeth's mind fluttered between the memory of his hands caressing her face and the image of his hands on *her*. Darcy had left so abruptly to tend his cousin. The protection Elizabeth had come to cherish was given to another, leaving her alone, feeling confused and dejected.

"What is the matter, Eliza?"

Elizabeth lifted her head to see Charlotte looking at her with concern.

"Nothing is the matter, Charlotte. I suppose I am just a little restless this afternoon. Forgive me for not being more attentive."

"Are you upset that Colonel Fitzwilliam did not call this morning? I should not think on it too much, Eliza. He is too smitten to stay away for long."

Elizabeth lifted her chin and narrowed her eyes in confusion. "What?"

Charlotte laughed. "Do not play coy with me. You must see how much he admires you."

"Who?"

"Colonel Fitzwilliam! This will be a very good match for you."

Elizabeth placed her sewing on the table and turned to better see her friend's expression. "You believe I will be matched with Colonel Fitzwilliam?"

Charlotte concentrated on Elizabeth for a moment. "You are not joking? Do you truly not realize he has been courting you?"

Elizabeth shook her head.

"Oh Eliza! You are so willfully blind to these things. Of course he has been courting you. He comes here every day, sits among your relations, tolerates my husband and flirts shamelessly with you. You seem to enjoy his attention."

Elizabeth nodded. "Colonel Fitzwilliam is a very amiable man."

"I just knew you would leave Kent engaged. I admit that I first believed Mr. Darcy would be the one, seeing as he could not keep his eyes off you when you were in company together. But, we have not seen him since we dined at Rosings and whenever we inquire about him, Colonel Fitzwilliam says he is with Miss de Bourgh."

The mention of that name was too much. Elizabeth's confusion over Charlotte's statement about Colonel Fitzwilliam gave way to irritation. She could stand no more. "Charlotte, please!"

"Eliza!"

"Forgive me. I am not well. Please excuse me."

Elizabeth left the room hastily and ran up the stairs to her chamber. She locked the door and sat on her bed, folding her arms over her stomach. The tears she fought since she left the grove stung her eyes as she struggled against the fear that threatened to overtake her.

She wanted go back to the morning, to the woods where she felt safe, where she was sure that Darcy loved her. She did not want to think about Colonel Fitzwilliam or Anne de Bourgh. She wanted the time back before they were interrupted, when he was speaking. What was he speaking? *You must allow me to tell you…*

She straightened and took a long, calming breath. Tell her what? He loved her? He wanted to marry her? Her heart answered yes to those questions. She could not have been wrong again. She wanted to trust that what they shared was as good and natural as she believed it to be, but their paradise had been penetrated, allowing doubt and fear inside, and she was no longer sure.

She rose and walked to the table where she had laid his gifts from that morning. She brought the sweetbriar to her nose and breathed in the scent. The tenderness in his eyes when he placed the flower in her hair was genuine, as was the nervousness when he presented her with the woven emblem. She picked up the necklace and traced the pattern. She had not noticed that he wove the blades into an intricate arrangement of hearts. She smiled.

She would not think him bad, not yet. But, she would have to use more caution until she knew his intentions. She also had to know her own. She had not thought about a life for her and Darcy beyond the woods. If he loved her and wanted her, she would have to tell him the truth. Lying to a beloved sister is hard enough. She knew she would not be able to deceive her husband.

With much apprehension mixed with her determination, Elizabeth decided her path. Her heart was his and she would give it to him completely. First, though, she must ask him about Anne de Bourgh, and then she would have to tell him the truth about Lydia.

Chapter 14

"You are quiet this evening, Fitzwilliam. Has my brandy left you dumb?"

"No, Aunt, I am perfectly capable of speech. What would you have me say?"

"You do not need me to put words in your mouth, Nephew. If you cannot not contribute to the conversation, perhaps you should retire."

"Was there conversation? I have heard none since we sat down. I could be mistaken, but I am reasonably sure your brandy has not affected my hearing."

The faces around the table all looked at him in disbelief. Fitzwilliam was often informal with his aunt, but he was never outright rude. Eyes moved from his casual demeanor to her ladyship, who never tolerated unveiled disrespect.

"You look very much like my brother when you hold your goblet that way. Mother never could break him of his tendency to act as if he belonged in the bowels of a ship. I see your mother had similar failings."

Fitzwilliam pushed his chair back just enough to free his legs. He did not stand but propped his boots on the table, just missing the elegant china.

"Shall we speak of failings, my lady? I believe that, *once again*, you have failed in your plans to tie my cousin to Pemberley. How many years has it been now? You have been pushing this alliance since Anne was old enough to say her vows before a blacksmith. Yet, she remains. I believe that is a much weightier fault than how I hold my glass."

"Fitzwilliam."

Darcy's warning tone was ignored as aunt and nephew stared each other down, each willing the other to concede. Finally, Lady Catherine shifted in her seat and turned her attention to Darcy.

"Your cousin, though seemingly out of his senses this evening, is correct. Too many years have passed in this fashion. I will tolerate your insolence no longer, Darcy. My solicitor can arrange for the license and we can dispense with the banns. You will marry Anne before the end of your visit. Mrs. Jenkinson can oversee the arrangements for Anne's removal to Pemberley. You need not be bothered with any detail."

Darcy looked to Anne, who was seated on his right, and she nodded. "I will tell you what I told your brother when he attempted to arrange my life to his liking: I will marry when and whom I choose. I do agree that this has gone on for too many years. So, understand me, Lady Catherine, that I bother with every detail of my life and after this visit, no aspect of my life will involve you."

His aunt gawked at him for a moment before she found her voice. "Darcy! You dare speak to me in such a fashion? Where is your honor? Your respect for the family? Do not forget that it was your mother's dearest wish that you marry Anne. You dishonor her memory with your refusal."

"I do not doubt that my mother entertained the idea of Anne and me marrying. It is probable she was more concerned with getting Anne away from you than of forming an alliance between the estates."

Lady Catherine placed her hands on the arms of her chair and leaned forward slightly. "You are upsetting Anne with this talk, Darcy. She has waited for you all these years and now you will break her heart? Speak Anne! Tell him how you feel."

"Darcy knows my feelings perfectly well, Mother. There is no need to speak of them now."

"Anne, tell Darcy how you wish for this union to take place. Now."

Anne sighed. "Very well. Darcy, you are truly the last man in the world I would ever wish to marry. Doing so would please my mother entirely too much."

"Anne! You obstinate, ungrateful girl. I should have you thrown from this house for your impudence."

Fitzwilliam no longer found the scene comical as Lady Catherine's menacing tone now matched her countenance. She had risen while voicing her threat and looked upon her daughter with an unnatural hatred.

Anne remained seated; Darcy and Fitzwilliam both stood to face their aunt. Fitzwilliam walked around the table to stand next to Anne and together, he and Darcy guarded her as she made a claim to her home.

"You may do whatever you chose tonight, Mother. I will leave if you wish, but it seems of little importance considering I will return in just a few days as mistress."

Lady Catherine paled as she stared at her daughter in disbelief.

"Did you think I knew nothing of my father's will? He told my uncle Darcy every detail of the plans he laid out for me. You are very fortunate he did not arrange for the estate to be sold and have you thrown into the hedgerows. Your place in this house will no longer exist in just a few days. You will be mistress of only yourself and what servants I allow you in the dower house."

Lady Catherine's lips curled into a snarl and her voice lowered. "You are too weak to be mistress of my home. You will ruin everything."

"I am weak, I will not deny it. I am aware my time as head of the household will be short. I have no doubt, however, that the woman Darcy brings home will care for the estate as I could not and they will rid Rosings of your influence and make this the home my father wanted."

"What do you mean the woman Darcy brings home?"

"Upon my death, Darcy will inherit Rosings and, as he said, you will not be part of his life. There is no hope for you to remain here. You may accept your fate graciously, or you will be dragged from your throne and placed under guard in the dower house."

"No other woman will be mistress of this house while I yet breathe."

"Do not tempt me, Mother. You will spend the next few days in your chambers while your new accommodations are being prepared."

Darcy turned to the footmen in the back of the room and nodded. They came forward and stood next to Lady Catherine.

"Please escort Lady Catherine to her chambers. She is not to leave for any reason."

"You have no right to order my staff around, Darcy." She turned to the footmen. "Return to your positions at once."

They did not move. Lady Catherine looked at them, finally noticing they were not the men who usually served during dinner. They were much broader.

"I am most seriously displeased with your treachery, Anne. My own daughter turns me out as if I were a common beggar? I am ashamed of you." She said no more, but turned and walked toward the door with the footmen trailing close behind. She turned to give one last menacing look, but the party in the dining room had ceased to pay her attention.

She watched as another servant removed her place setting from the head of the table. Darcy turned to Anne and bowed low then offered her his hand. He led her to the mistress's seat and she was nearly swallowed by the size of it. Lady Catherine smiled in satisfaction that she could at least see that her daughter could not fill her place. What she failed to notice was that Anne's eyes were filled with pride and excitement.

She could finally control her own life, and only death would take that from her now.

Elizabeth's feet felt as if they were weighed down by bricks as she moved slowly up the path into the woods. She had slept little the night before and when she did dreams of Lydia plagued her mind. She felt a particular longing for her sisters that morning. The comfort of their bond, even in times of struggle, was her only real constant. They were far away, however, and she would soon break her promise to one of them.

She stopped walking and closed her eyes as Lydia's pale, tear-stained face appeared in her mind. The first time she had told Lydia's secret, she learned her father's real character. She feared the same would happen with Darcy. She also feared his answer when she asked him about his relationship with Anne de Bourgh.

Before she started walking again, she heard a crunch on the trail behind her. Her chest filled with excitement, dread, and when she turned, disappointment.

"Colonel Fitzwilliam."

"Good morning, Miss Bennet. It seems we are of like minds this morning. I do love to explore the wilds of Rosings at least once a year. Shall we walk together?"

"I would not wish to intrude on your privacy, sir."

"Nonsense. I always enjoy your company, and there is something I wish to discuss with you."

"Oh?"

He gestured to the trail and they began walking. "Yes. I have been concerned with something for several days now but have not had the opportunity to speak with you privately. Miss Lucas mentioned Mr. Wickham is residing in the village near your father's estate. I am glad you have not fallen for his charms as so many young women have, but I feel I should give you a firmer warning. May I speak freely?"

"Of course."

"Thank you, and I do apologize if anything I say offends you. I believe the only way ladies can protect themselves from liars and rakes is if they know the full truth. Please stop me if I repeat anything Darcy may have already told you. I assume he issued some sort of warning to the fathers of Meryton?"

Elizabeth's throat was dry and she could barely form her words. She swallowed and tried to keep her voice even. "No, I do not believe he did. Not to my father, at least."

"Hmm. I should not find that surprising. Darcy does not like to air his private affairs, especially if they could ever paint him or his family in a negative light. You know they grew up together at Pemberley?"

Elizabeth nodded. "Mr. Wickham said he and Mr. Darcy were very close as children."

"That is true. I sometimes found myself jealous on my visits there to see my cousin with his favorite playmate. However, Wickham was wild and often got Darcy in trouble. Still, they remained friends until just last summer."

"Oh? I got the impression from Mr. Wickham that their grudge was of some standing."

"After my uncle died, Wickham ceased all pretense at being a gentleman and gave in to his true nature. He ran up debts in both Derbyshire and London and more than one poor girl had to be sent away. Darcy was always quick to settle the bills or any other disturbance Wickham might have caused. My cousin is very loyal and he did not stop caring for his friend even though his actions were becoming more dissolute."

He paused for a moment and looked at Elizabeth apologetically before he continued.

"Last summer, however, a permanent rift occurred. Wickham had become very friendly with a lady who was," He looked away then back to her. "Under Darcy's protection."

He paused again to give Elizabeth a moment to think about what he had just said. When understanding washed over her features, he continued.

"My cousin has many good qualities, but he is very territorial. Wickham trying to take this lady from him was unforgivable. I will not go into detail, but Darcy made his opinion on the matter quite clear. Wickham will no longer receive any kind of support from Pemberley."

Elizabeth stopped walking. Again she steadied her voice, but her tone displayed her anger. "Except for silence. Not exposing the man's true character allows him to continue in his degenerate ways."

"Yes, but you must understand that Darcy has his own interests to protect. He is very careful with the Darcy name. Pemberley is one of the largest estates in the country and Rosings will be his soon enough. He will not allow his legacy to be tainted by association with a scoundrel."

"And the rest of the world is of no matter?"

Colonel Fitzwilliam shook his head and sighed. "I have given you an unfavorable impression of my cousin. No, he is not so bad. He is proud, no doubt, and displays behaviors quite typical of his class. But, as I said, he is very loyal, perhaps to a fault and takes great care of his friends. In fact, he recently relayed to me how he saved Bingley from an unfavorable match."

"Indeed? I suppose the lady in question was not good enough for his friend?"

"I do not believe Darcy objected to the woman, but to her family. Apparently they were crude, unconnected and barely fit in the realm of gentility. Knowing a bride comes with her relations, Darcy advised Bingley to seek love elsewhere. Wealth and status will hide a multitude of sins, but this family has neither. They are certainly not the type that could be invited to Pemberley."

Elizabeth could no longer stand the sound of his voice. The previous afternoon she considered Colonel Fitzwilliam an amiable gentleman and perhaps even a friend. Now she despised him. She hated him because he spoke words she did not want to hear. Her stomach churned as the weight of those words settled upon her.

"Miss Bennet, are you well?"

"I am not, Colonel Fitzwilliam. I believe I am not suitable company at present. I will let you continue your walk, sir."

"No, Miss Bennet, I will not leave you in such a state."

"You will," She spoke with more emotion than politeness. "Please forgive my rudeness, but I only need air and quiet."

"Very well, but I will call at the parsonage later to see if you are well."

"Thank you."

Elizabeth watched him walk away and when she was sure he could not see her, she darted into the woods, desperately seeking the cover of the trees. She knew not in which direction she was heading and when she broke free of the woods she stopped. Her feet had brought her to the grove and her heart broke further at the sight of it.

Darcy rode his horse fast down the lane. He had been delayed by estate business and hoped Elizabeth had not been waiting long. Sleep had not come easy the previous evening though he went to bed exhausted from the events of the day. He was too anxious for the morning when he could claim Elizabeth as his own. They could finally leave the woods together though they would always hold a special appeal. He would walk with her to the parsonage and proudly state to Collins that he could have Longbourn, for Elizabeth would have Pemberley.

He led the horse to his usual spot and dismounted. He quickly secured the animal then set off in search of Elizabeth. He ran as fast as the terrain would allow and arrived at the edge of the grove out of breath. The sight of her waiting for him only exacerbated that condition. He took a moment to watch her as she stood beneath the great elm. She faced away from him, and he studied the line of her back as it gracefully dipped into the roundness of her posterior. She had such a beautifully enticing form that could only be challenged by the beauty of her spirit. He felt himself the most fortunate man in England to know her, to love her and, unless he was quite mistaken, to have her love in return.

He could wait no longer and as quietly as he could, he approached her. Mere words seemed an insufficient greeting, so he removed his hat, stood behind her and wrapped his arms around her waist. He felt her stiffen, then relax against him after a moment.

"Good morning, my dearest Elizabeth." He placed a kiss on the column of her neck. "I am pleased to see you have not left. Please forgive my tardiness."

Seemingly on their own, his hands traveled up and down her tiny waist, adoring the soft feminine curves and valleys. He reached to untie the ribbons of her bonnet then tossed it aside. When she turned around, her face was already tipped in anticipation.

Darcy smiled then bent down and placed a soft kiss on her full lips. He lingered there, enjoying the tastes and sensations as he tugged at her bottom lip, then the top. He then covered her whole mouth with his, gently opening her to his explorations. This was not the frenzied kiss from yesterday, but the slow and deep caress of a man who had an eternity to discover the treasures of the woman he loved.

The intoxicating feel of her small hands roaming his chest drove him on and he ran his palms over her back and shoulders. He was lost to her and the responsiveness of her body to his. He would have remained in this blissful capitulation but for the feel of her tears under his fingertips as his hands moved to stroke her face.

He pulled back in alarm, worried he had hurt or overwhelmed her with his attentions. His heart sank at the thought. Words of apology formed on his tongue but before they could be spoken, he felt a resounding slap across his cheek.

Chapter 15

Elizabeth was furious. When she arrived at the grove, she truly felt broken. In a short time, she had come to depend on Darcy for nearly every good feeling she experienced. His warmth and strength and gentleness had been her solace from the turmoil she felt over Lydia. She had fallen in love, but it had all been a fantasy. This pain was greater than any she had known; yet as she stood there mourning what never had been real, it was his arms that she craved. When she felt him suddenly surrounding her, she could not stop herself from giving in to his comfort and offering herself up to his ministrations.

But the strength of their ardor could not keep the unwanted images from her mind. The feel of his kisses was shadowed by the picture of him sitting astride his horse in Meryton, cantering away while Wickham stalked her sister. She grasped his lapels as the pain in her chest deepened. When her mind flashed to Lydia weeping in the orchard, she could no longer hold back her tears or her indignation and she struck him with all the fury she felt at that moment.

"Elizabeth. Forgive me, I did not mean to frighten you."

"What did you mean to do to me, Mr. Darcy?"

"What?"

"I am a woman without wealth or connections, certainly not suitable for a man of your social standing. At least not as a wife."

He stepped forward and reached for her but she moved away quickly.

"Elizabeth! Surely you do not question my feelings for you."

"Your feelings! No, sir, I do not doubt your feelings."

"I admit that words fail me at times, but surely my actions have spoken for me."

"Indeed they have, Mr. Darcy," She choked down a sob then gestured to the trees. "You pursue me in the shadows! You leave me before you can be seen by my relations. When we are in company with yours, you hardly acknowledge me. You ignore me while you hold the hand of the woman you are supposed to marry! Yes, your actions have told me everything I need to know about your *feelings*."

"You do not understand how I must behave with my family. They—"

"And what of your behavior with *my* family? Are they truly so low in your eyes that you care nothing for their well-being? Tell me, Mr. Darcy, did your friend love my sister?"

Darcy straightened his back and cooled his features in preparation for defending himself. "He believed he did."

Elizabeth let out a short breath. "And you corrected him? Did you consider Jane's feelings at all? He gave her all his attentions in Hertfordshire, set her apart from every other young lady in the neighborhood. He gave her every reason to believe he cared for her, yet he left at your bidding. You thought nothing at all of what was left for her when he departed. She was met with gossip and censure from nearly the entire village. But that is of no matter to you since my family is too far beneath you."

"I did what was best for my friend. I watched your sister with Bingley and saw no signs of a serious attachment on her part. I would not allow Bingley to be hurt by making an inferior match when the affection of one of the parties involved was inadequate."

"You made that judgment based on how many conversations with my sister? You did not know Jane well enough to come to such a conclusion."

She held her wrist as the pain of striking him began to pulse. She tried to concentrate on that feeling instead of the wounded expression he now wore. She faltered only a moment at his unguarded distress, but it was not enough to cloud her resentment over the treatment of her other sister.

"There was someone in Hertfordshire that you knew quite well, however. *Mr. Wickham.* In yet another show of arrogant disdain for the safety and welfare of those you deem unworthy, you said nothing of his character to any of the men in the neighborhood. He has caused much grief among those of my acquaintance."

Tears now flowed freely and her voice resonated every nuance of her heartache.

"You knew what he was. How could you not? You were raised together. Was Miss Bingley warned to stay away from him? Would you allow your cousin, Miss de Bourgh, to attend parties with him? You need not speak, Mr. Darcy, for I know the answer."

"Elizabeth there are things about these situations that you do not understand. If you will calm yourself and listen—"

She could hear his voice, but his words reached her ears as nothing but jumbled noise. The painful images persisted and she could hear nothing but Lydia's anguished cries.

"My sister is broken and it is your fault! That is all I need to understand. I will not stay here and listen to your reasoning. I foolishly gave in to your seduction. I will not hear your lies."

She turned and ran into the woods. Darcy made a few steps to follow her but stopped as he felt the full sting of what she had said. He was shocked, grieved, but also angry. He was prepared to give her the world, but she ran from him. All of her accusations could have been answered had she just listened.

The tingle from her slap drew his notice and he lifted his hand to touch his cheek. She held her wrist while she yelled at him, so it must have hurt her to land such a hard blow. Darcy stumbled back slightly, as if just then feeling the force of it.

He ran his hand through his hair as he tried to catch his breath. A dread was growing in the pit of his stomach, but he ignored it and concentrated on the injustice of her words. He had done the only thing he could. His choices were to court her privately or stay away from her. Perhaps the latter option would have been better considering her opinion of him.

And Wickham. He had cleaned up after that cad enough in his life. Should he always feel responsible for his degeneracy? To the best of his knowledge Wickham had, at least, never trifled with a gentlewoman until Georgiana. Protecting her was his highest priority. Of course, he did not hold the people of Meryton in higher regard than his sister. No one meant more to him than her. Except Elizabeth.

"Dear God."

He began pacing, refusing to give in to the anxiety caused by seeing her run from him. Yet, his mind would not stop. They had been meeting for weeks, why would these things be so important all of the sudden? Unbidden, a vision of Georgiana at Ramsgate entered his mind. He closed his eyes to it, not wanting to see the same sadness in her that Elizabeth had just expressed. *You pursue me in the shadows.*

The dread would no longer be ignored. It rose from his stomach and into his chest, consuming everything in its path. Darcy shuddered as the cold chill of realization came over him. He had lost her, and he had no one to blame but himself.

Elizabeth ran to the parsonage and straight upstairs to her room. She could not be in company with anyone at the moment and hoped Colonel Fitzwilliam would forget about his promise to call. What was she to do? She could not stay in Kent and risk seeing Darcy. The thought of being with him hurt just as much as the idea of never seeing him again. Her shoulders shook as she attempted to quiet her sobs. She tried to focus on Fitzwilliam's words, the memory of Darcy with Anne de Bourgh, the pain in her wrist, anything except the hurt she saw in his eyes just before she ran.

Doubt and hope warred against her better reason. She wiped her tears and shook her head. He would not have made her an honorable offer. Colonel Fitzwilliam as much as said Darcy would never accept her family. *A lady who was under Darcy's protection.* She was sheltered, but she was sure she knew what that meant. He must have wanted her to take that woman's place while he married Miss de Bourgh.

Elizabeth's tears returned. He had been so kind and loving toward her. He told her about his family and listened to her ramblings. He ran with her. But, it had all been done in secret, just as Wickham had done with Lydia. Darcy had always been gentle, though, and the kisses and caresses they shared had been quite chaste until—until she offered more. The memory of his kiss came upon her and she allowed it for a moment before she stood in renewed determination and paced about the room.

There was no excuse for what he did to Lydia. Darcy had apparently enabled Wickham's bad behavior for years then said nothing of his vile propensities even when she challenged him about Wickham at the Netherfield ball. No reason could be had to justify his silence. She stopped her pacing as a speck of thought broke through her anger. Unless--.

Her speculation was interrupted by a knock on the door. She said nothing, hoping whomever it was would leave.

"Eliza?" Charlotte spoke softly as she opened the door. "What is the matter?"

"I am not well, Charlotte." Elizabeth did not try to dissemble. She knew the stress of the morning must have shown in her countenance or Charlotte would not express such concern.

"Come lie down. Are you injured?" She nodded to the wrist Elizabeth held gingerly in her hand.

"Yes. I hurt myself this morning in the woods."

"Oh, Eliza. You must be more careful. Your mother would never forgive me if something happened to you."

"It is not so bad."

"You are flushed and breathless and you wince when you move your hand. I do not want you to leave this bed today."

"I will become restless if I am in the same room all day."

"I will have our cook bring you a pot of her special tea. It is very calming and will help you sleep."

Elizabeth nodded in acquiescence. Charlotte started toward the door, but Elizabeth stopped her.

"Charlotte? What does it mean when a woman is under a man's protection?"

"Why do you ask?"

"It is just something I heard and I wondered at the meaning."

"Well, in the most vulgar terms, it means a man keeps a mistress."

Elizabeth's heart sank.

"However, if you think about it, we are all under some man's protection. Whether a father or a husband."

"Or a brother?"

Charlotte nodded. When she saw Elizabeth would say no more, she turned and left the room.

Elizabeth tried to shut her mind to the confusion that brief conversation created. She was drained of all energy. Her body could not stand another onslaught of emotion. When the maid appeared with the tea, she eagerly drank two cups, hoping Charlotte was right about its effects. Thankfully, not long after the second cup was consumed, she fell into a deep slumber. She gratefully allowed sleep to serve as a shield against the beleaguering feeling that she had made a terrible mistake.

Chapter 16

"Eliza."

Somewhere in her twilight, Elizabeth felt the bed sink and heard Charlotte's concerned voice calling to her. She shielded her eyes with her hand and opened them slowly. Her head ached and she could not tolerate the light.

"Forgive me, Charlotte. I am still unwell."

"I can see that. You slept all day and night. It is now morning, will you rise?"

Elizabeth shook her head and once again closed her eyes.

Charlotte sighed. "Colonel Fitzwilliam is here. He asked to see you, but I informed him you were not yet well enough to come downstairs. He insisted I check on you to be sure. He did not want to leave without saying goodbye."

Elizabeth raised up on her elbow. "He is leaving Kent?"

"Yes, tomorrow morning. Mr. Darcy has been called to London on urgent business."

Elizabeth nodded then rested her head on the pillow. "Please give him my regrets and assure him I enjoyed making his acquaintance."

"Are you sure you will not come down? He will be disappointed."

"Yes, Charlotte."

"Very well." She rose to leave and Elizabeth called to her as she reached the door.

"Charlotte."

"Yes, Eliza?"

"Could you ask your cook to make another special tea for me, please?"

"Of course."

"Thank you."

Elizabeth rolled over away from the light. The tea she drank the previous evening did exactly as it should. For the first time in many weeks, she did not dream. Her mind remained black, void of all images and emotions. She was not yet ready to live beyond that space. She only wanted more dreamless sleep. The tea soon arrived with instructions from Charlotte to also eat some bread and cheese. She did as asked only so Charlotte would not disturb her.

She again slept in darkness and reluctantly roused when she heard Charlotte's voice the next morning.

"Eliza."

Elizabeth shied away from Charlotte's touch and buried her head under the linens.

"No, Eliza. You may have no more sleep. You must dress and eat. You have been called to Rosings this morning."

"Lady Catherine wants to see me?"

"No, Miss de Bourgh sent a note and a footman to collect you."

Elizabeth felt panic rise in her chest. Why would Miss de Bourgh want to see her? Had she somehow found out about her and Darcy?

"Charlotte, I cannot. I have not left this bed in two days. I am not fit to be in company with Miss de Bourgh. Please make my excuses."

Charlotte hesitated and examined her friend's face closely before her shoulders relaxed. "Very well, Eliza, though I do believe whatever ails you can be aided by movement and fresh air. Will you at least join us for breakfast?"

"Not yet, please."

Charlotte leaned in and placed a firm hand on Elizabeth's shoulder. "One more day, Elizabeth, then I will drag you out of bed myself."

Elizabeth had no intention of obeying her at that time but nodded anyway. "May I have some more tea?"

"No dear, you have had enough. If you have trouble sleeping then perhaps you can walk about the room, or better yet, come downstairs."

After Charlotte left, Elizabeth could not rest. The images lost in the void of sleep found their way to her waking mind. She still thought primarily of Lydia, but they were now joined by Darcy's pained expression when she spoke of Wickham. Why did she feel guilty for hurting him when he was at fault? She was again on the verge of tears when Charlotte re-entered the room.

"Oh Eliza, I am so glad you are awake. We must get you fed and dressed right away." She walked to the closet and pulled out the first dress she saw.

"Why? What has happened?" Elizabeth had never seen her friend so frantic. She immediately rose and began removing the nightgown she did not remember putting on.

"Miss de Bourgh's footman has returned."

Elizabeth's stomach flipped and she returned to sitting on the bed. Charlotte pulled her right back up.

"Did you inform her I am ill?"

"Yes. She sent another note along with the barouche insisting the air will do you good. I am sorry, Eliza, but you must go."

"Charlotte I cannot."

"Eliza! Something is happening at Rosings. One of the maids told ours that Lady Catherine has been moved to the dower house. Mr. Collins is frantic. Please, we must not upset Miss de Bourgh. It seems she is now my husband's patroness. Please, Eliza, get dressed."

Elizabeth arrived at Rosings a half hour later, regretting the muffins Charlotte made her eat. Instead of giving her strength, as her friend insisted, they churned in her stomach. She was sure she would not make it through the meeting without becoming ill. While the thought of losing her breakfast on Darcy's betrothed was somewhat appealing, she had to think of Charlotte and not upset the new mistress of Rosings.

She was shown to a room that starkly contrasted the rest of the manor, at least what she had seen. The dining room and sitting room where she was previously received were ornate and cold, furnished with grand and uncomfortable pieces. Those rooms were designed to intimidate. This room, however, was light and warm. The furniture was delicate and tasteful and overall the space was welcoming. The biggest difference was found in the lady who was receiving her.

Anne de Bourgh sat in the middle of the room next to her companion, Mrs. Jenkinson, with a soft smile adorning her pale face. She was not overly made up, nor was she standing next to Darcy and in the brightness of the room, Elizabeth felt as if she were truly seeing Anne de Bourgh for the first time.

She knew Anne to be sickly, both by others' estimation and her own observations, but the frail figure before her was not merely unwell. Her skin was stretched thin over her face, her hair was wiry and her countenance gave away her exhaustion as if the mere act of breathing was overly taxing. It seemed to Elizabeth that she was standing in that beautiful room surrounded by the sights and smells of life, yet looking upon the face of death.

"Miss Bennet, thank you for joining me this morning. Forgive me for not rising to greet you properly, but I find myself quite tired today." She gestured for Elizabeth to sit on the sofa next to her.

"Thank you for the invitation, Miss de Bourgh. It is my pleasure to be here."

Anne looked down where Elizabeth's hands were folded lightly in her lap, then back up to her anxious expression. "You do not have to worry about seeing my mother. She no longer lives here. Today is my birthday and as was stipulated by my father's will, I am now mistress of Rosings."

"Happy birthday, and congratulations on your—new position."

"Thank you. I had hoped to host a bigger celebration, but my cousins have left for London."

"You must miss them." The effort to steady her voice was taxing. She looked at Anne briefly then returned her gaze to her hands.

"I do. I asked them to stay longer, but Darcy needed to leave." She waited for Elizabeth to look at her, then spoke in earnest, but her tone was laced with confusion. "He was sad to go. I believe his attachment to Rosings grew this year. Now that it will be his, I think he sees it in a different light. He sees the possibilities rather than the many faults."

Elizabeth swallowed slowly and forced herself to maintain eye contact. She may have thrown herself at this woman's betrothed, but she would not be accused of impoliteness.

"Your estate is lovely. The grounds are particularly beautiful."

Anne smiled at the compliment and her voice moved from proud to pleading. "Thank you. They are nothing to Pemberley, I assure you. I have not seen it for many years, but I have no doubt Darcy has cared for it quite diligently. He has an estate in Scotland as well. With three estates and uncommon wealth, the woman he marries will never have to worry about her or her children's future. They will always be secure."

Elizabeth had looked away while Anne praised her cousin, but those last lines caused her head to snap back in her direction.

"What do you mean the woman he marries?"

Anne hesitated a moment in confusion at Elizabeth's abruptness. "Precisely that. Whoever he chooses will gain considerable wealth along with an excellent man. I do hope she will favor the man over the money, however."

Elizabeth felt all the air leave her lungs as she breathed out a shaky reply. "You are not engaged to Mr. Darcy?"

"Good heavens, no. Did you hear that from your cousin?"

"Yes, and others." She thought back to Colonel Fitzwilliam's words. He did not say Darcy and Anne were engaged. He said Rosings would be Darcy's. She assumed he meant through marriage.

Anne shook her head and reached for Elizabeth's hand. "Miss Bennet, no. Oh dear, is that why you quarreled; because you thought he was engaged to me? Forgive my intrusion, please, but Darcy was in such misery the last days he was here. I see that same anguish on your face now. Darcy is not engaged to me or any other woman. He is free to make his own choice."

Elizabeth was mystified as she looked into Anne's kind eyes. "Miss de Bourgh, I find myself quite confused at present."

"You poor dear. Perhaps this will help." She pulled a letter from the folds of her dress. "Darcy asked me to give this to you. Forgive the impropriety, but for Darcy to break the rules, it must be very important."

Elizabeth took the folded paper from Anne and stared at her name written in a close hand. Her fingers trembled as they traced over the letters.

"Will you stay here while you read it? I have reason to believe you will need my assistance once you have. Mrs. Jenkinson will show you to a room where you will have privacy. Please find me when you are ready."

Elizabeth was dazed but did as she was bidden when Mrs. Jenkinson gestured to her.

"Thank you."

Anne watched them leave with a heavy heart. She hoped the letter would solve whatever misunderstanding had come between Miss Bennet and her cousin. Darcy did not tell her what happened, only requested her help with the letter and apologized for leaving on her birthday.

"Forgive me, Anne, but I cannot stay."

The soft anguish in his voice and the dejected way he held his head told her more than words ever could. Elizabeth had rejected him, and he was running away.

Elizabeth entered the chamber and closed the door behind her. It was a beautiful room, done in dark, masculine tones. As she breathed in, she caught a faint smell of something familiar. She closed her eyes as she remembered being enfolded in the warm, spicy scent. Darcy. This must be his chamber when visiting Rosings.

As she walked toward a large chair nestled in the far corner of the room, she noticed a light-colored bonnet sitting atop a dark wood writing desk. She picked it up and examined it. She had forgotten in the grove when she and Darcy argued. He must have brought it back. Her heart broke a little further when she saw it was missing its ribbon. She hoped it was because he kept it.

She sat down and drew a deep breath, summoning the courage to break the seal. She finally did and unfolded the fine paper. It was dated the previous evening from Rosings.

To Miss Elizabeth Bennet,

Two charges you have lain before me, both of which, in your words, stem from a lack of regard for your family or anyone else outside my circle. I can only conjecture what lead you to make such a determination at that point in time. I thought we each had a certain amount of understanding in regards to each other's character. For you to chastise me so sternly, I can see I was mistaken.

I assure you that my silence in regard to Mr. Wickham had nothing to do with an intentional lack of consideration for the safety of your family, but with the responsibility of protecting my own, namely my sister, Georgiana.

What I am about to relay to you is a private family matter, and I trust you to keep it as such. George Wickham is the son of a very respectable man who served as my father's steward for many years. My father was grateful for his excellent service to the estate and, therefore, acted most kindly toward him and his son. George Wickham was educated as a gentleman and was given every opportunity to create a better life than his station otherwise would have allowed. You seem to have judged him correctly, so there is no need for me to list all the ways he wasted those opportunities. I never informed my father of Wickham's true character. When he died, one of the issues I struggled with most was how I could give Wickham the Church living my father had promised him, knowing what I did. Fortunately, the decision was taken from me when Wickham requested the sum of three thousand pounds instead of the living. I gave it to him gladly in hopes of never seeing him again. Unfortunately, that was not the case. He returned after having squandered the money I paid him and demanded I fulfill my father's promise of the living. I refused that request and each subsequent one. His resentment was extreme and he abused my name wherever he could. After this, all appearance of acquaintance was dropped. I did not see him again until last summer.

I have spoken to you before about my guardianship over my sister. About a year ago, I removed her from school and set her up at my home in London with a Mrs. Younge, who presided over my sister's routine. Last summer I was persuaded to allow Georgiana to travel to Ramsgate with Mrs. Younge. Wickham went there too, no doubt by design, for, unknown to us, a previous relationship existed between him and Mrs. Younge. Georgiana remembered him from her childhood and the attention he had paid to her then. She was persuaded to believe herself in love and to consent to an elopement. She was then but fifteen and cannot be blamed for the lapse in judgment. I joined them unexpectedly a day or two before the intended elopement and Georgiana told me everything. Knowing my affection for my sister, you may imagine how I felt and how I acted. Wickham and Mrs. Younge left the place immediately. If they had succeeded, my sister's life would have been ruined. She still suffers from her disappointment but is beginning to understand how she was manipulated. You must appreciate my need to protect her feelings and her reputation. A fifteen-year-old girl, who knows very little of the world outside her family should not suffer the rest of her life over the actions of an unfeeling cad. Exposing Wickham would risk exposing her to ridicule and conjecture, and I will not do that.

This leads me to the matter of your sister and my part in separating her from my friend. I have already admitted I convinced Bingley not to return to Hertfordshire and I told you my reasons why. I did not see any signs of a deep regard for Bingley in your sister. For as long as I have known him, Bingley's greatest desire has been to shed the taint of association with trade, purchase an estate and enter the first circles of society. Achieving two of those things would be made easier by a fortuitous marriage. Forgive me, but marriage to your sister would make that very difficult, if not impossible. How could I allow him to abandon the desires of a lifetime for a woman with no fortune or connections, who displayed no outward signs of affection, and whose mother very loudly proclaimed her joy at her daughter's success in securing a wealthy man. Forgive me, but the blame for the neighborhood's raised expectations could be put on that lady as much as Bingley.

I know my saying this will cause you pain, and for that I am sorry, but you cannot deny the general impropriety displayed on many occasions by your entire family, save you and your elder sister. Bingley's sisters, I admit, are little better. They demonstrate the best manners, but they are ambitious and need him to achieve his goals in order to meet their own. Bingley is of a gentle and modest nature. He will always be subject to their whims and life would have been much more difficult for him to have two sets of relations vying for his fortune and help in society.

All of this would mean nothing if she truly cared for him. A man can do anything if he is considered worthy in the eyes of the woman he loves. I am grieved beyond measure that you have found me lacking. I assure you, Miss Bennet, that it was never my intention to frighten or offend you. I courted you outside the view of our families only because doing otherwise would have put you in a precarious position. My aunt would never have tolerated me giving attention to anyone but Anne. I have no doubt she would have told Mr. Collins to send you home. I could not allow you to suffer humiliation for the sake of my attentions. I see now that my decision had other, unintended consequences.

Please be assured, my dearest Elizabeth, that since the first day we ran together in the woods, my only intention has been to love you. If we had not been interrupted yesterday, you would have heard my words of love as I asked you to marry me. I curse that interruption but more than that I regret that my actions ever gave you cause to doubt me.

*You asked me about the legend of the emblem I wove for you. If you look at the pattern, you will see it is a series of hearts entwined in a circle. It is a symbol of unending love, one that forever binds the wearer to the one who gave it to her**. So you see, Elizabeth, it is fixed. You are a part of me now, and more dear to me than anyone on this earth.*

I will ask my cousin Anne to deliver this letter to you. I trust her to be discrete. If you should so desire, I believe she would get one to me in return. I will only add, God bless you.

Fitzwilliam Darcy

Chapter 17

Elizabeth read each line again carefully, not wanting to misunderstand a single word. The suspicion that formed the night before was now confirmed. Wickham had attempted to harm Miss Darcy.

You must appreciate my need to protect her feelings and her reputation. A fifteen-year-old girl, who knows very little of the world outside her family, should not suffer the rest of her life over the actions of an unfeeling cad. Exposing Wickham would risk exposing her to ridicule and conjecture, and I will not do that.

Three lines were all it took to dispel her resentment. Three lines that she easily could have written herself. She could not be angry with him for doing precisely what she had done.

Nor could she be angry for separating Bingley from Jane. It was not the act that upset her, but the reasoning behind it, at least how Colonel Fitzwilliam had explained it. If the Bennets were not suitable for a man like Bingley, they certainly would not be acceptable to a man like Darcy. That had cast a very dark shadow of doubt over their time alone together. But the Colonel, apparently, was mistaken.

All of this would mean nothing if she truly cared for him. A man can do anything if he is considered worthy in the eyes of the woman he loves. I am grieved beyond measure that you have found me lacking.

She winced as the realization of how she had hurt him came to full view. Why had she not let him speak? He tried to tell her then but she would not listen. She cried for his grief and when she exhausted her tears, she rose from the chair and moved to the bed. It was beyond hope that his warmth would have remained several hours after he quit the room, but she could detect a trace of his scent. She found comfort in that small part of him that was still with her as she contemplated more of his letter.

Please be assured, my dearest Elizabeth, that since the first day we ran together in the woods, my only intention has been to love you. If we had not been interrupted yesterday, you would have heard my words of love as I asked you to marry me.

Oh, to have heard him speak! But, what answer could she have given him if he had managed those words? The lasting happiness of so many was tied to Lydia making it through her confinement without detection. Darcy had so carefully protected his sister's reputation, would he risk it now by marrying Elizabeth while Lydia's ruin lingered over them? Could she risk their reputations by accepting him?

I will ask my cousin Anne to deliver this letter to you. I trust her to be discrete. If you should so desire, I believe she would get one to me in return.

No, she could not, she concluded with much sadness. Wickham had finally left the Darcys in peace; she would not bring him back into their lives. She would not pollute the shades of Pemberley with the stain of a fallen sister. Perhaps after Lydia was safe, she could write to him. For now, she would protect Darcy's sister as diligently as she protected her own and pray that he would forgive her.

After sitting still for some time, she felt composed enough to leave Darcy's room and find Anne. She was again seated in the bright sitting room where she earlier received Elizabeth. When Anne saw her she smiled kindly.

"How are you Miss Bennet?" She gestured for Elizabeth to sit beside her then looked to Mrs. Jenkinson, who left them alone.

"I am still not quite sure, Miss de Bourgh."

Anne reached out and placed her hand on Elizabeth's arm. "Will you write to him?"

Elizabeth swallowed then shook her head. "I cannot."

"I promise no one will know. I will include it with a letter from me and send it by messenger."

"It is not that. I would not wish to raise his expectations."

"I see."

"There are things. . . differences between us. My family . . ." Elizabeth had told so many lies since the autumn, they should flow from her mouth without effort. She could not fathom why—perhaps she was simply too tired to think—but she could not lie to Anne.

"Do you not love him?"

Elizabeth raised her eyes to meet Anne's. This was a question she could not answer and still maintain her determination.

"Miss de Bourgh, I understand you feel a certain familiarity with this situation due to your closeness to Mr. Darcy, but you are not entitled to know my feelings."

The words came out much harsher than she intended and Anne looked so stricken by her words that Elizabeth immediately took her hands and apologized.

"Forgive me. I do not mean to be harsh. I am fatigued and short tempered."

Anne lowered her head. "No, you are right, I should not have asked. I am afraid I have little experience with conversation. My manners may be more relaxed than is proper at times."

"Think no more on it. We are new acquaintances and must learn each other's ways of speaking."

Anne nodded. "I would very much like us to be friends, Miss Bennet."

Guilt grabbed onto Elizabeth and twisted her already distressed conscience. She had brief moments of hatred and long moments of resentment toward Anne since she first saw Darcy sit with her at dinner. Seeing her hopeful face asking for friendship struck her through.

"I would like that, Miss de Bourgh. Will you please call me Elizabeth, or Lizzy? Or even Eliza, as Charlotte does?"

Anne smiled. "I like Lizzy. Please call me Anne."

When Anne spoke her name, Elizabeth suddenly realized why it had been so difficult for her to dissemble. Sitting beside her was the perfect embodiment of all her sisters. Anne had Jane's gentleness and Lydia's frailty; Mary's awkwardness and Kitty's eagerness to please. Though still feeling the pain of losing Darcy, Elizabeth felt comforted sitting there with his cousin.

"Thank you for giving me the letter, Anne. Again, I apologize for my uneasiness. I should return to the parsonage. Charlotte was anxious about my visit."

"Oh? Why is that?"

"They heard rumors of your mother's displacement. Mr. Collins is apprehensive about his position, I am sure."

"He should not worry. I could not rescend the living even if I wanted to. He should not change his routine at all." She smiled mischievously. "If fact, I believe he should still visit my mother as much as if she were mistress. If you will wait a moment, I will write a note telling him as such."

"Of course."

Anne completed her task quickly and gave Elizabeth the note along with one more plea on Darcy's behalf.

"Lizzy, I promise I will not berate you, but I ask you to reconsider your decision about my cousin. He is a good man and deserving of every happiness."

"I agree with you, Anne. That is why I will not write to him. Please, if we are to be friends, then you must not try to change my mind. It is done."

Anne nodded. "Very well. I will say no more, Lizzy."

Elizabeth pulled her into an embrace. "Thank you. Shall I come again tomorrow?"

"Oh yes, please do. And bring Mrs. Collins and Miss Lucas. We will have the cake I ordered for dinner tonight. It will be a delayed celebration."

"You are very excited about your birthday."

"Only because it means I no longer have to live with my mother."

The ladies laughed and Anne offered to have her driven to the parsonage. Elizabeth declined, feeling the need for a prolonged solitude. She began to regret her choice when she was about a half mile from Rosings. The burden of what all had happened descended upon her and she suddenly found it difficult to move forward on the path. Darcy and Lydia were both far from her reach and long months would pass before she could hope to see them. She stopped for a moment to rein in the panic that threatened to take her at that thought. She breathed deeply, but it was no use. The foreboding would not subside; she had to accept it as a companion.

Her steps to the parsonage were slow and tortured, and when she finally arrived Charlotte greeted her with much curiosity. Elizabeth assured her all was well and handed her the note.

"Thank you for going to Rosings, Eliza. I know you were not feeling up to it."

Elizabeth saw Charlotte's curiosity but could not find the strength for conversation. "Can we speak of everything in the morning? I believe I need one more night to rest and I will be fully recovered. Miss de Bourgh's note should put Mr. Collins at ease."

Charlotte hesitated but eventually acquiesced. "Very well, Eliza, but I do hope you will tell me what is wrong."

"I believe I am only fatigued, Charlotte. Will you allow me to have tea tonight?" Elizabeth tried to lighten her voice in hopes her friend might not push for answers.

"Prepare for bed. I will make your excuses to Mr. Collins and have the tea sent to you."

"Thank you, Charlotte. I promise I will be more like myself tomorrow."

Elizabeth spent another night in dreamless darkness and awoke with a determination to at least pretend to be cheerful. She knew she would not hold up under Charlotte's scrutiny. She was tired of the deceit and would simply have to avoid questions.

Her remaining days in Kent were spent in an air of pretense. She smiled and teased and excused herself as early as she possibly could at the end of the day. She still walked to the grove most mornings, accompanied by his memory. She conjured conversations and watched the memories act out in front of her, as if she were watching a play. She was content with the recollections, for the most part.

Occasionally, her mind would rebel and conjure images of future meetings. In these dreams they were not alone, but joined by a boy building bridges and a girl chasing toads. Every vision included the comfort of his arms and the passion of his kisses. As painful as they could be, these thoughts also gave her hope that his love was strong enough to allow forgiveness and that in loving him she would be able to forgive herself.

Each day after breakfast, the ladies of Hunsford called at Rosings. Anne seemed to truly enjoy her new companionship as well as the responsibility of managing the estate. Elizabeth hoped the new color she saw in Anne's cheeks would spread with a renewed health. More than anything, she hoped Mr. Darcy would never inherit the place.

She could no longer claim illness in order to have an excuse for cook's special tea. Her disturbing dreams continued, often waking her only a few hours after she retired. She kept a small box next to her bed that was filled with what she called her treasures. When her nightmare woke her, she would reach for the box. Opening it to see Darcy's gloves, the sweetbriar and the emblem would sooth her enough to once again sleep.

Elizabeth left Kent with a mixture of emotions. She was anxious to see her family, especially Jane. But, she would also see her father, with whom she was still very angry. The memory of his words to Lydia still haunted her, but those angry words were now juxtaposed against Darcy's words of love and protection. *A fifteen-year-old girl, who knows very little of the world outside her family, should not suffer the rest of her life over the actions of an unfeeling cad.* She was extraordinarily proud of him for taking such good care of his sister. It made her more determined to do the same.

Chapter 18

Darcy sat in a chair in the corner of his study at his London home. He rested his elbows on his knees as he stared into the darkened room. He left Kent nearly two weeks prior and the dread that sat like a weight in his stomach had not subsided. It was joined now by a constant throbbing in his head, no doubt aided by the entire decanter of port he had consumed that afternoon.

He rose and walked to his desk where he retrieved an open letter. He had anticipated that letter since he arrived in London. The last few days of waiting had been tortuous, knowing his hopes would be fulfilled or crushed with just a few words. As soon as he saw it, he knew which it would be. It was written in Anne's hand, but much too thin to contain two letters. Elizabeth had not written him.

His fear was confirmed upon reading. Anne told him that Elizabeth had read his letter, seemed quite upset over it, but would not maintain their connection. Anne did try to give him hope.

She said what lay between you is insurmountable at present. Darcy, I do believe she cares for you. She did not confide much to me, likely out of fear of me telling you. But, I can see she is unhappy.

Darcy walked to the fireplace and dropped the letter in the fire. He leaned against the mantle and watched it burn as the flames of grief and remorse consumed him. Hope had tortured him as he waited for her words of forgiveness. Now that he knew they would never come, he could only succumb to his future without her.

Never in his life had he felt so weak or so exposed. He was a methodic problem solver. No situation had ever arisen that he could not manage. But, how does one manage heartache?

He tried to understand what had happened. He was not quite sure what prompted her anger until he talked to Fitzwilliam in the carriage on the way to London.

"Fitzwilliam, when did you last see Miss Bennet?"

"I saw her when I was out making my usual tour of the grounds. I tried to call on her before we departed, but she was ill and not receiving visitors."

"What did you talk about?"

"You mostly, and Wickham."

"How did the topic of Wickham come up between you and Miss Bennet?"

"When I was at the parsonage one morning, Miss Lucas spoke of a letter she had received from Hertfordshire. It was filled with gossip, of course, some of it about Wickham. Apparently, the uncle of a young lady there felt compelled to remove his charge from Wickham's company. Miss Lucas seemed a little too relieved that Wickham was no longer promised to someone. I felt I needed to warn Miss Bennet to not get too close to the man."

"What did you tell her, exactly?"

"I did not expose Georgiana, do not worry. But, I did relay some of your history with him and told her she should be wary in his company."

"What else?"

"About Wickham?"

"About Bingley."

"Oh, you might be angry with me about this, cousin. I could tell you had a bit of a tendre for Miss Bennet. I tried to talk you up a bit. I told her what a true and loyal friend you are and used your dealings with Bingley as an example."

"You told her I separated Bingley from a lady recently?"

"I did."

"That lady was her sister."

"Oh God. Darcy, I had no idea. So, does she hate you now?"

"It would seem so."

"That is most unfortunate, Darcy. Miss Bennet is quite a woman."

Darcy had been tempted to throw his cousin from the carriage, but his anger soon gave way to self- reproach. He still believed that if he had not lost control, she would have spoken to him rationally. His father had been correct: one fleeting moment of indulgence could cost everything. He turned from the fireplace just as a knock came on the door.

"Enter."

Darcy's butler opened the door and announced a visitor.

"Colonel Fitzwilliam, sir."

Darcy nodded and the servant left the room as Fitzwilliam entered.

"Good God, Darcy! Are you ill?"

"I am perfectly well, thank you." Darcy stumbled back to the chair.

"Yes, so well you can barely walk." Fitzwilliam looked at the empty bottle on the floor next to his cousin's seat. "What has caused this sudden need to drink? You cannot be feeling the loss of Miss Bennet, surely."

Darcy looked sharply at his cousin. He still could not bear the sound of her name coming from his mouth. "Is there any particular reason you are here, Fitzwilliam?"

"Do I need a particular reason to visit my dearest relation?"

Darcy merely sighed and leaned further into the chair, placing his face in his hand.

"I came to see how you are doing. I have not seen you since we returned from Kent. It seems I should have come sooner."

Darcy still did not respond. His stomach, however, gave a loud rumble.

"When did you last eat, Darcy?"

"I know not. Sometime today, I am sure."

"Stand up."

"No."

"Come, Darcy. I am getting you out of this depressing room. I know exactly what you need and I will not relent until you have come with me."

Darcy had not the strength to argue, so when Fitzwilliam pulled at his elbow, he rose without protest.

"Where are we going?"

"To see a friend."

By the time they reached their destination, Darcy was convinced that the carriage ride was penance for everything he had done wrong in his life. His head spun and if they had not stopped when they did, he was sure he would have ruined his upholstery.

They entered a townhouse in a neighborhood Darcy did not recognize. He focused his vision enough to see it was richly decorated and filled with people he did not know. Voices of men and women mingled together and reached his ears as an intolerable ringing. They were shown to a room and presented with cold meats and bread. Darcy looked upon the food with disgust and instead reached for the wine.

Fitzwilliam chuckled. "You must eat a little something, Darcy. You will need your strength. Here, I insist."

Fitzwilliam placed food on Darcy's plate and stared at him until he ate what he was served. The food did nothing for his head, but his stomach did slightly calm. Darcy pushed his plate away and again attempted to take in his surroundings.

"Where are we, Fitzwilliam?"

"I told you, we came to see a friend. Come, let us go find some company."

"I would rather stay here where it is quiet."

"No Darcy. I insist on you being seen."

They walked down what seemed to be a ridiculously long hallway for a townhouse of its size. Just as Darcy was about to ask if the bloody thing ever ended, they entered a large room that seemed suitable for a ball, though no one was dancing. The air was thick with perfume and cigars and somewhere in his fogged mind, Darcy registered the sound of a woman's laughter.

Memories of Elizabeth's laugh cut through him like a blade, causing him to stagger. As he regained his balance, a figure appeared, gracefully walking toward him. He could not make out her face, but her form and lovely chestnut curls were somehow familiar. She came closer and he reached out, drawing her to him. He felt her small hand on his chest and he released a long, heavy breath.

"Mr. Darcy, I am so happy you have finally come. I have been waiting for you."

He lowered his head to hers and gave up the struggle to make sense of what was happening. He surrendered to the confusion and pulled the vision to his chest while gently caressing her back.

"Elizabeth."

She pulled away and Darcy protested, attempting to return her to his embrace. She laughed again, tugged on his arm and led him from the room.

Darcy's eyes fluttered as the thick blanket of sleep lifted from his mind. He yawned then flinched from the pain the movement brought to his temples. A wave of nausea rushed over him and he quickly sat and leaned over the bed. He waited several minutes for the feeling to subside then slowly lifted his head.

His eyes took in his surrounding as awareness began to overcome the fog in his mind. He looked down to see he was wearing trousers though his shirt and boots were removed. His eyes roamed the chamber and he saw his coat, cravat and shirt piled together on the floor next to the bed.

He rested his head in his hands as he tried to clear his mind. He had no recollection of retiring or removing any of his clothes. The last thing he remembered was--.

"Oh God."

Darcy looked around in a panic and was relived to recognize his chamber and that he was, blessedly, alone.

"Where did Fitzwilliam take me last night?" He had no clear memories from the evening, just shadows and a faint recollection of a laugh and the feel of a soft form in his arms. The thought brought on another bout of nausea. He was just recovering when he heard a knock on his chamber door.

"Enter."

"Good morning, sir. I hope you rested well."

Darcy thought he could detect a slight bit of judgment in his valet's voice, but he chose to ignore it for the time being.

"No, I did not. What time is it?"

"Not yet noon, sir."

"So late? Why did you not wake me earlier?"

"It seemed you need to rest, sir."

"I thank you for being so diligent about my comfort, James."

"Do not take your foul mood out on James, here, Darcy. He is not the one who drank half the port in London last night."

"Bingley?"

Darcy rose from the bed and walked around it to see Bingley standing next to his valet, wearing a very annoying smirk.

"What the hell are you doing here so early?"

Bingley laughed. "It is not so early and, if you must know, I spent the night. I thank you for your hospitality, now may I have a little civility?"

"You are having fun at my expense and I do not appreciate it."

Darcy left the room through a side door. Bingley turned to James and requested he bring his master dry toast and very strong tea. Darcy returned a moment later wearing a dressing gown and deep scowl. He walked through the chamber and through another door to his sitting room. Bingley followed.

"Since you spent the night here I assume you brought me home."

"Yes, I did."

"You were at that place, too?"

Bingley nodded.

"Did I –"

"No. I saw you with one of the ladies. I also saw the state you were in and interceded before you did something you would regret."

Darcy let out a long sigh of relief. "What were you doing there?"

Bingley raised his eyebrows and smiled. "Well, I am not quite the gentleman you are, Darcy."

Darcy shook his head. "You are a good man, Bingley, and a good friend. Thank you."

"You are welcome. I am glad I was there. The question is, Darcy, why were you? You never visit such establishments."

Darcy rubbed his hand over his face then through his hair. "Fitzwilliam took me there." He paused as his anger sent throbs straight to his temple. "I believe he was attempting to *cheer* me."

Bingley huffed in disbelief. "To cheer you? Darcy, you were so inebriated that any attempt at cheer would only have led to embarrassment. I did not see Fitzwilliam at all last night. He must have left you to your own devises. I can only imagine your mortification had you awoken there this morning."

Darcy's head ached further at the thought. "Again, Bingley, thank you."

Conversation ceased momentarily when James brought in the tray of toast and tea. Darcy dismissed him and Bingley began his inquiry.

"Why did Fitzwilliam think you needed cheering?"

Darcy took a drink of tea and contemplated how to begin. "Do you remember Miss Elizabeth Bennet from Hertfordshire?"

Bingley leaned back in his seat and smiled. "Of course I do! You took quite an interest in her, I believe."

"Was it so obvious?"

Bingley shrugged. "It was to me. You never flirt so openly, yet you *could admire her figure better by the fire*? I had to look to see if someone else had replaced you. Caroline certainly noticed your attentions to Miss Elizabeth. I wonder if that had something to do with her vehement objection to Jane."

"Jane." Darcy sighed. "Miss Elizabeth had much to say about my opinion of you and her sister."

"When did you see her?"

"In Kent. She was visiting her friend, the former Miss Lucas. She married my aunt's parson, Mr. Collins."

"And you grew to like Miss Elizabeth more while there?"

Darcy nodded. "Yes, very much" He sighed again. "I love her."

Bingley waited for him to continue and after a few moments, he did.

"Like I said, she was not happy about my advice to you regarding her sister."

"How did she know of it?"

"Fitzwilliam told her. It is a long story."

"Fitzwilliam again." Bingley poured himself a cup of tea and again leaned back in his chair. "I have all day."

Darcy told him of his time with Elizabeth, of his hopes and their argument, and how it seems she had decided he was the worst of men.

"You are no cad, Darcy. You had the best of intentions."

"But she did not know that. I should have spoken of my intentions that first day we were alone together. I did not think I had to. It sounds stupid now, but I truly thought she somehow just knew."

Bingley shook his head. "Women need to hear the words. Men hold all the power, even in a courtship where our hearts are engaged. They can only be sure of our affections if we speak them."

Darcy looked solemnly at his friend. "I am sorry for my interference, Bingley. I should never have presumed to know Miss Bennet's feelings."

"You were right about her lack of regard for me, Darcy."

"Bingley—"

"I saw her recently, here in London. She was walking in the park with her relations—and a gentleman. I spoke to them briefly and she implied they are engaged."

"Again, Bingley, I am sorry. I had no right to interfere. I hope you can forgive me."

"There is nothing to forgive. I saw the way she looked at him. I thought her an angel before, but the smile she gave him was truly beatific. She liked me, I am sure, and she enjoyed our time together. But, she *loves* him."

"How do you feel now?"

"I am happy for her. Truly. It took a little while, but I do not regret Miss Bennet."

Darcy nodded then looked down in confusion. "I do not understand. Elizabeth is very close with her elder sister. She would know if she was engaged. You say she looked happy?"

"Yes, very much. Perhaps Miss Elizabeth took your objections as a slight against her family and was offended on their behalf."

"I suppose so."

They were interrupted by another knock, followed by James entering the room with a note for Darcy.

"It is from my cousin Wakely. He heard I am back in town and has invited me to join him at his boxing club."

Bingley tilted his head in contemplation. "It is an odd time of day to watch men beat each other to a pulp, but why not? Perhaps we need a little physical pain to distract us from our broken hearts."

"I thought you were not hurt by your rejection."

Bingley rolled his eyes. "I am just trying to be supportive, Darcy. Let's go and get our hands dirty."

Chapter 19

"Lizzy!"

"Jane!"

Elizabeth was barely through the door at her uncle's home when she was pulled into a tight embrace. She and Maria left Kent that morning, accompanied by two servants, in Anne's carriage. Elizabeth assured her it was not necessary as they planned to travel by post, but Anne insisted on treating her friends.

"Do not be silly, Lizzy. You are far too important to be trusted to the post."

Elizabeth laughed. "I would hardly say that, Anne. I am no more special than the letters traveling in the same conveyance."

"To some you are."

Elizabeth knew that was a reference to Darcy. In spite of her admonishment, Anne continued to bring Darcy into the conversation whenever she could. Elizabeth was relieved to now be among people who knew nothing of the goings on in Kent. She had told Jane only that Darcy and Colonel Fitzwilliam were visiting Rosings and she had seen them a number of times.

"Oh, Jane. I am so happy to see you."

Jane released her sister and took her hand. "I am happy to see you, too, Lizzy."

Maria was greeted a little less enthusiastically but with warmth. Jane walked in front of them to the sitting room where she rang for refreshments.

"Aunt Gardiner will be home soon. She had some household business to tend to this afternoon. We did not think you would be here this early."

"Yes, traveling with a team of horses makes for a much shorter trip than going by post." Elizabeth was so lightened by seeing her sister that she actually felt hungry. For the first time in a fortnight, she filled her plate with her favorites. She smiled at Jane in gratitude.

"A team of horses?"

"Oh yes." Maria joined the conversation. "Miss de Bourgh—Anne--insisted we use her carriage. I have never sat in such luxury, except at Rosings, of course."

"Miss de Bourgh was kind to you, then?" Jane looked to Elizabeth in confusion. "Your letters made it seem she was not very nice."

"I am afraid I wrote that to you in ignorance. We had the opportunity to get to know Anne these last two weeks. She is quite lovely. She reminds me of you."

"That is wonderful. I am glad you made a friend. Will you correspond with her, do you think?"

"I believe so. She has become rather important to me." Elizabeth did not add that Anne was her only remaining connection to Darcy.

The ladies ate their fill while recounting their time in Kent. Jane was shocked when they told her how Anne banished Lady Catherine, but was soothed when they insisted the Lady deserved it. They soon retired to refresh themselves before dinner with the family. As expected, after a few minutes Jane joined her sister in their room.

"Lizzy. I must speak to you about tomorrow."

"Are you happy to be returning to Longbourn? You have not been home for several months."

"I am anxious, actually. Lizzy, Mr. Burton is escorting us to Longbourn. He is going to speak to Papa."

Elizabeth gasped and placed her hand over her mouth. Effusive congratulations followed.

"Oh, Lizzy! I do not deserve so much happiness. He is such a good man, and he loves me."

"Of course he does." Elizabeth hugged her sister tightly. "There is so much to love."

Both sisters were now crying. Elizabeth was overjoyed at the news, but something clawed at the back of her mind. She would have to think on it when she was alone.

"Lizzy, do you think Mama will be happy?"

"Of course. She is finally marrying off a daughter. Why are you concerned?"

"His income is not what she would wish, I am sure."

"Jane, Mama is not so mercenary. She will be happy so long as there is a room for her at his estate."

They both laughed. "Oh dear. She will inquire about that tomorrow, will she not? We must prepare him for what to expect from our parents. Pray, Lizzy, that we get him to the altar before something dreadful happens."

Jane spoke in jest and Elizabeth laughed dutifully. However, in her mind Elizabeth was doing just that.

Dinner was a noisy affair as they were joined by Mr. Burton and the Gardiner's two eldest children. Elizabeth took advantage of the chatter and asked Mrs. Gardiner if there had been any word from Lydia.

"I have not received a letter from Lydia, but my cousin wrote that she is better."

"That is all she said?"

"I am afraid so. I wrote her back asking for more detail. I also wrote to Lydia that we want to hear from her as well."

"I hope she will write to us. I am anxious for her."

"I know dear. I do have some good news, however. We will be able to see her sooner than expected. We will leave in early July and rent a house for us to stay in during her last weeks of confinement. You will see her in just six weeks."

"That *is* good news." Elizabeth looked down the table at Mr. Gardiner who was speaking to Jane and Mr. Burton. "I must thank my uncle for his troubles. He is going through considerable expense to house us for so long. Perhaps my father could be persuaded to help."

"No, dear. We will not ask him. Edward has enough worries; there is no need to add an argument with your father to them."

Elizabeth nodded and again looked down the table. "Aunt, how will it affect Mr. Burton if we are unable to conceal everything? Should we try to postpone the wedding until Lydia is home?"

Mrs. Gardiner shook her head and placed her hand over Elizabeth's. "You are a good sister to be concerned. I think we should do the opposite and encourage them to marry as soon as possible. Jane, at least, will be secure, even if the rest of you become tainted by association. Mr. Burton does not travel in a fashionable social circle. His sister is already married so there is no risk of ruined prospects there. His estate is so far from Longbourn that I doubt any rumor would have much effect on his social standing. That is, if they are married when the truth comes out. If it were learned before, he may wish to break the engagement."

Elizabeth found that scenario doubtful as she saw the loving looks Mr. Burton bestowed on her sister. Still, she agreed they should not risk it, even if it were improbable. She would miss Jane terribly, but would do everything she could to get her married and moved to Yorkshire within the month.

The smell of sweat and the sound of flesh colliding permeated their senses as Darcy and Bingley entered the room. Darcy's stomach rolled in objection to the odors but he gave no outward sign of discomfort. He scanned the room for Viscount Wakely while taking in the scene surrounding them.

Men of all sizes and in various states of dress filled the space. One of the men, a short yet broad individual, approached them asking what they wanted. Darcy told him they were there to see the viscount and the man nodded to the left. Bingley looked around curiously as they made their way to Wakely while Darcy maintained his dignified presence.

Wakely, in breeches and bare feet, circled another man with his fists raised. His hair had grown since Darcy last saw him, and it draped wildly around his face. His eyes held a look of intense concentration mixed with amusement. The circle continued for what seemed like long minutes when suddenly Wakely's opponent landed a blow across his jaw. Wakely stumbled only slightly before his right arm hooked in front of his body, drawing his fist across the man's chin. He barely flinched and the look of surprise on Wakely's face made Darcy and Bingley chuckle. The two men, along with another who had been observing, looked in their direction.

Wakely smiled good naturedly. "Find something amusing, gentlemen?"

"Indeed, Wakely. This man stands at least three inches above you and is about half a foot broader. That tap you just gave him must have been most irksome."

"Well, Mr. Bingley, if you can do better, then I cede my time to you, my man."

Bingley laughed. "Oh no. If my very expensive education served no other purpose, it taught me not to pick a fight I cannot win." He looked around the room. "Surely there is some little fellow here I can spar with."

Wakely pointed to an area close by where two other men were fighting. One seemed to be just the right size. "Let us see what he can do."

They all turned curiously to the match. Much like Wakely's, one partner had a distinct advantage in size. While they watched, however, the larger man did not land a single blow. The smaller of the two was able to escape his every effort and eventually he caught the man twice in the stomach and once in the jaw, sending him to the floor.

Bingley grimaced. "Perhaps a sickly one, then?"

The men all laughed then the one who had been observing Wakely spoke.

"As you see, sir, size will not guarantee advantage. You do not need great bulk to defeat a giant." He gestured to the roped off area Wakely had fought in and the man who still occupied it.

Bingley removed his coat and pulled at his cravat. "I don't suppose you have a slingshot?"

"You do not need one. Come, listen to my instructions and you may walk away from this unharmed."

Darcy and Wakely stood aside and watched as Bingley was sent to the floor time and again. Darcy could not help but laugh.

"Bingley is usually much better at following orders."

"Perhaps we should send for that sister of his. I would imagine she would give any man in here a run for their money. She would not even need her fists. She need only speak and half the men in here would hit the floor. Have I ever thanked you for that particular introduction?"

Darcy smiled. "I introduced you to *Bingley*. He cannot be blamed for his unfortunate relations. Do we not all have someone we are ashamed of?"

"I suppose you are correct. How *is* Lady Catherine?"

"Bitter, angry, vulgar and no longer mistress of Rosings."

Wakely raised his eyebrows in question.

"Anne sent her to the dower house. De Bourgh's will stipulated that if Anne was not married by the age of five and twenty, the estate would pass to her. She took charge the day we left Kent. Did Fitzwilliam not tell you?"

Wakely's countenance darkened. "I have not seen my brother since before you left."

"How did you know I was in town, then? I have not put the knocker on the door."

Wakely looked at him in bemusement. "Darcy, a man like you cannot visit certain establishments without the entire town taking about it. You have always *avoided* those places. After all this time, what brought you there last night, especially with that particular woman?"

"Your brother brought me there, and what particular woman?"

"I heard you enjoyed the favors of Olivia Wallace. She was one of the women my father had picked out for you. I suppose he tired of paying for two mistresses and sent her back to the brothel."

Darcy looked back to the match just as Bingley attempted to make contact with his fist. He missed.

"That is why she seemed familiar. I could not truly make out her features. I was rather impaired at the time."

Wakely let out a short laugh. "And my brother decided to introduce you to this particular debauchery while you were in such a state. Did he convince you to gamble away Pemberley as well?"

Darcy shook his head. "Nothing happened. Bingley was there and brought me home before I could do something I would regret."

"I would not say nothing happened, cousin. You may have remained upright but people are talking. You were seen inebriated and embracing a well-known courtesan. I would be surprised if it was not in the papers today."

Darcy cursed. "One bloody night that I can barely remember! That is all it takes to soil a reputation?"

"I doubt you are soiled, Darcy. In fact, you probably gained the respect of every gentleman there. You are now on their level, in their eyes, anyway."

Darcy growled. "I care very little for their opinion. What if Georgiana sees it?" *Or Elizabeth.* His headache returned.

"Georgiana is at Pemberley?"

Darcy nodded.

"I would not worry about it, then. I do believe you should be concerned about Richard, though. What was he thinking?"

Darcy shook his head. "I have not given much thought to his intentions. My head aches too much for consideration."

"Do you want to tell me why you imbibed? Did my brother have something to do with that as well?"

Darcy was quiet for a few moments, thinking about his reasons for drinking the day before. He accepted the blame for his argument with Elizabeth, at least in that he had given her reason to not trust him. But, Fitzwilliam's part in it was still questionable. He knew the words his cousin had spoken to Elizabeth, but Darcy now questioned his motivation.

"Perhaps."

"Perhaps?"

"We argued a great deal while in Kent. I did not approve of his behavior at times."

They were interrupted by a loud clap followed by a shout.

"Ha! Did you see that Wakely?"

The gentlemen turned to see a very proud Bingley pointing to his opponent who was shaking his head in confusion.

"No, I missed that, Bingley. Do it again."

Bingley's face fell as his friends laughed at him, but he raised his fists and continued.

Wakely turned back to Darcy. "He is not the boy we played with as children. He has grown covetous and wants what he cannot have. Whatever you treasure, you should shield from him as much as possible. Did I tell you Victoria has gone to the country?"

Darcy looked at his cousin's raised eyebrows then back to the match where Bingley was starting to get the better of his opponent. His mind wandered to the times he and Fitzwilliam had almost come to blows in Kent. Each time was over Elizabeth.

Darcy had been so sure of his decision to protect Elizabeth from his aunt. But, what if by doing so left her vulnerable to the machinations of another?

Richard Fitzwilliam leaned against the headboard as he strained to read the paper. He looked over to the woman who was sharing his bed. The dim light of the room served him well when he did not want to see her clearly. The few candles allowed the shadows to hide who she was not. It was not good however, for admiring his handiwork.

The prominent FD from Derbyshire was seen last night in the arms of a very popular lady. We suspect a liaison, but his inebriation could have caused him to stumble,

Most men could laugh at the follies that led to such a publication, but Darcy would be mortified. Everyone would now know his true character. For years Darcy had claimed moral superiority over the rest of the world. Yet, he enjoyed daily assignations with a gentlewoman while he thought no one was watching.

Fitzwilliam was enraged the day he saw them emerge from the trees together. He thought at first it must have been a chance meeting, but then Darcy leaned down and kissed her. Still, he doubted illicit behavior from the pair. He knew the look of a fallen woman, and Elizabeth did not have it. That is, until he and Anne came upon them in the grove. It was obvious to anyone with experience what they had been doing. Elizabeth could also not disguise the extreme jealousy she felt when Darcy left her side to tend to Anne.

He felt a slight twinge of guilt for using Anne to get under Darcy's skin. It was impossible not to care for her and respect her quiet dignity. But even she favored Darcy; so much that she will give him the thing that means most to her. It seems Darcy would be given the entire world if he waited long enough.

His cousin's interest in the lovely Miss Bennet was fairly obvious to Fitzwilliam even in the carriage on the way to Hunsford. Darcy never showed any such emotion, yet he was simultaneously frightened and angry. He had even admonished Fitzwilliam several times over his words about and behavior toward her. *You will not compare Miss Bennet to a whore.* He again looked to his partner.

"Oh, yes I will."

Elizabeth had played him for a fool with her sweet smiles and blushes. She made him believe she enjoyed his attentions, all the while carrying on with his cousin in the bloody forest. Had she ever even considered him, or, like Victoria, was she drawn in by the offerings of a first son?

Fitzwilliam picked up a cigar from the bedside table and took a long drag. He put it down and turned back to his bedmate.

"Wake up, love. You made the papers."

The figure beside him raised her hands above her head and stretched, giving him a view of her ample assets.

"What?"

"Here." He tossed the paper in her lap and watched her scan it until she found the correct passage.

"Hmm. He certainly did stumble—right out of my grasp. I almost had him to my chamber before that other man took him away."

Fitzwilliam scowled. Even this woman had been chosen for Darcy. It would seem she still preferred him.

"Must you sound so disappointed? Do you find a drunk eight and twenty year old innocent that appealing?"

"I find your father's money appealing. If I had succeeded last night he might have renewed my situation. I much prefer one man to half a dozen, especially for more money."

"And he is the one man you want?"

She smiled seductively and rolled over to press her bare chest against his. "Of course not. I only truly want you."

"You are a liar."

"Darling, you do not pay me to be sincere."

He rolled her back over and pressed her into the bed. "No, that is *not* what I pay you for."

Without preamble, he entered her in one long thrust. He took her wildly and every time it seemed he would finish, he continued on even harder. He concentrated on the growing sensations that took him to the edge of pleasure, but instead he found a growing void.

He closed his eyes tight to the image that would not let him rest: Elizabeth displaying the look of heartache that mirrored Darcy's the night before. Fitzwilliam ground into her harder, needing the release but feeling only grief.

Defeated, he finally relented and withdrew from her. He sat on the edge of the bed and listened as Olivia gathered her clothes and left the room. He would feel guilty about hurting her later. At present he had room for only one bit of remorse.

Chapter 20

Elizabeth sat in her father's study, waiting for the man to appear. Their party arrived safely early in the afternoon and had been greeted warmly by their mother and sisters, yet cautiously by their father. Elizabeth had not heard from him while she was in Kent and had written him only to give word of their safe arrival. After the effusive greetings calmed, Mr. Bennet asked her to meet him in his study after she was settled. Elizabeth was curious as to what her father wanted.

"Lizzy."

She turned her head and gave him a half smile as he came into the room. In spite of her lessened opinion, Elizabeth still loved him and did not like the tension between them. She could not live the next six weeks missing Darcy, worrying for Lydia, *and* resenting her father. Something would have to give.

"You wanted to see me, Papa?"

"Yes, Lizzy. I feel I have not seen you in some time, now. Even before your trip I rarely saw you."

"Lydia needed me with her. Papa, I will not pretend she does not exist."

Mr. Bennet nodded and looked down to his desk, toying with something there. He did not look up but spoke softly. "I would not expect you to. How is she?"

"I am told she is well."

He looked slightly alarmed and Elizabeth hoped he was softening to the plight of his youngest daughter. "She has not written you?"

"No, but Aunt Gardiner's cousin assures her that Lydia is better, though she is still often ill."

He nodded. "You mother was like that for a long while."

Elizabeth held her breath. Was he to acknowledge that Lydia was with child? As soon as the thought emerged in her, it seemed to vanish in him. He cleared his throat and sat up straighter.

"Well, tell me about Mr. Collins. Did he remind you often of the prospect you wasted?"

Elizabeth tilted her head. "At every opportunity."

"And what of the great Lady Catherine de Bourgh?"

"Everything you would expect, sir. You would have found her most diverting."

He smiled with every question and Elizabeth answered with some bit of amusement in her voice. Recalling her time in Kent with good humor was impossible at present, bur her father need not know that.

"Well, well, off you go then. I will not keep you from your mother. I am sure she wants to hear about the Collins' herself. Oh, Lizzy, one more thing. What think you of Jane's Mr. Burton?"

"I think he is a fine match for Jane, and she loves him. I hope you will help convince Mama not to prolong the engagement more than necessary." She looked at him pointedly, hoping he understood.

"Yes, a short engagement would be best. I will speak to her."

When Elizabeth joined the rest of the family in the sitting room she thought perhaps she should turn around and retrieve her father. Mrs. Bennet had begun her arguments.

"Oh, Jane how could you ever think of marrying so soon? No, it cannot be done. We must have at least two parties here at Longbourn plus the wedding breakfast, of course. Our neighbors will want to host you as well. Lady Lucas has been my friend for too long to slight her in such a way. Of course she will want to celebrate my eldest getting married."

"You did not host a party for Charlotte, Mama." Kitty observed.

"Mind your business, girl. That is of no matter. We must also wait for Lydia." She began crying. "Our poor Lydia. She will want to see her sister marry. You must wait until she comes home."

Jane, who had been determined to resist her mother's urgings, wavered at the mention of Lydia. She looked to Elizabeth for help.

"Mama," Elizabeth began. "Mr. Burton must return to his estate before the end of summer."

Mrs. Bennet interrupted. "That is well, then. He may go and then come back again when Lydia is here."

Kitty once again made an attempt at reason. "But will he not need to be here for the parties?"

"Kitty will you please be quiet? I am trying to plan your sister's wedding."

"Mama," Elizabeth began again. She leaned in close and spoke low.

"Yorkshire is a long way from here. Anything could happen during the journey. What if he became injured or worse? Jane would never escape the disgrace of having a betrothed die before the wedding. She would have to wear black without the privilege of being a widow. You know that is the one color that does not become her."

The women watched as Mr. Burton moved from his place beside Jane to the window. He rested his elbow against the pane and covered his mouth with his fingers.

"Oh, Lizzy! You should not say such things out loud. It is bad luck! Now we have no choice. We cannot tempt fate. Mr. Burton, you will stay here until the wedding. Kitty!"

"I am here, Mama."

"Kitty, go to your father and have him ride out to the church immediately to arrange for the banns to be read. Oh, we must wait until Sunday. Why cannot they be read on a Tuesday, I do not know. Mary! Mary! Oh, where is that child."

Mary stood from her seat beside her mother. "Yes, Mama?"

"Mary, come with me to my rooms and write down everything I tell you. We must make extensive lists of everything we. . ." Her voice trailed behind her as she walked up the stairs.

Elizabeth bit her lip and looked to the window to see how her future brother fared. She was relieved to see him fighting back laughter.

"Miss Elizabeth, I am not sure how I feel about you treating my potential death so casually. I suppose I should be grateful, though, that I do not have to wait until the autumn to marry." He reclaimed his seat and lifted Jane's hand to his lips.

Elizabeth laughed. "I am glad to see you have a sense of humor, sir. You will need it this next month. Mama has been waiting more than twenty years to plan a wedding. Hertfordshire may never be the same."

"Lizzy, do you not think Mama is correct, though? Perhaps we should wait for Lydia to return. I should like to have all my sisters at my wedding."

Both Elizabeth and Mr. Burton looked at her in alarm. They each waited for a moment to see if the other would object. Elizabeth was the first one to speak.

"Jane, Lydia would not want you to wait. I think she would feel guilty if you did so because of her. However, the promise of a visit to Yorkshire just might lift her spirits."

"Indeed, Jane, we could send for her as soon as she feels up to making the trip. We can invite all your sisters to spend a few weeks, if you like."

Jane beamed at her beloved. "Oh, I would like that very well. As much as I am looking forward to marrying, I admit to some apprehension about the distance between my new life and my family. Knowing I will see my sisters soon is a comfort. Thank you, Samuel."

"You are quite welcome, my dear."

Seeing the tender looks exchanged by the couple, Elizabeth felt she was intruding. She rose and walked toward the door.

"I need to see to a few things. I will return shortly." Mr. Burton smiled softly and Jane blushed bright red, but did not protest. Elizabeth turned to hide her smile and left to retrieve a book from her father's study. On the way she encountered her mother.

"Lizzy? Where are Jane and Mr. Burton?"

"Oh, they are still in the sitting room. I was just going for a book. I thought you were making lists." She hoped that would serve as a suitable distraction from the fact she had left them alone.

"Oh, you clever girl! Now, you musn't leave them alone for too long. But, he will expect some liberties and she must keep him interested."

"Mama."

"Oh, hush. I am glad to have run into you. With all the excitement over Mr. Burton accompanying you girls home, I did not have the opportunity to ask you if you have had a letter from Lydia."

"I have not, Mama, but Aunt Gardiner's cousin has sent word that Lydia is a little recovered."

"That is good. Still, I would wish to have a letter written by her, just to be sure. I wonder why she has not written any of us."

"Lydia has never been a faithful correspondent."

"That is what your father said, but I do not believe it. She has never had anyone to correspond with, given she has never been away from home before. She could, of course, write to you or Jane when you go to visit friends, but where is there interest in that? The ones who stay home have nothing to write about, except the workings of a house the reader already knows well. It is the one who has traveled that stirs curiosity. Now that she is the one who has gone, she should write."

The worry her mother felt for Lydia showed in the way she expressed herself quietly and without the demand for attention. Elizabeth could put aside her feelings toward her father to be sorted through at a later time. She could not do so with her mother's grief. It was too palpable and hung between them like a heavy shade. Elizabeth stepped closer and embraced her.

"Oh, Mama. We must have faith that she will be home soon." She released her before she continued. "We will be leaving to retrieve her a few weeks earlier than we planned. She may not be ready to come home then, but I promise to write so that you no longer have to wonder."

Mrs. Bennet's face brightened with the news. "That is good, Lizzy. Longbourn just is not the same without her. Now, let us retrieve those two for dinner. We are only having two courses since no one informed me of Mr. Burton's visit ahead of time. There will be enough time, however, for you to explain why I had to hear of your carriage accident from Lady Lucas."

Elizabeth had not wanted to worry her family so soon after saying goodbye to Lydia, so she made no mention of the carriage accident in her first letter after her arrival. In truth, so much had happened since then she hardly remembered it, and she forgot to write to them about it before Sir William returned. She received no letter of query from her family so the incident was soon forgot.

While seated at dinner, however, it seemed to be the only interesting topic. Everyone had questions. Her father wanted to know if she had been hurt. Mary asked if she had managed to confess her sins before the crash. Kitty was only interested in the men who came to her rescue.

"Was it very romantic, Lizzy?"

Before Elizabeth could answer, her mother exclaimed, "Do not be ridiculous, Kitty. It was Mr. Darcy. It must have wounded his great pride to have to help someone he considered only tolerable."

Elizabeth tilted her head and replied. "You should not say that, Mama. He was very kind and solicitous."

"Oh? He has changed since the autumn, then?"

"No, Mama. I believe in essentials, he is the same as he ever was. I found that in getting to know him more, I came to a better understanding of his disposition. He is a very kind and honorable man."

She could have spoken all evening on Darcy's good qualities, but doing so would draw too much scrutiny. Jane had already given her a curious look but thankfully asked nothing further.

The weeks before the wedding passed quickly and Elizabeth soon was to lose her eldest sister's company. The emotions that came with that fact ran between joy, jealousy, and fear. Most of all, though, Elizabeth was happy for

Jane. She had found love with a good man and would spend the rest of her life caring for him and the family they would create together.

One evening after dinner, Elizabeth sat at a little writing desk in her room, tracing the pattern on Darcy's emblem with her fingers. It had turned brown and in spite of her best efforts at preservation, it was falling apart. She sat it down next to a sketchpad she borrowed from Kitty, who had recently taken up drawing. Elizabeth picked up a pencil and tried to mimic the pattern. On her third attempt she was as satisfied with the result as believed possible.

The original was then folded into some paper and put it in her box of recollections. She placed the copy inside a journal she purchased on one of the many shopping expeditions they had made for the wedding. A long sigh escaped as she lowered her head.

She missed him. Her mother kept her busy with tasks for the wedding and in between she spent as much time with Jane as she could. But, his memory was always there in the recesses, waiting for its share of her attention. She wished she could share the details of her life with him. It was easy for her to imagine his smile when she told him about the way she laughed at Jane's moony eyes or his look of concern when she expressed how tired she was.

Her hands softly roamed over the journal as an idea formed in her mind. She could not speak to him with her mouth, so she would do so with her heart. Elizabeth opened the book and began writing.

My Dearest Fitzwilliam,

Since leaving Kent, my days seem exceedingly long. I retire soon after dinner each night and resist the pull of the morning. When I must be awake, I busy myself with wedding preparations and doing what I can to shield Mr. Burton from Mama. He has a cheerful, witty disposition and manages her effusions with good humor, but he is not yet her son. Mama has a way of estranging people who are not bound to her by blood.

He is a good man and I am happy for Jane. She will have a good life. I am a selfish creature, however, and indulge in my melancholy when I think how I am losing another sister. It is a strange combination of joy and grief that follows me through my days. I suppose that is what makes up love. Finding joy in another's happiness combined with the pain of losing them. I make every effort to concentrate on the good, for I am not formed for ill humor. There are times, however, when I wish I could somehow return to the days before last summer, when I lived in ignorance of the harsher aspects of life. But, then, I would not know you.

As write this I can hear my sisters downstairs at the piano. You told me once that Miss Darcy has a natural talent combined with passion for music. The same cannot be said for my sisters. Mary approaches the pianoforte as she does with everything—routine precision. I have never known anyone who could keep their sentiments so well in check. Seeing her attempt to teach Kitty, who is all uncontrolled emotion, to play is extremely diverting.

I am happy to see them together in any goings-on. They grew close without having three other sisters here to distract them. Papa has, thankfully, insisted on them staying home more and each had no choice but to look to the other for company. It seems they have found a treasure in their new bond. I do not know how that will change when Lydia comes home, but I pray they will love her as much as they now do each other.

I rarely see my father. He avoids the wedding planning that has taken over the estate as much as possible. There was a time when I would have hidden with him. It is probably very wrong of me to not try to regain our closeness, but I simply do not have the energy to feel anything else at present. Some part of the pain must remain in the shadows or else I cannot manage even the semblance of contentment. I would rather think on you and my sisters. Though there is grief, the joy I feel in loving you gives me hope that all will be well.

I do love you, my Fitzwilliam. I wish I could tell you how much. Until then, I remain forever, your

Elizabeth

Chapter 21

The pale light of dawn danced across his face. Still in slumber, Darcy attempted to wave away the annoyance, but the morning was persistent. With eyes still closed, he rolled onto his elbow and slowly rose. He paused midway as the pain in his side greeted him, reminding him he was not at home. The dark gray walls of the room contrasted with the warm rays now filling the space and Darcy's eyes finally opened to take it all in.

After watching Bingley and Wakely fight, Darcy decided to try it himself. He was bigger and, he thought, stronger than his friends and believed he would do better against the overly muscled lout who took them both down. He was incorrect. The result was a thorough beating. A cut on the chin and a bruised midsection served as reminders of his foolish arrogance.

The physical exertion, though painful, was a welcomed relief from the questions that plagued him. Wakely's words about Fitzwilliam wanting what was not his resonated in Darcy's mind. On the way back to the townhouse that day, Darcy recalled every conversation they had regarding Elizabeth. Twice they had nearly fought over Fitzwilliam's behavior toward her. Darcy's attention to Elizabeth in the carriage should have been enough to tell Fitzwilliam of his interest. The fact that he became so angry at the smallest slight to her could only confirm it.

It was not difficult to believe that Fitzwilliam would hold an attraction for Elizabeth. What Darcy did not want to believe was that his cousin would want to purposely harm him. The idea of it went against everything he knew of Fitzwilliam. He was on the verge of dismissing the idea altogether when he arrived home and saw a note waiting for him.

Darcy,

I am glad to hear you have finally made use of my gift. You may not be marrying Anne, but I forgive you. Now that we have more than blood in common, perhaps we can finally be friends. Come see me when you can.

Matlock

There was no longer any doubt: his best friend had ushered him into the arms of his enemy. Matlock now had what he wanted—a chance to see Darcy be less than what he was raised to be. He was one of them, even if only for a night. He immediately wrote to Fitzwilliam, asking him to come to Darcy House, but the demand was rebuffed.

My duties do not allow for a visit at this time. I still hope to see you at Pemberley later this summer.

Darcy was angry and wanted to hear the truth from Fitzwilliam--that he had taken him to that place to cause his humiliation. More than that, Darcy wanted to know if Fitzwilliam purposely said things to Elizabeth that would cause her to hate him. He did not deny his own fault in their argument; he should have spoken his feelings. But he increasingly found it suspect that her anger over Jane and Bingley should have erupted so violently when it did.

He rose and strode through the sunlight to the vanity. The room was sparse, with only the essentials needed for sleep and hygiene. He poured water into a basin and splashed his face and hair, allowing the coolness to chase away the remaining sleep from his mind. His hand ran down his face, over the beard that was growing thick. He had left his valet behind at the townhouse; his current accommodations did not require the dress of a gentleman. A rudimentary meal would be served later in the day and Darcy would eat it without tasting. Like everything in the room surrounding him, food merely served a function. Quickly pulling on a pair of breeches and a shirt, he completed his ablutions and left the room.

The sounds of flesh striking again filled his ears as he entered the same room where he fought that first day. It was now common, along with the sights and smells he had previously found savage. With no cravat, an open shirt and bare feet, he quite fit the picture.

After reading the notes from his uncle and cousin, a kind of agitation came upon him like he had never before experienced. He felt the need to move, to strike, to run. The only place he could run to was Pemberley, but he was not prepared yet to go there without the hope of her joining him. Instead he returned to Wakely's club and received instruction from Mr. Steele, who had observed him the day before. The man's surname was rather apt, in Darcy's opinion, given his physique, formed from years of pugilistic exercises. He could likely do the work of an ox, and his disposition matched his burley frame. Darcy was again matched with the man who beat him before, and again suffered many cuts and bruises.

On his third visit, he decided to take a room at the club. He felt suffocated in the townhouse. The air was too thick with regret and what could have been. More than once he thought how he should be celebrating his engagement. At least the club was a place where he never imagined Elizabeth. The only visions of her there were in his dreams.

After two thrashings, Darcy was determined to triumph over the brute who had bested him both times. Mr. Steele convinced him to begin his training against a more appropriate opponent.

"Smith has already learned you, Mr. Darcy. You must become someone else if you are to beat him now. Let us begin with Jones here."

He pointed to a man roughly the same size as Smith and just as menacing. Darcy looked at Steele doubtfully.

"He does not yet know you. Perhaps you can tire him before he learns your movements. Remember, your feet are as important as your fists." He waved and Jones moved toward them dutifully.

Darcy removed his shirt and instantly regretted it as his opponent's eyes landed on his bruises. The fight had not yet begun and he had showed his weakness. They circled each other as they had been taught to do, examining the flaws and determining the best course of action.

For Darcy, that was putting up his fists and blocking the first strike. He had learned from his bouts with Smith that the more experienced fighters were eager for quick victories against the unproven newcomers. Ego was a fragile thing, even for those with many wins behind them. Humility would not serve Darcy in this fight. He had to believe he could slay the giant.

Darcy moved quickly, as Steele had advised, and mostly managed to avoid being caught by Jones' fists.

"That is good, Mr. Darcy. Your ability to avoid a blow and even to take one without falling is excellent." Steele watched closely and would often comment and correct as the fight progressed.

Darcy continued to avoid a strike until Jones drew his attention to one fist while the other landed hard on his side. Air escaped his lungs and he momentarily became lost to the throbbing. Steele stepped in between them and sent Jones away.

"Do not be afraid of the pain, Mr. Darcy. It will make you defensive. The stronger the ache, the greater the need to protect. You knew where the weakness lay, yet you left it open to an attack. Do not do that again."

Still struggling for breath, Darcy looked in his eyes and nodded. When he retired to his room that evening, he reflected on Steele's words.

You knew where the weakness lay, yet you left it open to an attack.

He had done that with Elizabeth. He was so distracted by the need to protect her from his aunt that he left her open to the manipulations of his cousin. Not only to his manipulations, but his attentions as well.

Darcy was sure Fitzwilliam visited the parsonage almost daily. Elizabeth was captivating and while he easily understood any man's attraction to her, the mere idea of it made his stomach coil into a tight knot. He had allowed another man to court her favor while he hid in the blasted woods.

The anger Darcy felt over the situation did not dissipate with a night's rest. He arrived downstairs the next morning full of rage and eager to put his fists to work. He asked Steele for a chance to face Smith but was again refused.

"You are not yet ready, Mr. Darcy. What good is starting a fight you cannot win? As I said, you must become someone different. You avoid blows well and manage not to fall when hit, but it is not enough."

Jones stood in front of him again and this time Darcy did not wince as he removed his shirt.

"Remember, Mr. Darcy, be quick and reflexive, protect and strike."

The men took the proper stances and again circled each other. Darcy kept his movements quick and light as instructed. Jones made the first move, but Darcy quickly dodged before his fist could land. This happened several times and Darcy could see his opponent's frustration. Jones tired after a while and Darcy saw an opportunity to strike as he left his jaw unguarded. He hesitated slightly, which was enough to alert Jones who covered his weak spot and landed his only blow that day. It was enough to cause Darcy to stumble.

"That is enough for today. Thank you, Jones."

"I am not finished," Darcy protested.

"Yes you are. You read him well, Mr. Darcy. You saw he had protected his jaw through the match. But, when he forgot and exposed it, you were too slow to take advantage. Hesitation cost you the victory. You will not win if you are afraid to strike. You will always be a step behind if you concentrate solely on defense."

Hesitation cost you the victory. Darcy was tired of protecting himself from the hits he anticipated and more tired of defending himself against the ones that surprised him. He was quite familiar with this dance. It was time to end the pattern.

For the next few weeks he continued to follow Steele's instructions and yesterday he managed to lay Jones to the floor. Today, he would take on Smith.

Darcy said not a word to anyone as he walked through the room. He stopped in front of Mr. Steele and tilted his head toward Smith, who was standing behind him. Steele moved away and gestured for them to take their positions.

Darcy did not waver in making the first strike. He quickly studied his opponent and noticed an almost unperceivable change in breathing when he leaned to the right. At the first opportunity, Darcy hooked his left fist into Smith's side. Rather than pull back and wait for a reaction, Darcy immediately landed a second punch to his now unprotected jaw.**

The giant of a man stumbled back slightly but quickly reversed his momentum and brought his fist around to heavily land on Darcy's mid-section. Darcy had not anticipated his quick recovery and struggled for a moment to catch his breath. He did not, however, relent. Before Smith could block him, Darcy again attacked his weak spot, temporarily sending the man to his knees.

The exchange of blows lasted for some time. Darcy was quick to block and dodge most of Smith's attempts and he could see signs of fatigue in his movements. Darcy moved faster, pushing his own body to the brink of exhaustion. He'd had enough, he determined, and moved to finish. Two short, well timed jabs to the stomach followed by a bone-cracking hit to the jaw, and Darcy's victory was set.

When he saw Smith acknowledge defeat, Darcy lowered himself to the floor, propping one arm on his knee. His breaths were shallow and caused sharp pains up his chest. He startled slightly when he felt something cold and wet under his hand.

"Here, Mr. Darcy." Steele placed two pails of ice on either side of Darcy. "Put your hands in here, it will help with the swelling."

"You have never done this before."

"I suppose now you are worth the expense." Steele smiled and gestured to his left.

Darcy saw a small crowd of men, gathered around, watching him. He had not noticed them before, but assumed they had watched the match.

"You have made me a small fortune today, Mr. Darcy. Few were willing to bet against a man like Smith, not even those who witnessed you defeat Jones."

"You believed I would win? That was quite a gamble, was it not?"

"Not particularly. I have often seen that men fighting their own demons are more willing to take the necessary hits as well as land them. You did an excellent job of drawing his punches and tiring him. So, tell me: was it a betrayal or a woman that had you fighting? Or perhaps both?"

"How long must I do this?" Darcy nodded to the pail. He had no intention of laying his heart out before anybody.

Steele chuckled. "A while. We can take these to your room if you like. You will need to rest a few days before you fight again. If you wish to fight again."

Darcy looked around the room. "I believe it is time I rejoined my own kind."

"Who is to say we are not your kind, Mr. Darcy? We may now be a civilized nation, but those primal forces of our ancestors are still within us. The gentleman must find a way to reconcile with the man inside or they will always be at war, causing one to behave foolishly. A gentleman is taught to protect, while a man recognizes the need to fight. As you have seen, only the combination will achieve victory."

Steele rose and offered his arm to Darcy, who grasped his elbow and pulled himself up. Darcy nodded then picked up the pails and walked to his room. As he waited for the swelling in his hands to subside, he contemplated staying on at the club a little longer. He had enjoyed his time away from civilization, even if it had left him bloodied and bruised. Doing so, however, would mean he was hiding. That thought settled like an iron weight in his stomach. He could not hide from his regrets or his responsibilities. He must again become the gentleman, but hopefully with a better understanding of the man he wanted to be.

Chapter 22

"What do you mean you are not going?" Mrs. Bennet was suddenly thrown into a state of panic. Her husband just informed her, a mere seven hours before a party at Lucas Lodge, that he would not be attending.

"I mean precisely that. I will not attend tonight. Please give my apologies to Lady Lucas."

"Mr. Bennet, must you be so irksome? This is the final party before the wedding—you must be there!"

"Why is that, Mrs. Bennet? I am sure it will be no different than the other thirty parties we have been to since the engagement was announced." He sat behind the desk in his study and watched as his wife fluttered about the room.

"*Five*, Mr. Bennet. We have had just five parties in four weeks. Oh, this short engagement! This is the most important for it is at Lucas Lodge. The entire neighborhood will be there."

"I will see the entire neighborhood at church." Believing that to be the final word, he turned his attention to his ledger.

"Oh, who wants you there anyway? Just remain here alone with your smelly books."

He looked up and tilted his head. "I will not be alone. Mary and Kitty will be here."

Mrs. Bennet gasped and stepped closer to the desk. "They most certainly will not. The officers will be there and the girls have not had a dance in weeks."

"They may dance at the wedding breakfast."

"With whom? You would not allow me to invite many young men. We will only have the Lucases."

"That is perfect, then. With our nephews from London, we will have just the right number of single gentlemen for our girls plus one left over for Maria Lucas."

Mrs. Bennet was so overcome with nerves that she could no longer argue. She left the room in a hurry, calling for Jane to do something with her most vexing father. Mr. Bennet let out an amused chuckle.

"Papa, surely you could have managed to not upset her so." Elizabeth had come to the study for a book just before her mother entered and was privy to the entire exchange.

"Lizzy, she is in a constant state of upset. There was nothing else for it. I am sorry to send you to Lucas Lodge alone. I do not want your sisters around the officers, but I cannot state that publically without raising eyebrows. Stay close to Burton and Jane, though I hardly believe it will be necessary. Not even Wickham would be so indecent as to show up at a party celebrating our family."

"He has done worse things." She rose from the couch and placed her book back on the shelf. "Please excuse me; I must help Mama calm."

Elizabeth was grateful that her father had kept the girls away from the militia while she was gone. He said it had been no hardship on Mary and Kitty only complained for the first month. He would not tell them why they were limited socially, only that he had heard some rumors in the village of improper behavior and did not want them exposed to it.

Still, she was disappointed that he would not go to the party. He was leaving it up to Mr. Burton, who knew nothing about what happened to Lydia, to protect his daughters from exposure to Wickham. The way he continued to tease her mother upset her as well. In the past, she would be amused by it, even believing she deserved it for her silly ways. Since Lydia's illness, however, she began to see her mother differently.

Mrs. Bennet was ridiculous. Elizabeth could not deny her lack of proper manners and decorum. She had been embarrassed by her mother more times than she wanted to remember. That had kept Elizabeth from seeing that her mother was a human being. More than that, she was a woman. She carried five children for a husband who showed her no respect and treated her as a joke for two decades. Children are taught to respect their parents and obey their wishes. Wives are subservient to their husbands. Why are men not more obligated in their behaviors?

She pondered those thoughts while she prepared for the evening. Before she left her room, she picked up her pen and asked Darcy.

Why is it, sir, that a man is allowed to do whatever he wishes and be judged very little? If my mother behaved in the same manner toward my father as he does with her, she would be considered a shrew. If the truth about Lydia were to come out, she would be ruined in society while Wickham could just move on to the next village with little harm done. The unfairness of this world can be much disheartening if dwelled upon for too long. Forgive me, I am not asking for a solution, merely giving voice to my frustrations.

She wrote to Darcy every day, mostly about the mundane details of her life at Longbourn. She felt closer to him this way. In one of her early passages, she told him everything about Lydia. Even if it was only on paper, it was a relief to tell him and to explain why she had been so angry that day. He may never see the words, but at least in her heart she had shared them.

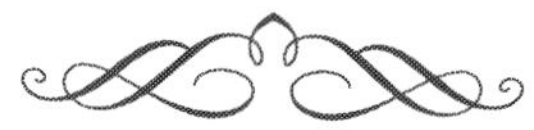

Lucas Lodge was decorated beautifully with all the blooms of the season. Mrs. Bennet was correct when she said the entire neighborhood would be there. Jane had requested the wedding breakfast not involve a large crowd, so this was the last chance for more than half the people there to see Jane before she left for Yorkshire.

Elizabeth found it difficult to remain with the happy couple, as their attention was constantly needed. She spied several of the officers but so far had not seen Wickham. Perhaps her father was right and he would not come. No sooner had she thought those words did the man step behind her as she helped herself to a glass of punch.

"Please allow me to get that for you, Miss Elizabeth."

Elizabeth did not look up from her glass. She had not seen him since November, but still recognized the smoothness of his voice. She had found it charming then, but now it caused her back to stiffen and defenses to rise.

"As you see, I am done."

She began to walk away, but he grabbed her elbow to stop her. Elizabeth looked around the room. She could not see her sister or mother. No one else was at the punch table, but at least they were in plain sight.

"Please do not leave me, yet, Miss Elizabeth. I have not had the pleasure of your company in months. I heard you recently returned from visiting Mrs. Collins in Kent."

"Yes, I did." Elizabeth's gaze remained fixed on the crowd.

"And how did you find the inhabitants of Rosings?"

"Interesting."

"Will you not look at me, Miss Elizabeth?"

She did not respond and he took a step closer.

"I hear Miss Lydia has been ill. I do hope it is nothing too serious. Where is it they sent her off to?"

This got the response he undoubtedly sought. She turned to him, her usually warm expressive eyes turned cold.

"My sister's illness and whereabouts are none of your concern, Mr. Wickham."

He smiled and spoke in a light but quiet tone. "I believe we both know they are. Lydia and I became good friends last autumn. I do miss seeing her in Hertfordshire. She was always so lively."

Elizabeth again attempted to walk away, but once more he prevented her departure.

"Do not leave so hastily, Miss Elizabeth. You do not want to cause a scene."

"What do you want?"

"Merely to speak to you. Sir William told me Darcy was also in Kent."

"He was."

"And how did you find him?"

"Interesting."

"You have already said that. You must use a different description for Darcy. He is as entertaining as watching mud dry."

Elizabeth stepped to the side and turned to look at him. "Again, you speak of Mr. Darcy. You take an eager interest in his affairs. Why are you so fascinated with the gentleman, Mr. Wickham?"

"I would not say I was fascinated, Miss Elizabeth." His voice suddenly lost its charm.

"No? What word would you use, then? I can think of several that could apply to your position where Darcy is concerned. Jealous. Inferior. Servant."

"I was never his servant." He spat the words out bitterly.

"Perhaps not, but neither were you ever his equal. That knowledge is the root of all your resentment toward him, is it not?"

"Miss Elizabeth, we are in a room full of your neighbors. Perhaps it is not wise to provoke me when I know your secrets."

Elizabeth lifted her chin and held his gaze. "I am not afraid of you. I admit there was a time, even earlier today, when I was frightened by you and the power you have over my family's reputation. As I stand here with you tonight, however, I realize something. You are a particular type of evil, one that preys on the favor of others. You feed off their goodwill and their hesitancy to think ill of someone who was supposedly wronged. You have the ability to commit gross indecencies and convince others that you are the victim. You did it with the late Mr. Darcy, here in Meryton, and I am sure everywhere else you have ever resided. You will say nothing about Lydia for this is a game and you will not spoil it before it is complete.

"I will think about you no more, Mr. Wickham. I believe people do get what they deserve in this life. When it is your time, I hope you pay at Darcy's hands and that Lydia and Miss Darcy bear witness. One day, we will all be satisfied with your ruin."

She walked away and did not look back. If she had, she would have seen that her words had the desired effect. She subtly let him know that her relationship with Darcy was more than it had been in November. Wickham could have exposed his actions with Miss Darcy but as far as she knew he never had. She could only hope it was some fear of Darcy that kept him from doing so and her implied intimacy with the man would offer her family some protection as well.

She found Jane and managed to smile and enjoy much of the evening. She was anxious to return home and relay the night's events to Darcy. She was warmed through by the thought that he would be proud of her.

Just over a fortnight later, Elizabeth once again stood in front of Longbourn saying goodbye to her family. It was not the sad occasion that was Lydia's departure or the joyful one of Jane's. They all expected Elizabeth to return soon and so their goodbyes were not as superfluous.

"Now, Lizzy, I want you to take this for Lydia." Mrs. Bennet handed Elizabeth a thick letter. "It has some new hair ribbons and I told her all about the wedding. Tell her we will have all her favorites when she comes back."

"I will Mama. I am sure she is happy to be coming home."

"And take every opportunity of enjoying yourself while you are there. You may never again be at the sea side."

Elizabeth laughed. "I will try, Mama." She held her mother's hand tightly. "We will be home in just two months."

"Yes, and perhaps when you return we will have new neighbors. I will always regret Mr. Bingley. But, Jane has done well enough with her Mr. Burton. He is not as rich as Mr. Bingley, but—"

"My dear sister, we must be leaving," Mr. Gardiner interrupted. "Thank you for hosting us since Jane's wedding and for taking on the children while we are away."

"Oh, brother!" Mrs. Bennet embraced him. "What would our poor Lydia have done without you to arrange for her stay? You are too good to us."

"There, there, Fanny. We were glad to be of service, but we must set out to retrieve her."

He pulled away to allow his wife to say her goodbyes. While Mrs. Gardiner fussed over her children, Mr. Bennet approached Elizabeth.

"Well, Lizzy, you are off again. I wish you safe travels."

"Thank you, Papa." He seemed to want to say something. He stopped and started a few times so she waited.

"You and I have not spoken much lately, what with the wedding and all. I just want you to know that, well, I miss our conversations. I look forward to everything going back to normal when you return."

His placed his hands on her shoulders and kissed her forehead. Elizabeth let out a sigh of disappointment but managed a smile. He just did not understand that nothing could be the same now. *She* was not the same. Unfortunately, he was the man he had always been.

"Goodbye, Papa. I will write."

Elizabeth embraced both her sisters and her mother once more before turning to enter the carriage. The Gardiners followed behind.

Once they began moving, Elizabeth let out a sigh of relief. "Saying goodbye to Mama feels like falling down a never ending hill. I believe she grows tired of these farewells."

"Well, my dear, hopefully, she will not have another one for a while. Once Lydia is home, I cannot imagine a scenario in which any of you will leave Longbourn again shortly. That is unless some dashing gentleman comes and sweeps one of you off your feet."

Elizabeth laughed. "Oh, Aunt, I do not imagine that will happen anytime soon. It is enough to lose one sister, I am not prepared to lose more at present."

"And what of you?" Her uncle teased. "You will turn some man's head before long, I have no doubt."

Elizabeth blushed. "Uncle, we have a long journey ahead of us. Can we not discuss my sorry marriage prospects until we are less than five miles from our destination?"

Mr. Gardiner's laugh filled the carriage. "As you wish, Lizzy. But we must have some conversation. If I cannot tease you then, you must pick a topic."

"Very well. Let us discuss Derbyshire. I am curious about this place you that you love so much, Aunt. Most particularly Lambton."

Mrs. Gardiner sighed. "Derbyshire is the most delightful county in all of England. I do not need to visit the rest of the country to know that. It is lush and green and home to some exquisite estates. Indeed, Pemberley is but five miles from Lambton."

"Five miles?" Elizabeth had not been aware of the close proximity of Pemberley to Lambton. She was unsure if she were more frightened or hopeful that she might see him.

"Yes, dear. The village owes a large share of its prosperity to that great estate though the family is rarely seen there. You renewed your acquaintance with Mr. Darcy in Kent, did you not, Lizzy?"

"Yes, but I could not say we are friends. I do not believe I could secure an invitation."

"I was not suggesting you try, just thinking perhaps you might like to tour the place since you are acquainted with the owner. It is quite majestic with woods and groves that might even satisfy you, Lizzy."

"Oh?"

Elizabeth listened as her aunt talked enthusiastically about Darcy's home. Mrs. Gardiner had toured it once and told Elizabeth as much detail as she could remember about the grounds and manor.

"Of course, this was years ago when Lady Anne Darcy was still living. The current master could have changed things, or he could be waiting for his own wife to do so."

Elizabeth went pale at the thought and Mrs. Gardiner took her hand in alarm.

"Lizzy, are you unwell? Should we stop the carriage?"

Elizabeth was lost to the thought of Darcy's wife and the likelihood that it would be someone other than her. She determined when she left Kent that she would write to him after Lydia was home, but she could not be sure of his understanding or forgiveness. The hurt in his eyes the day of their argument haunted her. She was now traveling to his county and would be a short carriage ride to his home. Even if she did not see him, she could find some solace in the knowledge that he was close by.

"Lizzy," Mrs. Gardiner asked again. "Should we stop the carriage?

Elizabeth shook her head. "No, I am well. I do not wish to delay us, even by a moment."

A hard rain fell over the cottage, bringing a tapping sound into the room where Lydia sat, gripping the edge of the bed. The quick taps fell in time with her heartbeat as she attempted to calm. She stared at the door and its keyhole, which was empty. She could not lock it. She could not keep him out.

He was going to come for her, he as much as said so. She had been in the kitchen, scrubbing plates over the basin when she felt him behind her. His rough hands grasped her hips and he pulled her back against him.

"You are too thin." He hissed disapprovingly. "You just might break underneath me."

She squirmed and twisted in an attempt to break free, but Mr. Baines held her tighter and laughed.

"You cannot claim to be shy." One hand moved from her hip up to her rounded stomach. "This tells me you know exactly what to do."

His breath was thick with drink. The smell mingled with her fear and brought on a powerful wave of nausea. She turned her head to the side as her body expelled all she had consumed that day. He released her immediately, shoving her forward enough that she almost fell into the basin.

"Try to keep better control of yourself. I will find you later."

She managed to complete her chores though her body trembled the rest of the day. She jumped at every noise or movement, thinking he had come back to finish what he had started. She escaped to her room as soon as she could, but now as she stared at the door, she knew she was not safe there.

Tears streamed down her cheeks as she began to panic. Her mind brought forth images of November when Wickham came over her in the barn. The pain had been unbearable and it was going to happen again. Her tears gave way to sobs and her body shook. Through her despair, a sharp pain on her side got her attention.

She put her hand over her stomach as the pain moved from her side to the middle. She rubbed over it as she nodded her head.

"Alright sweet one, we will go. He will not hurt us."

She stood and looked around the room. She was confused and more than a little frightened, but she tried to form a plan. If they saw her go, they might come after her. She had to help prepare dinner but would not be expected to join them since Mr. Baines was home. She never understood why Mrs. Baines allowed her company on the nights he was not there. She always acted as if she would rather not see her. It was of no matter now. She must think.

The money Mr. Gardiner gave her was in the bedside table. She retrieved it along with Elizabeth's necklace and put them in her reticule. She lifted her skirt and tied the small bag to the trim on her chemise. She pulled at the knot as hard as she could to secure it.

The trunk full of her clothes would have to remain. She knew not where she would go. There was no one whom she could ask for help. The cook never spoke to her and always left as soon as the meal was ready to be served, likely to return to her own family. Adam was her only friend and there was nothing he could do for her. She would have to pray that help would be found along the way.

"Lydia!"

Mrs. Baines' loud voice caused her to jump. It was time to start dinner. One hour and she would leave.

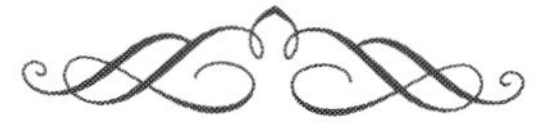

Lydia shivered as she pulled the old work coat tighter against her body. The garment was heavy, but she was grateful for the protection against the wind. It was hanging on the door in the kitchen and she grabbed it without much thought as she hurried outside.

By her estimation, she had been walking a couple of hours. The rain had stopped and the moon lit her way. She had no idea what direction she was going in. She just hoped to find a barn or some sort of shelter for a few hours of rest. Soon, her swollen feet would no longer cooperate with the mud. She hobbled to the closest tree and sat between two large roots at its base.

Before she left the kitchen, she wrapped a piece of bread and some dried meat in a cloth and put in the coat pocket. She was not hungry but forced down the bread to keep some energy. She would save the meat for next day. Hopefully, she would find a way into the next village where she could write to Mr. Gardiner. She worried they would be angry for not telling them sooner that she was frightened of Mr. Baines. She had attempted many times to write her family. Mrs. Gardiner had twice sent packages filled with letters from her mother and sisters. She read them over and over, but never could bring herself to respond. What could she write of--loneliness and fear? Her mother wanted to know of the sea. How could she write of something she had never seen?

Regret and doubt once again invaded her mind. Perhaps it would be better for her family if she never returned. They could tell people she never recovered from her illness and died at the seaside. Her sisters would never be ruined and her father would not have to welcome a fallen woman back into his home.

She fell asleep with those thoughts plaguing her mind and woke to a wet morning. The long branches of the trees had given her some shelter, but she could feel the water in her boots. She slowly made it to her feet and walked forward into the rain. Somehow as she slept she decided she would indeed never return to Longbourn. She would dissolve in the mist that now surrounded her. Lydia Bennet would only be a memory to those who cared about her. She would walk until she found a church, where hopefully the minister would be kind and help her find a safe place to birth her child. She would leave him there and disappear.

The rain gave way to the sun as it rose on the horizon. Wanting to feel some of its warmth, Lydia removed the coat, then let the soaked covering fall to the ground. She shivered but walked steadily toward the rays. The light would deliver her. She had taken two steps forward before dizziness caused her to stop. She knew the pattern. Nausea would now come followed by expulsion. She fell to her knees as her body rejected the bread from the night before. She shook from the violence of it.

She tried to stand, but her legs would not lift her. She was too weak. The muddy earth collided with her cheek as blackness overtook her.

The darkness still claimed Lydia, but she could hear voices coming from the night. They sounded hurried and sharp. A pressure surrounded her and she stiffened and tried to push it away.

"Shhh, little one. I have you."

Lydia stopped struggling and gave into the calmness of the voice and the warmth that now enveloped her. She must have made it to the sun. Her fogged mind could conjure nothing else and she soon felt the warmth shift. She was moving; perhaps floating into the light. But darkness once again claimed her and she fell into a deep sleep.

"You must drink, little one. Here."

The voice was back and she could again feel the warmth, this time trickling into her body. Tea—she could taste it—sweet and creamy just like she preferred. Had she come home?

"Lizzy?" She choked on the word and began coughing. Strong hands lifted her and held on until the fit passed. Her eyes fluttered as she leaned back into the softness underneath her. She grew tired before she could focus and again succumbed to oblivion.

I have laid down my plan, and if I am capable of adhering to it—my feelings shall be governed and my temper improved. They shall no longer worry others, nor torture myself. I shall now live solely for my family. You, my mother, and Margaret, must henceforth be all the world to me; you will share my affections entirely between you.

A different voice spoke to her now, telling her of sisters. She stretched her arms and groaned at their heaviness. The fog was lifting as more words became clear.

"Brother, I believe she is waking."

Lydia felt a weight beside her and a now familiar touch on her hand.

"Are you ready to join us now, little one? We have been anxious for you."

The burden that had kept her eyes closed was gone and she opened them slowly. She kept her gaze down and saw she was in bed, covered with soft, warm linens. The firm hand covering hers gave a gentle squeeze and she moved her eyes up.

"Please do not be alarmed. You are among friends. Do you know who I am, Miss Bennet?"

Lydia focused on the face for a long moment before she could nod. "Mr. Darcy."

Chapter 23

Darcy looked at the girl in front of him. She had been with them for several days and he still could not comprehend what had brought her there.

After taking a few days to heal, he had returned to the townhouse to find a stack of letters from both his steward and his sister. Georgiana's letters had urged him home to Pemberley. Her words of loneliness drew him from his own self-pity and he knew it was time to again focus on her. He set out the morning after he returned to Darcy House but was slowed by heavy rain. He was a few miles from Pemberley's gate when his driver stopped unexpectedly.

"Pardon me, Mr. Darcy," the coachman called from outside the carriage door. Darcy opened it and stepped out. "There seems to be someone on the road here."

Frustration built within him as he assumed some inebriated ruffian had passed out on the road. He walked around the carriage and stopped when he saw it was not a man, but a young girl beside whom his driver was crouched, seemingly afraid to touch her.

"Is she alive?"

"Yes sir, she breathes. I do not know who she is. Likely a servant girl."

Darcy kneeled beside the girl and looked carefully. She wore no bonnet and her dress was caked in mud. Blonde curls covered much of her face. Darcy carefully moved them and took his handkerchief from his pocket. As he wiped away some of the mud from her face, she seemed somehow familiar. The assumption that she must work at Pemberley gave way quickly as he finally recognized the poor soul splayed on the road.

"Good God." Darcy put his arms under her and gently raised to his feet. "Help me get her into the carriage, then drive as quickly as you can to

Pemberley. Take us to the side entrance and as soon as we are inside I want you to fetch the doctor."

"Yes, sir."

Lydia groaned and began to flail as they sped down the road. Darcy held her tighter against him, fearing she would hurt herself.

"Shh, little one. I have you."

What was Elizabeth's sister doing on his property when she was supposed to be at the seaside? She was certainly ill; he could feel her fever through her clothes. They quickly arrived at Pemberley and Darcy stepped from the carriage, still carrying Lydia though his coachman did move to help. He shook his head then ascended the steps as quickly as his burden would allow. He was greeted at the door by his housekeeper.

"What is this?"

"Mrs. Reynolds, I need a fire lit in one of the guestrooms and maids to help tend her."

"Yes, sir." The elderly woman called out orders then quickly followed behind her master. At the top of the stairs, she turned in the direction of the guest wing to find that Mr. Darcy moved in the opposite direction and entered a chamber in the family wing, across from his sister's rooms.

"Move quickly, she is ill." He laid her on the bed and left the room so the maids could tend her. After taking a close look at the girl, Mrs. Reynolds followed.

"Mr. Darcy?"

He turned to see her questioning gaze. "We found her lying in the road." He let out a long breath. "She could have been trampled."

"Do you know her?"

Darcy nodded. "She is the sister of a dear friend. I expect her to be tended most diligently."

"Of course. Shall I send for the doctor?"

"I sent a man already."

"Mr. Darcy, I believe we must also send for a midwife."

Darcy stared in disbelief. "She is a child."

"She is *with* child, sir. That makes this situation all the more precarious."

Darcy stared for a moment, thinking on her words. "Who is with her now? Can they be trusted?"

"Yes, of course. Pemberley's staff is always trustworthy."

Darcy stepped forward and expressed all the authority of a master. "I want no one tending her except those who have already seen her. Make it clear to them that they will lose their positions if word of this ever leaves this house. Miss Lydia's reputation must be kept safe."

"Miss Lydia?"

"Yes. Lydia Bennet from Hertfordshire. I will send an express to her father."

"I believe you should wait, sir. Miss Bennet is far from home. It may be they do not want news of her."

Darcy immediately understood what Mrs. Reynolds was saying. Lydia must have been turned out from Longbourn.

"You are correct. I will wait until I speak to her." Darcy ran his hands over his face. He could hardly comprehend that Lydia Bennet was with child and in his home.

"Brother, what is happening?"

He turned to see Georgiana standing in her doorway. Darcy immediately pulled her into an embrace. More than ever he felt the relief of his sister having been spared such a fate. He would have to explain what she had just overheard.

"Let us go to your sitting room." He turned to Mrs. Reynolds. "Come to me when they are finished tending her."

He noticed the housekeeper's hesitation. "I care nothing for the propriety of it, Mrs. Reynolds. I will see her when she is ready."

Darcy took his sister's hand and led her to a couch in her sitting room. He relayed the events of the morning and she was understandably shocked.

"Oh no! What could have happened to her?"

Darcy shook his head. "I hope to get that information from her when she wakes. I am afraid I am at a loss for any possible explanation."

Georgiana lowered her head. She did not look at her brother as she spoke softly. "I heard Mrs. Reynolds say she is with child."

"Yes."

She raised her eyes slightly. "How old is she?"

"I believe she is your age."

Georgiana finally met his eyes. This could not be an easy conversation to have with an elder brother and Darcy would himself been more uncomfortable were he not still in shock.

"I would like to help tend her. I believe our staff is loyal, but the fewer people who know of Miss Lydia's condition, the better. Mrs. Annesley will help, too."

Darcy's eyes filled with pride as he took her hand. Her compassion had overruled her any discomfort she likely felt.

"We will both tend her as best we can."

The doctor and midwife both examined Lydia and came to the same conclusion—she was in a dangerous predicament and it was unlikely both she and the child would survive delivery.

"That is simply unacceptable." Georgiana had stated firmly. "I am determined she shall be well."

Darcy agreed. Elizabeth's sister would receive the best care and would recover. He simply could not allow otherwise.

Darcy and Georgiana spent most of their time over the next days in Lydia's chamber, reading to her and attempting to bring her fever down. Lydia drifted in and out of consciousness. She would call out for her sister and Darcy's heart sank each time. Elizabeth had been distraught over Lydia's illness. Did she know the truth?

After what seemed like an eternity, her fever broke and she was now fully awake and looking at him in confusion.

"Miss Lydia, you are at Pemberley, my home. We found you lying in the road unconscious. Can you tell me how you got there?"

Lydia pulled at the counterpane and looked down. "He was going to hurt me, so I ran away."

"Who was going to hurt you?"

"Mr. Baines." Her attention was drawn to Georgiana, who was standing next to the bed. Lydia placed a hand over her stomach and looked down. "There is much to tell."

Darcy turned to his sister. "Georgiana, could you please see to some refreshments for Miss Lydia?"

She hesitated, but nodded and left the room.

"That is my sister, Georgiana. She has helped us care for you while you were sleeping. You called out for your sister. Does Miss Elizabeth know . . ." He looked down to her stomach then back up. "Everything?"

Lydia nodded then burst into tears. "Mr. Darcy, please do not think ill of my sisters. They should not be tainted by me. Lizzy is the only one who knows what happened. She took care of me when I was still at Longbourn and would be with me now if she had been allowed."

"I do not doubt that, Miss Lydia. I saw her recently in Kent. She agonized over the distance between you. You need not worry about my good opinion. I assure you it is quite immovable. Please, tell me everything so that I might better know how to help you."

Lydia took a deep breath and calmed. "I am with child."

Darcy nodded. "Can you tell me by who?"

Tears came once again. "I did not know what he would do, Mr. Darcy. He was always so charming, I never thought he might hurt me."

Words became sobs and as Darcy waited the words of another surfaced in his memory. *You knew what he was.* His heart sank to the floor as the reasons behind Elizabeth's anger became apparent. Still, he must know for certain.

"Miss Lydia?"

She looked at him and he took her hand, as much for his own comfort as for hers.

"Please tell me." He paused to catch his breath. "Was it Wickham?"

She breathed in deep and nodded. "Yes."

Darcy ran a hand over his face then rested it on his mouth. He closed his eyes and made an effort to calm his thundering heart.

"I am sorry, Miss Lydia. I am so very sorry."

A knock sounded behind them and Georgiana ushered in Mrs. Reynolds and a maid carrying trays. Everything was laid out on a table by the fire and no one spoke until the girl curtsied and left the room.

"It seems your dinner is here, Miss Lydia."

"Our dinner, brother. I thought we would join our guest if she is not too tired for company."

Darcy smiled at Georgiana's eagerness. "Miss Lydia, may we join you?"

"I do not wish to eat at present."

"You must eat. The doctor said you are too weak."

Lydia lowered her head. "I am often ill when I eat."

"I thought that might be the case, Miss Bennet, and asked cook to prepare some special things that might be easier on your palate."

Lydia looked at Mrs. Reynolds and Georgiana, then to Darcy.

"Forgive me, you have not been introduced. Miss Lydia Bennet of Longbourn in Hertfordshire, may I present my sister, Miss Georgiana Darcy."

Georgiana immediately took the seat on the bed her brother had just vacated. She took Lydia's hand and gave it a gentle squeeze.

"I am pleased to meet you, Miss Bennet. My brother said he met you when he visited Mr. Bingley last autumn."

Lydia nodded and again looked down at the counterpane.

"This is our housekeeper, Mrs. Reynolds."

"Miss Bennet, if there is ever anything you need, please ring for me." She pointed to the cord behind the bed. "I am at your command while you are with us."

Lydia fidgeted with the trim on the counterpane and still would not look up.

"I am fatigued still and would like to sleep."

Darcy could see that Lydia was growing uncomfortable under their scrutiny. He was in need of solitude himself but would remain to see her consume something.

"We will leave you to rest after you have eaten."

Mrs. Reynolds arranged some things on a tray and brought it to the bed. Lydia propped herself on the pillows and looked down at the food. Her stomach rolled.

"I am sorry, but I cannot."

"You must, Miss Lydia. I will not leave this room until you do."

"You had best listen to him. When he uses that voice, there is no use arguing. It is the same one he uses for his horse."

Darcy was on the verge of admonishing Georgiana for her tease when the sound of Lydia's giggle stopped him. He looked at her and saw she had picked up her spoon and was slowly eating the clear broth Mrs. Reynolds had put in front of her.

"I must tend to some business so I will leave you ladies in peace. I will be back shortly, though. I realize you are tired, but we must finish our conversation."

Lydia nodded and Darcy strode from the room. She returned her attention to the broth and managed to finish it.

"Very good, Miss Bennet." Mrs. Reynolds stepped forward to take the bowl. "Now some bread, please."

This time Lydia did not protest. The broth was sitting easy on her stomach and she believed the bread would do the same.

"I am told you have four sisters."

"Yes, Miss Darcy, I do. Jane, Elizabeth, Mary and Kitty. I am the youngest."

"It must be a great comfort to you to have so many."

"I did not always think so, but I do miss them."

"I am envious. I always wanted a sister."

Lydia thought about the family she left behind at Longbourn and her heart ached. She had never truly appreciated what a beautiful gift she had been given. Her thoughts then wandered to the man who had treated her with such care and kindness. For the first time in months, she felt safe.

"I believe I should like to have a brother."

The shadows of the room enveloped Darcy as he sat in contemplation. He leaned over his knees and laced his fingers then rested his head upon them. His breaths were shallow and his eyes were glossy with remorse.

My sister is broken and it is your fault.

Darcy had erroneously believed Elizabeth was speaking of Jane when she shouted those words to him. Not Jane, but Lydia, and she was indeed broken. He could scarcely believe she was the same energetic, boisterous girl who had so fearlessly demanded a ball from Bingley in the autumn. Elizabeth could never possibly forgive him for allowing Wickham to prowl Hertfordshire unchecked. Georgiana's reputation was safe, but at what cost?

Wickham was a deplorable man, but Darcy had never known him to bother with fortuneless gentlewomen. He had been far too mercenary to waste his time with a woman who could not provide him with an easier life. It would seem his quest for pleasure had prevailed over any decency he may have once had.

Darcy shook his head. Why did he find it surprising that Wickham's character would further deteriorate? The man had nothing to lose and lord knows no one had ever tried to stop him. The Darcys were responsible for creating that monster; they should have taken more care to see him pay for his actions.

Silence enables bad behavior and inaction only allows further destruction. Darcy had always believed Wickham would destroy himself with his wicked ways, but he gave little thought to the ones who would be hurt in the process. Elizabeth's sister now faced the consequences of his failure.

He must write to her and tell her of Lydia's situation. She will want to come to Pemberley to care for her sister. Darcy wondered how he could face her, loving her more than ever, yet knowing she would never be his. Hope was persistent and tortured him even now as he grappled with regret. He must try. He must show her by every effort in his power that he had changed, that he would no longer merely react to life's challenges, but be a man who could better control them.

With a renewed determination, Darcy rose from his chair and set out to speak to Lydia. He would see her well no matter the cost or effort, and above all else, he was determined to earn their forgiveness.

Chapter 24

Darcy had returned to Lydia's room after he composed himself. His calm was short lived when he heard Lydia's tale. What Elizabeth must have gone through keeping this secret. No wonder she felt the need to run. If he had known earlier, they could have brought Lydia to Pemberley before she was forced to escape the Baineses. Elizabeth could not have known that, though. Given the way her father reacted, she was likely reticent to trust anyone else.

After Lydia had told him about life with the Baineses, they were both too exhausted to continue. He promised to return the next day after breakfast. When he arrived, Lydia was refusing her tea. Darcy sent the maid away and prepared her cup himself. He hovered until she drank it all then proceeded to ask about her Uncle Gardiner and how he could get a letter to him. She quickly became agitated.

"What is it, Miss Lydia?"

"Mr. Darcy, I ask that you not write to my uncle. My sisters' reputations will be safe if I do not return to Longbourn. I ask instead that you help me find a place for my child, then allow me to go."

"Go where?"

"I know not. I only know I cannot go back to Meryton. My father will not want me and I do not wish to live the rest of my life under the glare of his disapproval."

"Miss Lydia, I promise I will do everything I can to see that no one ever knows of this and that those who do say nothing. I will find a place for your child. I will not send you back to Longbourn if you do not wish it, but I will write to your uncle. Remember I was with your sister in Kent. She worries for you and misses you. I cannot allow you to disappear when it is in my power to return you to her."

Lydia shook her head and began to argue, but Darcy interrupted. He could see the guilt and shame in her features and knew that was behind her wish to flee.

"Listen to me. What happened with Wickham was not your fault."

Lydia was startled for a moment, then shook her head. "How can you say that? I flirted with him and met him in secret. I let him kiss me. I should have known better."

"He did know better, Miss Lydia. Wickham was raised among gentlemen but chose instead to behave like a brute. None of this is your fault. You should have been better protected."

Darcy saw her struggle. She had been blamed for Wickham's actions by the man closest to her and then sent away from everyone she loved. It would likely take time for her to see the truth of the matter.

She continued to look at him as she relaxed into the pillows. "Lizzy and my aunt and uncle were to travel here to be with me during my last weeks of confinement. I am afraid I do not know when they will arrive. It should be soon, I think."

Darcy smiled in relief. He would never have complied with her wishes, but he would rather not keep her against her will.

"I will send a man to Mr. Gardiner's home in London and one to Lambton to see if they have yet arrived. Hopefully, we will find them before they go to the Baineses'. They will be frantic if they find you missing."

"I did not want to cause more trouble."

"Shhh. All will be well. Please just concentrate on getting better. I must go write those letters. Rest for a while, little one."

Darcy sent his fastest messenger to London to seek out Edward Gardiner of Gracechurch Street. He also dispatched a man to Lambton to inquire at the inn and one to locate the Baineses' cottage. With any luck, Elizabeth would be reunited with her sister within the week.

"What do you mean she is not here?" Mr. Gardiner's angry voice resonated through the cottage. They arrived in Lambton and after disposing their belongings at their rented house, hurriedly traveled to the Baineses' where they were told Lydia was gone.

"I mean, Mr. Gardiner, that your niece has run off. She has not been here for several days." Mrs. Baines held her back straight and her features were hard. She could not, however, look at the man in front of her. He turned and went up the staircase to the room where he last saw Lydia.

"That is impossible. Lydia would not just run off without saying anything." Mrs. Gardiner looked at her cousin in disbelief.

"Well, she did, Maddy. Perhaps you should ask our stable boy about her whereabouts. She seemed friendly enough with him."

"You are a liar." Elizabeth stepped forward and closed the gap between her and Mrs. Baines. Panic struck her the moment they entered the house. She knew Lydia was not there; she would have been waiting for them. "Where is my sister?"

"Her trunk is upstairs." Mr. Gardiner returned to see Elizabeth standing too close to the woman who was near twice her size. He pulled her back gently and stood between them.

"I suppose she could not carry it with her." Mrs. Baines remained stoic.

"Indeed. She could barely carry her own head on her shoulders when I left her with you. Where is she?"

"I do not know! She left without saying anything."

"Where is Mr. Baines? I want to speak to him."

"He is working in the fields today. I doubt you will be able to find him."

Mr. Gardiner stepped forward, but his wife's hand on his arm halted his movement. "Come, Edward. She will tell us nothing. We must look for Lydia while it is still day." Mrs. Gardiner turned to her cousin once more and with a voice that countered her gentle nature, hissed. "I trusted you with her. If any harm has come to my niece, I will see you pay."

They rushed back to the carriage and gave orders to return to the house.

"Elizabeth, I want you to stay there while your uncle and I look for Lydia."

"Why must I stay? I can help you search for her."

"My dear, you are understandably distraught. We cannot tend you and look for her at the same time. I know this area well and can cover more ground without having to stop and give you directions. Please, just remain at the house until we return."

They arrived and the Gardiners soon set out again with the aid of two servants. The maid Hannah was left to tend Elizabeth, who paced the floor in alarm.

"Can I get you something, Miss? A cup of tea perhaps?"

Elizabeth was about to dismiss the girl when a thought occurred to her. "Hannah, we are close to Pemberley are we not?"

"Yes, Miss, less than five miles."

"Do you know if the family is in residence for the summer?"

"Yes, Mr. Darcy arrived a few days ago, I believe. My brother is an undergardener there and it is always such a fuss when the master arrives."

Elizabeth stepped toward the girl and spoke quickly. "I will need a carriage, Hannah. How soon could you arrange for one?"

"I would need to walk to the village. That will take about an hour."

"Go. Go as quickly as you can and return with a carriage."

Hannah hesitated. "Mr. Gardiner said not to leave you alone."

"Very well, I will come too." Elizabeth gathered her things then turned back to the girl. "Be quick, Hannah."

They made it to the village in just under half an hour, leaving Elizabeth to wonder how slowly the maid would have walked if she had not come, too. A conveyance was easily procured though she had to empty her purse to get the man to hurry.

She was soon on the road to Pemberley. Her anxiousness for Lydia overruled her nervousness about seeing Darcy. He had made her promise to seek his help if she ever needed it. Hopefully, his anger toward her was not so great that he would not oblige.

Though her thoughts were occupied, she could not help but marvel at the landscape as they drove along. The natural beauty of the land was in no way marred by the presence of the estate. When the manor finally came in to view her breath caught in her throat. Never had she seen a home that seemed so in unison with the nature that surrounded it. She could not imagine a more perfect place.

The jolt of the carriage coming to a stop brought her back to the situation at hand. Her emotions were once again shaken at the thought of Lydia being alone and possibly harmed. She exited the carriage and ascended the stairs quickly. Apparently her arrival had been noted because the doors opened on their own.

"Can I help you, Miss?"

"Yes, I need to see Mr. Darcy."

"Are you Miss Bennet?"

Elizabeth blinked in surprise. "Yes. I am Elizabeth Bennet."

The butler nodded and gestured for her to hand him her outerwear. She did so though she was confused by the fact he knew her.

"Follow me, please. Mr. Darcy gave instruction to interrupt whatever he was doing when you arrived."

"I do not understand. You say Mr. Darcy is expecting me?"

Before the butler could answer, the man himself appeared coming down the stairway.

"Miss Bennet!"

Seemingly on their own, Elizabeth's legs propelled her toward him. They came together at the bottom of the stairs and Elizabeth had to fight the natural urge to fall into his arms.

"Mr. Darcy. My sister—"

"Yes, she is here. This way please."

He took her elbow and guided her up the stairs. She stopped after a few steps and looked up at him with much confusion.

"My sister is here? Lydia?"

"Yes, did you get my note?"

"No."

"Then why . . ."

"I came to ask your help."

Darcy swallowed then took her hand and resumed walking. "Come. She is anxious to see you."

"I am afraid I do not understand."

"I will explain later and perhaps you can offer some explanations of your own?"

She nodded as they came to a halt outside a door. She turned to go inside, but Darcy stopped her and clasped her hands in his.

"Miss Bennet, I feel I must warn you that your sister is much changed. She is pale and her face is quite thin. But, she is already much improved from when I first found her. Please do not become distressed when you see her. I assure you she is being well cared for."

Elizabeth nodded and he gave her hands a gentle squeeze. "Thank you, Mr. Darcy."

She retrieved her hands from his and walked through the door. Elizabeth heard a soft voice reading aloud and could feel Darcy beside her as she intrepidly moved closer to the large bed in the center of the room. They were unnoticed until they reached the foot.

A young girl sat in a chair close to the bed reading from a novel. Elizabeth barely glanced at her, but knew she must be Darcy's sister. Her own sister looked up and, first seeing Darcy, offered a soft smile. Her eyes then moved to Elizabeth and she gasped in surprise.

"Lizzy?" She asked as if she could not trust the vision.

"Liddy!"

Elizabeth rushed to the bed and embraced her sister tightly. The feel of Lydia's thin frame startled her, but she was so glad to feel her at all.

"Oh, my dear girl. I have missed you. I was so frightened when we could not find you this afternoon."

"I am sorry, Lizzy. I have so much to tell you."

"Indeed you do. Start by telling me how you feel."

"I am better than I was a few days ago. The Darcys are very kind and have taken prodigious good care of me."

Elizabeth turned to Darcy and flashed a grateful though tear-stained smile that earned a tentative one in return.

"We will give you privacy now. I suspect your aunt and uncle will arrive soon."

Elizabeth rose from the bed and stepped toward him.

"Mr. Darcy, I remain quite confused over the circumstances that brought my sister to you. But, I am grateful for all you have done."

Darcy cleared his throat. "It is an honor to be of service to you, Miss Bennet, and to Miss Lydia."

They stood looking at each other for some moments before a movement at his side drew Darcy's attention.

"Miss Bennet, this is my sister Georgiana."

After a curtsey, Miss Darcy spoke. "I am much honored to make your acquaintance, Miss Bennet. I have heard such lovely things about you."

"Thank you. I have heard many nice things about you as well. Thank you for your kindness toward my sister."

Georgiana blushed. "As I am sure you know, she is easy to care for."

"Come, Georgiana. Let us see to Miss Bennet's stay." He turned to Elizabeth. "I hope you will stay at Pemberley as our guest while your sister recovers."

"I would not wish to inconvenience you." The polite response seemed rather silly given their situation and they both smiled.

"It is no inconvenience to have you here. We have anticipated your presence for some time."

Elizabeth swallowed and offered a soft "Thank you."

The Darcys left and Elizabeth returned to her seat on Lydia's bed.

"What happened, Liddy? We arrived at the cottage today and that Mrs. Baines implied you had run off with the stable boy. I know that is not true. Tell me."

"Oh, Lizzy. I was so unhappy there. I was sick all the time and no one would talk to me. Mrs. Baines was mean and the cook never would even look at me unless she had to. The little boy, Adam, was the only good thing there. Still, I would have stayed like I was supposed to if not for Mr. Baines."

"Mr. Baines?"

Lydia nodded. "I was afraid he would hurt me the same way Wickham had."

"Liddy." Elizabeth took her sister's face in her hands. "You must have been so frightened. I am so sorry you had to go to that place. Oh, those horrible people. They promised to take care of you."

Elizabeth took a moment to calm as she fully took in Lydia's appearance. She could see why Darcy would warn her. Lydia was even gaunter than when she left Longbourn. The contrast of her thin upper body to the bulge in her abdomen was stark.

But Darcy had said that she was better than when he found her. She must be healing. Elizabeth was determined to remain hopeful that all would end well.

"Mr. Darcy said he found you."

"Yes. I did not know where I was going. I do not remember stumbling onto a road, but that is where he found me. He brought me here and has seen to my care, mostly through giving orders, but he has read to me and kept me company. He hovers over me to be sure I eat and brought in a doctor." She paused. "And a midwife. He knows everything that happened yet he allows Miss Darcy in my company. He told me it was not my fault and that he will not send me back to Longbourn if I do not wish to go. I do not remember much about him from the autumn, my mind was engaged elsewhere. But, he seems to be a good man."

"He is, Lydia. He is the very best of men and I thank God he found you and will keep you safe."

Lydia smiled, but Elizabeth could tell she was tired. "Shall I let you rest, dear? I will just refresh myself and return in a little while."

"I am glad you are here, Lizzy," Lydia whispered as she sank into the pillows.

"And I thank God for you, my dear girl."

Elizabeth stayed for a few minutes more and watched as Lydia's eyes fluttered in sleep. She forced herself to stand. Leaving even for a moment felt wrong, but she knew Darcy would be waiting to speak to her. She must face him sometime and there were holes in Lydia's story that needed to be filled.

Her hand rested on the doorknob and she tried to gather strength to turn it. She had hurt him and continued to do so every day that she did not write. Yet, he took Lydia into his home, protected and cared for her. He was indeed good and kind, but could he forgive her?

Chapter 25

Darcy did not go far when he left Lydia's room, just to a bench at the end of the hall. He found he could go no further knowing Elizabeth was there. She would have questions, he was sure, and we wanted to be at her disposal. Rooms needed to be prepared, however, and he sent Georgiana to fetch Mrs. Reynolds.

"I heard Miss Lydia's sister has arrived. Thank God. Having her here will make such a difference, I am sure."

"Yes, they were relieved to see each other. Miss Bennet will be staying with us for some time. I want the green room prepared for her right away."

Darcy did not miss the housekeeper's raised eyebrows but chose to ignore them.

"Also prepare rooms for her aunt and uncle. I believe they will want to be close to Miss Lydia as well. Alert the staff to be at their disposal. I want Pemberley to be displayed at its very best advantage, Mrs. Reynolds."

"Of course, Mr. Darcy. Your guests always leave happy."

The point, of course, was to make at least one of those guests want never to leave. He was formulating how best to communicate that to Mrs. Reynolds when he saw Elizabeth come into the hallway.

"Have her room readied at once. She is likely tired." He did not wait for a reply and walked to Elizabeth.

"Miss Bennet." Words failed him as he looked into her watery eyes. Even in her sadness she was beautiful. He had been starved for the sight of her and now that she was in front of him all he could do was stare. When he did finally open his mouth, it was at the precise moment Elizabeth chose to speak.

"Mr. Darcy, I—"

"Miss Bennet—"

They smiled and Darcy began again only to be interrupted.

"Excuse me, sir."

They turned to see the butler standing there.

"A Mr. and Mrs. Gardiner have arrived. They are waiting in the east drawing room."

"Thank you." Darcy nodded and the butler turned to leave. They stood together for a brief moment before Darcy gestured for Elizabeth to follow him.

"Your sister has been with us for a few days, but was unable to tell me what all happened until this morning. My first thought was to send an express to Longbourn. I knew how worried you were for her. It was brought to my attention, however, that given her condition and her whereabouts, she might not be welcome there. She told me you and the Gardiners were to come to Lambton, but she was unsure when, so I sent men to London and the village, hoping to get word to you that she was here."

"One of your men must have found my aunt and uncle, then."

Darcy stopped and turned to her. "But not you. You came to me on your own."

Her eyes met his and she spoke honestly. "I did. I knew you would help me."

A fire ignited in his chest, driving away part of that cold ache that had returned after their argument. It could only be described as hope, perhaps mixed with a little pride. She trusted him enough to come to him for help. That was something, indeed far more than he would have expected.

There was so much more he wanted to say but did not know how to start. How could he express his great regret for what happened to Lydia? How could he tell her how much he loved her when the specter of his inaction still hovered between them?

He took her hand and placed a gentle kiss on her fingers. Elizabeth closed her eyes and let out a soft breath. He was pleased to see his touch was not rejected. He would speak to her, but first they must see the Gardiners. He kept her hand in his until they reached the drawing room and reluctantly released it just before entering.

"Lizzy!" Mrs. Gardiner's hand replaced Darcy's. "What is happening? Your uncle received a note that Lydia is here?"

"Yes, Aunt. Let me introduce you and Mr. Darcy can explain." She turned toward Darcy. "Mr. Darcy, these are my aunt and uncle, Mr. and Mrs. Edward Gardiner."

Darcy bowed. "Welcome to Pemberley, Mr. and Mrs. Gardiner. I wish I were making your acquaintance under better circumstances. Let us sit down."

He led them to a sitting area and waited for Elizabeth to choose a seat, then sat in the chair closest to her.

"I have been in London these many weeks and was just last week summoned home. I would have arrived a day earlier if not for the heavy rains. When I was about a mile from Pemberley's gate, my driver stopped when he saw a girl lying in the road. When I realized the girl was Miss Lydia, I brought her here and called for the doctor.

"I knew she had been ill, but I did not know the reason. I was told she was at the seaside so I was quite confused about how she was instead on my property." He looked at Elizabeth while he spoke this, but she kept her head down. He continued.

"After walking some distance in the rain, she was quite weak and feverish. Just yesterday she was lucid enough to eat a proper meal and tell me what happened. The people you left her with—the Baineses—were not as kind as you, no doubt, expected them to be. Miss Lydia had particular reason to fear Mr. Baines. I do not think she told me everything that happened, but she did run away before he could hurt her."

By this time, both Elizabeth and Mrs. Gardiner were crying and Mr. Gardiner had begun pacing.

"This is my fault. I was too preoccupied when I left her there. I did not even wait to speak to Mr. Baines before I got back in the carriage. Lydia must have felt I abandoned her."

Mrs. Gardiner rose and walked to her husband. "No, Edward. You cannot take the blame. I mistakenly trusted my cousin. I arranged for her to come to Lambton when I should have found some way to care for Lydia myself. I sent her to strangers. I am no better than her father."

Mr. Gardner led his wife back to the sofa and held her hand in comfort. Darcy looked at them, then Elizabeth, wishing he had the right to provide the same sort of support. Tears ran from her closed eyes and she held one hand over her mouth. Guilt further penetrated his conscience now that he could see the full extent of Elizabeth's pain. He turned back to Mr. Gardiner.

"You are both admirable for wanting to take the blame, but I am afraid it rests solely on me. Miss Lydia never would have been abused had Wickham's true character been exposed. I have known it for years, but remained silent, not wishing to bring pain to my father, who loved Wickham, or embarrassment to my family. Miss Lydia is paying the price for my silence, and I am truly sorry."

Darcy held Mr. Gardiner's gaze for just a moment before he lowered his head. The days that Lydia had been with them brought many realizations.

When Lydia told him of Wickham's actions, his first thoughts were of Elizabeth and the hurt she had endured watching her sister shrink into despair. Now he could see his failure reached beyond Elizabeth and Lydia to anyone who also loved them.

"You take too much on yourself, Mr. Darcy." Elizabeth's sweet voice brought his attention to her face, marked from crying, but still lovely. Her gaze did not waver from his as she spoke. "We all feel some level of guilt over what happened to Lydia. I willingly believed that man's every lie and manipulation simply because he played to my vanity. I have felt the culpability of that for months. But the truth is, Mr. Wickham alone is responsible for his actions. I realized this after I had the misfortune to be in his company recently. He wakes up every morning with the same choice as the rest of us—to use his talents for good or evil. You did not create the blackness that is in his heart. It is not your fault, Mr. Darcy. You reacted the way we all have—with great care and concern for the people you love."

Darcy took a moment to steady his emotions. He could not believe she was offering him absolution. The warmth in his chest grew. "Is that how you truly feel, Miss Bennet?"

"Yes." She took in a shaky breath. "I am sorry you were ever made to feel otherwise."

Darcy shook his head and looked down, then back to her. "You are too generous. I cannot dismiss my guilt so easily, not when I can see the pain my silence has caused."

"Do try, Mr. Darcy. Regret is such a heavy burden."

They looked at each other for some time, each trying to gain an understanding of the other. Finally, the gaze was broken when Mr. Gardiner cleared his throat. Darcy reluctantly turned his attention to the other occupants of the room.

"Forgive me. It has been a trying day and you must be in need of rest. I have had rooms prepared for you. We can send for your things--that is if you would like to stay. The doctor and midwife agreed that Miss Lydia should remain in bed. I assumed you would want to be close to her."

"Yes, Mr. Darcy. We thank you for your kindness. I know what you are risking by having Lydia here."

"Mr. Gardiner, I am risking nothing. I have taken precautions to ensure Miss Lydia's privacy. Even so, if word were to get out, Pemberley can stand the weight of it. We should, however, discuss the Baineses. Perhaps tomorrow morning?" Darcy watched as a cloud of anger settled over Mr. Gardiner's face.

"That is agreeable to me, sir."

"Good. Shall we?"

They rose from their seats and Darcy walked next to Elizabeth as he led them all to the staircase. They stole looks as they moved but were silent. Neither of them could find the proper words to express the hope that refused to diminish—that the other could forgive and accept the love each was desperate to give.

When they reached the top of the steps, Darcy realized he did not know which rooms had been prepared for the Gardiners. Thankfully, Mrs. Reynolds had anticipated him and appeared to guide them to their chambers. Elizabeth's room, though in the same wing, was down a different corridor. Darcy guided her there and along the way gathered his courage. Elizabeth's quiet gasp as they entered her chamber gave him a bit more confidence.

"This was my grandmother's room after she left the mistress' chambers. It has not been occupied for quite some time. I hope it meets your approval."

"I think there are few who would not approve. It is lovely."

Elizabeth turned her head to fully take in the décor, done in various shades of green. She felt as if she were outdoors in a beautiful glen rather than inside an elegant manor house.

"I am glad to know I chose correctly."

She turned around and looked at him. The day had brought so many different emotions and as she stood there with him, she suddenly felt very fatigued. As much as she wished to speak to him of all her regrets, she lacked the strength to do so at that moment. He must have noticed.

"You are tired."

His face fell and Elizabeth could see both disappointment and concern in his eyes as they drifted across her face.

"I am. I have not rested well at the inns the past few nights. It was noisy and I was anxious about Lydia. Thank you, Mr. Darcy. It seems I always have a reason to feel gratitude toward you." She tried to smile, but exhaustion was claiming each action.

"I wish you would not. Of all the things you should feel toward me, gratitude is hardly one I would expect."

Elizabeth shook her head. "You rescued my sister. She would have died—"

"Miss Bennet," Darcy interrupted. "We have much to discuss and I am anxious to do so, but not at the expense of your health. Please rest for a while. I am not sure what we will do about dinner. Georgiana and I have been taking our meals with Miss Lydia. She needs encouragement to eat. Now that you are here, I am sure she would rather have you with her. But soon, very soon, we will speak."

He continued to stare at her with that same intense gaze that used to cause her such confusion. Elizabeth wanted very much to speak more of her gratitude. He had not told her about encouraging Lydia to eat to illicit a response, she was sure, but, regardless, her heart beat wildly at the thought that he had cared for Lydia in her absence.

He bowed and vacated the room and Elizabeth was sorry for it. She had not had the time to enjoy his presence, yet she immediately missed him when he left. The beauty of the room beckoned her to explore, but the call of the bed was greater. No doubt she could ring for a maid, but she did not bother. As she settled into the bed, Elizabeth stilled her mind and willed her conscience to be quiet long enough to regain some strength through sleep. Lydia would need her now more than she had at Longbourn. Elizabeth found great comfort, however, knowing she was no longer alone.

Darcy stood outside Elizabeth's door, unable to command his feet to move. Just as it had been after the carriage accident, leaving her alone was difficult and felt wholly unnatural. His longing for her was too great and had been of too long a duration to be satisfied with just a couple of hours and a few words. He wanted to hold her and reassure her with his touch as well as words that all would be well.

She was tired, had been for months and now he knew the full reason why. He could not be selfish and make demands of her time at present. He had so many questions to ask and explanations and apologies to offer, but they would have to wait. Elizabeth was at Pemberley. For now, that would have to be enough. With great effort, he moved away from her door and walked downstairs to his study.

There was much that required his attention. He had not been faithful to his duties during his time at the club, nor since he had returned. Estate business was ignored a moment longer as he picked up his pen to write a note to his solicitor. Lydia had told him the Baineses ran a farm. It was unlikely they owned it themselves, but he wanted to know for certain. He knew it was not one of his but was determined it soon would be.

More than an hour later, Darcy was somewhat satisfied with his progress. He had sorted through his letters and responded to the most important ones. The sound of his stomach grumbling alerted him to the fact it was nearly time for dinner. As if reading his mind, Mrs. Reynolds knocked on the door and was called to enter.

"I have arranged for dinner, Mr. Darcy but need to know where to serve it. I have been informed by Miss Darcy that the ladies will all eat with Miss Lydia."

"Even Georgiana?"

"Yes, sir."

Darcy smiled softly. "Good. I worried she would hide when Miss Lydia's family arrived. She has grown much these past months. Mrs. Annesley has been a good influence, I believe."

"If I may say, Mr. Darcy, having a most excellent brother and guardian is what has made the most difference."

Darcy smiled a little more at Mrs. Reynold's obvious bias. The compliment was made not out of a desire to gain favor. Rather, it came from the genuine affection of one who'd had a hand in raising him.

"Mrs. Reynolds, Miss Lydia has asked me to find a place for her child. We have some time, still, but will you think on it and have some suggestions ready for me in a few days?"

"Of course. I will also arrange for a nurse and everything the babe will need after he arrives."

Darcy was unsure what those things would be so he merely nodded, trusting her to take care of everything.

"Ask Mr. Gardiner to join me in here for an informal dinner. Keep it simple. We have much to discuss and I would rather do it without footmen present."

"Yes, sir. Will that be all?"

"Yes, thank you."

Mrs. Reynolds left the room and Darcy leaned back in his chair. He spent the few moments of solitude lost in the memory of holding Elizabeth's hand that afternoon. Her skin was as soft and warm as he remembered. He had, of course, felt more of her—her blushing cheek, the gentle curve of her waist, her soft full lips. The kisses and caresses they shared in the grove starred in his dreams nightly, but he believed they had frightened her and caused her to run from him. After seeing her reaction to his touch today, along with her words of trust and forgiveness, Darcy believed they could find their way back to the comfort they felt in the woods. They only needed time and patience. One they had, the other Darcy was never long on. For her, though, he would wait until the end of time.

Chapter 26

Elizabeth watched as Lydia lifted the spoon to her mouth. The utensil shook as if its user found the weight of it unwieldy. She had offered once to help her eat, but Lydia insisted on doing it herself. Elizabeth first interpreted Lydia's insistence as her way of expressing anger or disappointment toward her for what had happened. The guilt she carried would always cause Elizabeth to look for ways to feel worse, even when nothing was really there. After noticing Lydia look at Miss Darcy as she too lifted her spoon, Elizabeth realized Lydia was simply grasping for some form of normalcy—to be in any way similar to the sixteen year old girl sitting beside her, even if only by holding her own spoon.

After a few more sips, Lydia pushed the bowl away and promised to eat more after she rested. Elizabeth knew very little about childbirth but was educated enough to know it would take much more energy than Lydia had just expended by eating. The relief she felt earlier in the day was quickly being replaced by a gnawing fear that her sister would not survive.

Elizabeth felt a gentle pat on her arm and turned to meet Mrs. Gardiner's concerned eyes. She was doing a poor job of hiding her emotions. Her aunt raised her eyebrows and smiled, reminding Elizabeth to do the same.

"I do not know if you received my letters, Lydia. Would you like to hear news from Hertfordshire?"

"Yes, I would, Lizzy. I did get your letters. Please forgive me for not writing. I cannot say why I did not, only that it seemed I couldn't."

"It is of no matter now, Lydia. Do not think of it again. Now, shall I tell you of Jane's wedding?"

"She is married?" A lovely smile graced her features. "I am so happy. She wrote of her engagement, but now she is married. I met Mr. Burton briefly in London. I liked him."

"He is a good man and will make Jane happy. There was talk of us all going into Yorkshire later in the year."

"That would be lovely." Her eyes drifted closed as she spoke, leaving the other ladies in the room at a loss as what to do next. At length, conversation began in hushed whispers.

"Miss Bennet, you know your sister well. You must tell me what I can do or provide for her comfort. I have been reading to her, but I cannot tell if she enjoys what I have chosen. Does she like music? I can have a pianoforte brought in, or a harp."

Elizabeth smiled sweetly at the young woman. She was so eager to please. "I have only seen Lydia enjoy music when dancing was involved. I have never seen her willingly pick up a book, so I have no advice on what you should read aloud. I am afraid the diversions you and I would likely prefer would not hold her interest. Lydia is a social creature and loves noise and action; dancing and gossip were always her favorite pastimes."

"Oh, I can provide gossip. It would not be about anyone she knows, however. Is gossip interesting if one is not acquainted with the subjects? I have never thought so. You know Miss Bingley? She can go on about this lady and that for hours it seems. I am sure I can remember some of her stories if I think about it hard enough." She paused and bit her lip in contemplation. "Perhaps I can tell her stories about my own family. Though, I am sure my brother would not approve. Oh, I know the perfect thing. My grandmother wrote down all the tales her mother and grandmother told her as a child. Some of them are quite sensational. The book is kept in your room, Miss Bennet. Would it be alright if I retrieved it?"

Before Elizabeth could answer in the affirmative, her aunt spoke.

"I could use some movement at present, Miss Darcy. If you tell us exactly where to find it, Lizzy and I will bring it back."

"Of course. It is on the bookshelf. It is an old journal bound in leather. There is no title, but you will know it by the writing. It is the only one there written by hand."

"Thank you. We will return shortly."

She rose and looked at Elizabeth to do the same. When they reached Elizabeth's chamber, Mrs. Gardiner let out a small gasp similar to the one her niece released upon entering there for the first time.

"Oh, Lizzy. This room could not be more perfect for you if you decorated it yourself."

"It is lovely. Mr. Darcy said it was his grandmother's, which is why, I suppose, her journal it here." Elizabeth held up the object, which she retrieved while her aunt looked around. She made a move toward the door, but Mrs. Gardiner stopped her.

"While we are alone, Lizzy, would you care to tell me what the situation is between you and Mr. Darcy?"

"I beg your pardon?"

"Do not dissemble with me, Elizabeth Marie Bennet. I would generally not pry so openly, but Lydia's predicament has made me overly sensitive, I suppose. No man would do all Mr. Darcy has done for Lydia if not moved to do so by some powerful emotion. Anyone with sight can tell he is in love with you, Lizzy. There is much, I feel, you have not told me."

"I have nothing to tell, Aunt." Elizabeth was not yet willing to reveal to anyone other than Darcy the full extent of her feelings.

"Forgive me for being indelicate, but do the two of you have an understanding?"

"No."

"Why not?"

Elizabeth let out a sigh of frustration at her aunt's refusal to relent. "Truly, Aunt, I have nothing to say on the matter. If anything changes, I promise to tell you. Cannot that be enough for now?"

Mrs. Gardiner's shoulders dropped in disappointment. "If you will not confide in me, then I suppose I must trust you. But, Lizzy, if anything untoward has happened—"

"No! Mr. Darcy is everything good and honorable. Please do not pain me by making such suggestions. I assure you, our lack of an understanding is entirely my fault." Elizabeth looked up to the ceiling, trying to keep the tears that had formed from falling. "May we please go back to Lydia, now?"

"Forgive me, Lizzy, I did not mean to upset you. I am only concerned."

Elizabeth saw her aunt's distress and embraced her. "Thank you. Tell me quickly what you think of Miss Darcy. I was led to believe she was shy, but it seems she is quite comfortable with us."

"It may be that caring for Lydia has given her some sort of confidence. I believe when this is over, they will become great friends."

"Aunt, tell me, truthfully, do you think Lydia will be well?"

"I know not, my dear. I worry she will not regain much strength while the child is with her. It seems to be taking everything from her. We can only wait and pray."

Elizabeth nodded. She wanted someone to tell her both Lydia and her child would be well, but no one could. They returned to her and spent the rest of the evening tending to Lydia while listening to fairy stories and old Irish legends. Elizabeth's mind naturally wandered to the emblem Darcy wove for her. A symbol of unending love. He had proven his love for her in a way she never could have imagined. Her heart was as fixed as his, she need only an opportunity to tell him.

"I promised Miss Lydia I would not send her back to Longbourn. You may feel that officious of me, but I do feel some responsibility, given I was the one who found her. Do you think it will be difficult to convince Mr. Bennet to allow her to stay here?"

Mr. Gardiner sighed and took a drink of brandy. They had discussed the situation throughout dinner and now had come to the subject of what would happen to Lydia after she gave birth.

"To be honest, Mr. Darcy, I think he would be relieved to not have Lydia back. He could go about his days without being reminded of how he failed her. Bennet will always take the easy way. If you are willing to take on Lydia, he will not object. However, there will be talk of exactly why Lydia is here. You have no stake in her well-being, after all."

"Is it not enough that I would feel compassion, or that she would be a good friend for my sister?"

"No, Mr. Darcy, it would not. I was angry with Bennet for how he handled the situation, but I could sympathize with his predicament. I find it harder to excuse his actions, and mine, now that I see what you, a virtual stranger, are willing to do. You must truly be the kindest man in all of England. That is unless you have some other motivation?"

Darcy's mouth set in a straight line as he looked away from Mr. Gardiner. He did not believe the man was questioning his honor, but rather challenging him. Still, he did not answer.

"Perhaps the happiness of my other niece has been the true incentive. Is there anything you would like to ask me, Mr. Darcy?"

Darcy stood and paced the room for some moments before answering. "I have nothing to ask at this time."

"Why not?"

Darcy was incredulous at the man's directness. However, he believed Elizabeth's uncle was asking out of concern.

"There are things that must first be said to Miss Bennet." He paused for a moment then returned to his seat. "I cannot court her while her sister struggles so."

"Of course you can, and you should. These past months have been tortuous for Lizzy. Her letters from Longbourn were filled with grief and worry. I am surprised she did not make herself ill. When she wrote to us from Kent, however, there were more signs of her usual liveliness. You were there, too, were you not?"

Darcy nodded.

"Lizzy needs to feel something good in these coming weeks. Knowing she has a future with a good man could help soften the blow if the worst happens. Am I assuming too much, Mr. Darcy?"

"No. No, you are not."

They were silent for some time and Darcy knew Mr. Gardiner expected him to say more. It seemed wrong, somehow, to voice his feelings to anyone except Elizabeth. He would ask the question Mr. Gardiner anticipated, but he must speak to Elizabeth first.

"Is it enough for now that I assure you my intentions are honorable?"

"I will accept that—for now. You must think I am brash, but I am only thinking about Elizabeth. Mrs. Gardiner and I noticed how the two of you looked at each other this afternoon. If it is in your power to give her any sort of happiness, please do not hesitate. She has had little of late."

Darcy contemplated Mr. Gardiner's words for a few moments. Hesitation on his part could indeed cause distress. Had he not learned that lesson repeatedly over the last weeks? He had thought expressing himself would only add to Elizabeth's worries. Could it, instead, make her happy?

"Thank you, Mr. Gardiner." The men rose and shook hands. "I will think about what you said."

They parted ways for the evening and as Darcy readied for bed, he chastised himself for nearly falling into his old habit of merely reacting. If he and Elizabeth were to come to an understanding, he must deliver the first punch.

"Liddy."

Elizabeth awoke with a start and quickly rolled over in search of her sister. She could not immediately place her surroundings, but as the fog of sleep slowly gave way, her heart slowed and she calmed. She was at Pemberley. Lydia was safe and Darcy was close by. She need not be alarmed.

The bed curtains were not drawn and she could see bits of dawn breaking through the shadows of the room. Elizabeth threw her legs over the side of the bed and, as she stood, she heard a soft knock on the dressing room door. She opened it to find Lucy, the maid who had tended her the night before, standing on the opposite side carrying a tray.

"Good morning, Lucy."

"Good morning, Miss Bennet. I hope I did not wake you. I did not want to keep you waiting this morning, but I forgot to ask you last night what time you wished to rise. I hope you will forgive me."

Elizabeth smiled reassuringly. "There is nothing to forgive. You did not wake me. Your timing is perfect, actually."

The girl seemed pleased with this. "Thank you. I have brought tea if you wish for a cup before we begin your toilet."

"That would be lovely, Lucy. Thank you."

Elizabeth watched as she placed the tray on a table in the seating area. Lucy poured a cup then curtsied.

"I will prepare your toilet if you are ready."

Elizabeth smiled again. Every servant she had encountered at Pemberley had been most anxious to see to her needs. She wondered if it was because Darcy paid them well or threatened them. She knew that latter was not true and that more than likely, he simply inspired their best work.

"That will be fine."

The girl hurried away and Elizabeth sat and picked up her cup. Before she brought it to her lips, she paused as a piece of folded paper caught her eye. She returned the tea to the table and reached for the note.

She fingered her name on the outside. It did not read *Lizzy* in her aunt's handwriting, or even *Miss Bennet*, but Elizabeth. She knew the lettering well, had memorized every loop and line over the last weeks. Her fingers trembled as she turned it over and broke the seal, and her eyes watered when a ribbon woven into a knot fell out.

Elizabeth,

I have just left Miss Lydia. She had her morning tea and is once again sleeping. I have left instructions for her to be woken for breakfast. I will spend the morning in the rose garden. Its paths provide sufficient exercise and are close enough to the house that I can be easily summoned if needed. If it will not offend you to walk among such cultivated vulgarity, will you please join me?

FD

A soft chuckle escaped her. He was so dear. As she fell asleep the previous evening, she tried to imagine ways they might meet and discuss everything that had happened. He anticipated her, however, and even saw to Lydia's comfort, likely knowing it would aid hers.

The note was carefully folded and her tea was quickly drunk. Elizabeth rose from her seat and walked to a large armoire where her belongings had been stowed. She brought her box of mementos with her though it meant leaving books and an extra gown behind. She placed the note and ribbon inside, on top of her journal. Smiling, she walked to the dressing room while unbraiding her hair.

"Lucy, let us be quick this morning. I will wear my green dress."

"Is that one not too nice for the early morning?"

"I suppose for most mornings, but not this one. Do be quick. I will start on my hair while you retrieve it."

Elizabeth picked up a brush from the vanity, but the girl looked so crestfallen that Elizabeth paused mid-stroke.

"Lucy, I do not doubt your ability. I am merely in a hurry and want to take as little time as possible. I am one of five daughters who all share one maid. You will find me doing things on my own without thought. I assure you that when it is done, it will be out of habit and not dissatisfaction. Now please hurry with that gown."

Elizabeth was sure she had never dressed so quickly. Eschewing gloves and bonnet, she moved as quickly as she could through Pemberley's corridors and down the stairs. A footman greeted her when she reached the bottom and showed her the exit to the garden. She thanked him and sent him away before he could open the glass door.

Darcy was several steps away, standing still while drawing something on the path with his walking stick. She saw that he, too, had left his hat and gloves. The rest of him was immaculate as always. Everything on him was well tailored, polished and perfect--except for one stray curl above his forehead. She was quite familiar with that vagrant lock. It hovered over his brow, separate from the others as if teasing them to join it. He never toyed with it or tried to make it take its rightful place with the rest. He seemed to accept that deviant strand as a part of himself.

Elizabeth felt a desire to run her fingers through those dark curls, not to tame the stray but to bring disorder to the rest. In her mind, she did just that. As she admired her work, a warmth welled up inside of her; the feeling was both exquisite and terrifying. She shook herself out of her reverie to find Darcy staring back.

Chapter 27

Darcy looked up to see Elizabeth staring at him. She had come. He smiled and stepped toward the door just as she opened it.

"Good morning, Elizabeth."

Darcy took her hand and bowed, placing a light kiss on her fingers before he rose. He did not release her, but ran his thumb lightly over her knuckles, to her wrist and back again. He did not know if her lack of gloves had been intentional, but he was pleased to be able to feel some part of her.

She was so lovely—and nervous. Darcy saw it in her eyes. He wished to take her in his arms and kiss her doubts away. Memories of the more enjoyable aspects of their last encounter came to mind as he drank in her appearance. A battle waged inside him between the desire of the gentleman to respect her sensibilities and the raw, consuming need of the man who wanted to be close to her, to have some sort of physical connection after so many weeks of believing he would never see her again. However, he believed the lack of propriety he had displayed caused at least some of her anxiety that day. He would have to be content with the small indulgences of holding her hand and speaking her name until he was sure she wished for more.

"Good morning, Mr. Darcy."

"Thank you for joining me. I hope you slept well."

"I did, for the first time in many weeks. Thank you."

Darcy laid his walking stick against the door and placed her arm through his. Pulling her closer, he pressed his free hand on hers and led her up the path between the hedges.

Elizabeth greatly enjoyed the feel of his fingers on hers. Until he kissed her hand the day before, she had not realized how much she needed his touch to feel secure. They had been so free with their affection in the grove, but she was afraid her harsh words to him that day would cause him to withdraw from her. She was pleased with his gentleness and adored hearing him say her name, but she wanted to feel the strength of his arms around her. She supposed she would have to earn his forgiveness before he held her like that again.

They were silent for some time, each trying to form the right words. As the moments wore on, Elizabeth became anxious. She had so much to say, but she knew not how to begin. She struggled to form words of apology, but eventually conceded to her nerves and instead asked about her sister.

"How were Lydia's spirits this morning? I must say I was surprised to read that she had already woken. Even before, she was never an early riser."

"Mrs. Reynolds believes if Miss Lydia has something in her stomach early and then goes back to sleep, she will not become as ill throughout the day. I do not understand how tea and toast before dawn reduces any upset she might feel in the afternoon, but it seems to have worked so far. I tend not to question Mrs. Reynolds on these things. Her experience shows, and I trust her. I hope you do as well."

Elizabeth let out a long breath and clutched his arm a little tighter. He was rambling and she supposed he was anxious as well. How could she ever have found him arrogant and unfeeling? Even after their time together in Kent, she had misjudged him so badly. Yet, he had done much for Lydia. Her appreciation was so great it brought tears to her eyes.

"Mr. Darcy, I tried to express my gratitude yesterday, but you would not let me. You must allow me now to thank you on behalf of all my family, for they will never know the service you have provided to them by caring for Lydia as you have. I do not know any man who would have acted as you did. I could never have imagined such kindness, especially after how I spoke to you." Her voice cracked with those last words and she had to look away.

"Elizabeth, please. I am not so very noble. Surely you must know, you must see." He stopped and turned to her, taking her hands in the process. He looked into her eyes and spoke with great feeling. "It is true, I would have stopped to help anyone in distress. If I were acquainted with them, I would have brought them here and called for the doctor. But Lydia is in the room across from my sister, being cared for by my most trusted staff as well as myself, being treated as family because that is how I see her. I care for your sister because I still have hope that she will soon be *my* sister."

With that, Elizabeth could no longer hold back her tears. Her hopes were confirmed. The happiness she sought was there, waiting to be claimed, but her guilt rendered her limp and disbelieving.

"How? How could you still want me after all I said that day? I was so cruel."

"No, my love. What did you say to me that I did not deserve? You were correct to chastise me. I did not treat you as you as a gentleman should and that caused you to doubt me."

"No! No, it was never you. I was confused and jealous and I allowed my hurt to overrule my head. You tried to explain that day and I would not let you. I yelled and accused and—"

"You ran from me."

Elizabeth nodded, too overcome with tears to speak. The gentleman be damned. He could not look upon the woman he loved, see her crying with such force and simply hold her hand. Darcy took her arm and walked along a different path where the hedges were taller. He pulled her into his embrace and held her tightly until she calmed.

"I should have run after you. I started to, but the truth of your words struck me before I could take two steps. I thought of how you looked after you slapped me. The confusion and pain in your eyes was much the same as I saw in Georgiana's at Ramsgate." His deep voice trembled slightly and he closed his eyes to the memory. "I did not realize it at the time, but I was behaving no better than Wickham. I courted you in the shadows, as you said. You had every reason to doubt me."

Elizabeth attempted to pull back but Darcy did not allow it. He could not let her go, not even for a moment. The feeling of her in his arms again was too sweet, too precious to allow even light to pass between them.

She did not try again, but spoke from his chest.

"Do *not* compare yourself to him. Does intent not matter? A man stealing bread to feed his family is not the same as a man stealing for his own pleasure. You told me in your letter that your intention was always to love me."

He nodded the kissed the top of her head. "And it remains so."

"Then please do not say such things. I treasure our time in the woods. I will not allow it to become something to regret. We had one day, one terrible day filled with doubt and fear. But we had many others that were beautiful."

Darcy's hand ran down the length of her back and up to where his arm wrapped around her shoulders. His ministrations were comforting and when he felt her relax, he did as well. He loosened his grip enough that she could run her hands up his chest. Elizabeth tilted her head to look at him, then closed her eyes and placed a kiss over his heart.

"I missed you."

She looked back into his eyes with such undisguised hurt and longing that Darcy instantly acted to take it away. He cupped her face with his hands and did not hesitate to bring his mouth to hers. That one motion, the soft gliding of his lips over hers, provided the consolation they had sought since their last embrace. Nothing they had tried in their separation—neither her written words, nor his fists—had brought healing. True solace was in each other.

Darcy's hands moved from her face to her neck then to her hair. Several curls came loose around his fingers as he threaded them through the lightly woven coiffure. He continued the pattern as their tender caresses deepened into a slow burning need to possess and consume.

Too soon, Darcy felt himself slipping under as desire came over him in waves. His need for her was overwhelming, but his love was stronger. He slowed his pace and she reluctantly followed. After a few more moments lost to sensation, they broke apart.

"Elizabeth." Darcy's labored breathing made his words sound heavy in the still morning air. "We should walk and continue our conversation."

"Can you kiss me while we walk, sir?"

"No, madam, I do not believe I possess such talent."

"Then I would rather remain here. I understand what you mean to do. But, I feel safe and cherished when I am close to you like this. The memory of being in your arms has sustained me these last months. I love you, Fitzwilliam, and I need your touch to feel complete. Please do not tell me I have to do without now."

Darcy was comforted by her words. He had been so afraid that he had frightened her by showing the strength of his affection. Knowing she felt just the opposite, that his love gave her strength, erased all his anxieties regarding his great passion for her.

Elizabeth rose up on her toes and wrapped her arms around his neck. Darcy could not deny such an invitation, and again their lips met in an exquisite dance that left them both longing for a closeness that was yet out of their reach.

Darcy clutched her waist and rested his forehead against hers. "Please take care, Elizabeth. You do not know the power you wield. Have mercy on me, love, and let us walk."

She looked at him and after drawing a deep breath, nodded. She reached behind to adjust her hair then took his arm. It was some time before Darcy could again find his voice.

"We shall not argue over our share of the blame for that day. It is futile, for it seems we are determined to hold each other blameless. I do wish you had told me about Lydia. I would have done everything in my power to take that burden from you, or at least share it so you were not so weighed down"

Elizabeth's eyes focused on him for a moment, then dropped to her feet. "I was going to. I was sure you were going to propose that day and had determined I could not lie to you."

"And you would have accepted me?"

Elizabeth nodded.

"What happened?"

"I saw Colonel Fitzwilliam when I was walking to the grove. He said several things to me and I am afraid I misinterpreted them all."

Darcy stopped and looked at her for a moment before walking again. "I am not so sure."

"What do you mean?"

"Let us sit."

Elizabeth expected him to lead her to a bench or back inside, but instead she was treated to a sight she had sorely missed. Darcy took off his coat and spread it next to a hedge. He sat and held his hand out for her. Instead of helping her to sit beside him, he pulled her down into his lap. She immediately curled into him as his arms circled her.

"Will you tell me what he said to you?"

"You will have to give me a moment to recall. I am afraid I have not thought about Colonel Fitzwilliam or that conversation much since I left Kent. After reading your letter, nothing he had said really mattered."

Darcy was shamefully pleased with that information. A small smile appeared but was quickly controlled when Elizabeth began speaking.

"I suppose I should first explain my state of mind that morning. When I left you the day before, you were with Anne. I am ashamed to say that I was jealous of the attention you paid her. You had just kissed me and I was still lightheaded from the sensation, but you left my side to go to her. In my resentment, I did not allow myself to see how frail Anne really was or that the walk had been so taxing for her. All I saw was your concern. I thought about it all that day and evening.

"I convinced myself, eventually, that I should ask you about Anne before I made any assumptions. I had made so many erroneous ones in the past. I also decided that I had to tell you about Lydia. That caused me much anxiety. After my father's reaction to what happened to her, I swore that I would tell no one else. Not even Jane knows. We told only my aunt after we suspected Lydia was with child. I did not know what to do. Anyway, I had worked myself up into quite a state when Colonel Fitzwilliam came upon me.

"I do not remember his exact words, but …" she paused and took a deep breath, "he said Rosings would soon be yours. I, of course, assumed it would be through marriage to Anne. Mr. Collins had implied more than once that you were meant for her. Coming from Colonel Fitzwilliam made it more plausible."

"But he gave no indication of just how I would come to own Rosings." The deep, smooth voice that had just spoken of his love became cold with anger.

"No. I did not understand the truth of that particular matter until I spoke to Anne." She pushed away from his chest and looked at him. "I pray most fervently that that estate will never be yours."

"As do I, love." He kissed her and guided her head back down over his heart. "What else did he say to you?"

"He warned me about Wickham. He had heard Maria say something about him being in Meryton and felt he should warn me. It was unnecessary, of course. I knew Wickham's story about the rift between the two of you, but Colonel Fitzwilliam told me more. He said you felt responsible for Wickham and continued to pay his debts and such until last summer.

"Please forgive me, Fitzwilliam, for assuming the worst." Her tears resumed as she remembered her horrible assumption. "He told me that Wickham had betrayed you by trying to take away a woman under your protection. Of course, I know now that he spoke of Miss Darcy, but at the time—"

"He said that?"

Elizabeth startled at the strength and bitterness of his tone.

"He said *those* words? 'A woman under my protection'? What else would you think? He made you believe I was marrying Anne and that I kept a mistress. What else? He told you I separated Bingley from your sister."

Elizabeth again leaned away from his chest so she could see his face. She had never seen him angry before. He was quite severe. His jaw tightened and his lips set in a thin line. She leaned in and kissed him lightly until he softened and returned her attentions with a bit more ardor. She pulled back and answered his question.

"Yes. I was not upset about that, not really. Mr. Bingley is responsible for his own actions and Jane is happy. But your cousin said you had strong objections to the lady's family, that they were not the sort of people who would be allowed at Pemberley. My thoughts were that if the Bennets were not good enough for your friend, then we certainly were not good enough for you. I am ashamed to say I questioned exactly what kind of proposal you were going to make. I am so sorry."

Darcy's anger did not dissipate, but his tone was laced with hurt and disappointment. "He chose his words well, did he not? Listening to that would convince anybody I am a cad."

"I believe, in his way, he was trying to be helpful. I must have misunderstood him."

"No, dearest. Something happened in London that made me question his friendship. This only confirms that he set out to purposely hurt me."

Elizabeth ran her hand over his chest in a way he hoped would become a habit. "Why would he do that? You told me he was your best friend."

He placed his hand over hers and held it against his heart. "Did he visit you often at the parsonage?"

"Yes."

"Did he flirt with you?"

"No! Well, maybe a little, but I think that is just his way. I would never take him seriously."

"He wanted you, Elizabeth. I have no doubt of that."

Elizabeth sighed and rested her head on his shoulder. "Charlotte said something similar but I dismissed it. I never thought of him in that respect. To me he was only your cousin. I would never give false encouragement to any man."

Darcy stroked her hair and kissed her gently. "No, you would not."

"I am sorry."

"You have nothing to be sorry for. You are a victim of the war between Pemberley and Matlock. It seems Fitzwilliam has chosen sides."

"I do not understand."

"It is a long story and of little matter at present."

"It seems to matter a great deal to you."

"Not as much as you do, love. In the end, Fitzwilliam's words would not have had the impact they did if I had behaved differently."

"We agreed not to argue blame, did we not? It is over."

He nodded. "Can you tell me why you did not write to me?"

Again, she nodded and tears pricked her eyes in response to the pain in his voice. "After I read your letter I felt I had to protect you and your sister. I would not risk your name or bring Wickham back into your life. You both had suffered enough because of him."

"Elizabeth." He wiped away her tears and pulled her closer. "I love your fierce, protective nature. I am pleased and honored that you love me and wished to shield me. You need to know, Elizabeth, that I will always protect you. You will never have to face grief and uncertainty alone. I ask only for the truth, no matter how painful it might be. Believe in me, Elizabeth, and in my love for you and I swear I will never again give you cause to doubt me."

She drew his face down and kissed him. He returned her sweet affection with raw, desperate need. The desire to mark her as his overpowered his senses. Once again, his fingers dislodged her hairpins, sending long curls down over her shoulders. His kiss became deeper and more insistent and Elizabeth held on to him, trying to match his movements. After some time, she relaxed in his embrace, allowing him full control. Darcy moaned at her acquiescence and drew her bottom lip into his mouth, sucking gently as his hand roamed over the buttons on her spencer.

He wanted to feel her skin and love every beautiful inch of her. Some small part of him was still aware that she was not yet his, not fully, and he could not claim her body as he so desperately desired. Elizabeth was so loving and generous, and so perfectly innocent. She had no idea what her displays of love did to him. She was merely expressing her affection in a way that was natural for her. He had to be strong for them both.

He slowed his movements then pulled away and rested his forehead on her chest. He could feel her fingers stroking his hair and he began to calm.

"I am so sorry I hurt you."

Her sweet voice penetrated his foggy senses and he felt like weeping. She understood. He *had* been hurt—deeply. At times the agony had been so strong he believed he would never get out from under it. But the pain made him better. He would no longer be a timid lover, or fail to act as a man in love should—openly and not under the protection of the trees. His honor was not only bound to Pemberley and the Darcy name, but to her—her loyalty and her goodness, her trust and her love. He would strive to be worthy of those gifts for the rest of his life, starting by freely giving and accepting forgiveness.

He brought his head up to hers. "It is over now. Let us be done with the apologies and regrets. I only want to love you and feel your love in return. We cannot do that if we dwell on the hurt we caused each other. Let us think of the past only as it gives us pleasure."

Elizabeth laughed lightly and brought her hands to his face. "You, my darling, brooding man, could never practice such a philosophy."

Darcy smiled and relaxed further as he relished the adoration shining in her eyes. "You are correct, but I will try. It will be your job, my dearest, loveliest Elizabeth, to remind me of the joys in the present when I remember the past, and bring me out of my brooding when I am unconsciously lost in it. You bring me such happiness, Elizabeth. How can I ever thank you for choosing to love me?"

She wrapped her arms around him and hugged him tightly to her, then released him and looked in his eyes.

"It is my pleasure to be of service to you, Fitzwilliam."

Chapter 28

Morning continued to bloom around Darcy and Elizabeth as they took a respite from the emotional upheaval of their conversation and simply enjoyed each other's company. She remained in his lap, though for the sake of his sanity, he had slightly adjusted her position. Their touches had gone from passionate to light, but their hands and lips were always exploring.

Elizabeth traced his long fingers as she rested her head on his shoulder. She could smell the roses surrounding them as they opened for the sun. Though she still preferred the smell of the woods, she could appreciate the perfume of the cultivated garden. Elizabeth was especially pleased that Darcy had chosen a place where they could be alone but close by in case Lydia needed them.

They had been there for some time and Elizabeth began to wonder if the gardeners would happen upon them.

"Should we be concerned about accidentally being beheaded by shears, Mr. Darcy? We are very close to this hedge."

"Do not worry. The workers will not be out here this morning."

"Really? I suppose you have ordered your staff away from the garden?"

"Under threat of death."

Elizabeth laughed. She loved the not-so-serious side of him. "Is that why they are all so attentive? Fear of the gallows?"

Darcy smiled. "Indeed." He captured her hand and brought it to his mouth. "I am glad to hear they have seen to your needs."

"Yes, most proficiently. I have never seen such eager workers. I believe they all want to please you."

Darcy nodded in agreement. "Usually. I think now, they are most eager to please *you*."

She raised her eyebrows in question.

"I am sure it has been speculated—especially after I told Mrs. Reynolds to put Pemberley on its best display—that the future mistress has arrived."

"Oh?"

Elizabeth's voice was soft with a trace of shyness Darcy had not expected, especially given the activities of the morning. He found it endearing and his chest swelled with tenderness.

"Yes. Has their diligent attention to your needs been enough to make you stay?"

Elizabeth tilted her head in contemplation. "I do appreciate a well-run staff, but that is hardly an inducement to matrimony."

Darcy lowered his head and set his mouth in a straight line. "That is unfortunate. They will all be disappointed." He lifted his head and knit his brows. "What of the house? Have its comforts and charms impressed you so much that you could not bear to leave it?"

She sighed and toyed with the knot in his cravat. "The house is beautiful. I have never visited a home more lovely or grand than this one. I would perhaps be sad to leave, but you will find I am not overly sentimental about dwellings."

"Hmm. As you see, the gardens are well maintained. You could fill your chamber with blooms every day of the summer and not deplete their supply."

"I do love flowers and I must say that your garden here is quite beautiful and fragrant. I would even say that you have the least vulgar roses in all of England, but I could never be swayed by hedges and thorns."

She expected him to laugh, but instead Elizabeth suddenly found herself displaced from Darcy's lap. He stood and then not so gracefully pulled her up.

"Come."

Darcy took her hand and walked hurriedly past the hedges. Elizabeth began to worry that she had gone too far with the game. She was ready to tell him she would stay for no reason other than him when he stopped just outside the formal garden. Darcy turned her around, stood behind her and wrapped one arm around her waist. With the other, he pointed across the lawn.

"See the trees just there?"

They looked upon a vast wooded area that must have covered many miles. The trees stood tall and she could hear a slight rustling of the leaves as if they were calling to her.

"All of that is ours, Elizabeth. You may escape civilization as much as you choose and run as fast as you can without fear of censure. I imagine you will find plants and creatures that are entirely new to you. You can walk these woods for years and never see the same scene twice." He pulled her closer and she could feel his heartbeat pounding against her. "*This* is the beautiful and rare, Elizabeth, and I offer it up to your exploration."

Elizabeth knew he was speaking of more than just the woods. Somehow, more tears formed as she realized all this man was offering her.

"Will you explore with me, Mr. Darcy?"

"Yes, my love. Every day of my life."

She turned in his arms and he brought his hands to her face.

"Marry me, Elizabeth."

She smiled with heartbreaking tenderness.

"Yes, my darling Fitzwilliam. I will command your excellent staff, manage your beautiful home, walk in your perfectly manicured gardens and run wild amongst your trees."

He bent down for a lingering kiss then rested his forehead on hers.

"And I will cherish you always, my beautiful Elizabeth."

They managed to enter the house with as little attention being called to them as possible. Before he escorted Elizabeth to her room, Darcy inquired as to the whereabouts of his sister and the Gardiners. He was relieved to hear that none had yet emerged from their chambers.

"I like your uncle and I would rather he not call me out before breakfast."

"Do not be silly, Fitzwilliam. Dueling is how gentlemen settle disputes. My uncle would just shoot you without ceremony."

Seeing his blank expression, Elizabeth laughed. "I am teasing you. My uncle is as gentle as a kitten—most of the time."

They arrived at her chamber and Darcy opened the door but did not follow her inside. They lingered in the doorway for a little while, their fingers slightly touching as they hesitated to say goodbye.

"I should repair my appearance before anyone sees. Let Lucy tend to me before my aunt wakes."

He nodded and ran his thumb over her still swollen lips. "Have her fetch you some ice, that should help." He smiled as he watched a dark blush move up her neck.

"I will have breakfast with Lydia, but I will see you later?"

He nodded. "I will invite your uncle to dine with me again. I must tend to some estate business afterward, but then I will find you. Perhaps you would like a tour of the house while Lydia rests this afternoon?"

Elizabeth smiled happily. "I would like that very much."

He took her hand and kissed it. "I will see you then, love." He watched her retreat behind her door then turned toward his own room. After changing, he gave orders to his valet concerning breakfast then walked through the doors that connected his room to the mistress chambers.

Several of the family's jewels were kept in a locked cabinet in the dressing room. Darcy had retrieved the key before entering and unlocked it to look upon many familiar pieces. He recognized some from the portraits that hung in the gallery. Some were more than a century old, but a few pieces were given to Anne Darcy by her husband. Those would go to Georgiana. He picked them out to put in a safe in his study until she came out.

He also found several items that had come from Matlock. His mother had rarely worn Fitzwilliam heirlooms, choosing instead to display the Darcy legacy. Darcy wondered if that had been a conscious effort on her part. He fought the urge to toss the jewels to the pigs. Anything associated with that side of his family was abhorrent to him at present. The desire to harm him seemed to flow in the Fitzwilliam veins.

As angry as he was with his cousin, he could not forget that his mother was part of that family and she had been good and kind in spite of it. Anne and Wakely were also far superior to their parents. It was Richard who had chosen to be otherwise. Darcy put the Fitzwilliam jewels to the side for Elizabeth to decide their fate.

Darcy continued looking, hoping the piece he searched for was there and not in London. He wanted to give Elizabeth something special to mark their engagement and he thought the brooch his grandmother gave to his mother when she became the mistress of Pemberley was perfect. It contained diamonds and emeralds that had been taken from other, older pieces, and set into silver threads woven into vines and leaves. Quite ideal for his wild rose.

Darcy opened the last drawer in the cabinet and was relieved to find the brooch nestled in with several hairpins. He smiled at a memory from earlier that morning. Elizabeth had struggled to right her hair after his attentions had sent it cascading around her shoulders. She could not find all of her pins afterward and teased him about how shocked his gardener would be to find frippery among the hedgerows.

He took the jeweled pins from the drawer and put them in his pocket.

He would carry them with him in case she ever again found herself in need of replacement. His smile grew, knowing that would likely happen again very soon.

"Lydia." Georgiana whispered from the edge of the bed. "It is almost time for breakfast."

A groan came from beneath the covers as Lydia rolled onto her back. She slowly pulled the blanket off her face and rubbed her eyes.

"Good morning, Georgiana." She pushed herself up onto pillows and looked curiously at her visitor. It seemed unusually early for Georgiana to be there. "Are you well?"

"I am. Well, I am a little anxious. But, yes, I am well. How are you? How did you sleep?"

"Well enough, I suppose." She shifted her weight to find a comfortable position. "Why are you anxious?"

"I wanted to talk to you about something, but I am afraid I might upset you."

Lydia pulled a pillow from behind her back and sighed. She had remained contented for all of a minute. "I wonder why you would bring it up, then."

"Well, I think it is important for you to know. That is if I am correct."

"About what, Georgiana?"

"I know my brother very well and can usually understand why he does things. He is very compassionate so it did not surprise me that he brought you here. I did wonder, though, why he treated you with such care, just as he would with me. That is until I saw him with your sister yesterday. I believe he is quite enamored of her."

"With Lizzy? Well, he should be." She thought for a moment then smiled. "Lizzy and Mr. Darcy? Mama is going to faint. Why did you think that would upset me?"

"Not that. I am taking too long to make my point, I believe. The look on his face when he was with your sister yesterday was one I had never seen before. However, since you have been here, I have noticed that, more than once, he gets a particular look that I recognize well. It is one of disgust mixed with regret."

"Oh?" Lydia's voice dropped to a whisper.

"No! No, not for you. I am sorry. It is for someone else."

Lydia huffed. "Georgiana, you are making me dizzy. If I promise not to swoon or scream, will you please just tell me whatever it is?"

Georgiana sighed then blurted out. "My brother only gets that look when he has to deal with Mr. Wickham. Am I correct in thinking that he is the one who put you in this predicament?"

Lydia nodded then looked away.

"I am sorry if I am upsetting you. I just wanted you to know that I understand how very charming he can be. How he can make everything you are doing feel wonderful and exciting. That is, until the moment you realize it was all a lie."

Lydia sat up. "Georgiana? Did he--?"

"No. My brother came before anything irreparable could happen." Georgiana tearfully relayed the events of Ramsgate.

"Oh Georgie, he could have taken everything from you."

She nodded. "He is a predator. He lured me away from Fitzwilliam, through Mrs. Younge, and pounced on me like a lion would its prey. The things he said to me … it was as if he knew the exact words that would cause me to react the way he wanted. He spoke to me of my father, how much he had loved him and how he always considered Fitzwilliam a brother. I think the memories of them that he shared is what appealed to me even more than his flattery."

Lydia nodded in agreement. "He made it all seem fun and exhilarating. I was always so bored in Hertfordshire. He promised he would take me to London where he would buy me lovely gowns and we would dance. I truly thought we would marry. After, I was afraid I would be made to marry him. He turned cruel so quickly after he took what he wanted. Your brother said what happened was not my fault. Wickham and my father said otherwise. I do not know what to believe."

Georgiana took her hands. "Let us both believe Fitzwilliam. Lydia, I think you and I are meant to be sisters so that we can always remind each other that things could be so much worse. One of us could have him for a husband. No matter what he might have said or done, we are worthy of good things. We will not let him make us weak."

Lydia began to sob. "But I *am* weak, Georgiana, and I am frightened. I am so far from who I used to be that I may as well not be anything."

"No, Lydia. If that were true, you would have died instead of being found. Good things will come from this if you allow it. Wickham teased me with thoughts about family, but the joke is on him because I will have a sister. And you will have a brother who will always take care of you. I have gained much strength since I have been at Pemberley and so will you."

Lydia was too tired to argue, especially since she wanted to believe every word Georgiana spoke.

"What do you want me to say, Georgiana?"

"That you will not give up, even when you feel you cannot go on. I know that my experience with Wickham can hardly compare with what you have been through. But, I do know how it feels to think you are not good enough and how that drains you of every good thing. But, it is a lie. I want you to say you believe me and *we will not let him make us weak.*"

Sweet, obliging Georgiana looked so determined at that moment that Lydia would not dare defy her. She rubbed one hand over her stomach and squeezed Georgiana's hand with the other.

"No, Georgie, we will not let him make us weak."

Chapter 29

"I will need to write to Bingley soon. He and his sisters were to visit next month, but I must ask them to postpone their trip. Fitzwilliam was to come as well. I will have Georgiana write to him."

Elizabeth, once again comfortably seated on Darcy's lap in the garden, ran her hand along his chest in comfort. She knew he felt his cousin's betrayal deeply though he tried not to let it show.

"Will you never write to him?"

"No. What I will say to him needs to be done so in person."

Elizabeth knew she should encourage Darcy to forgive his cousin if for no other reason than for his sister's sake. Georgiana adored Colonel Fitzwilliam and spoke of him often. The pain was still too raw for both of them, however. She chose instead, to change the subject.

"Did you see Lydia this morning?"

"I did."

"Does she not look better? Her face is fuller and her cheeks have some color."

"Eating properly and being free from at least some of her worries has helped, I am sure. Not to mention the rest doing her good."

"Yes. You have not told me what happened with the Baineses."

"No, I have not." He paused to find the right words. He and Mr. Gardiner visited the Baines farm the previous day. Threats were made and Elizabeth need not know the specifics. He thought back to her comment about her uncle being as gentle as a kitten. That was hardly true the day before. "I do not believe we have to worry about them. They will not speak of Lydia."

"What about the little boy? Lydia seemed fond of him."

Darcy smiled a little. "We saw him. He was happy to hear Lydia was safe. I will remember him. When he is older, I will bring him here to work if he would like."

"That is very generous of you."

She kissed him on the cheek and he smiled.

"I think it will make Lydia happy. But, dearest, I must speak to you about something. I am afraid you will not be pleased."

"We have only been engaged a week and you are already displeasing me? This does not bode well for the future, Mr. Darcy." He smiled only a little at the tease. "You are serious?"

Darcy had been reluctant to approach the subject and had put it off for several days. Mornings in the garden were the only times they were alone together. The Gardiners were pleased with news of their engagement but were stern chaperones. Thankfully, they were not early risers. He did not want to mar their time together with talk of his departure.

"I will need to travel to Hertfordshire soon."

Elizabeth had been leisurely playing with the curls that rested on his collar. She stopped her ministrations and pulled away.

"I am one-and-twenty, Fitzwilliam. You need not seek my father's permission."

"I know, but I will be taking away two of his daughters. I should inform him of that."

"You could write to him."

"I could, but your uncle said the letter could sit on your father's desk for a month before he opened it."

"That is true, but have you thought about what you are going to say to him? Lydia and I are supposed to be at the seaside, not in Derbyshire."

"I would not wish to lie to him."

"I know and you would not have to. You or Uncle Gardiner can write to him and explain everything. But, Mama cannot be trusted with this. Papa can be the one to tell her the lie, but I am afraid we will have to make it up ourselves."

Elizabeth watched him contemplate her words. She knew it was hard for him to intentionally deceive anybody. His honor could not make it easy and she hated asking him to do so.

"What town did you say Lydia went to?"

Before replying, she kissed him in gratitude, knowing he would do or say anything to keep her safe.

"We never named a town. Simply saying the seaside seemed to be enough."

"It is fortunate for us that England is an island. We can say that you decided to tour the lakes on the way back to London. It is feasible that Mrs. Gardiner would want to visit old friends in Lambton while she was in the county. It is more feasible that I saw you and determined I could not let you go for the third time."

"Third time?"

"Yes." Elizabeth was shocked to see him actually blush. "I wanted you in Hertfordshire, only I was too much of a coward to do anything about it."

"Truly? I had no idea. I thought you looked at me only to find fault."

"How could that be so, when there is no fault to find?" He accompanied that statement with a sly grin.

"Oh, I like that answer, Mr. Darcy. You are entirely too charming at times."

He chuckled. "I am glad you think so, dearest. No one ever has before." He sighed and stroked her hair. "All those dinners and balls where all the single gentlemen and ladies were put on display, no one ever caught my attention. I never had the occasion to practice my charm. If you did not see my interest while we were both at Netherfield, then that proves how lacking I am in that area."

"You lack in no areas, my darling man."

"Ah, now who is being entirely too charming?"

She turned so that she could more easily touch him. She ran her fingers through his hair and smiled.

"What is it, love?"

"I believe I would like a lock of your hair, should you wish to give it to me."

Darcy brought his mouth to hers and kissed her, slow and deep, leaving her panting when he pulled away.

"You may have any part of me you desire, dearest Elizabeth."

They adjusted their positions so that she was on her knees between his legs.

"Do you have a pen knife?"

He nodded and thankfully was able to retrieve it from the inside pocket of his greatcoat without moving her from her current position. Her breasts were displayed to their great advantage in front of him. He would not move for the world.

Elizabeth reached back with both hands to release a ribbon from her carefully pinned hair. Darcy watched her movements in a daze. She was naturally sensual and had no idea what her graceful movements did to him. His hands gripped her waist and with a great feat of willpower, he managed to keep them from moving up.

Elizabeth watched the subtle changes in Darcy's expression as she pulled the ribbon from her hair. She had not worn a spencer, deciding to risk a chill to feel more of Darcy's touch when they were alone. He seemed to appreciate its absence.

When they were together in Kent and her feelings for him were growing deeper, she did not resist the urge to touch him or allow his gentle caresses in return. Her physical expressions were born from love and a need to feel safe and protected. It was natural for her to express affection through physical contact and doing so with Darcy had always been easy.

Those feelings were changing into something stronger—something that pulled at her most sensitive places and left her longing for more of him. She was sure *desire* was the name given to these feelings. But such a small word seemed inadequate to describe the need she felt to disappear in him and the pleasures she received from his touch.

She leaned into Darcy and he placed his head on her shoulder. His lips barely grazed her skin and she felt his warm breath on her neck. She grasped his shoulders to steady herself, as the sensations caused by closeness made her shudder.

She slowly moved her hands across his shoulders to his hair. Her fingers ran through his dark curls over and over, loving the feel of the soft strands. Finally, she tied off one curl and cut through the lock with the knife.

Darcy did not immediately lift his head. His grip on her waist tightened slightly, then loosened as his hands roamed down to her rounded hips. At the same time, his lips began gently caressing her shoulder, then her neck and cheek then down again. Her skin was sweet and he paused to taste more at the base of her neck, lingering there while his hands continued to explore.

Unhurriedly, purposely memorizing the terrain, his hands moved around to her back and traveled up to her hair, where they found another ribbon. He removed it, along with several pins. Curls fell around her shoulders and Darcy finally ceased his ministrations to inspect her locks for the perfect token. Finding it, he tied it off then ran his fingertips down Elizabeth's arm to the hand that held the knife. He took it and wrapped his arms around her, positioning the knife at his chosen curl. As he cut through, Darcy leaned in to kiss her full, pink lips. He placed the knife and curl on either side of him, then reached up to hold her face, deepening the kiss into one of complete capitulation. He would be hers forever.

Without breaking the kiss, Darcy rose to his feet, bringing Elizabeth with him. Reluctantly, he pulled away but took a moment to savor the sight of her flushed cheeks and swollen lips. The regret that she was not already his wife had never been greater. He retrieved his coat, then placed her hand on his arm and led her back inside and upstairs to her room.

Darcy opened the door to her chambers but did not usher her inside. Instead, he wrapped his arm around her waist and placed a lingering kiss on her forehead. He looked inside her room then back to her. Without a word, he turned and walked away.

Elizabeth walked through the door and closed it behind her. Lucy appeared and, noticing her mistress's dazed expression, immediately asked what she required.

"Only ice, Lucy. A great deal of ice."

"What are you doing over there, Charles? Are you writing to Mr. Darcy?"

Bingley sat in a small drawing room in the Hurst townhouse trying to concentrate on his letters. His sister had joined him a quarter of an hour earlier and rather than tend to her own occupations, apparently decided to annoy her brother instead.

"Caroline, one day I hope you will begin a conversation with me that has nothing to do with Darcy." He lifted his head and tapped his finger on his chin. "What did you ever speak to me about before I made his acquaintance?"

"Do not be ridiculous, Charles. We speak of many things." Her attention drifted briefly to her skirts before she again addressed her brother. "I have not yet forgiven you, you know, for not informing me when Mr. Darcy returned from Kent."

"It is of little matter, Caroline. He was busy while he was in town."

"Yes, I know. I read all about it in the papers."

Bingley rolled his eyes but did not bother to correct his sister. Caroline was not one to be offended by the behaviors of men. She would likely hand pick an entire harem for Darcy if it meant she could be mistress of Pemberley. He was just returning to his letters when his other sister appeared.

"Charles, I must speak to you about Caroline."

Mrs. Hurst handed her brother a note and was about to speak again when her sister made her presence known.

"What about me, Louisa?"

"Oh. I did not realize you were in here. Oh well, you might as well know. My husband has informed his mother of my delicate condition. She insists on returning to town to see that I am being cared for."

Louisa had suspected for some time she was with child but had only recently told her husband. He displayed an uncharacteristic amount of joy at the news and declared her housebound. They would not travel, and he would have his mother come to oversee the household so that his wife would not tax herself. Louisa would have been moved by his attentions if she believed they were in any way brought about by concern for her wellbeing. She was sure, however, that he was more concerned that this child would come into the world strong, healthy and male, thus ensuring he would not have to participate in making another one.

Caroline sighed dramatically. "I suppose she will be staying here?"

"This *is* her house, Caroline. She has every right to stay here. Furthermore, she has the right to eject any guests she does not like." Louisa looked pointedly at her sister.

"What do you mean?"

"She says you are rude, snide and behave as if you are mistress of this house. She arrives next week and expects you to be gone before then."

Caroline gasped. "Charles, say something. I cannot be sent away. Where will I go?"

"You could go back to Netherfield. I know how much you enjoyed the society there."

"Louisa, should you not go lie down? I believe your *delicate condition* is affecting your mind."

"Netherfield is not an option as I have given up the lease. Louisa, will Hurst's mother not take some pity on us? It will be difficult to find other accommodations in just two days."

"No, Charles, she is quite adamant. Apparently she has had complaints from the servants."

Bingley groaned. That was nothing new. Caroline never could keep a maid for long and several of his staff at Netherfield quit before they reached the end of the first month there.

"I suppose I must quickly find a house to rent. I should warn you, Caroline, nothing is likely to be available in the areas you wish to be."

"Why do we not remove to Darcy House? I am sure Mr. Darcy would love to have us."

"He has gone to Pemberley. There is no time to write and ask for use of his townhouse before we must vacate this one."

"Oh, let us go to Pemberley, then. It is only a few weeks early. He is such a dear friend, he will not mind."

Bingley contemplated the idea for a moment. If he were traveling alone, Darcy would not hesitate to welcome him at any time. Accepting Caroline with equanimity, however, usually required preparation.

"Colonel Fitzwilliam was to travel with us. I do not know if he can rearrange his plans so easily as you, sister."

"Well, write to him and ask, dear brother. If you will excuse me, I will see to our packing." After giving her sister a scathing look, she left the room.

"Charles, when you write to Mr. Darcy, please let me know so I can include a note of apology. I had looked forward to being at Pemberley again."

"Ah, but a child is much more exciting than an old house. You are wise to stay behind."

"I am merely following orders."

"Are you not happy, Louisa? You will be a mother. Our own mother was dear; surely you would want to be like her."

Louisa smiled at her younger brother. Sometimes, at least when Caroline was not around, she could not help herself.

"She was dear to you, Charles, because you were the youngest and could do no wrong. Caroline and I were treated much differently. She was determined we would be ladies."

"Well, I needed her comfort. Father put just as much pressure on me as Mother put on you. But now, I look forward to being an uncle. Really, what is better than a soft little bundle to bounce on your knee? I know many men do not pay attention to the little ones, but I shall be overjoyed to spend time with yours, Louisa."

"That is good Charles, perhaps you can act as a nurse and save us the expense."

Bingley laughed then sighed somewhat wistfully. "I would not go that far, but truly, children are a joy and I look forward to my own in the near future."

Louisa patted him on his shoulder. "I will let you get back to your letters, Charles. Since you are such a kind brother, I will return the favor and keep Caroline from you until dinner."

Bingley smiled as she left the room then tried to concentrate his business. Ever since he saw Jane Bennet in the park, something pulled at him, like an anchor trying to weigh him down. He knew his flighty ways would eventually come to an end, but he had expected to have a reason, an estate or a wife, to inspire the need to settle down. Instead, it was coming all on its own. Perhaps this was good. This way, rather than trying to keep up with whatever change was coming, he would be prepared for whatever life decided to give him.

Chapter 30

Lydia adjusted the pillows behind her back for the hundredth time that afternoon. Try as she would, she just could not get comfortable. Her legs tingled and as much as she bent and stretched, she found no relief. For a distraction, she began looking around the room. A wave of annoyance hit her when she saw the seating arrangement in the far corner.

"Mrs. Reynolds, will you please come here?"

The housekeeper, along with Mrs. Annesley, were sitting with Lydia, attempting to make her happy. Lydia had already requested solitude after driving away Darcy, Elizabeth, Georgiana *and* the Gardiners. She found it difficult to tolerate their voices. Darcy sent in the two people least likely to speak or be offended by Lydia's increasing irritation.

"Yes, Miss Lydia? Can I get you something?"

"I do not like the looks of that chair there. Please move it."

"Very well, where would you like it placed?"

"I care not. You may put it in the fireplace if you wish, but I do not want to look at it again."

Mrs. Reynolds did as asked. The chair was light and she was able to move it into the hall without help. Lydia's annoyance did not wane.

"I need to move. Please help me up."

"Miss Lydia, that is not wise. You are not strong enough."

"I must leave this bed for a while. My legs ache for movement. Please help me."

With both Mrs. Reynolds and Mrs. Annesley assisting, Lydia rose from bed for the first time in many days. Her knees instantly gave, but the women managed to keep her upright.

"Miss Lydia, please return to bed."

"No. I only wish to take a turn about the room. I am not going to plow the fields. Let us move to the table there."

Slowly and deliberately, the three women walked to the table where meals were served to whoever was sitting with Lydia at the time. She grasped the corner for support but did not sit as requested.

"No, I do not wish to sit. I want to bathe. Mrs. Reynolds, will you please call for water? And I want to wear a real dress, my pretty pink one if it has been retrieved."

"Very well, Miss Lydia. I will return shortly, but please sit in the meantime."

Mrs. Reynolds and Mrs. Annesley shared a knowing look. The coming days would be a trial.

"What is it, Mrs. Reynolds?"

Those who had been dismissed from Lydia's room at various times that day were gathered in Pemberley's smaller dining room, partaking in a casual luncheon.

"Forgive me for interrupting, sir." She looked to the footmen who were serving the meal. Darcy noticed and dismissed them.

"Is it Lydia?"

"Yes, sir. I believe it is time to bring in the midwife."

Elizabeth looked up in alarm. "But it is too soon! Aunt, is it not at least a month too soon?"

"Calm down, Lizzy. Babes come when they want—sometimes early, sometimes late. Lydia's time has been peculiar. Mrs. Reynolds did not say it is time, only that we should be prepared." She turned to Mrs. Reynolds. "Is she in pain?"

"No, but she is inflicting plenty. Miss Lydia is very agitated and cannot remain still. She has requested a bath and to dress. She also wishes the furniture to be rearranged."

"How is that unusual? She has been in bed for a long time now. She must be restless."

"She is nesting, Mr. Darcy. Instinct is driving her to prepare for the baby."

Darcy rose and walked toward Mrs. Reynolds. "I want the doctor and midwife brought here immediately to stay until the child arrives. Do whatever you must to see to her comfort. Surely this agitation is not helpful. If

Lydia wishes to move the furniture, then move the furniture."

Everyone still seated around the table looked at Darcy, slightly confused by his abruptness. Mrs. Reynolds, it seemed, understood and smiled softly.

Darcy took a deep breath and spoke in a lowered voice. "What do we do?"

"We wait."

"A letter for you, sir."

Fitzwilliam had just left his father's study and was anxious to quit the house altogether when the butler stopped him. Annoyed, he grabbed the letter from the tray and continued walking. Asking his father for assistance was never an easy task. Matlock always expected something in return, and he had rarely needed anything from his second son. The earl must have been in a good mood that afternoon because he responded favorably to his son's request without much thought, which annoyed Fitzwilliam more than if he had made demands.

He decided to stop by the drawing room to see his mother before he left. He had attempted a visit prior to seeing Matlock but she was entertaining some duchess or other and he was in no mood for polite society. He stopped outside the open door and looked inside. The countess was alone and hunched over sleeping, her morning dose of opium doing its job of sedating reality. Letting out a long breath, he walked in the room and pulled a stool in front of her chair. He sat and studied her.

Lady Sophia had been a striking woman in her youth. Fitzwilliam remembered thinking as a child that his mother's hair was so beautiful it must have been spun from gold. Now she was streaked with grey, seemingly all over. Her mind was listless and her sapphire eyes, which he inherited, were draped in weariness.

Fitzwilliam remembered his father's words about her having been meant for the deceased first son. He wondered if the slow decline he had witnessed in her all his life was caused by grief over having lost the man she loved or if self-destruction had simply become a hobby.

Remembering the letter, Fitzwilliam turned it over and broke the seal. Bingley needed to leave for Pemberley a few weeks early. He rubbed the back of his neck as he contemplated the change in plans. Considering his recent decision, it actually worked in his favor to travel to Pemberley early, but his stomach twisted at the thought of seeing Darcy.

Their last encounter had played in his mind over the last weeks so often that Fitzwilliam knew every word and movement by heart. The gratification he felt at seeing Darcy act the fool had steadily waned and he now only felt dread and discontent. He had not seen Olivia since his last failed attempt at forgetting and the memories of Victoria no longer held the same attraction. Like the effects of drink or his mother's opium, the elevated feelings that came with the infatuation with that lady had been empty and fleeting. His pride had been affected far more than his heart.

The same could possibly be said of Elizabeth Bennet. He had certainly been filled with pride when he thought she preferred him. Of course, that preference had never existed. Fitzwilliam did wonder how things would have been different if Darcy had not been at Rosings. Could he have touched her heart if the temptation of wealth and connections not been so strong? It was of no matter now.

He would have to go to Pemberley. He wanted to see Georgiana even though it meant facing the consequences of his actions. Darcy had not written to him again since his refusal to come to Darcy House. Fitzwilliam knew Darcy's anger would not be dissolved with a few jokes and a half-hearted apology. This visit would likely bring a confrontation and though he had been so keen for one at Rosings, he now only wanted to ride away from Pemberley without the shadow of regret following him.

Looking upon his mother one last time, Fitzwilliam rose and walked to a writing desk in the corner of the room. He remained standing and bent slightly while he scribbled out a reply. He left the room and gave the note to the butler along with instructions to have his belongings packed into trunks and sent to his quarters with the regiment. Without looking back to Matlock House or thinking any more on those inside, Fitzwilliam descended the steps and disappeared into the crowded streets of London.

The melancholy sounds of Georgiana's playing filled the rooms where several restless residents of Pemberley waited. Mrs. Annesley sat in the music room with her charge, attempting to keep her stitches straight and her mind occupied. Mrs. Reynolds worked in her office, methodically going over household accounts, pausing occasionally to look at the clock or sigh in time with the music. Mr. Gardiner was attempting to concentrate on a very dull book of history, but his companion made it difficult.

Darcy paced about the room, occasionally stopping to glance at a book or some papers on his desk. The slightest noise would cause him to stop and look at the door, expecting someone to enter with news. A week after the midwife had taken residence in Pemberley, she was summoned in the middle of the night to tend to a crying Lydia. Twelve hours later, the babe had not yet arrived and the last report the men heard was that Lydia was exhausted with the process and in so much pain she kept crying for her mother.

"Darcy, it could be hours still before this is all over. Why do you not go for a ride? The air will do you good."

"I do not wish to leave the house."

"I know you are anxious for Lydia and for Elizabeth's feelings as well. But, it seems you have something else worrying you. It may be better for your peace of mind, as well as your carpets if you talk about it instead of pacing like a caged animal."

Darcy sighed and ran his hand over his forehead then down his face. He looked at Mr. Gardiner for a moment, then sat across from him.

"Pemberley has seen more than its share of death. My younger brothers are buried alongside my parents, grandparents and every Darcy who ever existed since the land was granted to us. I am afraid the situation with Lydia has brought up some painful memories. My mother was weakened by Georgiana's birth and never recovered. I do not want Elizabeth to watch her sister fade as my mother did, but I am just as powerless to stop it now as I was then. This *waiting* is torture."

"Indeed, it is, Darcy. I could spew platitudes in an attempt to calm you, but we both know the precariousness of the situation. Lydia is weak and the babe is coming early. In this instance, and every time you find yourself awaiting such an arrival, you have to accept your own uselessness and trust in a higher power. Lydia should have already died once, but you saved her. I do not believe that was for nothing."

Just then a knock came followed by Elizabeth coming through the study doors. Both men rose with a question in their eyes. She shook her head.

"Nothing yet, though I think it will be soon. My aunt would not let me stay any longer."

Darcy's own anxiety was forgotten as he beheld the look of his beloved's exhaustion. He took her hand and led her to the sofa and sat beside her.

With Mr. Gardiner there, he could not take her in his arms as he wished, so he kept hold of her hand and offered every comfort he could.

"What can I get you, Elizabeth? A glass of wine perhaps, or some tea? Have you eaten anything today?"

Elizabeth thought for a moment. "I do not believe I have. I went to Lydia right after I rose this morning. I did not think about eating."

Rather than ringing and then waiting for a servant, Darcy stepped out the door and gave instructions to a footman. He returned to Elizabeth, sitting closer this time.

"Dearest, you cannot risk your own health. After you eat, I want you go to your chamber to rest."

"I do not believe I could, Fitzwilliam. My mind is too busy. She is in so much pain and my heart breaks each time I hear her whimper for Mama. My sister is upstairs laboring as a woman, yet calls for her mother with the voice of a child. Sleep will not shut that sound out of my mind."

He gripped her hand tighter. "No, I suppose not."

"Darcy, I know you wanted to travel to Hertfordshire and speak to Thomas in person. However, I think I should write to him."

Darcy looked at Mr. Gardiner and nodded, guessing what was on his mind. "Tell him everything and ask him to bring Mrs. Bennet to Pemberley. She will not be here for the birth, but perhaps she can provide some comfort after. I will send the letter by rider and do what I can to make travel easier for them."

Elizabeth smiled softly through her tears. "Thank you, Fitzwilliam. I know you are trying to give Lydia what she wants, but we cannot bring my parents here. It is natural, I think, for Lydia to crave the warmth of a mother when she is in pain, just as it was natural that I should seek a father's strength when I was so frightened. I am afraid, however, that their characters do not allow for such comforts. Mama would be hysterical and Papa would ignore the seriousness of the situation. As much as we may need them to be different, we must accept their limitations. Expecting anything more would only lead to further disappointment. I cannot trust them with my sister." She turned to Mr. Gardiner. "Uncle, you know this to be true."

He nodded. "You are very wise, Lizzy. Still, I will write to Thomas. I will tell him our tale of visiting the lakes and ending up here. My sister needs *some* news of her daughter. I will go to my chamber and write to him now. I will not be long."

He gave Darcy an understanding, yet stern look and exited the room. Darcy immediately brought Elizabeth to his lap. She turned her head into him and sobbed quietly.

"I am so frightened for her. While I was with her this morning, my mind kept wondering about her future. What kind of life will she have? Will she ever marry or have other children? What will happen to her if no man would wish to marry her now? All this time I have been scared she would not survive, I had not given a thought to what would happen if she does.

"All of this has made me see my mother differently. If I am this fraught with worry for the future of one sister, how much more must she feel for *five* daughters? That would be enough to drive any sensible woman to a fit of nerves. Add a careless husband and I am surprised she has maintained any of her sanity."

"She was relieved when Jane wed?"

"Yes, I told you—"

"What?"

"I was going to say I already told you how she reacted, but I remembered that I did not. At least not to your face. I wrote to you of it."

He frowned. "I would remember if I received a letter from you, dearest."

Elizabeth smiled sadly and kissed his cheek. "I wrote to you in a journal, nearly every day while I was at Longbourn. I missed you terribly and felt closer to you while writing. I have it here; I will bring it to you if you wish."

"You would not mind me reading your journal?"

She shook her head. "As I said, they are your letters. I want you to read them."

"I should like that, Elizabeth." He leaned down and kissed her gently. "Very much."

He kissed her again then rested his head on hers. Just as they had started to doze, a knock alerted them that their tea had arrived. They assumed a more proper position on the sofa and soon after Elizabeth had fixed their cups, Georgiana joined them.

"I do not believe I have played that much in one sitting since I returned to Pemberley. My fingers hurt."

"You sounded lovely, Georgiana."

"Thank you, Lizzy." Georgiana reached out and patted her hand. "I know you are worried for Lydia, but she will be well. I know she will for we have made a deal. She and I are to be sisters and we will not let that horrible man ruin us. We will seek our revenge on him by living happily."

"Lydia agreed to this?"

Georgiana smiled broadly. "She did. She will not give up, Lizzy."

Before long, Mr. Gardiner returned after having written a lengthy letter to Mr. Bennet. He had been sorely tempted to break through his brother-in-law's shield of ignorance with the entire truth of Lydia's situation, but decided Elizabeth's chosen path of silence was best.

They ate mostly in silence as fatigue and concern won out over politeness. After a while, Mr. Gardiner urged them all to retire.

"None of us will be any good to Lydia if we do not rest. I have been through this four times and know you must sleep when you can. Nothing will happen without your knowledge, I promise."

The four of them all retired to restless dreams as their uneasiness followed them in their sleep. Dawn broke and brought with it the news they had been seeking. Elizabeth rushed to Lydia's room while Mr. Gardiner once again returned to his. He decided to amend his letter to include word of the *birth of a girl*. She was small but managed a mighty wail. Her mother had fought hard through the night to bring her into the world and was currently, in spite of all she had experienced, resting comfortably.

Chapter 31

Lydia lay on her side and watched as the sun's rays drifted through the room. She had watched the light change from dim to bright and now it was retreating into the shadows. The tenderness in her lower body caused her to wince as she slowly turned over then sat up on her pillows. She pushed the counterpane down to her hips and pulled her nightgown tight around her abdomen. She wondered how long it would take to get used to the fact that her child was no longer there.

A knock sounded on her door and she quickly covered herself just before Darcy entered the room.

"You wanted to see me, Lydia?"

"Yes." She looked down and toyed with the trim that had become frayed from her nervous fidgeting. She did not look at him when she spoke. "Where will she go?"

Darcy sat down and looked at her sadly. "To a family whose estate is about twenty miles from here. I know them fairly well. They have a son close to your age. My father had the opportunity to be of service to them years ago and Mrs. Reynolds reminded me of their continued desire to return the favor. It will be said she is an orphaned cousin. She will be raised among the genteel."

Lydia shook her head. "But she will not be considered one of them. She will always be on the outside. My daughter is illegitimate; she has no gentleman father to give her credit of any kind and her genteel mother has given her away."

"I wish I could do more. If Elizabeth and I were already married—"

"No, Mr. Darcy. Her origin will always be questioned. I would not have it speculated that you are anything but honorable. I am grateful the family you have chosen is willing to risk any gossip that might arise when they take her." She looked down at her hands for a moment, then back to Darcy. "We should have died. We would have, if you had not come upon us and brought us here."

"Lydia—"

"No, Mr. Darcy. I should not have survived this. I honestly never expected to, not from the day I first became ill. And now, what do I do?"

For months, Lydia had felt she and her child were in peril. Now that the danger had passed, she must face all that had happened. She was no longer the same girl from before and the person she was to become stood somewhere in the distance. The gap between the two now seemed like an expansive divide, and Lydia was too fatigued to contemplate the first steps.

Darcy leaned forward and took her hand. "You heal, Lydia. It will take time, but you will be relieved of this burden. Elizabeth said you asked for your mother. As soon as you are able, we will take you to Longbourn. Would it help you to see your mother and sisters?"

Lydia's heart beat faster and her palms suddenly became sweaty. She swallowed hard and shook her head. "I cannot see them, not yet. I do not know what they would expect from me. They would be disappointed to see me so altered, I think. I will write to them, assure them I am well, but I can't pretend to be who I no longer am."

"We could send for Jane. I am sure Elizabeth would like to have her here for the wedding."

Lydia thought for a moment then began to cry. "I would like to see Jane, very much. Will you write to her today?"

Darcy's eyes softened and he nodded slightly. "Whatever you wish, little one. You need not worry about anything other than getting well."

"Thank you."

Darcy left her to rest and Lydia retreated beneath the covers, her anxiety somewhat mollified for the moment. Feeling grateful for being allowed to simply just be, she closed her eyes and waited for sleep to take her.

Darcy stared at the paper in his hand in disbelief and frustration. If he were interpreting the poor lettering correctly, Pemberley would have guests within the next few hours. The letter was dated a week ago, but Bingley had written the direction so ill it must have been lost, as Darcy was just now receiving it.

"The man has written me here a hundred times and *this* is the letter that goes astray." He spoke to himself as he walked from his study to the drawing room where Elizabeth sat with Georgiana and the Gardiners. Without ceremony, he entered and handed Elizabeth the letter.

"Forgive me, sir, but I am unfamiliar with whatever language this is written it."

Darcy huffed. "It might as well be its own language. The letter is from Bingley, informing me that he needed to alter his travel plans. He, his sister and *my cousin* are to arrive today."

"I thought you wrote to him asking him not to come."

"I did. He must not have received it before he left."

"Oh no. Well, there is nothing to be done about it now, Fitzwilliam. We must simply act as if nothing has happened. We will tell them the same story we related to my father, except we must explain Lydia's illness."

"You are correct, of course." He turned to Georgiana. "Will you please ask Mrs. Reynolds to prepare guest rooms as far away from Lydia as possible?"

"Of course. Do not worry, brother. The worst is over. You may enjoy having Richard and Mr. Bingley here. Your best friends will attend your wedding!"

Before Georgiana could leave to have the rooms prepared, the butler entered and announced the Bingleys' arrival. They entered the room and Bingley immediately and very excitedly spoke.

"Darcy! It is very good to be back at Pemberley." Bingley's next words were halted as he noticed that the room was occupied by more than just his friend. Any annoyance Darcy felt at Bingley's unexpected arrival was erased when he saw the look of surprise, then joy that spread across his features when he recognized Elizabeth.

"Miss Bennet!" He stepped forward and bowed over her hand. "How wonderful to see you here at Pemberley."

He looked at Darcy with a question in his eyes. Darcy smiled and Bingley looked again at Elizabeth.

"Yes, I am very pleased indeed."

"Thank you, Mr. Bingley. I am delighted to see you as well."

A noise behind Bingley reminded them of the other guest who had arrived. Everyone in the room turned their attention to the woman whose face had turned a brilliant shade of red. Unlike her brother, Miss Bingley was anything but pleased.

Richard Fitzwilliam sat on his horse, overlooking Pemberley from a nearby hill. He had deliberately lagged behind the carriage carrying the Bingleys, then took an alternate path to the estate. He stared straight ahead, ignoring the lake in the distance where his Uncle George had taught him how to steer a boat and the large tree to his left that he and a distraught Darcy climbed to try to escape the grief after Lady Anne died. He had as many childhood memories of Pemberley as he did of Matlock, and most of them were far more pleasant.

Reaching inside his coat, he brought out a flask and took one last shot of fortification. He would not dwell on the memories; they were not why he came. Fitzwilliam had fought through the resentment, guilt and pain to ride to Pemberley for a single purpose—to see Georgiana one last time. He kicked his horse forward toward the manor. With each step, his stomach twisted tighter, but he did not stop until he reached the front steps. After emptying his flask, he took a deep breath and entered.

"Imagine my great surprise to find you all here, Miss Eliza. Why, I had no idea you were so closely acquainted with the Darcys. Please tell me, however did you manage an invitation? Surely you have not seen Mr. Darcy since we left Hertfordshire together."

Georgiana and Bingley were speaking to the Gardiners, with whom he was happy to now be acquainted. His sister, however, barely acknowledged them, preferring instead to interrogate Elizabeth. Darcy stood beside his betrothed and watched as Miss Bingley attempted to unsettle her.

"Mr. Darcy and I renewed our acquaintance while we were both in Kent."

"Oh yes, your cousin is a parson there. What a coincidence you were there at the same time. I am surprised he had time to visit you at all. It is my understanding that he is quite close with his relations, particularly with Miss Anne de Bourgh."

"Miss Bennet knows this quite well." Darcy turned to Elizabeth, annoyed with the way Miss Bingley was speaking as if he was not staring down at her. "You and Anne became good friends, did you not?"

Elizabeth smiled. "Yes, we did. She was a great comfort to me after your departure."

"How is it that you are here, Eliza?" Miss Bingley's annoyance overruled any effort at politeness.

"Mr. Darcy invited us to stay here while we were touring the area. Unfortunately, my sister fell ill and is still recuperating."

Miss Bingley rolled her eyes in exasperation. "Good heavens! Does a Bennet girl always become ill while visiting a grand home? I suppose you must extend your stay while she recovers."

"*Caroline.*" Bingley finally heard his sister's tone and sought to correct her, but Darcy spoke first.

"At my request, Miss Bennet has agreed to extend her stay at Pemberley. In fact, she will be here long after you have departed, Miss Bingley."

Not acknowledging the warning tone from Darcy or her brother, she blurted out, "Just how ill is this girl?"

"Very, if you must know, but that is not the only reason Elizabeth will remain at Pemberley. You see, Miss Bingley, I have finally met a woman who is worthy of the Darcy name. I must ask your congratulations for Miss Bennet has agreed to be my wife."

The room fell silent as all the occupants awaited Miss Bingley's reaction. She stood, looking at Darcy in confusion, as if he had just spoken in Russian or some other language with which she was completely unfamiliar. She tilted her head as her mouth made movement as if to speak, but no words came out. She was saved from her efforts by the butler, who came in to announce another arrival.

"Colonel Richard Fitzwilliam."

"Cousin!"

Georgiana quickly moved to embrace Fitzwilliam. "You are finally here."

He smiled broadly. "Good afternoon, Georgie. I apologize for my tardiness. The grounds were irresistible and I lingered too long."

His gazed moved from Georgiana to seek out his other cousin. When he looked up, however, his eyes rested on someone wholly unexpected.

"Fitzwilliam." Darcy saw where his cousin's eyes landed and was quick to draw his attention. "You remember Miss Bennet."

"Of course." He bowed but did not remove his eyes from her. "How nice to see you again, Miss Bennet."

"Colonel Fitzwilliam." The mention of his name and a brief curtsey was his only greeting.

"Let me introduce you to the rest of our party. Mr. and Mrs. Edward Gardiner, my cousin, Colonel Richard Fitzwilliam."

Pleasantries were exchanged and attempts at conversation were made, but the tension in the room made the flow of words difficult. Georgiana eventually remembered to have rooms prepared and ordered refreshments. She sat close to her cousin and attempted to draw words from him, but his usual loquaciousness was stifled. He was too occupied with thoughts about his other cousin and the lady sitting next to him. Before long, Darcy stood and begged the ladies would excuse the men for a while.

"I would like to show them something in my study. I hope you do not mind. We should not be long."

"Mr. Darcy." Elizabeth looked at him with concern. He brought her hand to his lips and leaned down to whisper in her ear.

"Do not worry."

Darcy motioned for the gentlemen to follow him and led them to his study. No one spoke on the way, but Fitzwilliam, who was the last through the door, began upon entering.

"Well, Darcy, it appears you and Miss Bennet have recon--"

Before he finished his thought, Darcy's fist made contact with his face, sending him to the floor. Mr. Gardiner stood shocked, looking down at the colonel. He turned to Bingley, who shrugged his shoulders, then took a seat. Mr. Gardiner sat beside him. Bingley did not take his eyes off the scene before them, but leaned in so Mr. Gardiner could hear him.

"Do not be alarmed. I believe this has been coming. I will not let it go too far, but Darcy needs to do this." He then folded his arms and leaned back to enjoy the show.

"You know, Darcy," Fitzwilliam rose from the floor and wiped the blood from his lip with the back of his hand, "it is not gentlemanly to strike a man when he is not expecting it."

Darcy stepped closer. "You should have expected it the moment you saw Elizabeth standing next to me. No, before then—when you first spoke your lies in Kent."

"I do not know what the lady has told you, cousin, but I never lied to her."

"No, you chose your words carefully, did you not. Wickham tried to 'take away a woman under my protection'? You could have phrased that a number of ways and not give up Georgiana. You said what you did to hurt Elizabeth and make her think ill of me. You have certainly lived up to your surname. Your father must be proud that he finally made you his puppet."

Fitzwilliam stepped closer and raised his voice. "I am not under my father's control. I do my own bidding, just as you do. I suppose her being here means you are making an honest woman of her. After all that time you spent alone in the woods, you had no choice, being that you are such an *honorable* man."

This time, Darcy's fist landed in Fitzwilliam's stomach before he pinned him to the wall.

"Keep talking, Fitzwilliam, I beg you. *Please* give me a reason to call you out."

"Darcy." Bingley called from across the room. "You've just promised Pemberley to Miss Bennet. You cannot give it to her with blood on its grounds. Besides, Miss Darcy does not yet know her cousin's true character. She may not understand if you run him through."

Darcy nodded and released Fitzwilliam. He stepped back but his eyes remained locked on his cousin.

"Would you care to offer an explanation? Why would you seek to destroy my happiness then try to pull me down even lower after you succeeded? My mind has worked on these questions for weeks. What did I do to you, Fitzwilliam, that could possibly justify your actions?"

Fitzwilliam shook his head and spoke calmly. "How could there be anything, Darcy, as perfect as you are? You have been given the world, and now, it seems, you have won Miss Bennet. What was it, exactly, that secured her forgiveness? I am sure everything I said to her was forgotten the moment she saw the grounds of Pemberley."

Darcy resisted the urge to throw another strike, knowing he was being baited. "Your words prove that you do not know her at all. Elizabeth chose *me*, Fitzwilliam—the man, not the fortune. If she had ever wanted you, Elizabeth would have been willing to live in a tent on the battlefield. But, she did not.

"And you say I have been given the world? That may be true, but the second son of an earl hardly has cause to repine his station in life. You have the privilege of choice, Fitzwilliam. You can be happy with a comfortable living and highly coveted connections, or be a miserable sot wallowing in bitterness over not having been born first."

Darcy waited for a moment to see if his cousin would respond. When Fitzwilliam remained silent, Darcy continued.

"You have two days, Fitzwilliam, to rest your horse and see Georgiana, then you will leave Pemberley. I will not host you here or in town. You have proven yourself a master at spinning tales, so I leave it to you to explain your forthcoming absence to Georgiana. And in the meantime, you will not look at or speak to my betrothed more than politeness requires."

"Do you really feel she needs to be protected from me, cousin?"

"I would say *you* are the one who needs protection. You do not want to be on the receiving end of her ire."

"As it turns out, Darcy, your edicts are not necessary. My father has assisted me in obtaining a new commission. I will be leaving for Canada in a few weeks."

"Canada?"

"Yes. So you see, you and your wife will not have to tolerate my presence at all." He bowed slightly, then left the room.

"Well, that was interesting." Mr. Gardiner broke the silence after a few minutes.

"I apologize for the display, but I wanted you in here to keep me from killing him."

Bingley laughed. "I doubt there was any true danger in that, no matter how tempted you might have been."

"I take it he caused some sort of misunderstanding between you and my niece?"

Darcy nodded. "The situation is a bit more complicated, but, yes. If not for his interference, I believe Elizabeth and I would already be married."

"Unfeeling bastard."

"Do not be so quick, Mr. Bingley. I believe the colonel feels a great deal of guilt."

Both men looked at him disbelievingly.

"He made no attempt to block your hits, Darcy, nor did he hit back. He said some malicious things, but they were rather weak, really. It may be that he knew he deserved your anger. I am not saying you should welcome him back into your good graces. You are certainly right in keeping him away from Lizzy. But, it seems to me that your cousin might be struggling with his behavior. Perhaps he will find redemption in the New World."

"I have given him the benefit of the doubt too many times. I will not waste my time thinking of his possible redemption. Whatever becomes of him, it is his own business."

"Well said, Darcy." Bingley smiled and leaned forward. "Now on to more agreeable news. How did you and Miss Bennet come to an understanding? You believed it was hopeless when you were in London."

Darcy took a moment to form the right words, knowing he could not tell Bingley everything. "We talked, honestly and openly for a long while. When she told me all Fitzwilliam had said to her, everything finally made sense. There are no more barriers between us, and we will wed as soon as Lydia is well enough to attend the wedding."

"I am sorry to hear of her being ill. I look forward to seeing her when she is better."

Darcy looked at his friend and saw genuine concern. Not for the first time, he wondered just how he and Miss Bingley could be so different. He marveled at how so much time in her company had not altered Bingley for the worse. He may not have always found the strength to control his sister, but he was always true to himself. He was much like Elizabeth in that way.

"Bingley, if your sister continues to act rudely to Elizabeth, or extends the behavior to Lydia, I will ask her to leave. I had to tolerate her biting remarks against Elizabeth and the Bennets while in Hertfordshire. I will not allow it in my home."

Bingley sighed. "I apologize for her Darcy and I will speak to her. Perhaps now that she can see her cause is lost, she will behave better."

"Well, if not, let us hope Elizabeth can still laugh at the foibles of others. If not, Miss Bingley may find herself wishing she, too, was going to Canada."

Chapter 32

Darcy stood at the kitchen entrance of Pemberley and watched a small conveyance carry away Lydia's child. He had planned on delivering her to her new home himself after a few days. Having unexpected guests descend upon them had caused a change in plans. They could not keep her at Pemberley any longer. Both Miss Bingley and Fitzwilliam were vindictive enough to expose them if they happened upon the truth.

Their arrival also meant he would have to stay behind. He would not leave while Fitzwilliam was still there. Instead, he sent Mrs. Reynolds with a nurse, a maid and all the supplies the babe would need. Only Mrs. Reynolds would return.

Darcy continued to watch the carriage until it disappeared from view, then entered the manor with a heavy heart. No child had ever been sent away from Pemberley. Regardless of how she was sired, Lydia's child was family and he could not feel easy about surrendering her to the care of others, even if it was necessary.

Lydia's tearful goodbye just an hour earlier tugged at the hearts of everyone who was there to witness it. In spite of how the child came to be, Lydia loved her daughter and that assured Darcy that Elizabeth's sister would grow to become something truly good.

He made his way to the rose garden and to his great relief, Elizabeth was waiting there. She turned to him and gave a slight, quivering smile. She, too, had been affected by the morning. Darcy opened his arms and she rushed and fell into them. They stood there in the quiet of the garden, not speaking or worrying about who could see them and allowed their tumultuous emotions to settle into quiet acceptance.

"They are quite charming, are they not?"

Fitzwilliam jumped at the unexpected sound coming from behind him. He had inexplicably been drawn to the gallery that morning. Walking through a room while every Darcy in history looked down upon him was not his idea of a pleasant time. Yet, that is precisely where his feet had taken him.

After braving the judgment of generations caught in portrait, he had paused at a window hoping to see the colors of dawn break over the horizon. Instead, he was treated to the sight of Elizabeth alone in the rose garden. He waited for the stirrings that should have accompanied the sight of her lovely figure walking among the blooms. They did not come; he felt only the hollow longing that always remained after he had failed to secure what he thought he wanted. It truly had all been a game to him.

Darcy appeared in the garden and Elizabeth turned to him. Fitzwilliam could not make out her expression, but her joy at seeing Darcy was made evident a moment later when she ran into his arms. Fitzwilliam closed his eyes. The regret he kept fighting was making ground and it seemed useless to continue to resist.

Turning around, he greeted his visitor. "Good morning, Georgiana. You are up early."

She smiled somewhat sadly and looked away. "I suppose I am, a little. What do you think of them, Cousin?" She pointed out the window. "Is not my future sister delightful?"

Fitzwilliam shrugged. "Darcy certainly finds her to be."

"Do you not like her?"

"It does not matter whether or not I like her, Georgie. You and Darcy are the ones who will be living with her; yours is the only opinion that matters."

Georgiana tilted her head and looked at him curiously. "Did you sleep well last night, Cousin?"

He brought her hand to his lips then placed it on his arm and led her down the gallery. "No, I did not."

"Perhaps your decision to leave England is weighing on your mind. Is it too late to change your plans?"

He had broken the news to her at dinner the previous evening. She had fought back the tears then just as she was now.

"It is too late and I do not regret my decision. I realize it is hard to understand why I would want to leave. For some time, I have felt an anxiousness, a need to do something."

Georgiana nodded and squeezed his arm. "I can understand that, Cousin. I felt much the same when I was in school. Mrs. Annesley believes that restlessness was part of the reason I fell for Mr. Wickham's lies. Perhaps you are right to make a move before you do something foolish."

He cleared his throat. "Indeed."

Fitzwilliam allowed Georgiana to lead the way and without realizing where he was going, he suddenly found himself outside, walking toward Darcy and Elizabeth.

"Georgiana, I do not believe they would want to be disturbed."

"We will only greet them then move on. I do not wish to be indoors this morning."

Fitzwilliam noticed an immediate difference in their posture when Darcy and Elizabeth saw his approach. If Georgiana had not been there, he believed Darcy would likely hit him again.

Georgiana greeted the two warmly. "We will not keep you from your stroll, Brother. I hope you are having a good morning?"

"All is well, Georgiana."

Fitzwilliam found the exchange rather odd as if there was a deeper meaning behind their words. Before he could contemplate it much, he felt a tug on his arm.

"Shall we continue on, Richard?"

"Yes." He took a step but then stopped and turned to Darcy. "I am sorry, Darcy, truly sorry to have—disturbed you." He looked to Elizabeth. "Miss Bennet, please forgive my intrusion."

He bowed and after taking in each of their looks of disbelief, followed Georgiana up the path. He spent the entire morning with his ward, happy to eschew the rest of the company. They spoke of her studies and she related all she knew of Canada. Those hours were the best he had spent in some time and the next day, as he again sat on his horse overlooking Pemberley, he thought of the innocent way she continued to think of him. Georgiana still looked at him as the man he should have been. That look would haunt him far more than the hurt that came from Darcy and the cold indifference that came from Elizabeth.

After taking one last survey, he turned his horse and galloped as fast as the animal was capable, leaving the expectation of goodness behind with the reality of his deceit. Perhaps in the future he could return and attempt to make amends, but the pull of freedom was now too strong for him to dwell further on regrets. The past was gone and he would only concentrate on what was ahead.

Jane Burton looked at the passing scenery outside the carriage window. She had fallen in love with the terrain of her new home. Yorkshire was not entirely different than Hertfordshire, but the nuances were enough to make it special for her.

She began the journey in good spirits, but the movement of the carriage was making her stomach roll. She leaned her head against the seat and tried to ignore the growing nausea. She forced her mind to focus instead on the letter she had received the previous day. It had come by rider and Jane immediately feared the worst—that something had happened to Lydia. Instead, Elizabeth wrote to inform Jane of her betrothal to Mr. Darcy and to request their presence at Pemberley. The letter was brief but contained the promise of an explanation. Jane was prepared to leave immediately, but her husband insisted they wait until morning.

The carriage hit a bump, sending Jane's stomach to her throat. She placed a hand over her abdomen and closed her eyes.

"Samuel."

Mr. Burton looked at his wife then knocked on the carriage ceiling and called for the driver to stop. He quickly opened the door and ushered Jane out just in time for her to be sick in the grass beside the road. The violence of the expulsion caused her to stumble, but her husband steadied her as she finished.

She lifted her head and looked down at her clothing as her husband handed her a handkerchief.

"I will need another spencer from my trunk."

He brushed the hair away from her face and spoke with much worry. "Jane, why are we traveling while you are ill?"

"Because my sister is getting married. It is not even a half day's drive. I can manage it well enough."

Burton sighed in frustration. "Yes, you were managing quite well just now. What is the matter? You have been ill all week. Do you think you have contracted whatever ails your sister?"

Memories of Lydia's illness had followed Jane all week, beginning with the first time she lost her dinner in the middle of the night. Jane had been thoroughly educated on the eventual results of active participation in marriage. She was sure she was not merely ill. But, the similarities between how she was now feeling and what she had observed in Lydia could not be ignored. Her stomach turned for an entirely different reason.

"Yes, Samuel. I greatly fear that I have."

They returned to the carriage and spent the next few hours talking softly about what to expect when they reached Pemberley. She confessed a concern for Elizabeth's seemingly quick decision to marry Darcy. While she appeared to have softened toward him while in Kent, Elizabeth had never confided a *tendre* for the man, much less a desire to become his wife.

"Lizzy is very sensible, she would not make this choice lightly." Burton tried to reassure his wife, but she was not mollified.

"She *is* sensible about most matters. However, she never has been when it comes to Mr. Darcy. She determined she hated him before they ever had a single conversation. Now, she is marrying him. I can't help but wonder if it has something to do with Lydia."

"I do not understand."

Jane sighed and shook her head. "Neither do I. I suppose this conjecture will do no good. I will know all soon enough."

"Soon indeed. Look."

They had reached the manor and were both taken aback by its grandeur. When they pulled up to the steps, they saw the residents of the house had come to greet them. They exited the carriage and Jane walked as fast as she could to her sister.

"Lizzy!" Jane embraced her tightly, then stepped back to look at her. "You look very well."

"Why are you surprised, Jane?"

"I am not sure. I admit that I am a little unsettled." She suddenly remembered that she and Elizabeth were not alone. She turned to see that her husband and Mr. Darcy had been introduced by Mr. Gardiner. She looked back to Elizabeth.

"What is happening, Lizzy? Where is Lydia?"

"She is in her room. She is well. There is much to tell you, Jane. For now, please know that I am very happy."

Jane nodded, accepting her sister's assurances for the present.

"Mrs. Burton." Jane again turned to Darcy. "I am very pleased to see you again. May I offer my congratulations on your marriage?"

"Thank you, Mr. Darcy. I must offer you mine as well. I hope you do not mind me saying you are the most fortunate of men."

Darcy smiled broadly. "Indeed not, for I wholeheartedly agree. Shall we?"

They all walked into the entrance hall and the ladies excused themselves to go to Lydia. Darcy offered Mr. Burton refreshments in his study while their rooms were prepared. Elizabeth had written in her journal that Burton was an amiable, intelligent man who was easy to like. He found that to be so and enjoyed an instant conviviality that was rare for most men and entirely unheard of for Darcy.

"Thank you, Mr. Darcy. This is a charming little place you have here. Have you been in the neighborhood long?"

"Not long, only a couple of centuries."

"Ah, do not worry, you will feel settled in no time."

Lydia sat in a chair close to the window and listened as Georgiana spoke of her conversation with her cousin. She painted such a vivid picture of Colonel Fitzwilliam that Lydia regretted not meeting him. She was feeling better. The slight fever that developed soon after the birth had gone and the soreness was waning. She was beginning to feel restless, but the idea of socializing with the Bingleys kept her fixed firmly in her chambers.

One person she desperately wanted to see was her sister Jane, so when she entered the room, Lydia could not contain her joy. She slowly rose from the chair then clung tightly to her sister when she approached. After several moments, they separated and Lydia sat back down. After a quick introduction to Georgiana, Jane kneeled in front of Lydia and studied her closely.

"What has happened, Lydia? Please tell me the truth."

Lydia looked to Elizabeth and Mrs. Gardiner, then back to Jane. She would not lie to her anymore. She began to relay the story and noticed Georgiana had quietly walked toward the door.

"Georgie, please stay."

The girl nodded and stood by Elizabeth, holding her hand tightly.

Lydia watched a complex display of emotions play across Jane's face as she told her everything, beginning with Wickham's flirtations and ending with waking at Pemberley. Both ladies were exhausted by the end and the room was silent for some time. Finally, Jane's soft voice was heard.

"Where is the child now?"

"Mr. Darcy made arrangements for her. She is nearby and will want for nothing as she grows."

"Oh. I would like to have seen her."

Lydia drew a shaky breath. "She is beautiful and loud. Such a small thing makes so much noise. She has big, blue eyes and no hair at all. I am sorry you did not get to meet her."

Jane shook her head and wiped her eyes. "I am happy to see *you*, dear sister. I am so sorry for everything you have gone through."

Lydia smiled softly, grateful for Jane's sweet, calming presence. "I am glad you are here, Jane. Did you know Lizzy is getting married?" She was eager to change the subject and made no attempt at subtlety.

"Yes, I heard." She stood and straightened her skirts. "What I do not know, is how this engagement came to be. The last I heard she was not particularly fond of the man."

Jane's voice had become light and teasing. She was still concerned about how quickly this understanding seemed to happen, but after hearing how Darcy helped Lydia, she was inclined to support the match.

"That is not true, Jane. You heard me speak kindly of him at Longbourn."

"I did and I must say I was surprised, but you did not elaborate so I assumed there was nothing more to tell."

"We spent a great deal of time together in Kent. I loved him then, dearly, but we had a misunderstanding."

The ladies waited for her to continue, but she did not.

"Oh, Lizzy, you are terrible at telling stories. Thankfully you are not the one writing novels." Lydia complained, sounding more like her old self.

Elizabeth laughed. "Well, it is my story and I am keeping it close to me. It distresses me to think about our argument and the time we were apart. I would much rather think about the present."

"Well, that is good, Lizzy, because we must think about the wedding. You have not been fitted for a new gown, yet. Will you travel to London to have one made?"

"No Georgie, I will see the dressmaker in Lambton. Mr. Darcy has written to his solicitor about obtaining a special license so that we may marry here at Pemberley rather than at the church."

Lydia smiled and touched Elizabeth's hand, knowing that decision was for her benefit.

"As soon as it arrives, we will marry."

"Oh my goodness! I need to arrange for seamstresses to come here tomorrow. Have you spoken to Mrs. Reynolds about the wedding breakfast?

I must look and see what flowers and fruits are ready for decoration. I wonder which room we will use . . ."

They all looked at Georgiana in amusement. "She often gets stuck in a ramble. Give her a shove and she will right herself."

Georgiana took a breath and narrowed her eyes at Lydia. "Is this how sisters treat each other?"

Simultaneously, all the Bennet girls replied, "Yes."

Georgiana rolled her eyes and walked to a small desk and sat. "I am going to make a list. You all may continue to tease me from over there, but I will be too busy with my work to notice." She smiled as everyone laughed.

"I will help you, Miss Darcy, if you like."

"Oh, yes please, Mrs. Gardiner. We must not forget anything."

As Georgiana and Mrs. Gardiner planned, the three sisters continued to enjoy being together again. Jane, using the prerogative of an elder sister, fussed over the health of the youngest.

"Lydia, how long have you been in this room?"

"Weeks," Lydia groaned.

"It is time you left it."

Elizabeth nodded. "I agree with Jane. I know you are apprehensive about being in company with the Bingleys, but I am not asking you to tolerate them for long. Georgiana has opened a sitting room on this floor so you would not have to walk far. Will you join us for a while after dinner tonight?"

"I would like a change of scenery. I do not know how sociable I can be, but if you two insist upon it, I shall."

Later that day, Lydia regretted her promise to Elizabeth. As she prepared for the evening, she took a long look in the mirror. Though she felt better, she still looked ill and had little practice at socializing for months. For the first time in her life, she actually thought about how she should act. Her nerves were getting the best of her and if she had the strength to run from the room, she would.

Miss Bingley's shrill voice could be heard coming down the hall. Lydia wiped her hands on her skirt and slowly rose. She forced a tight smile that became genuine when she saw her sisters come through the door.

"Lydia," Jane reached her first and took her hands. "I am so glad you joined us."

Mr. Burton came up beside his wife and kissed Lydia's cheek. "Good evening, Sister. I am happy to see you feeling better."

Though surprised to see the men had joined them, Lydia's smile grew. If Jane told her husband all that had happened, he gave no indication of it.

He greeted her with the warmth and affection of a brother. It seemed her angel sister had married a prince.

"Lydia, you remember Mr. and Miss Bingley?" With Elizabeth on his arm, Darcy gestured toward the other guests. Lydia replied in the affirmative and curtsied. Miss Bingley responded with a nod and simple greeting. Her brother more than made up for her lack of enthusiasm.

"Miss Lydia." Bingley bowed gallantly. "What a great pleasure it is to see you again."

"Thank you, Mr. Bingley." She looked at Darcy, who gave her an encouraging smile. "Are you enjoying your visit?"

"I am indeed and it is made much more pleasurable now that you are able to join us. Let us sit. We must get to know each other again after all these months."

Lydia noticed Miss Bingley roll her eyes as she sat down across from them. She saw Lydia looking at her and smiled. The gesture was so obviously forced that Lydia did not bother to return it. Instead, she attempted to focus on what was being said by the gentleman at her side. Mr. Bingley spoke hurriedly the way Georgiana did at times but did so with much more confidence in what he was saying. She listened attentively without adding much and was grateful when Darcy engaged Bingley's attention. She was content to sit and observe, something she had rarely done in the past.

She could hear voices all around her, primarily from Darcy and Bingley, who sat closest to her, but also from Elizabeth and Jane. The rest of the party sat further away, but occasionally she caught her uncle's deep laugh. The one person she did not hear was Miss Bingley.

Looking across from her, Lydia could see every nuance of Miss Bingley's expressions as she stared at Jane and Elizabeth. Lydia knew the look Miss Bingley wore. Although she had rarely felt it herself, it had been directed at her often by the girls in Meryton. It was jealousy mixed with a good amount of hate. Lydia watched as Miss Bingley looked around the room for a moment then focused again on her sisters, particularly Elizabeth.

"Eliza, I heard that dear Georgiana is bringing in a dress maker to tend to your wardrobe. You must be relieved to have her superior knowledge of fashion at your disposal."

"I am glad that Georgiana will be my sister for many reasons, Miss Bingley."

Lydia admired the way Elizabeth returned Miss Bingley's ire with politeness, though what she actually wished to see was someone deliver the woman a firm set down. The exchange lasted another moment or two and Elizabeth never lost her temper. Lydia, on the other hand, had had enough.

"What an interesting brooch you are wearing. It is so old-fashioned." Miss Bingley smiled condescendingly at Elizabeth.

"It is not old *fashioned*, it is *old*," Lydia replied before Elizabeth had a chance. Using a voice that sounded much more like Jane's than her own, she continued. "Mr. Darcy gave that to my sister. The jewels have been in his family for many generations. The last two mistresses of Pemberley wore it, so it fits that he gave it to Elizabeth." She paused and looked down at Miss Bingley's hands. "That is a lovely ring you are wearing, Miss Bingley. It is certainly of the newest fashion." She tilted her head. "Did your brother give it to you?"

Miss Bingley seemed confused, but answered coldly, "Yes, he gave it to me when I came out."

"Oh, my mistake. It is not so new, then."

Mr. Burton's sudden cough was the only sound heard in the room. It continued with such force that Jane rose to tend to him. Miss Bingley also rose, and with as much civility as she could force, asked everyone to please excuse her. Those who could bid her a polite goodnight. The rest succumbed to their laughter as soon as the door closed.

"Lydia." Darcy attempted a reprimand but had to bite his lip and turn away. Jane had better success.

"Lydia Bennet, that was most uncivil."

"Please do not admonish her, Mrs. Burton. My sister deserved it." Bingley turned to Lydia and smiled. "Well done, Miss Lydia."

Lydia blushed and looked down. "Jane is right. I should be more like my sisters and always respond with more civility."

"Why? Everyone treats Caroline with civility though many are cold towards her. She will never change. However, I believe Caroline will have a headache and keep to her room until I am able to put her in a carriage back to London. The momentary embarrassment she likely feels will at least keep her from our company. Again, I say well done. Not everyone will respond to politeness. Perhaps you need only learn discernment."

Lydia tilted her head and smiled in amusement. "Mr. Bingley, of all the people now residing here at Pemberley, I would never have expected a lesson on behavior from you."

"Ah, Miss Lydia, the greatest wisdom always comes from unexpected places."

He looked so serious that Lydia could not help but laugh. The sudden sound echoed around them and brought peace to every heart in the room.

Chapter 33

"Well, she certainly made *that* difficult."

Darcy looked up from his book as Bingley walked into the room and dropped unceremoniously into a chair.

"I take it your sister has departed?"

"Yes, finally. She was not happy to have been ordered away from Pemberley. She blamed Mrs. Burton and Miss Bennet, of course, and had many unkind things to say about Miss Lydia."

"It is good I remained here, then."

"Yes. I told Caroline she should really be grateful Miss Lydia spoke when she did. I believe you were on the verge of saying something far worse."

"It is true. I was going to speak, but Lydia was quicker. I have learned that the Bennet sisters are quite protective of each other and do not hesitate to strike when necessary."

"It must be a wonderful thing to have someone love you that much."

Darcy smiled. "Indeed."

Bingley graciously fought the urge to tease his friend about the look currently residing on his features.

"Thank you, Darcy, for helping me secure a place in London for Caroline so quickly. I was unable to find accommodations for her before we came here."

"You are welcome. I thank you for staying to stand up with me instead of going to see her settled."

"It is my pleasure, Darcy. I would much rather stay among the company here than travel three days in a carriage with an angry Caroline."

Darcy laughed. "I suppose anybody would make that choice. Has it been uncomfortable for you at all, being in company with Jane and Burton?"

"Not really. At first, maybe, but I knew they had married, for it was in the papers. Caroline was quick to point it out to me. You need not fear me carrying any tender feelings for Mrs. Burton. It is my hope that we will all be great friends." He clapped his hands and leaned forward. "Now, tell me, Darcy, are you at all nervous?"

"About getting married? Not at all."

"Not even about the wedding night?"

"Bingley."

"Now, do not get all lord of the manor with me, Darcy. I am not trying to embarrass you. I know how you like to be prepared, so I am offering you my expertise, should you want it."

"I am not discussing your *expertise*, Bingley. It is enough that Wakely took it upon himself to give me advice through a letter."

Bingley laughed. "Now, there is a man with enough practice to be a true proficient. I believe I would like to see that letter. I would wager it is more interesting than Fanny Hill."

Darcy relaxed a little, laughing quietly at Bingley's joke. "He actually did say something useful."

"I cannot wait to hear it."

"He said that, as in all aspects of my marriage, putting Elizabeth's needs first is paramount."

Bingley folded his arms across his chest and raised his eyebrows. "That is all?"

"No, Bingley, that is not all, but it happens to be the least detailed line in the letter. I do not think I can see Lady Victoria again without turning at least three shades of red."

Bingley laughed again, louder and longer than before. "I will leave you be, Darcy, for I can see you have made up your mind to keep your own counsel in this matter. I have no doubt you have studied every book in Pemberley that could give you any insight on the subject. If you made notes, please share them. I am always looking for ways to further my education."

Darcy threw the book he had been reading in Bingley's direction, hitting him directly in the chest. Bingley continued to laugh as Darcy's mind wondered back to Wakely's letter. He mentally underlined each passage he found interesting, hoping that however he expressed his love for her, Elizabeth would accept his attentions without hesitation and return them with equal enthusiasm.

Elizabeth stood in her room with Lucy going through her old gowns to see what could still be worn by the mistress of Pemberley. Miss Bingley spoke nonsense mostly, but one truth that passed her lips was that Elizabeth would need to fill out her wardrobe with pieces that reflected her new station in life. Ideally she should go to London to purchase a wedding gown, but traveling would delay the wedding and neither bride nor groom accepted that as an option.

Instead, the dressmakers in both Lambton and Kympton were commissioned to provide as many new gowns in as little time as possible. Elizabeth and her sisters spent two exhausting days picking out patterns and fabric and the results were well worth the effort.

Elizabeth was about to give her maid instructions when they heard a knock on her door. Assuming it was Jane or Georgiana, Elizabeth called for them to enter. Her maid's quiet gasp was followed by the sound of a deep, commanding voice.

"Leave us, Lucy."

Elizabeth turned around as a red-faced Lucy exited through the dressing room. She placed her hands on her hips and gave her visitor a serious pout.

"Mr. Darcy, you have scandalized my poor maid. Her cheeks may never return to their normal color. Why are you in my room, sir?"

He wrapped an arm around her waist, pulled her close and pressed kisses along her neck. "I wanted to see you."

Elizabeth sighed and tilted her head. "A simple note would have alerted me to that, Mr. Darcy."

"I cannot kiss you through a note."

"No, you certainly cannot. I believe that would be the point."

"I also have things to give you."

"Mr. Darcy! I had an enlightening discussion with my aunt last night and I believe those things you wish to give me will have to wait two more days."

Darcy laughed and stepped back. "You are quite brazen today, my love."

She smiled. "You are the one who came to my room, Mr. Darcy. I must be bold to ward off your advances."

"I must inform you, my beautiful Elizabeth, that your boldness would not deter me; quite the opposite, actually."

She blushed and nodded to the table where she had seen a package that he must have brought in. "What did you bring me, Fitzwilliam?"

"You have a letter from your father. He included it in one to me."

"Oh." She walked to the table where Darcy had placed the letter. Somewhat reluctantly, she picked it up and broke the seal. After a brief perusal, she sighed and put it back on the table.

"I have battled my conscience for months over my incorrect judgment of people's character. As it turns out, it is just as painful to be right. He is unhappy to be informed of our engagement through a letter but has resolved to accept it all with equanimity since it was all done with little expense or inconvenience to him. He makes little mention of Lydia, just that he informed Mama of her betterment in health."

"He wrote something similar to me and said he has no objection to Lydia living with us. He did assure me the letter from your uncle was burned. You were right. It is good they are not here."

Elizabeth nodded. "What is this?"

"My cousin has sent you a package, a gift, I think."

"From Anne?"

"No, from Lady Victoria, my cousin Wakely's wife. He wrote their regrets that they are unable to come for the wedding. But, she sent this."

He handed her a neatly wrapped package tied with twine. She opened it carefully to find the most beautiful ivory silk she had ever seen along with a letter.

"What does she say?"

"She welcomes me to the family, tells me you wrote of my many admirable qualities and she hopes I like the fabric. If I cannot use it for my wedding dress then perhaps I will have a ball gown made for she will be hosting a ball for us in her parent's home as soon as we are all available. She sounds lovely."

"Wakely thinks so. I have only been in her company a few times, but I believe she is genuine."

"After such a generous gift, I am inclined to think very well of her."

Elizabeth held up one end of the silk and the light from the window revealed its transparency.

"I will need to use this as an overlay."

Darcy stepped toward her and again wrapped his arm around her. "Or for a gown only seen by your husband."

She dropped the fabric back on the table and placed her hands on his chest. "Mr. Darcy, now *I* shall be scandalized."

Darcy smiled then pulled her closer. "Tell me more about this talk with your aunt."

"I cannot, it is too embarrassing." She lowered her head to his chest.

"Even with me?"

She looked up. "*Especially* with you."

He raised his eyebrows in question.

"She described what happens in the marriage bed. I confess I was not altogether ignorant of the mechanics, but she divulged more details about . . . certain parts."

His hands traveled from her waist to her bottom. He usually did not allow himself to roam so far, but as the days dwindled before their wedding, he became more adventurous. Pulling her against him, he leaned down and spoke in a low, gravelly voice.

"You have sat on my lap nearly every morning for weeks now, Elizabeth. I believe you have been made aware of *certain parts* on occasion."

Elizabeth said nothing, just closed her eyes and enjoyed the feel of him against her. She had indeed felt him beneath her and even before her aunt explained, she knew it was the way his body naturally expressed its need for hers.

"I must confess, dearest, that my education on this particular subject is incomplete. I am not altogether ignorant, either. Men do talk and there are natural instincts to consider."

His hips remained pressed against her and his hands came around to land on her ribs, then slowly moved up to the curve of her breasts and down to her hips. Over and over, his palms glided up and down while his thumbs blazed a heated trail between the places where she ached the most.

"I know that my hand is naturally inclined to wander to the areas that will give you pleasure. I know that certain parts of me crave certain parts of you with a ferocity that keeps me up at night trying to imagine how it will feel when I am finally joined with you. I know I have been mad with desire for you since the morning you walked three miles to Netherfield. I had never wanted anything as much as I wanted to be the reason for your wild hair and flushed cheeks."

His lips descended on hers as his hands continued on their path. She pressed against them, trying to guide them to where she needed to be touched, but he would not allow it.

Somehow, he was able to break away. Her soft whimper when his lips left hers almost sent him in for more, but he managed to step back and mutter a few words of apology for having to leave.

"Soon, my love. Just two more days and we may explore."

After one long last kiss, he turned and quickly left. All at once, Elizabeth was angry at his departure and thankful for his resolve. After a few moments of attempting to calm, she rang for her maid. When Lucy entered, it was all Elizabeth could do not to laugh out loud in gratitude when she saw her with a basin of ice. Darcy's staff was truly efficient.

The days leading up to the wedding passed pleasantly and quickly. A familial atmosphere flowed through Pemberley, allowing the party to strengthen their bonds and simply enjoy each other. The house bustled with activity as the staff prepared for its new mistress. Rooms were re-organized, the wedding breakfast was planned and the dower house was turned into a honeymoon cottage where the dear couple would spend their first week as husband and wife.

Wife. Darcy repeated that word over and over in his head as he waited for Elizabeth at the make-shift altar. She would be his wife—his partner, his companion, his lover. *His*. The thought that she could have been so months earlier threatened to dampen his mood, but he would not allow it. Today, he would feel nothing but gratitude.

Early morning light filtered through the space, giving everything it touched an ethereal quality. When Elizabeth entered the room, the sun shone beautifully around her and danced off the shimmering material of her gown. She was no mere woman, but his magical wood nymph made up in human clothes. The light carried her to his side and he took her hand and placed a reverent kiss on the back.

"My Elizabeth. My beautiful bride."

Her radiant smile remained in place as the parson's words of faith and fidelity wrapped around them. The vows Darcy spoke became part of him as the truth of the words penetrated every layer of his being. Love, comfort and honor; forsaking all others. Only Elizabeth. *His wife. His, forever.*

Elizabeth looked down at their joined hands then to Darcy's eyes as the final blessing was said over them. The intensity in those dark, beautiful pools could so easily overwhelm her, but it was a sensation she welcomed. By drowning in him—in his strength and love and passion, she had found life.

Without warning, she suddenly found herself in his arms, her feet dangling off the ground and his lips firmly pressed against hers. Over the wild beating of her heart, she could hear the laughter of her family, who were no doubt surprised to see Darcy's affection expressed so openly. She knew however, that this unexpected action was merely a drop in the great depths of his love for her, and that his passions, when truly on display, had the power to make her forget her own name. She greatly looked forward to the evening, when she was sure that the only name she would be able to recall would be his.

Darcy's eyes fluttered open as a soft breeze played across his face. He felt a shiver on his chest and looked down to see goose bumps covering his wife's skin. He pulled his coat over her shoulders and kissed the top of her head.

"Wake up, love. The sun is behind us now. I do not want you to get chilled."

Elizabeth was lying almost completely on top of him, with her head resting over his heart, and her hair splayed wildly over his shoulder. They had entered the woods late that morning with the intention of exploring its treasures but had ended up exploring each other.

Darcy felt her leg slide up his as she lifted her head and smiled. His heart beat wildly at the sight and as her leg continued to move on his, something else began to stir. Elizabeth's smile grew, making the picture of her dark hair against her bare, pale skin even more enticing. She grasped his shoulders and pulled her body over his until every inch of her touched some part of him.

"I do not mind the chill, Fitzwilliam, for my husband knows exactly what to do to make me warm."

Wrapping his arms around her shoulders, he rolled them over and proceeded to warm her most thoroughly, first with the heat of his mouth, then with the strength of his ardor. As they laid there afterward, with his weight resting gently on her, Elizabeth began to laugh.

Darcy raised up and with a slight hint of indignation, asked what she found so amusing. His tone caused her to laugh more.

"I just find it humorous now that I told you it was unnecessary to bring a blanket. I did not want to do without the treat of watching you remove your coat. Now that you are completely naked, it seems a silly notion."

Darcy's deep laugh echoed through the woods. He slowly lifted himself off her and stood then offered her his hand.

"I am afraid it is time to return to civilization, dearest. We want to make our way out of these woods before night."

He looked around for their clothes then, much to his wife's displeasure, pulled on his shirt and breeches.

"Must we, Fitzwilliam? It has been such a pleasant week, with nothing to do but love each other."

Darcy smiled and helped her into her chemise and gown. "Yes, dearest wife, we must begin this horrid life we will lead together."

Elizabeth laughed while she watched him struggle with his boots. Once they were on, he offered her his knee to sit on while she donned hers.

"It will be horrid, will it? Exactly what should I expect, sir?"

Darcy gathered his coat and the blanket then took her hand and began walking.

"There is our wedding trip to Brighton, and you know what must be done there."

Elizabeth nodded in affirmation.

"When we return we will undoubtedly be plagued by neighbors and well-wishers."

She gasped. "Oh, dear, and they will wish us to be civil and appreciate their hopes for our happy life together? Terrible, awful people."

Darcy looked down in an attempt not to smile. "Indeed and we will have to host many of these people at dinners and perhaps even a ball, where I will be forced to introduce the new mistress of Pemberley and parade her around the room with great pride."

"You poor man. And I suppose we must take part in the London season next year?"

Darcy groaned. "Yes. We will visit museums and attend plays and reviews where you will wear enticing gowns and hold my hand during performances. Not to mention making love in every room of our London home. It will be unbearable."

"Mr. Darcy, I am afraid I have not the constitution for such happiness. To live in splendor, be well-liked by our neighbors, enjoy cultured activities and be loved by the very best of men? No, sir, it will not do. I cannot abide civilization. Something must be done. What say you, Mr. Darcy?"

"Well, Mrs. Darcy." He stopped and tossed the coat and blanket aside to be collected some other time. Tugging on her hand, he tilted his head slightly toward the trees. "I say we run."

~the end~

Epilogue

A fortnight later, in Brighton--

"Ah, not a bad night, if I do say so myself."

Wickham leaned back in his chair and propped his feet on the table, disturbing the stacks of notes and coins.

"Nearly twenty pounds and a nice romp I didn't have to pay for. A good night, indeed."

He looked over to the bed and the girl who was lying there. She had been fun, but dawn was approaching and he was not sure he wanted to see her in the light of day.

"Oi, time to get up sweetheart." She did not move so he shouted as he stretched out his leg to kick the bed. "Come on, love. I want you out of here before your father comes looking for you."

He watched her rise from the bed and gather her clothes. She dressed quickly without saying a word or even looking at him. When she walked around the bed, Wickham saw her eyeing his winnings. He stood up and grabbed her elbow.

"Do not even think about it. You paid your brother's debt last night, now get out before I decide to take more."

She broke away from him. "You are a brute."

"Ah, love, you had your chance." He grabbed her and kissed her hard while pulling her bodice down. His hand had just made its way to her breast when he suddenly felt her knee come up hard in his groin. Before he could react, she grabbed some notes and ran out the door. Wickham hobbled back to his chair.

"Still overwhelming them with your charm I see, Wickham."

He leaned back in his chair as the pain began to subside and looked at his unexpected guest. He smiled smugly and crossed his hands over his chest.

"Darcy? What brings you here, my friend?"

Darcy walked around the small room for a moment before taking a seat across from Wickham. "I am staying in the area for a few weeks. I heard the militia was quartered here and I thought I would pay you a visit."

"Well, I am flattered, especially since the last time we saw each other, you did not acknowledge me at all."

Darcy stared at him without expression. "That was a mistake."

Wickham faltered a little. He believed he knew how to manage Darcy well enough, but the unexpected visit combined with his strange demeanor, gave him pause. "What exactly brings you to Brighton, Darcy?"

"I recently married and my wife expressed an interest in traveling to the seaside."

Wickham laughed. "I thought you had a different air about you. Congratulations, my friend. Would I happen to know the fortunate woman who won your heart?"

"Indeed you do. Miss Elizabeth Bennet is now Mrs. Darcy."

Now able to move his legs, he again propped them on the table. "I thought as much. She had some heated words for me when I last saw her. It led me to believe you had made an impression on her."

"So it would seem."

They stared at each other for a few moments before Wickham decided to move whatever game this was forward. "Alright, Darcy, I can guess why you are really here. I suppose you want me to marry that girl. The youngest one. . . Lydia. I have no objection, but I do not believe I could support her on an officer's salary."

"No, you could not. It is of no matter, however, because you will not be an officer much longer."

He placed his feet back on the floor and leaned forward. "Ah, I do like the sound of that. Are you to finally give me the living I was promised?"

"No."

Wickham tilted his head and raised an eyebrow. "Darcy, I will not marry that girl without proper recompense."

"Wickham, you will not marry her at all."

"Has marriage made you addled? I do not understand you. You said I will no longer be an officer."

"That is correct. Tomorrow morning you will be found after having deserted the militia. You will then be subjected to whatever punishment they deem necessary. So, you see, marriage to my sister is impossible."

Wickham became somewhat alarmed. He had expected Darcy to handle the situation the way he always did, with money. "They execute deserters, Darcy."

"Yes, I have heard that."

Wickham laughed. "I see the lovely Miss Bennet, rather, Mrs. Darcy, has helped you find a sense of humor. You would not deliver me to the firing squad, Darcy. You are far too honorable to get your hands dirty in such a way."

"This is true. I *am* too much of a gentleman to dispose of you in the way you deserve." He stood, walked to the door and opened it. "These men, however, have no such limitations."

Wickham watched as a man roughly the size of a house entered the room, followed by another of equal size.

"I will leave you now, Wickham. These men will see you to your destination. Farewell, *my friend*."

"Darcy!" Wickham called out, but he had already closed the door.

Darcy walked down the stairs of the inn and over to a man sitting alone at a table.

"You were right, Colonel Forster. He is here. Thank you for your help in locating him."

"You are welcome, Mr. Darcy. It was a fairly easy guess, knowing his propensities. If he was not at camp, I knew he would be here."

"What happens now?"

Colonel Forster raised his eyebrows. Darcy reached inside his coat then handed him a small package.

"I do not want him killed."

"You are taking a risk that he will somehow manage to free himself."

"He is currently in the company of some acquaintances of mine from London. They know how to render a man immobile."

The colonel leaned back in his chair and looked at him questioningly. "I will do what I can to see that he is put on a boat. I wonder why you did not do that yourself."

"I suppose I want him to be frightened—to know how it feels to believe he will die."

Colonel Forster smiled. "Well, perhaps that will inspire reflection."

"As long as he breathes, redemption *is* possible. However unlikely it may be, one can always hope."

Spring 1815

"Brother!" Georgiana walked hurriedly into the sitting room, waving a letter in the air. She stopped short when she saw her sister resting on the sofa.

"Oh, Lizzy, you are green."

"Thank you for that observation, Georgiana. When you make the next one, could you be a little quieter?"

Georgiana walked over and gave Elizabeth a kiss on the cheek. "Forgive me, Lizzy. I am just excited to share some news."

Elizabeth shook her head and sat up. "No, Georgie. I am sorry for my ill temper. I just tire of this constant sickness. Please share your news."

Georgiana looked at Darcy, who had just moved to take a seat next to his wife. "I have a letter from Richard! Can you believe it? I have been so worried since we have not had one from him in over a year."

Darcy looked at Elizabeth then back to his sister. "What does he say, Georgie?"

"He is married and has a son! Look." Georgiana handed him one of the two pieces of paper she held. "His wife's name is Helen and she is a widow with two young boys. She is quite accomplished at drawing and sent this sketch of their little one."

She handed the drawing to Elizabeth, who looked at it and smiled before giving it to her husband.

Darcy studied it for a few moments, looking for similarities between father and son. He glanced at Elizabeth, then back down. "The letter says the child's name is George, after my father."

He handed the sketch and letter back to Georgiana. "Thank you for sharing that with us. It is good to know he is doing well."

"You are welcome, Brother. If you do not need me for anything, I believe I will go to my sitting room and respond. I have much to tell him."

"Go ahead, Georgie. We will see you at dinner."

After the door was closed, Elizabeth crawled in Darcy's lap and rested her head on his shoulder.

"What else was in the letter?"

"He said he named his son George to remind him of the man he should be, not the one he was inclined to be. He added a jest after that, likely for Georgie's sake."

"Yes, but the line about 'the man he should be' was for you."

Darcy nodded.

"Write to him, Fitzwilliam, and include my best wishes for their continued health and happiness. We need not carry this grudge, especially since it is likely we will never see him again."

"You are correct, of course. I will write to him and perhaps Georgiana can draw Annie as well."

"That is a lovely idea." Elizabeth sighed as her husband's hand ran down her thigh.

"Now, tell me wife, are you very ill?"

She sat up and pressed her chest against him. "I *am* quite ill and in desperate need of distraction. Could you provide that for me, Fitzwilliam?"

"I am at your service, madam."

Lydia strolled up the path from Meryton on her way back to Longbourn. She had just left Kitty and Mary with their Aunt Phillips, using an excuse of having a head ache to escape the company. She was home for the first time in three years, having come for Kitty's wedding. She was marrying a barrister she had met while visiting the Darcys in London. Lydia was not fond of Kitty's choice, believing Mr. Cummings cared more for the connection to Darcy than for Kitty, but she said nothing. Kitty was too happy to be getting married to care about anything else.

As she walked, she noticed how little things had changed in the village. No one had moved in or out of the neighborhood, no new shops had opened. The only real change, it seemed, was her. She had refused every invitation from her mother to come to Longbourn, saying she preferred London or Pemberley. Instead, Darcy had hosted the Bennets twice in London. The invitation to come to Pemberley was an open one, but Mr. Bennet would not travel that far.

Lydia had been apprehensive about seeing her father again. When in London, he remained in Darcy's library for much of the time and she had been occupied with her sisters. There would be more opportunity for interaction while she was at Longbourn, but he hid there, too.

She did not have Elizabeth's memories of a doting father to make her regret his absence. Her pain over his reaction to what Wickham had done slowly changed to anger, and even that was beginning to subside. She was determined that, eventually, she would feel nothing at all.

The path ahead of her forked—one trail led directly to Longbourn while the other wound around the estate and would take her past the orchards and the barn where she had last seen Wickham. Her skin flushed and her hands began to shake as she stepped forward. Before her mind could convince her body to take the path on the right, she heard a voice behind her call her name. She turned around and could not help but return the joyful smile she saw on her friend's face.

"Good morning, Mr. Bingley. I would not have expected to see you. Have you come to Meryton for the wedding?"

"Indeed I have. Your mother invited me. I believe she must have seen me talking to Mr. Cummings at the Darcys' and assumed we were friends."

Lydia laughed. "No, Mr. Bingley. You were invited because my mother has two available daughters and you have five thousand a year."

"I am more than my fortune, you know." Bingley attempted indignation, but Lydia did not buy it.

"Not to my mother, you're not." She laughed louder. "Oh, Mr. Bingley! My sister Mary will be your constant companion in the next days, whether either of you like it or not. Mama is so disappointed with Kitty's choice. She cannot brag to Lady Lucas that Kitty's marriage will throw her girls in the path of other *barristers*. No, Mama must have at least one more rich son-in-law to balance the one who must earn a living."

"And why are you so sure Mrs. Bennet has chosen me for Mary and not you?"

Still smiling, Lydia looked at him and saw something in his expression for which she was entirely unprepared. She looked away quickly and began walking.

"Because I have already informed Mama that I have no plans to ever marry."

"You are young, Miss Lydia. Is it not too soon to make such a statement?"

She shrugged. "I do not see why I should marry. I have the privilege of living at Pemberley and I may visit Yorkshire and London whenever I wish. There is little chance that I will grow bored with the company in any of those places. Thanks to my brother, I now have a dowry that I can live on and with five sisters, I am sure to always have a niece or nephew with me. I am quite determined."

"As I said, you are young. You may change your mind."

She shook her head and spoke softly. "I would not count on it, Mr. Bingley."

They walked a while in silence. Lydia was trying to think of something clever to break the tension when Bingley spoke.

"I have not had a letter from Darcy in a while. Did they make the journey for the wedding as well?"

"No, Lizzy cannot travel at present. She has been ill since they came back from Kent. At first she believed she was merely upset over Miss de Bourgh's passing. No one knows, yet, but I will tell you. She is expecting again. She wanted to come for the wedding, but Darcy has her under strict regulations."

Bingley laughed and Lydia was happy to have the mood lighten. "I would expect nothing less from my friend. Perhaps little Annie will have a brother to play with. Darcy did not send you to Hertfordshire alone, did he?"

"No, I came with Jane and Samuel. I will go back with them and spend most of the summer in Yorkshire."

"Oh, you will not be at Pemberley?"

There was no mistaking the disappointment in his voice.

"Not until August. Were you to visit?"

"Yes, but perhaps I will wait. When in August will you return?"

"The very beginning, but you should not change your plans."

With a firmness she did not know he was capable of, he spoke. "No, Miss Lydia. I will wait."

Before she could think of a suitable reply, Lydia looked around and saw they had walked further than she had realized. Just in front of them, to the right of the path, was the barn where it had happened.

For the past three years, she had struggled to put a name on what had occurred. Could she say she was violated when she had willingly met him in the barn? Was it a seduction even though she did not know how it would end? She did not consent, nor did she say no.

She stood there as if in a trance until she felt Bingley touch her arm. Lydia looked at him, and the concern she saw genuinely touched her. Looking back to the barn, the one word she needed came to mind. *Over*. Whatever it had been *then*, it was over, and all that mattered was *now*.

Lydia stepped back, turned to Bingley and smiled sweetly. Doing so changed his countenance so much that she was tempted do it again and possibly never stop. She was not ready to run toward a certain future, but she *would* take steps.

Summer 1817

"I want to marry her, Darcy."

Darcy looked up from the papers on his desk. Bingley had asked his advice on some business matters, but had been very quiet since entering the study. He should have been surprised by Bingley's statement, but somehow was not.

Bingley had yet to purchase an estate, preferring to visit Pemberley as much as possible. Darcy had not thought much about it until one afternoon about a year prior when he saw Elizabeth's soft look directed at Bingley. He was on the lawn and embroiled in a pretend sword fight—with Lydia. When she bested him and threw her head back and laughed gaily, there was no mistaking the look on Bingley's face.

Although his friend seemed genuinely taken with Lydia, Darcy did not then become alarmed. He had often seen Bingley in love and Lydia did not appear to encourage him, so Darcy dismissed it as a passing fancy. Yet, Bingley still visited often and he was now asking for her hand. Darcy's back stiffened. Best friend or not, Bingley would have to address the matter properly.

"You want to marry whom, Bingley?"

Bingley straighten in his seat. "Miss Lydia."

"I see. Have you asked her?"

"Yes. She said she needed to think about it. Do you know how it feels to lay your heart bare to a woman only to have her say she would *think* about it?"

Darcy would have laughed if Bingley had not sounded so defeated. "There are things that you are not aware of, Bingley—"

"She told me everything." He rose and paced in front of his chair. "The child. *Wickham*. Please tell me he is in the bottom of a ravine somewhere."

Darcy leaned back and tapped his finger on his desk. "He has been dealt with."

Bingley nodded then returned to his seat. "What if her answer is no, Darcy? I had thought myself in love before, but she has become essential to me. For five years this has grown. I thought she would be ready now."

A quiet knock was heard and Darcy bid the person enter. A footman handed him a note and then retreated to stand by the door.

Darcy contemplated the missive for a moment then addressed the footman. "Have a curricle brought around, please."

He then turned to Bingley. "Lydia would like you to meet her in the entry way." He stood and continued in his firmest voice. "Bingley, I am allowing this because it is important to Lydia. I expect you to act like a gentleman."

Confused, and slightly frightened, Bingley immediately left to find Lydia.

A half hour later, Bingley found himself in the driver's seat of a curricle, looking questioningly at his companion.

"Where are we going, Miss Lydia?"

"Follow the west road and I will give you directions from there." She smiled softly. "I want you to meet her."

He smiled, then clicked the reins to get the horses moving. It was a beautiful day for a drive and Bingley would have enjoyed it if he were not so nervous. He glanced at Lydia and saw she was nervous, too. Taking the reins in one hand, he reached over with the other and gently squeezed hers.

"Do you visit her often?"

She shook her head. "Not too often, but enough that she recognizes me." She looked down to a small package in her lap. "I have some doll's clothes for her. I think they will make her happy."

He brought her hand to his lips. "I am sure they will, sweetheart."

Lydia smiled and laid her head on his shoulder, gently toying with his sleeve. Bingley had become her best friend in the years since she left Longbourn. Being someone who bored easily, she had never wanted to remain in one place for very long. Everywhere she had traveled to over the last five years, he had been, too. Somehow he would manage to secure an invitation from whoever was hosting her at the time and, even if only for a little while, they would be together. She had come to depend on the comfort that being close to him brought her. The need to roam was waning. He made her want to be still.

"Miss Lydia!"

A mass of petticoats and blonde curls came running to greet them as they walked into the garden. Lydia scooped the girl up and kissed her cheek.

"Good afternoon, little one. Were you swinging?" Lydia nodded to the nurse who quietly walked to another part of the lawn.

"Yes, but Nanny would not push me very high."

"Oh dear. What is the point of swinging if you cannot go high?" She twirled the girl around until they were both out of breath and dizzy.

"Let us sit for a while. I would like to introduce you to a friend." The two sat on a bench with Lydia holding her daughter in her lap.

"Mr. Bingley, I would like you to meet Joy.* Can you tell Mr. Bingley good afternoon?"

Joy dutifully stood and turned to Bingley, then offered a low, wobbly curtsy. "Good afternoon, Mr. Bingley."

He bowed graciously and smiled. "I am very pleased to meet you, Miss Joy. You have lovely manners."

The girl beamed. "Thank you, sir. Nanny says I have to learn to be a lady. You can tell her you think my manners are good. Perhaps then she will push me higher."

Bingley looked at Lydia and she shook her head. Joy could not be more like her mother if Lydia had been the one raising her. He was instantly charmed.

"If you promise not to tell Nanny, I will push you higher myself, but you have to promise to hold on tight."

She squealed her agreement and ran for the swing. Lydia watched as her daughter fell in love with the handsome man behind her. It was then that she realized she had, too.

They spent the next hour playing in the garden, until it became painfully obvious that Joy needed to sleep. With a tight embrace, a kiss on the cheek and a promise to return soon, Lydia and Bingley said goodbye.

"She should come live with us."

They had spent some time in quiet thought after they returned to the road, both of them now feeling the weight of separation.

"What?"

Bingley guided the curricle off the road and turned to her.

"If you decide you want to marry me, Joy should come live with us. You love her and if you will take my name, I will give it to her, too."

Lydia's voice became shaky as tears fell down her face. "You would give my daughter a name?"

"Yes. We could move far away, to a place where nobody knows us. No one ever need know she is not my daughter."

Lydia could not help herself in that moment and kissed him full on the mouth. Bingley was gentlemanly and resisted the urge to deepen the kiss for an entire second before he succumbed to temptation. With great effort, he broke away slowly.

"Does that mean yes?"

Lydia looked at him sadly and shook her head. He was immediately heartbroken.

"Please listen, Mr. Bingley. We could not take Joy. Your sisters would know that she is not yours. Caroline would not hesitate to spread rumors about Joy's origin. I will not have you or her spoken of maliciously. Also, I cannot take Joy from her home. You see how happy she is and it is because she is loved.

"I accepted a long time ago that she could never be mine. Not every story will have a happy ending, Mr. Bingley. It has to be enough for me to know that *she* is happy."

She reached for his face and pulled him down for another kiss.

"But I will marry you, Charles."

Bingley attempted to kiss her again, but his smile was too great to allow it. She again rested her head on his shoulder as they drove back to Pemberley, talking excitedly about their future life along the way.

"Are you busy, darling?" Elizabeth stood at the door of her husband's study, watching the emotions play across his face. He had given Bingley permission to marry Lydia, and was brooding.

Darcy rose from his desk and walked to her. "Never too busy for you, love."

"That is good. I thought you could use a visit from these two."

Elizabeth stepped aside to allow the children entry. Darcy smiled as he picked up his youngest daughter and leaned down to give the eldest a kiss.

"This was just what I needed—a visit from my girls. Where is Matthew?"

"Sleeping soundly. Given how his nights have been lately, I did not want to risk disturbing him."

"That is understandable." Darcy looked down when he felt a tug on his trousers. Annie quickly corrected her behavior when she saw her father's stern look.

"Excuse me, Papa. May I use the pencils?"

Darcy immediately softened. "Yes, little one, but you must share with your sister."

"Thank you, Papa. Come on, Beth."

Annie held out her hand as her little sister wriggled out of her father's arms. Darcy sighed as he watched Annie help Beth into a chair.

"What must we do to ensure they never leave Pemberley?"

Elizabeth came up to him and wrapped her arms around his waist. "Aside from putting every young man in the country on a boat to China?—nothing. No matter what we do to discourage them, one day they will leave us. It is the natural order of things."

"I do not like it."

"No, I suppose you do not. We have many years before we have to think about this. You should not worry too much, though. It is unlikely our girls will ever marry."

"Why do you say that, dearest?"

"You may not know this, but a woman compares every man she meets to the one who loved her first. No man in England will ever compare to their father. After taking time to thoroughly sketch your character, I know that you, my dear, loving husband, are the very best of men."

Notes

I based much of Lydia's pregnancy on my experience with baby number three. It may be rare, but it is possible to become ill very early on and remain so through the rest of the pregnancy. Like Lydia's little one, mine was born five weeks early and miraculously healthy.

The Celtic Heart legend Darcy speaks of was borrowed from a booklet that came with a necklace I purchased a couple of years ago. I had hoped to site a reference, but I was unable to find this particular legend in books or online.

Pugilism was very popular among the upper classes in Regency England. The combination punches we see in Sketching Character, however, were not used until the Victorian Era.

Joy was not a common name during this time period. It did not become popular until later that century.

Acknowledgements

I want to send a big thank you to my cold readers, Ruth, Kathy, Anji and Joy and editor Kristy Rawley. Thank you for making my book better.

I am fortunate to be part of a community of Janites who support and encourage each other to be their very best. Thank you all for the laughs, hot men pictures, brownies and love. You make me want to do this forever.

Last but not least, I send love and gratitude to my two partners in crime: My husband Lance and my Vanity and Pride Press cohort Cat Gardiner. Thanks for always having my back.

Other Austen-inspired books published by Vanity & Pride Press

Lucky 13
by Cat Gardiner

Winner of Austenesque Reviews Favorite Modern Adaptation for 2014: "What a phenomenal read!! The attention to detail and the clever way the author immersed her audience in the story was such a terrific experience!"

A Contemporary Austen-inspired, Pride and Prejudice novel - New York City advertising executive, Elizabeth Bennet is determined to find a respectable date to take to Christmas dinner with her insane family. So, what's a girl to do with only 26 days remaining? She and her best friend embark on a mad-cap dating blitz. Speed dating and blind dates become a source of frustration when one man continually shows up, hell-bent on either annoying her or capturing her heart. Fitzwilliam Darcy, wealthy, hunky, part-time New York City firefighter is Elizabeth's new client, one of thirteen men chosen for a fundraising, beefcake calendar.

Sparks fly and ignite as misunderstandings abound. Sit back and laugh for an unforgettable, hot, holiday season in the Big Apple.

Denial of Conscience
by Cat Gardiner

"Denial of Conscience smolders with action, adventure, and romance. Darcy and Liz are hot together! I'd beat down Jane Austen herself for this Darcy!"

A fast-paced Contemporary, Austen-inspired Pride and Prejudice novel - Fitzwilliam Darcy is steel, rock-n-roll, and Tennessee whiskey. Elizabeth Bennet is orchids, opera, and peaches with cream. Thrown together in a race against time to save her kidnapped father, they are physically and emotionally charged TNT, ready to explode!

Dearest Friends
by Pamela Lynne

"Dearest Friends is one of those rare stories that quickly grabs hold of the reader and never lets go; it is a thrilling ride filled with danger, seduction, romance and humor. I never wanted it to end."

A heartwarming, Pride and Prejudice Regency Variation – Fitzwilliam Darcy and Elizabeth Bennet have both experienced betrayals that have caused them to reconsider many of their preconceived notions of life and love. When they see each other again in London, they bond over a shared grief and begin a courtship in spite of Mr. Bennet's insistence she marry another. They are supported by an unlikely group of friends, and as they follow Darcy and Elizabeth on their road to happiness, connections are formed that will change their lives forever.

Find more from Cat Gardiner and Pamela Lynne on social media

Twitter:
@pamelalynne1
@VPPressnovels

Facebook:
Vanity and Pride Press
Pamela Lynne
Cat Gardiner

Made in the USA
San Bernardino, CA
25 October 2015